THE

MULHOLLAND DIARIES

A novel

L'vette Sonai

DAISY SCOUT PUBLISHING

Nashville   Los Angeles

The Mulholland Diaries

Second Edition

ISBN-13: 978-0692541135 (paperback)

ISBN-10: 0692541136

Library of Congress Cataloging-in-publishing Data is available upon request.

Book design by The Dream Squad

Front cover image used by permission

Daisy Scout Publishing

Nashville   Los Angeles

www.lvettesonai.com

This book is dedicated to women of all walks of life. Through our strength, our integrity and our desire for love, we share a sisterhood.

Acknowledgements

I want to thank my entire family for the love, lifelong guidance and inspiration. I love you all so much, and am blessed to share these bloodlines. *Pillow Hill for life*. My "baby bro" Tommy, you are my heart and I love you. Mom and Dad, thank you for loving me no matter how stubborn and hard headed I've ever been. I heard every single thing you said, and I took it to heart. I love you both very much. Marcy, you are my true and loyal friend, my sister and I love you deeply. Felicia, thank you for the boost I needed to start this crazy adventure. Really, how did this happen? I was just kidding when I said I would write this. You were truly motivating, and I love you.

To my darling husband, the love of my life~ I know I'm a handful, but I love you and appreciate you for being the man who loves me like you do.

To Candice, Bebe and Rayne: you chicks can finally get out of my head - for now.

L'vette xo

There is no greater form of make-believe than Los Angeles, the City of Angels. Mulholland Drive is the yellow brick road spanning from the Hollywood Hills to the San Fernando Valley, with Beverly Hills holding court as its modern day Oz. The streets are money green, and the glittering drives are the causeways to the good life. Fantasy is built around the people. The sun always shines, and life is perfect. It's the city of dreams. Women are willing to sell their souls to live behind these gilded gates. We swim in the fountain of youth, seeking eternal beauty, while hoping for a little bit of love along the way. To onlookers, we are living the dream. For some of us though, the dream has evolved into a nightmare.

THE MULHOLLAND DIARIES

CANDICE

I was thirty-one when I met the man of my dreams. We were an unlikely match, and quite honestly I was terrified to let him in. But, on that fateful January night in Chicago, the entire course of my life was altered forever. Still, if I had it to do over again, no matter how much I loved him, I'm not sure I would make the same decisions. Eventually a woman reaches a point where she asks, is it worth it?

Thirty should be a positive turning point in your life. Instead, there I was, feeling stuck and unfulfilled. At the same time, being the contradiction that I am, I'd become satisfied with the way things were. I lived for everyone except myself. Well no more. Though I loved my family it was high time to do ME, and that had nothing to do with Chicago anymore.

Everyone knows Chicago winters can be unforgiving. January especially, is known to be bitter and frigid. This particular night did not disappoint. It was two degrees outside and the wind-chill at least minus ten. The kind of night you just want to stay inside and curl under a blanket and drink a nice glass of wine, my Pinot Grigio was chilled and ready. That's exactly what I had planned. But, instead I was headed out because my best friend all but bribed me to meet her. I thought, 'I swear this is my last winter in this town. I'm done!'

I'd lived in suburban Hoffman Estates all of my life and had big plans of living in the city after high school. That vision always beckoned from the visible distance, as I could see the Sears tower from the freeway. After high school, I entered DePaul University where I earned my BA in Journalism. I just knew I would be the black Maria Shriver. I got a little sidetracked though, taking minutely fulfilling jobs and dating a variety of guys who were all my prince charming. I actually started to believe that crap.

For almost ten years, I was caught in that web. That is until the prospect of grad school entered the picture. The only problem being, I was torn between staying in Chicago or finally realizing my dream of going back to Los Angeles and entering USC's school of Journalism. Working in one of the most promising public relations firms in Chicago, I was also up for a promotion and felt I'd be crazy to let that pass. But one thing was for sure, taking that job would put grad school on the backburner and I felt that in a few more years I might have to retire my dreams. It was now or never.

With all of that on my mind, the last thing I wanted to do on a cold Friday night was waste time hanging out with people I didn't know; especially Faith's boyfriends. She'd always been like a sister to me, but that girl worked her hustle to the bone. Everyone served a purpose in her life. Even me.

Standing in front of the dressing mirror securing myself in the warmth of my plush parka, so many doubts flooded my mind. You see, being the sensible and worrisome girl I was, I questioned why I constantly followed along with other folks' big ideas. They almost always went wrong. From getting a nose job with a friend when I was nineteen years old, to bailing out an ex-boyfriend whose credit was so bad, that at age twenty-five I leased an apartment in my own name so that he would have a place to live. Uh huh! You guessed it! He stiffed me on that one and I was stuck with the debt. To this day I can't believe I fell for that. I felt sorry for him and hoped he'd realize how much I cared, enough to risk my reputation to help him. I saw him years later and he was still a fast talking loser.

Yes, so back to Faith. Once again, there I was, the responsible one who supposedly had it together, feeling like her babysitter. That night was bound to be no exception and I honestly dreaded it because girlfriend had an angle. I wondered what it was, but was sure it would end with me being bored and frustrated.

"God, I'm so sick of this!"

Struggling with the buckle on the jacket, it only got worse. I removed the scowl and the irritation from my eyes, and brushed bronzer on my face to give a little more color to what Faith described as my too-yellow complexion. Then painting on my signature smile as I headed out of my bedroom, bolting down the stairs of the townhouse I shared with my older sister Anne.

"I'm gone! I'll be a little late… I love you!"

Anne yelled back from the kitchen, "Love you too, and watch out for my car when you back out!"

After a few minutes of staring at the steering wheel, I drove off in my Nissan, dialing on the cell phone. Faith picked up immediately. "Are you on your way?"

"Yes, I am. I should be there in half an hour."

I was nervous about the night. I'd watched friends, especially Faith, work men like pros. I tried to get out of going to that party but Faith actually whined, 'No...please go. This guy is classy and he's loaded. Pretty brown girls like us deserve the good life, the HIGH life!'

I hated that she lumped me into her schemes, because those weren't my thoughts. I was raised to do it for yourself or don't do it at all, even if I didn't always follow that advice. Still, I thought about what my friend was saying and it worried me. She sounded as if she was ready to go to any length for this so-called good life.

"Hmmm, so Faith, who are these people again?"

"Just some really nice men I met at dinner last week. You need to branch out, Candice."

I turned on the interior light and checked my reflection in the rear view mirror, licking my lips and rubbing my manicured pinky across the lower. You have to make sure your mouth looks good. Anyways, there I was driving to Lake Forest with no knowledge of whose party it was. She'd told me earlier that the host was really nice and all of that. He was having some friends over for a game night at his place.

"Faith, black people don't live in Lake Forest. What if I get lost?" I laughed because I knew my saying that would get under her skin.

"Candice, shut up. God!" That's when she got all excited. "...and just wait until you see this house. Excuse me, mansion!"

I felt panic set in, "Faith, I don't want to be set up with anyone, you hear me? And when I'm ready to leave, I'm leaving!"

After a forty minute drive and me secretly wishing I was at home, I finally turned onto Sussex Lane. A long, two-lane road of which each estate I passed, the next seemed more lavish. My GPS announced that I was approaching my destination and I entered the open gates that welcomed me. Even covered in snow, you could see the grounds were massive and I think my jaw dropped. I couldn't help but think, oh my god, who lives here?

I picked up my cell and dialed Faith, "Okay, I'm here. I need to know who this person is and what he does. He's not some drug dealer, right?"

There was a brief silence. I think Faith was actually offended. "You know I don't roll with drug dealers...not that I know of, anyways." She giggled, "I'm kidding, come on, Candice!"

Glancing out of my car window towards the house, I was relieved and sighed, "Just tell me who he is and what he does because this place is incredible."

Faith quickly rolled off the credentials as I took mental notes. "Look Candice, he's a successful businessman, completely legitimate. You've heard of Swann Pharmaceuticals, right? The name is all over hospital equipment too. Well, he's *that* Swann. Honey, I've seen the pictures around his house. I mean, he's freaking golfing buddies with Donald Trump. People part like the Red Sea when he walks into a room." She went on and on and on...

Although I was getting that nervous feeling in my stomach, I also began to relax since I now knew I probably wouldn't be in danger, so I dismissed the Scarface images from my mind. Then I started worrying that I wasn't dressed right, hoping I didn't look like I was trying too hard; too label whorish. I had on black Ann Taylor slacks and a snug fitted charcoal v-neck cashmere Tse sweater, along with the Chanel handbag that was a gift from my dad. Then I thought *just be yourself, Candice. Who cares what they think?*

I reached the entrance, rang the bell and a stone faced housekeeper answered, "Good evening, ma'am."

I remember hesitating because she looked less than impressed.

"Good evening, I'm Candice Kane and I'm a guest of..." While wishing I hadn't felt the need to explain why I was there, the woman gave me a once over, and all I could do was hand her a casual smile.

"Of course. Come in, please."

Stepping inside the impressive grand foyer, I glanced up at the winding staircase and crystal chandelier which I silently admired. I'd never been welcomed by so much grandeur. I'd been in beautiful homes before and I grew up in what my friends called the perfect Leave it to Beaver style house, but this was intimidating; like old money can be. My head started spinning like crazy.

The woman led me into a large sitting room that was the size of a grand hotel lobby and up wide wooden steps that led to the open billiard room. There was a small group of people playing poker across the room. Faith was sitting at the table and waved me in. But right away my eyes fixed on two men on the opposite end; one leaning over the pool table focusing on his shot, while the other stood nearby gazing at me as I entered. He was a cute, preppy black man in his mid-forties.

"Hello, you must be Candice." He waved me over, "Come on in. You're just in time."

I graciously spoke and adjusted my handbag on my arm while trying to read his facial expression. I can only imagine that I was fidgeting at the time. Then the other man finished up his shot and glanced up. I was stunned by how blue his eyes looked and how gorgeous he was. He just stared at me, smiling. He put his pool stick on the rack and made a beeline over to where I was.

"So you're the beautiful friend? I'm glad you could make it."

My first thought was *oh my god; don't single me out, please.*

Extending his hand out to me he said, "Welcome, I'm Frank."

I giggled, "You sure are…sorry, I'm Candice." I remember that because I knew it sounded corny.

It was a pretty uneventful night. Frank Swann and his friends were entertaining with intriguing yet sometimes dull conversation, which I tried to engage in so as to not appear bored. Then the guys started swapping industry war stories. Wealthy men are so silly sometimes and it would have been so easy to take advantage of them without feeling guilty. All night, I caught Frank watching me, but I don't think I was really flattered. For some reason I was ready to leave.

We took the party out to the patio just off the billiard room, where the chef grilled king crab legs and lobster tails. It was an open patio, but there were heaters built in that kept it around a toasty seventy degrees. It's amazing the cozy accommodations that money can provide. I especially enjoyed the Krug champagne,

5

both glasses. I tried my best not to be impressed, but I appreciated the presentation. Not to mention the backdrop of the u-shaped manor wrapping around us was magnificent as the lights in the courtyard below shone onto the house. I mentioned how nice it all must be in the summer.

Frank didn't miss a beat. "It is...you'll have to see for yourself."

He wasn't subtle in the least and I gave him a sassy smirk. I didn't respond to the flirtatious comment, but enjoyed it just the same. I wondered how in the world Frank had met Faith. Or what he felt he had in common with her. God bless her, but she's a little rough around the edges.

As I was leaving, Frank discretely handed me his card and wished me well. When I got in the car, I tore it in half and shoved it in the bottom of my bag. *Not interested!* Besides, I was still trying to stay focused. Men always threw me off course. My mind was on the promotion among other things. I had a plan and was on the fast track to stick with it, unlike my more free spirited friends like Faith, who stayed there after I left.

Just before midnight, I got that expected phone call on my way home.

"Candice, so what did you think of Frank? He's nice, isn't he? Not a thug like you thought."

"Sure Faith, he was alright." All the while, thinking how good looking Frank was. "We stayed too long, though. Are you leaving soon?"

"No, I'm hanging out a while. They're starting up another poker game and I'm watching."

Undoing my hair from the ponytail and fingering it loose, I warned her, "Well just be careful. Don't stay too long. You don't want to look desperate." I meant that.

I was tired and focused on the drive back to Hoffman Estates. The champagne had gotten to my head and I was crashing quickly from the sugar high.

"...and Faith, you shouldn't have to ask a man out, silly girl! Just flirt a little, and if he's a gentleman, he'll beat you to it. Keep it classy."

Earlier when we were on the patio, I'd heard Faith whispering with Frank's friend, asking him to dinner and I wondered what that girl had gotten herself into. All I could do was shake my head.

When I got home, I went to my bedroom and fell back on the bed, staring at the ceiling and thinking about work, then about the night I'd just had. I turned towards my handbag on the bed, grabbed it and fumbled through it until my finger tips found the pieces of the torn card that read *Frank W. Swann, Chairman, Swann Pharmaceuticals Inc.*

I wondered about this Mr. Swann and how Faith had met him. It's funny, I'd never really heard of him, so curiosity led me to Google his name. What I found shocked me. There was his image, his bio which told me he was forty-seven, and then the company website along with a string of articles, including many on the World's Richest People. That perked me up more than I care to admit. What can I say? I'm a girl, and I'd be lying if I denied being flattered to have a guy like that show a spark of interest. I had flashbacks of his smile and those eyes. Pursing my lips and biting the corner of the bottom lip, I felt my curiosity increasing. I wanted to know more.

It reminded me of when I was a kid and had one of my first brushes with a famous man; specifically the head honcho.

I was thirteen years old and my family went to see Smokey Robinson, with the Temptations on the same show. I was standing in the corridor of the Arena waiting with my parents for the concert to begin. All of a sudden, my little cousin came up, "Look! This man just put this on my shirt!" My eyes fixed on the little square sticker that read SMOKEY ROBINSON BACKSTAGE. My overbearing uncle snatched it off my cousin's shirt and then I quickly spoke up, "You're taking me!" I dashed off after him, leaving my own mother, a huge Smokey Robinson fan, in my dust just standing there. When we got backstage, my wide eyes roamed the room looking for a famous face. Out walked a Temptation then another who chatted briefly with my uncle and spoke to me politely. Not impressed, I nodded but eyes still roaming for 'the star'. Standing in the crowded hallway, I saw him walk out of a room, a dressing room I assumed, but there he was...Smokey Robinson. I gasped and hit my uncle's arm, "There he is!" Now, I had no real idea what Smokey Robinson meant to a lot of people. I kind of knew a few recent songs because my mother played them all day. But what I did know was that he was the headliner for the night's show and that's what impressed me. I wanted HIM to greet me. Not someone from the opening act. Smokey was the one all of those women in the front of the house had come to see. Now he was standing right in front of me, smiling with the greenest eyes I'd ever seen, asking me, "How are you?" I blushed and shyly said hello, because he was really a good looking man but I was more star struck than anything because there was no way I'd think of liking a man that old. As far as I was concerned he was another notch on my celebrity meet and greet list. Meeting Ronald McDonald when I was eight was just small fries, literally. I didn't really care about anything that Mr. Smokey Robinson was saying to my uncle, and he didn't really acknowledge me anymore as far as I could tell. Why would he? Even though I looked older, I was a kid! The other men in the room hadn't realized that though, because the Temptation with the deep voice, said of me to my uncle, "This is a cute blonde you got here." What did that mean, anyway? Boy did he piss me off. I thought to myself, 'You washed up has-been!' My uncle laughed and said, "Oh, she's my twelve year old niece." I barked back, "I'm thirteen! Can we go now?" I was bored since I'd already gathered my story to tell the kids at school on Monday.

The same intrigue was rising in me about Frank Swann. He was at the top of the chain. But at the same time, I was a little put off because I sensed he assumed I was impressed by him. But fact of the matter is, I knew there was a possibility that he was messing around with Faith, and it threw me, because they were so mismatched. Again I love her, but Faith could be just a little bit ghetto. Sure she's beautiful and even smart, but always hustling. Thinking back, she had her reasons.

It was getting late, so I put the two pieces of the business card in my top desk drawer and went to bed.

I woke up at around eight on Saturday morning and went down to the kitchen and started breakfast, which I usually did every weekend. I used to treat Annie to a full breakfast on Saturdays. Our kitchen had all the trappings of a suburban wife in the making. It looked like a Cuisinart commercial. I wasn't sure about all of that taking care of the man stuff like in the movies, but I enjoyed the feeling I got using the dual ovens and stainless steel appliances. I always said it's so pretty you just want to cook.

Somewhere in the middle of stirring the eggs for the French toast I was making, I started feeling guilty. Something told me that Faith was hoping to settle into Frank's world, nice and cozy like. Still, even though he came off a little forward, there was something about him that I couldn't shake. Caught off guard by my thoughts, I just kept stirring, trying to push them out of my mind.

The gentleman always wins

"That's correct. They're to be delivered tomorrow. Not today - tomorrow. Alright, thank you very much." As Frank hung up the phone, the knock at the door startled him. "Come in."

The statuesque brunette walked into her boss's office, carrying a box of files and placed them on the corner of the desk.

"Mr. Swann, here is their entire file that goes back twelve years. I'm sure this will be helpful."

Frank cut his eyes at the stack and went back to staring at the monitor without so much a word.

The company's vitamin supplement division was facing an impending lawsuit from a rehabilitation center in Arizona that claimed they'd received a product that put their senior clients at risk. Actually, what really happened was they'd decided to go with another company and wanted to cancel their commitment to Swann. They'd even threatened to contact the networks. Swann attorneys spent weeks engaging them, but Frank had enough of the threats. He did the unthinkable, and decided to squash the games himself. Something he never did.

He turned back to the mounting stack and shook his head. "You know what, just send that back please. They're not getting away with this! Contact their legal department and schedule a meeting for me with the administrator anytime over the next couple of weeks."

She looked puzzled, "Are you sure, Sir? We could send Legal to do this."

Leaning back in his chair, he smirked, "That's what they think is going to happen. No, we're going. I'm handling this myself. Thank you, Stacy."

Swann Pharmaceuticals became an industry leader in medical supplies because they stand by every product. Never compromising, and certainly not kneeling to a small fry like those guys in Phoenix.

That's the type of shrewdness he learned from his father, Frank W. Swann, Sr. and his great grandfather Howard F. Swann who founded the company back in

10

1892. They have a saying: *Think beyond the bluff and do what's right for the company.* He passed that on to all of his executives and field employees, and now Swann Pharmaceuticals is a sixteen billion dollar a year empire.

It's also that type of confidence that prompted him to locate a young woman named Candice Kane. For all he knew, she'd call and curse him, but he chanced it because he sensed her curiosity towards him the night they met. Frank hoped he was right.

Candice: They don't give freely

The drive into work that Tuesday was no easy feat for me. I was meeting with two of the partners to interview for the project manager position. One of only two other black women on the team, I had initially thought I was the experiment. But, I'm smart and dedicated, and my work product is stellar. So, I was pretty confident that the position was mine if I wanted it.

Wishing I could take a longer route to the office, I almost dreaded it and only because I wasn't sure if I actually wanted that promotion. It wasn't really my field and the prospect of attending grad school still loomed. Taking on this new position might have been more of a setback than a blessing. I didn't know what I wanted to do.

I got to work that morning dressed in my dark blue Armani skirt suit, put my things on my desk, and headed down the long hallway. I stood outside of the conference room and said a quick prayer for guidance. I didn't pray a lot, but it felt like one of those moments where I really needed God's help. I was torn between practicality and desire for a new adventure.

Well as it worked out, the partners did offer me the position and I quickly accepted. But, walking out of that conference room I couldn't shake the feeling of disappointment in myself instead of being excited. I knew I wasn't staying in Chicago. I impulsively accepted. I didn't want to be stuck, and at the same time didn't want to disappoint the people who believed in my ability.

At the end of the day I got a call from Anne as I packed up to leave the office. "Hey sis, are you on your way home?"

I put her on speaker, "Yeah Annie, is everything okay? You need something?"

Anne giggled a little, "No, but there was just a delivery for you."

I stared at the phone, "Okay, what is it? Well...come on." I hated when she stalled like that.

I could hear ruffling in the background as Anne was obviously walking through the house. "You'll see when you get here. But hurry, because I want to hear about what's going on, Can." I shook my head not sure what my nosey sister was hinting at, but I was irritated that she wouldn't tell me.

When I got home, I walked through the kitchen door, sat my bags on the island and crept around the house, ending up in the living room. Immediately I spotted a huge crystal vase filled with perfectly bloomed red roses. I was awestruck.

"What in the world?" A blushing grin came to my face as I touched them and leaned in to inhale the aroma that filled the room. I pulled apart the little card that accompanied which read *I couldn't find anything as splendid as you...hope these will do. ~Frank Swann.* Spoken like a man who couldn't wait to have sex with me.

Blinking my lashes, I was a little stunned. If he was attempting to woo me, he had succeeded. Yet, I was also a little put off by his presumptuousness. I wondered what made him assume he could send me flowers. And how did he get my address? No matter, I was certain men of Frank Swann's stature didn't give freely and I couldn't help but wonder what he wanted from me.

My sister and I were raised by hardworking middle class parents who taught us the basics of life: how to be honest, dignified, strong women. My father had his own business and instilled in his girls the importance of making our way, while at the same time, not turning our backs on opportunities granted us.

Our mother always said, it doesn't make you less of a woman. Just make it known that you don't *need* the door to be opened for you, it just helps when someone extends the gesture. Strong families come from the strength of the women. She wanted that for her daughters. Anne is a divorcee but her marriage ended because her husband couldn't handle that she could think for herself and refused to be his puppet. So he went out and cheated on her. Getting out of that marriage was the best thing that happened, because he abused his headship with his mind games. She now runs her own website design business and is doing well. Most of all, she's happy with herself, which is what I wanted for me.

Lying on my chaise in the den, I was swarmed with thoughts. Mostly wondering how I was going to break it to my family that I had decided not to take the promotion after all and was planning to move to Los Angeles. I needed a new scene and that included entering USC's graduate journalism program. I even had a roommate; a high school friend who invited me to stay in her condo until I got settled.

Then I thought about Frank Swann and his roses. I hadn't spoken to him since that night at his house. I felt suspicious about his grand gesture and before I knew it was mumbling, 'what does he want? He can't assume I'm that easily bought.' Inside, I knew that wasn't what he was trying to do.

Although I was a little skeptical, I was still intrigued by him. Part of me wanted to know more. He was interested in me and I wondered just how much. Powerful men still had a pull on me. I enjoyed the attention of men who were so-called important. Although I knew they were mostly selfish egotistical pigs, they filled a need, and I think the innocence that I projected attracted them. I'm sure a psychologist somewhere would have a lot to say about that.

My phone was ringing in the bedroom down the hall and I rushed out to grab it. When I saw it was Faith calling, I quickly picked up to take it. I didn't expect the greeting I got.

"Hey what's going on?"

"I don't know, Candice. Is there anything you want to tell me?"

I could feel the angst and sarcasm through the phone and braced myself for what was next. My mind was racing on fast forward trying to come up with fitting answers.

"Not really. I decided to turn down the promotion. The timing is…"

Faith abruptly cut me off, "Candice, what's the deal with you and Frank?"

"What are you talking about? There is no deal!"

Faith started talking fast, without taking a breath between sentences, which told me she was about to flip.

"Frank called me today. I thought he was inviting me out or something, but you know what? All he cared to discuss was you."

I closed my eyes and sighed. "Look Faith, you're the one who insisted I come out to Lake Forest with you. I didn't want to be there. Next thing I know he sends me flowers! How'd he get my information anyways, Faith?"

There was an uncomfortable silence. "He sent you flowers? Okay whatever... bye!" Faith was mad. Not hurt – mad, like she had lost a competition.

The line went dead and I was left conflicted. How'd I get into such a mess? I hated to let a man come between me and a friend. Especially a man I didn't really know. I had to try to fix the situation. At least that's what I told myself, because deep down I was dying to know what would come next. I wasn't sure if it was real interest or an insatiable curiosity towards Frank. Either way, let's face it - Frank knew exactly what he was doing when he sent me those flowers.

Hollywood Schmooze

"*I* want to avoid those cameras out front Renee, so what can you do?"

"Of course, Mr. Swann. I'll go around to the other entrance." The driver continued past the red carpet and bright hot lights that welcomed the celebrities arriving to the event.

"Thank you." Scrolling through emails on his phone, Frank was bored already. The entertainment industry, especially the schmooze fest surrounding award shows, is just not something he was interested in. "I'm only here for the drinks, you know what I mean?" The driver looked in the rear view laughing with him.

It was the eve of the Grammy Awards and Frank was attending the Clive Davis party at the Beverly Hilton. He socializes with some showbiz big shots, but wants no real part of it. Though he respects the business part of it, he feels the rest is a silly waste of time. Frank was making a brief appearance as the guest of super producer and composer, Derek Fabian, a long time family friend from back East.

Entering the ballroom, he spotted Derek and his wife Bebe seated in a plush banquette chatting with musician Alicia Keys. They waved him over as an over eager cocktail waitress interrupted his path, offering a glass of champagne.

"No, but I'll have a martini. Dry, please. Thank you."

"Frank buddy, you made it!" Derek leapt up and greeted him with a handshake, draping his arm around a shoulder. "Alicia, I'd like you to meet my friend, Frank Swann. Frank...Alicia Keys." Derek turned back to Alicia, "You should be talking with this guy, Alicia. I'm a nobody!" The group laughed, not with Derek but mostly at him. He was a little tipsy.

"Glad to see you've finally accepted that fact, Derek." Frank chuckled, exchanging friendly intros with Alicia before leaning down to greet Bebe with a kiss. "You look beautiful, Bebe."

Bebe's smile appeared for probably the first time that evening, "Thank you darling. Are you here alone?" She peered around him for a possible date.

Bebe Fabian looked elegant in the ice blue satin Nicole Miller dress. Her wavy platinum hair, brushing against her shoulders, almost glowed. Frank thought what a lucky man Derek was to have her. She'd been a good friend to him when he needed a listening ear. There were few trustworthy people in their world, but Bebe was the real deal.

"Yes, I just got in from Chicago last night and I haven't had time to do much besides come here tonight."

"Well we're happy you did." She crossed her legs and cut her eyes at Derek who was now chatting up recording artist Morgan Bryant and his wife. "Oh, Frank I don't think you've met Morgan and Rayne. They're absolute sweethearts." She dangled her slender diamond encrusted hand in the air, "Rayne? Rayne darling!"

The music was pulsing and loud and the buzz around the room even louder. They almost had to shout.

Rayne came over and grasped Bebe's hand, "Good to see you again. How are you?"

"I couldn't be better. You look gorgeous. I want you to meet a dear friend, Frank Swann. Frank...Rayne Bryant. Her husband Morgan and Derek have been working together recently. They're nominated for...how many Rayne? Two I think?"

Rayne nodded, "Yes, that's right. He's so happy about it." Turning her attention to Frank, she flashed him her megawatt smile. "Frank, it's very nice to meet you."

Frank cupped her hands with his, "The pleasure is all mine." He nonchalantly admired her perfect cocoa complexion and curvy, petite frame and smiled, "Congratulations on the nominations, I'm a fan." He lied, albeit in an elegant manner.

"Oh, yeah...thanks." She gestured towards Morgan and Derek who looked on. She didn't seem too interested in her husband.

The wait staff finally brought their drinks over.

"Excuse me for a moment, ladies?" Frank grabbed his martini and left them.

When he walked away, Rayne sat down quickly, "Is that THE Frank Swann? He's like a zillionaire or something, right?" She giggled.

"Well, yes that's our Frank. He's a darling and his ex... she's a fool for what she did to him."

"Huh! She must be." Rayne watched Frank as he caught the attention of other guests as he walked across the room. He stopped to talk to some skinny blonde actress who seemed a little out of place, but from the looks of her body language, knew him fairly well. "He seems nice. Not an asshole like most moneymen."

Bebe giggled, drinking her champagne.

Frank left the party after an hour. He made the courteous appearance, but the Hollywood Schmooze was not his thing.

RAYNE

I'd just checked in on my babies after coming home from the Grammy party. The nanny had gone to bed, and I made sure to spend a moment with them before I turned in. Every night, I kiss each of them before they go to sleep. Morgan always thought I coddled our kids too much. He went directly into the home studio to play back a track he'd just written. The song couldn't wait until the next day. You'd think after all of these years I'd be used to coming second to what really turned him on, which was usually his music. Notice I said usually.

Morgan and I got married right after college, and I pretty much carried us while working as an accountant, and he pursued his music career. He held gigs as guest vocalist for a couple of jazz bands and earned an impressive solo reputation on the club circuit. All the while he was working on his own music. Writing and arranging. He was destined to be a star. Hey, I was no fool. I sincerely loved him, but I knew full well that my sacrifices would pay off one day. I was right. Now he's Grammy award winning singer, song writer, Morgan Bryant, and he provided a comfortable life for me and our children. That life was in the Mulholland Estates enclave of Beverly Hills, in a sprawling eight thousand square foot home nestled on almost two acres.

We had a perfect family life. Or so it appeared.

Candice: The Chase

I finally got around to telling my parents about the plans to move to LA. I have to admit, I was a little disappointed because they weren't as upset as I thought they would be. My mother was shocked, but didn't even cry. It's like she didn't care. I think my sister was just happy to be getting her privacy back. I still don't know why Anne needed so much privacy. It's not like she was getting any action in the dating department. I used to tease her that she'd end up an old, lonely lady with a hefty bank account because Anne never spent any of her money on anything fun or risky. I surely didn't want to be that girl. Already in my early thirties, I felt it was high time I got out of Chicago and lived my own life. Not the one my parents wanted me to live.

In the midst of putting on moisturizer after my shower, I heard my phone ringing. I sprinted into my bedroom and grabbed it off the bed.

"Hello, this is Candice." I sat on the bed, turning my head away from the phone, to catch my breath.

"Candice, Frank Swann. How are you?"

I was so caught off guard, since I never returned his call or even thanked him for the flowers.

"Oh, um... hello. I'm good, how are you, Frank?" Pulling the loosening towel tightly, I waited, curling my feet underneath me.

"That depends on you, Miss Candice." His voice was soothing, and I enjoyed being on the receiving end.

Giggling under my breath I asked, "Is that right? What does that mean, Frank?"

He laughed, "It only means that you left my home rather quickly last week and I was hoping to get to know you better - as friends."

I didn't say anything. I was rapidly dissecting, replaying and reading into every word he'd just spoken.

"Actually, I would like to take you to dinner."

No! He wasn't going to transition so easily. I paused for a few seconds more. "Well, it's just... first I need to clarify something, Frank."

"Okay..." He responded in a tone that said uh oh, here it comes.

Though I felt a little hypocritical for asking the following, I knew I had to.

"I realize Faith and you are acquaintances, but...are you involved? I mean, in any way? You do understand why I'm asking?"

He paused. "Of course. Faith is a beautiful young woman, but that's not the nature of our friendship. So come on, give a guy like me a chance to know you."

I loved his voice. He had that distinct dialect reflecting a polished Northeastern upbringing. I was confident that I was right about that. I enjoyed the way he smiled as he spoke to me. I also had to give him a few points for how smoothly he brushed past my concern about Faith.

"You're funny. Well, I'll think about it, okay?"

"How long do you need...sixty seconds?" There was no subtlety with him.

I laughed and nervously tightened my towel. "At least ninety." I rolled off that girlish giggle again, "Alright, dinner sounds great."

"Good. I'm in LA right now, but I return to Chicago on Thursday, so let's say Friday evening? I'll pick you up at seven."

"Sure. See you then...and Frank?" I nervously pressed my lips together.

"Yes, Candice?"

"Thank you for the roses. I love them."

"My pleasure. Goodnight."

I stared at the phone, blushing as I hung up. At this point I was thinking less and less about Faith and wondering more about what to expect out of Frank. He knew just how to charm me; like the way he picked up on my interest in him. Now, I had two days to prepare for our date. I hoped I knew what I was getting into.

Looking at my reflection in the dressing table mirror I thought out loud, "What are you doing?"

I tried my best to self-talk out of it; thoughts like he was trying to get me in bed, nothing else. But the truth was that inside I didn't really feel that at all. There was something about Frank that I trusted. He was at least fifteen years older than me so perhaps that was it. That he was past the game playing phase. Still, it was completely against the rules I was used to following.

BEBE

Everyone in this town knows me. At least they think they do. Who I am, what I think, and what I stand for. The media touts me as an accomplished, beautiful society queen, appearing to have it all with my Grammy Award winning songwriting career, beautiful homes and solid marriage to virtual star maker, music impresario Derek Fabian. The darlings of Beverly Hills are how they describe us. Well, they sure know how to write fairytales, don't they?

I have to say, my life is a far cry from my early years in Nashville, but many a time I've wanted to cash it all in. I've often felt like I was being choked by the life we'd built. I wished I could run away, but couldn't. There was too much invested in being Bebe Fabian, and more than that, so many people depending on me to be perfect. Or else, the ideal doesn't work.

My early morning runs have always been my only real escape from it all. I lead a fairly simple life outside of my social commitments. So each morning, which usually starts at six am, I throw my hair into a ponytail, grab a yogurt from the Sub-Zero and prepare for my run. It's a ritual - the time I get to spend alone. No cell phone, no Derek, nothing, just me, the sputter of sprinklers and the chirping birds that sang out over Beverly Park. It's rare for any of the women in our ritzy enclave to get out of bed before ten, but I never saw myself as one of the women. I've actually worked hard for everything I have.

There's a lot of heartache behind these gates and I especially, have never shared mine over tea. I learned much better than that, years ago. The southern girl inside of me keeps home business, at home. This brings me to my husband, Derek. During this time period, something was going on with him that I couldn't quite put my finger on. I was sure it was dirty whatever it was because he'd changed for the worse. I just hoped it wouldn't tear us apart. We were teetering on the brink as it was.

During the first few years of our marriage, we were nearly inseparable. We wrote songs together, appeared at public events holding hands and stealing moments to cuddle at award show parties. A lot of which would end up in the tabloids: Hollywood's Sexiest Couple. They were waiting for one of us to mess up.

It's like you're not allowed to have a real marriage in this town. Unless there's a public fight or one of us is caught sneaking out of a bungalow in the middle of the night, we're not "normal".

I admit neither of us had walked the line perfectly. But then, I started noticing drastic changes in Derek's behavior. Something had gone completely wrong. I couldn't place it, but we started living separate lives under the same roof.

No woman should ever feel so alone in her own home. I wouldn't have wished this dark time on my worst enemy.

Candice: The catch

*A*fter two hours of switching dresses and accessories, I finally decided on the right outfit to wear to dinner. My sister had suggested I dress for cocktails. I wanted to be more professional looking but Anne told me, "You may as well admit that this is a date, little sister!"

I just laughed her off, "It's not! He's back in town and we're having dinner, is all. I just want him to know I'm not what he's expecting. You know, take the flowers and lay on my back."

It was just going to be a nice dinner. Anne nodded and left the room while I finished dressing. So I finally decided on the black knee length Diane von Furstenberg wrap dress. I threw on my pearl necklace and earrings along with black ankle strapped heels and my favorite cobalt blue Michael Kors python clutch to add fun color. I wanted to look like a lady, and not some gold digger, which is what he was probably used to.

At seven o'clock sharp my sister whisked into the room. "Candice, Frank is here. I saw him pull up!"

Annie's smile was huge and she was all excited. The bell rang, so she went to answer it. I was still standing in my bathroom fighting with my hair, which I wore down with loose, wavy curls. The self-talking continued. "God, I hope I'm not making a huge mistake. Here goes."

As I approached the landing at the top of the stairs to the living room, I heard my sister talking and laughing. Then I spotted Frank standing in the doorway with a hand in his pants pocket. He was wearing a black two button sports jacket, with a white shirt unbuttoned at the collar and slacks. I thought how good the jacket looked against his leftover California tan. Not to mention his shortly cropped, dirty blonde hair and graying temples. He appeared a lot better looking than I'd remembered. When he looked up and saw me approaching, he softly smiled and I wondered where he hid those delicious dimples before. He was too good to be true and I was waiting for the other shoe to drop. No man so debonair proved to be sincere. Not in my recollection anyways.

When I walked into the room, Anne was still talking, while Frank watched me the entire time. The same as he did on our initial meeting. He released his hand from his pocket and extended it to me as I approached him, lightly clasping my fingertips. I couldn't deny the tingle I got from that.

"Hello, you look gorgeous." He leaned in, giving me a light hug, but pulled back before it lingered too long. As if he perceived I wouldn't like that. Not out the gate.

I felt his eyes on my skin. I also knew he was checking out the dress on the sly. I was fine with that. It's why I wore it…for him. I know how to work it, and that dress hit my lean but curvy body perfectly. He enjoyed me I could tell, because his eyes told me so.

Modestly I blushed a little, "Aw, you know just what to say, Frank." Intentionally not returning the compliment like women often feel obligated to, I grabbed my shawl off the chair.

Walking out the door, I almost got light headed when the first thing I saw was a soft blue Bentley GT parked out front. He paced himself ahead of me to get my door. I realized the car had already started and I think I purred as I settled into the plush leather that smelled like clean crisp bills. I was still cynical and thought that must go over well with the ladies.

When he got in, Frank just stared at me for a second while Marvin Gaye crooned from speakers.

"I'll tell you one thing, Candice. I'm glad I cleaned up tonight."

His smiling blue eyes, and the way they crinkled at the corner caused my suspicious thoughts to fade away. I decided it was okay to enjoy Frank's company.

Averting my eyes to the mahogany console, I calmed down. "You look pretty good yourself." I looked up at him, "So, where're you taking me?"

He raised a brow, "Yes, well, a place I know you'll love. The food is incredible."

I nodded, smiling, "Okay…" I couldn't help but wonder what we'd talk about at dinner and I hoped he was really being himself with me.

We arrive at downtown Chicago. Turning onto North Lakeshore Drive, Frank told me he was taking me to The Seasons, which was one of the city's most posh restaurants. I'd never eaten there, and would never have gone with my sister or a female friend. It just seemed like a very romantic spot.

"I've always wanted to bring someone here for dinner. It's very elegant and the chef..." Frank claimed to have only dined there with business colleagues, but was going to make the night special for me. I wondered how he would do that.

The valet met the car and we got out and went inside, to the second level of the building, where the cordial host greeted us.

"Mr. Swann, welcome. Good evening, Miss Kane." He then escorted us to a private dining room that was set for two.

I'd been in many a upscale establishment, but this was by far the most impressive because firstly, the Maître D' greeted me by name, then a private wait staff catered to our every need. I felt uncomfortable only once, and that was when one of the servers cut her eyes at me. A fair-haired female and I imagined it was just out of jealousy, so I ignored her.

Dinner was beautiful and the chef pulled out all the stops. We enjoyed a five course meal that included rack of lamb and rib eye, which I sort of picked at. The wine helped me to relax even more. Frank's sense of humor was refreshing too. He wasn't like any man I'd gone out with before.

Then...in the middle of telling him about my move to Los Angeles, the conversation took a turn that I swear I could have only dreamed up. I almost wished it hadn't, because it unfairly caused me to question my own motives regarding him.

Somewhere between the third glass of wine and the crème brulee, I brought up my applying to USC. Frank had told me he attended Stanford where he studied biochemistry before in his words, 'the grueling years' at Harvard, earning his MBA.

"Congratulations! You know, you'll have endless options once you're done Candice."

I smiled at him, flattered that he showed interest in my plans. "I hope so. I mean, I already have my BA in Communications, so I think this will be a good move for me. The school is very hands on and I love that. Not to mention LA is a good starting point with so many possibilities, you know? I even have a place to stay off campus, which I prefer. A friend offered me to stay in her house." I must have rambled on and on like I was in an interview.

Frank continued, sipping his coffee, "It's the perfect location; New York or LA...especially in your field." He nodded, looking directly into my eyes which made me self-conscious. I averted my eyes towards my plate, and then looked back up.

He paused, dabbing the corner of his mouth with the napkin and leaned forward with his hands clasped on the table. "The friend you mentioned, she lives near the campus or...?"

I quickly cut in, "Yes, she has an apartment in Mid Wilshire, so it's like fifteen minutes, which works good. I'm just grateful she's willing to let me live there."

He grinned, "That's really nice. Actually my daughter lives in Malibu." He giggled, "She loves the beach, and you know how that goes."

A little surprised, I asked, "Oh, you have a daughter, Frank?"

Nodding he continued, "Yes, Karoline. She's twenty-one and a little off course. She's a great kid, don't get me wrong, it's just...she has her ups and downs. It's probably my fault. I don't say no enough." His focus drifted off, then back to me.

Not sure how to respond, I listened and continued eating my dessert and then thought about it. "Well, she must be pretty responsible if she lives there alone." I wanted to ask him more, what he meant about Karoline, but I held back.

"She's a very responsible girl. It's just that she's young and her friends... I'd just feel better if she didn't live alone, but she doesn't trust her friends enough to roommate."

Even though Karoline's story was poor little rich girl sad, little did Frank know that my interest pretty much peaked when he started talking beach property, because I could only imagine living on the beach and how peaceful it must be. I think he read my mind.

"Maybe you could live there, Candice. She'd really like you. I do."

He looked away, waving for the server. I studied his face to see if he was serious or jesting in conversation. I realized the man was indeed serious.

"Well now, there's an idea!" I enjoyed another swallow of wine.

He looked at me convincingly, "I'm serious, Candice. You two would get on well. I'm sure of it."

Even though I was tempted to jump in head first, I also thought he was pushing his life on me a little too quickly. We weren't really friends yet, and now he'd offered me a place to live? There was so much to be done with getting prepped for school like the entrance interview, financials and not to mention gathering letters of recommendation. I didn't have time to think about his last minute invite.

"I don't think that's a good..."

He waved his mint flavored stirrer as he spoke, "Would you at least considerate it? Grad school can be tough, you'll appreciate the beach after classes, trust me." He chuckled, watching my facial expression. "I'll talk to Karoline. It'll be fine." He continued on with his coffee.

It's as if he'd already decided my future, and I didn't like it. I was intrigued, but wanted to make my own decision.

When I got home after dinner, I couldn't stop thinking about LA. I was more excited than ever at the prospect of entering USC in the fall. I had all kinds of thoughts.

Settling into a hot bath, I fought hard to push Frank out of my mind. I didn't want to get myself in another situation where I'd be on the receiving end of disappointment and humiliation.

The realist that I am, I couldn't fight off the nudging thoughts that said, here I am - a middle class black woman from Chicago being seduced by Frank's glamorous world of prestige, power and money. I couldn't wrap my head around it. And on top of it, he was offering me to live in his house while I went to school. I wasn't sure I could be comfortable with that because there had to be something else he really wanted from me.

"I've seen it a thousand times, but I'm not going to be so easily bought Frank Swann...so no thanks to you and your gorgeous blue eyes!" I giggled out loud, punting the bubbles up with my feet, and then submerged myself under the water.

In all seriousness, it was a way out of Chicago and a chance to get a jump on what my life was meant to be, with grad school being the number one priority. If I got wined and dined by a man like Frank now and then, that was cool too.

I had some serious decisions to make, in a short amount of time.

Rayne: Having it all

"Come on in, Morgan. You don't have to knock!"

Looking up at my husband standing in the doorway of the master bath, I brushed the bubbles away from my top half, teasing him. "You like?"

A sexy little smirk appeared on his face as he walked over behind me, knelt down and reached his hands underneath my arms, stroking and cupping my naturally full breasts. I've never even considered implants. Fortunately there was no need. I rolled my neck at the sensation that his touch gave me. Like the feeling I got when we first married, only now it occurred less often.

"I have to drive out to Studio City 'cus I'm working on something with Rod." I couldn't help but wonder why he scratched the back of his neck as he told me this.

His collaboration with young hot mega producer Rod Jamz would almost guarantee Morgan's new record platinum status out the gate.

I leaned forward, "What? Morgan, it's like nine o'clock already. Can't it wait until tomorrow?"

"What can I say, he likes to work late, baby. Come on, Rayne. I won't be long, I promise." He kissed my neck, stood up and shook the excess bubbles off his hands.

"Alright." I laid back, leaning my head against the pillow, reaching for the remote to turn on the television perched from the ceiling. It was time for Criminal Minds, my favorite TV show.

Morgan looked up at the screen with sarcasm, "You and Shemar Moore!"

"Don't be a hater...and pull the door back on your way out!" I closed my eyes and mumbled something out of frustration.

Being married to the king of R&B, Morgan Bryant for nearly eighteen years hadn't been easy. In fact it had been a test of my sanity. When we met in college, he was literally a starving artist and I was the girl who believed in him. Even then he possessed one of the strongest voices I'd ever heard and a vocal range that rivaled his idols, Michael Jackson and Stevie Wonder. We moved to LA a year after getting married, to follow his dream.

In all the years we'd been together, I'd never resented Morgan more than I did at this time. Adding more Grammys and AMA's to his repertoire didn't help. He was at the top of his game while the bottom was falling out of our marriage.

I know people sometimes envy the life we lead, but what they don't know is that I'd trade places with them in a heartbeat. I was a lot happier when we had to sit down in our two bedroom Leimert Park apartment and figure out whether to pay a bill off or invest in studio time. We valued the little luxuries we were able to scrape together, and because I would make personal sacrifices to help him accomplish his goals, he also valued me. Then Sony called. The rest, as they say, is history.

Morgan began to take me for granted. I felt more like his live-in girlfriend. He spoiled me materially, but like this night, played his little sexual mind games to buffer his actions of staying out all night, "in the studio". If I complained he'd say 'Look at our life, Rayne! What are you bitching about?' As if he'd done me this huge favor. He didn't get it. But I guess with this life, you can't expect to have it all.

Your wife will thank me

*D*ing! The elevator leading to the twelfth floor of the Marquis Lofts & Towers in downtown Los Angeles stopped and a young woman in her mid-twenties decked out in a tailored Chanel suit, stepped off. She strolled down the dimly lit hallway with a key in hand. Her charcoal lined, seductive eyes, full mouth and chiseled cheek bones caught the attention of a random guy coming out of an apartment with his girlfriend, who nudged him with a frown on her face. The sexy temptress softly smiled and looked away, but not before doing a quick assessment of his watch and then his shoes. She scowled at the slight scuff on one. Thinking to herself *don't worry honey; he can't afford me* she continued on like a tigress searching for her prey.

Stopping at the large door at the end of the hallway, she inserted the key and lightly tapped as she entered the apartment. There was no one inside.

Surveying the open space, Sexy Miss walked over to the bedroom area and just as she requested, found the unsealed envelope tucked neatly under the flower vase. She sighed, "I just love fresh tulips..." Then leaning in to inhale the aroma while her manicured fingers slid the envelope out, she quickly counted the crisp notes and tucked the stash away in her Chanel tote.

"Hmmm..." She released her bag and removed her jacket and skirt, revealing 38D breasts cradled in the lavender and black tulle bra and matching suspender bottoms. The skirt dropped to the floor and she stepped out of it, fluffed her hair and sashayed over to the bed where she lay on her stomach, enjoying the feel of the exquisite Egyptian cotton against her skin, and waited. While playing with her emerald ring, the door clicked. She glanced at the entryway then looked away. "Is that you?"

"Yes, please don't be angry."

The man's voice, while masculine, became intentionally weak, begging her for mercy as he grew hungrier for her beauty, watching the muscles of her tanned, rounded ass flex as she swung one of her legs up and back.

"Come here!" She ordered him without acknowledging him visually. "You're five minutes late."

"I'm sorry Holly, I…"

"Oh shut up!" She rolled over with one knee bent, the heels of her five inch Giuseppe Zanotti peep toes penetrating the bedding, and lightly gliding the tips of her fingers across her buxom chest. "Do you know what this means?" She possessed huskiness in her voice that was both sexy and intimidating. This girl meant business.

Standing there unapologetic, he shrugged and exclaimed, "I'm sorry, what do you want me to do?"

Pointing to the floor, she ordered him, "I want you to beg for forgiveness."

The gentleman removed his sports jacket, nearly sweating of humiliation, while she watched his every move.

Holly sat up on the bed, "Kneel right there. Do it!"

There he was, a man who is considered a titan in his industry, kneeling. "Please…"

She licked her lips, biting the corner and raising her eyebrow, "No." Shaking her head she took a hand and rubbed the top of his head, like a pet. He reached out to touch her arm, but she pushed his hand away scolding him, "Don't touch me!"

It wasn't until he felt the utmost degradation did he get a massive hard on. If anyone else had been there, they would have been embarrassed for him.

At that moment, Holly allowed him to look her in the eye. "My time is precious too, but you're too selfish to realize it. Now get up here!"

With a hungry look in his eye, he sheepishly started to rise and crawled onto the bed from the floor as she stood in the middle of it looking disgusted. He unbuckled her shoe strap and kissed and licked her foot.

Her face softened, "Mmm, that's better…"

He pulled her down towards him grinning, while she straddled him in a controlling position, pinning him down with her subtle gyrating hips. "You never keep a woman waiting. Do you understand, baby?"

"Yes Holly, now come here…" He licked at her cleavage in desperation.

"You dirty boy… I'm going to teach you a lesson."

"Yes, teach me, please. I've been so inconsiderate."

His manhood was attentive beneath her as he rubbed his hands across her fleshy thighs, unsnapping the suspenders.

She smirked looking at him with a teasing grin, "Remember, I'm not doing this for you. Your wife will thank me one day."

Holly leaned over him, and he grabbed her face, planting a wet, forceful kiss, as she received his tongue between her lips and open mouth.

Professional escort Holly Taste spent two hours in a cycle of humiliating and rewarding her gentleman for his obedience, before adding more degradation to their scenario. The highly respected and celebrated man had just been demoted to a sex slave and felt it was worth the two grand he'd just dropped to be with her.

After she showered and dressed, Holly sat at the edge of the bed and handed him the cocktail she'd made for him. "We're friends and whenever you need me, I'm here for you." She rubbed his face with the back of her open hand as if petting her puppy goodbye.

He lay back, against the mountain of plush pillows, sipped his vodka and watched her walk towards the door. He winked as she waved and left. His craving had been satisfied and he eagerly awaited their next tryst.

Candice: Caught in the middle

Out of the blue, the doorbell rang and it was Faith. We hadn't spoken in over a month and honestly, I wondered why she had stopped by. The last conversation made me feel like crap and I wasn't sure if I wanted to deal with that again. Of course I opened the door.

"Faith? Hey, come in…"

Somehow Faith found out about dinner because she walked in with that tone of hers and started in on me with the repeat of, "So why Frank, Candice? You knew we were hanging out!"

I turned and walked towards the kitchen. "Come on Faith. Let's talk because you've got this all wrong." She knew me better than that and besides, Frank was just another mark as far as she was concerned.

Faith followed me into the kitchen and helped herself to a juice from the refrigerator, "Okay, so talk."

I sat on the stool at the counter looking at Faith's pretty, but hard face. "Why do you always do this? You hover around these men just because they have money. You don't have to do that…you're smart and you're beautiful. You don't need them!"

On the defensive, Faith jumped in, "Look, this isn't about me, alright! It's about YOU and how you maneuvered your way in to Frank's face."

I shook my head, "You know what? We're not fourteen. You made me come to his house! I guess you wanted to show off as usual. You insisted that I meet your rich guy friend and well…I met him. Besides, he's a grown man and has a right to have the friends he chooses. Actually it's none of your business!"

Deep down, I felt like I had shoved Faith off her bike and taken off with it. Still, while I loved my friend, at the same time, I couldn't wait to see Frank again, so I laid it out.

"Faith, you don't even like him. You like the *idea* of him and everything that comes with it. You know I'm right!"

Faith was left speechless. I'd hit the nail on the head and she couldn't fire back with anything. She put her slender, manicured hand on her hip looking puzzled, "Damn, Candice, Frank basically told me the same thing you just did. I just don't get it. He saw you all of what, five minutes?"

I got up and hugged her. "Faith, we're best friends. I'm not letting anyone come between us, but girl you know you're not that into him. I know you." We laughed.

"No, no I am...but not like THAT. I mean, Frank is fine as hell, but I just don't enjoy sleeping with white men." She twisted her mouth like she used to when we were kids and she was back peddling a story.

"You're a nut!" Giggling at my blunt friend, I figured it still wasn't a good time to tell her that Frank offered me to live in his beach house in LA. She'd surely go through the roof.

"Oh shoot! Girl, my friend is waiting in the car. I have to get out of here, but um...let's do something next weekend, okay? I do miss you."

We hugged and promised to make plans. When Faith walked out the door, I watched her climb into a black Cadillac Escalade which some guy was driving. The license plate read 1CHISTRM.

"Ahhh...Chicago Storm..." I assumed he was a pro basketball player. Needless to say, my guilt subsided instantly.

Angels do exist

"Yes, Mr. Green, it will be an honor to be there tonight. We can't wait to see the children."

With the call on speaker, Bebe drove up Santa Monica Boulevard in her Mercedes S-Class, towards Fairfax Avenue, where she was meeting her associates at the Arts Center.

Reaching into the console, she clutched the Chanel No.5 bottle, and lightly sprayed into the air, fanning her hands.

"I'm ten minutes away and I believe..." Keeping her eyes on the street, she reached over and flipped open her schedule planner on the passenger seat. "...a gentleman by the name of Horace will meet us out front with his guys and all of the goodies." Bebe's smile could have lit up all of Hollywood that afternoon. "Great, see you shortly."

"Dial Sheila!" Her voice prompt dialed her co-chair's number.

"Hello, this is Sheila."

Fluffing her hair with one hand, Bebe called out, "Darling, hello. Listen, how close are you?"

"I'm pulling into the lot right now, Bebe."

"Good, I'll be there in five. Thank you, Sheila."

"Of course, see you in a few, dear."

Turning onto Fairfax Avenue, approaching the West Side Performance Arts Center, Bebe could see two black vans parked inside the gated lot. She turned in, and Sheila greeted her at the car.

"Bebe, honey. everything is here. It's perfect!" Sheila's voice always sounded as if she was in a bubble bath. Relaxed and stress free.

Sheila Ericson, one of foundations most dedicated Angels, is the former wife of R&B record label chief and mega producer, Keith Ericson. After winning a settlement of close to forty million in the divorce two years before, she vowed to continue the fight to keep performing arts in schools. Their divorce was fairly amicable and Keith was still one of her biggest supporters. To make it even cozier, he purchased an estate within jogging distance from Sheila, who still lived in their Holmby Hills mansion. All to assure that their teenage daughter, a student at the prestigious Mount Mary High School, kept her routine as emotionally balanced as possible. Talk about a friendly breakup.

"Fabulous!" Bebe climbed out of the car, smoothed the skirt of her St. John suit, and hugged her friend. "I can't wait until they see all this stuff."

Bebe becomes animated with excitement when she's bringing what she calls, "gifts" to the kids. On this night, there was going to be a performance of Oliver Twist. Talented kids from all over LA were given the chance to excel in music, dance, visual art and acting classes, to name a few. The majority would not have that opportunity had it not been for the people like Bebe Fabian, who never took credit of her own. *The arts are instilled in all of us at birth* is her motto, and she makes sure every child possible has a chance to nurture those talents.

"Ladies and gentlemen, Mr. Green, we'd like to thank your staff and these wonderful parents and amazing students for allowing us to be here tonight to represent the Angels of Music foundation. I don't want to bore you with a long speech, so...guys, bring out the toys!"

Bebe and Sheila gestured for the kids to come forward, grasping their hands, and handing out hugs as they all anxiously waited for the surprise.

The gentlemen rolled out a new piano, cellos, wind instruments, violins and other equipment. Sheila took to the microphone.

"These are just a few things we were told you guys wanted." The cheers were almost deafening, and Sheila waved her hands, laughing. "But...but, we realized there are costumes, props and much more that you will need, and you're better suited to pick that out. So, it's our honor to present the West Side Performing Arts Center with a check for thirty-five thousand dollars."

Mr. Green, the Center's director, was in tears as the children crowded around him, jumping up and down. "Ladies, you've just made their dreams come true. So many children will have the opportunity to come alive on this very stage because of your generosity."

The audience came to their feet in applause. The group left the stage, as the curtain was about to rise. Those boys and girls gave the performance of their lives.

Off stage, Bebe whispered to Sheila, "See, this is why we do what we do. This is what really matters, the children and their smiles. Look at them!" Sheila's eyes were misty as she agreed.

Driving back to Beverly Hills that night, Bebe started reminiscing about being a student back in Nashville, in the Seventies. The music classes she'd spent hours a week in and the performances on that stage. She was determined to help as many kids as possible have a jumpstart at achieving their goals. Money was not going to be their obstacle if she could help it.

Candice: They had their chances

*U*sually a basketball game excited me because I love the game, but this night was a crazy mess. Faith invited me to the Storm game since she had great seats. Dating a pro basketball player has major perks and a courtside seat is one of them.

We arrived at the Chicago Mecca and parked in the secured lot at the rear entrance. Walking through those doors you were in the spotlight. The women dressed like they were attending the Player's Ball. Full length mink coats, exclusive designer handbags and shoes, and the three thousand dollar hair weave...all courtesy of the Association's payroll. We gathered in what was called The Family Lounge and snacked on catered food, which included premium alcohol. Faith had a few too many.

"Girl, I want you to meet Kai. I just met her a week ago and she's so freaking nuts! I think she's a pill head...and always assuming somebody wants her nasty ass man. I heard he's bisexual anyways - so serves her right!" Waving her over to us, Faith yelled and pasted on a fake smile, "Heyyy, Kai!"

Kai, a walking man trap with jet black chin length hair, porcelain skin and emerald eyes, rushed over to us with her boot heels clicking and long black diamond mink flowing behind her. Sure it was mid February, but it wasn't freezing outside. That was all for show, flossing her latest gift.

"Hey honey. How are you? And, who's this?" Taking a bejeweled finger to pull her hair behind an ear, she looked me up and down, with a nearly sincere smile.

Faith answered in step, "This is my best friend Candice."

I extended a hand to Kai, and she reciprocated. Kai was a Wifey which means she was the girlfriend of a ballplayer. Not his wife...just a live-in play wife. Her guy was a starter for the Storm and he treated her like a princess. At the same time, he cheated on her to no end which is probably what made her so suspicious of any attractive girl, or guy for that matter, who came within a thousand feet of that court floor.

"Where are you guys sitting? I'm 101." I figured it made her feel just a little superior saying those words.

Checking our tickets, Faith said, "Oh, so are we. We'll go out together."

The families usually sat in sections 101 or 102 just behind courtside floor seating. Kai wrapped her fur covered arm through mine, which was already taken over by my oversized Marc Jacobs bag.

"So, why haven't I seen you before, Candie? Are you with one of the guys?" Kai's unnatural baby voice rivaled Latoya Jackson's, and it was getting on my nerves.

I wanted to pull away so badly. "It's Candice...and no, I'm not. I've been there, done that. You know how it is."

Faith recognized the look in my eye and rescued me from Kai's reckless clutches. "It's almost tipoff so let's head out." I must have looked at her like, get this chick away from me!

Being in that environment gave me flashbacks of when I was going out with then superstar hoopster Casey Headway in the late Nineties. I was just twenty years old and we were crazy about each other, but we were pretty much doomed from the start.

I met Casey while I was standing outside the family room after a Storm game. He was on the opposing team, and they were walking out of the locker room heading towards the buses. I was leaning against a wall with a family friend while she waited for her sports reporter husband to come out of the Storm locker room. Bored and ready to leave, I heard someone standing over me saying, "Why you standing here looking so mean?"

I was about to fire back something smart, but looked up and saw him smiling at me with the cutest face I'd ever seen. "I'm not mean, just tired..." I looked away towards the door hoping it would open and my friend's husband would come out.

He held his hand out, "I'm Casey." It's a good thing he said his name, because I really didn't recognize him under his cap.

I couldn't help but smile, "I'm Candice. It's nice to meet you, Casey."

Kids were trying to get his autograph. Some guy, team personnel of some sort, was directing him to the exit. Casey took a kid's pen and paper and jotted his phone number on it and handed it to me. I thought that was so lame, but had no intention of throwing it out. Two weeks later I called him. "I just wanted to check if the number was actually yours." He seemed amazed that I'd called and said he had been thinking about me.

Soon after, he flew me to Florida to visit him. I brought my sister Anne with me as sort of the guardian. Besides, I didn't want to give him the wrong impression. After that weekend, we saw each other as often as his schedule allowed. The romance went on for over a year. There were gifts, trips, you name it. The guy was generous; generous to a fault because apparently he was doing the same thing for someone else in Miami.

Out of the blue, a girl called me asking questions about Casey, and where I lived. She was dignified, not confrontational or anything; just confused, like I now was. The world of basketball wives and girlfriends is a small one. They talk, and news gets passed on until it reaches the one who should know the truth.

I wouldn't take Casey's calls for a couple of weeks and one day I was watching TV and saw him on that stupid animated commercial. I called right then, and broke it off with him.

"No Kai, no more ballplayers for me. They had their chances and they blew it."

Kai shrugged her shoulders and the roar of the crowd escalated at the announcer's voice: "Are you ready for your Chicago Stoooorrrrrrrmmmm?"

The music and spotlights started pumping. It was Showtime!

Rayne: Meet Trey Chic

"*H*ey, what's up, Rayne?"

Trey's voice was always confident and upbeat, like he had the dish on something, which he usually did.

"Trey, how are you? You guys still in Chicago?" I had the schedule on the kitchen desk, so the kids knew where their father was at all times - geographically anyways.

"No, we just rolled into Milwaukee." Looking at the clock on my night stand, I realized it was a little past midnight, two in the Midwest. "Sorry girlfriend, I got your text after the show, but we left out pretty quick, then I fell asleep on the bus. This hotel is alright. You'd like it."

I didn't know why Trey was talking about the hotel when he knew I wanted to know where Morgan was. I hadn't tried to call him because it had gotten frustrating, calling and have him not answer, or some bodyguard answer his cell phone and make excuses.

"How was the show? How was his voice tonight?"

"He was on! Sick or not, Morgan is a pro. You know how your husband is. Never misses a note."

"That's for sure; he takes care of his instrument."

"YOU need to be out here taking care of his instrument, girlfriend!"

Trey always got on me about attending so few shows. He told me that women were always lined up backstage throwing themselves at Morgan. Sometimes even during the show, which I used to find amusing.

When I did go on the road, Morgan asked me to sit further back, around the fifth row or so. He wanted his most eager fans up front. In other words: the hoochie mamas. They're the ones who follow him city to city, with their titties falling out, hoping for their big chance. He'd say, "It's fantasy baby, like I'm singing to them. You have me in real life, so let them have two hours."

44

So I did. I handed him over to the women who daydreamed about sleeping with him. Or at the least, that he was singling them out as he crooned to the crowd. I've seen more cleavage than any woman needs to, not to mention hearing girls actually yelling over my head, how they wanted to be with my husband. Female fans can be so delusional. They actually believe in the eye contact they make with celebrities. But, the sad part is, a fan will sometimes, on just the right night, hit the jackpot.

At first, I couldn't understand how Trey and I hit it off. But he's like my gay husband. We laugh, shop and gossip about everyone, including Morgan. Which is how he became my inside man. My third eye, so to speak. Trey always thought Morgan was a trifling hoe, as he so flamboyantly called him. He felt sorry for me, which is how my eyes became opened to what was really happening. He's a little out there, but I thank God I met Trey.

A year before, we spent a week in New Orleans, leading up to the Essence Music Festival. The kids, the nanny, all of us and I was relieved to be back home. It was a rare chance to cut loose and hang out with girlfriends and family, and enjoy the wild animation of Bourbon Street.

I got a kick out of treating my friends to exclusive access, like being stage side during the sound checks, which in my opinion boasts the best performances because the artist is raw and uninhibited. That Friday, Morgan did an impromptu duet with pop diva Sasha Childs. There were around two hundred fans invited in for the sound check, and they got to witness a tear jerking gospel number that wasn't on the set list. I was so moved and proud of him at that moment. Sasha's voice was like a melodic wind chime and Morgan took it back to the church. I hadn't witnessed that passion since early on in his career. As he left the stage, I saw his eyes were red. Quickly walking past us, he grabbed my hand, and then headed straight to his trailer. Two hours later, Morgan Bryant brought the house down with his full band and backup singers.

After his set, I walked into the lounge backstage and immediately spotted two girls in tight spandex dresses, with laminated passes. Not meet-n-greet, but special guest passes, which you don't get unless you know someone. Groupies – plain and simple. One of them, a busty Latina in her twenties, couldn't stop watching me. Her overly lined eyes literally followed my every move, and I noticed she whispered to her friend, who was too ignorant not to turn her head towards me. I assumed they knew I was family or a girlfriend, as most of the guests waiting in the area were. Funny, I've always allowed myself to forget that Morgan is a celebrity and people recognized not only him, but me. She knew who I was, and the look on her face said, she didn't appreciate my being there.

I made it a point to stay out of Morgan's way when he was working. Not be the possessive wife. So, my friends and I decided to go hang out in the lounge to grab a bite before going back out to watch Sasha Childs' headlining performance.

In walked the cutest brown skinned boy toy I'd ever seen. I shouldn't say boy, but it was obvious he was young, fashionable and gay. He strolled in with his Louis Vuitton man bag draped across his thin frame. He had a strut fiercer than even mine when I wore five inch heels. Trey didn't shy away from the stereotype. He saluted it.

"Ladies..." His facial expression said all eyes on me. His light brown eyes looked me up and down, appraising my outfit. Just as I was amazed at how he worked the skinny jeans that slung at his waist and hugged his tiny butt. He stopped and pointed, "Love the Birkin, baby girl..." He was so animated. Trey fixed himself a veggie plate and then eyeballed the girls in the corner of the room, cutting his eyes away, unimpressed. He took his free hand and rubbed the skin of my prized handbag. "I just have to touch it."

I didn't mind. "It's okay." I giggled.

"I'm Trey, and you are..." He put the plate on the table.

"Rayne and these are my friends. It's nice to meet you Trey." I silently thought he must be the boyfriend of someone in the show.

"Excuse me, Mrs. Bryant he's asking for you!" One of the security guys yelled across the room at me. I nodded.

The light bulb went off in Trey's head. "Oh, you're the wife. Hmph! You're too cute for Morgan." He giggled and revealed that he was brought onboard as the new wardrobe stylist. "I'm just kidding..." He leaned closer and whispered, "...and because I like you, Imma keep an eye on them two thangs over there." Trey indiscreetly gestured, as the girls rolled their eyes at us. Still, I had a sick feeling regarding one of those girls.

"I think you're my new best friend Trey." I patted his arm, "Maybe I'll see you soon."

"Oh for sure, and here…I live in LA. Call me, we'll hang." He handed me a card he'd just yanked from his bag. Reading it, I was tickled. I thought, no he don't call himself, TREY CHIC.

And, that he was. I still get a kick out of that first meeting.

"Trey, I can't just leave my kids every time Morgan needs a babysitter."

"His suite is down the hall, but he's alone Rayne, so don't worry, alright?"

"I'm not!" I snapped at him for no reason. "Sorry…"

"It's okay, boo-boo." He yawned a little, probably as a signal for our conversation to come to a close.

"Call me when you get back in town, Trey. We'll do some damage."

"Alright, mama, see you."

Trey is the friend who tells it like it is. The gay boyfriend every girl needs. He called me his big sister, and I love him just the same.

Candice: The porcelain turtle

"So Candice, how's your friend?" Anne flipped through the channels searching for a movie.

I knowingly asked her, "Which friend...you mean Frank?"

Anne giggled, glancing around at our mother across the room who blurted, "Yes, Frank!"

I was laid back with my feet propped up on the sofa in my parent's family room, but sat up, "Look, I came over here for a girl's night, not to be interrogated." I was only half kidding, and tossed a pillow at my sister.

"Okay, I get it." Anne rolled her eyes up and went back to watching TV.

With a more concerned look on her face, Mom turned her full attention to the subject at hand. "You're so private about him. Usually we know everything by now."

Anne chimed in, "Frank seems like a decent guy, so why are you hesitant about him?"

"What am I supposed to do, Annie? Jump all over him because he has money?" She looked at me like I was crazy as I lowered my eyebrows, visually frustrated. "What is this?"

"Who's talking about money? And why are you so defensive? We're just asking about him." Annie was outwardly irritated with me.

Then the real issue came forth from my mother's lips. "He's older right, like almost twenty years?"

"No, seventeen...you two, please stop!" They knew too well that I'd rather walk out of that house than let them pry, because I certainly didn't welcome their input. But, they were right about my hesitation.

"Honey, Annie and I just want you to be open and honest with yourself. You don't have to hide the fact that you like him."

"Right, Mommy! Remember the last time I listened to you about a man?"

I threw my hand up and couldn't help but think about that dark period in my life. I ended up with a boyfriend who was mentally battering. It took me three years to get past that experience.

I was in the middle of a brunch at one of the swankiest hotels in Chicago when someone came up behind me, pointing to the lavish spread, and said, "This is one of my favorite dishes, try it." I looked up and saw a guy who was so cute he knocked me off guard.

"I um, I think I will."

He had nice eyes. My last boyfriend certainly didn't have that.

Kevin was a chef in Le Rouge, one of the restaurants on site. That was impressive - a man who cooked. I could also tell he was intelligent and somewhat cultured. I know now that he was a very skilled smooth talker and should have an Oscar on his mantle, because he was certainly charming.

His birthday was approaching and he invited me to dinner. Something told me he didn't have a dime to his name, but I fell for him instantly. On the first date, he kissed me and that's when I really jumped in. He treated me like I was the girl he had searched for his entire life.

Then he met my family. Needless to say, Mom and her sisters loved him and urged me to take him seriously because he was 'so charming and we can tell he cares about you. Make sure you don't push him away.' I still can't believe they said that to me. It didn't matter to them that he was broke and had nothing to really offer except his pseudo charm.

Well he turned out to be a serial boyfriend who conned women out of money, was a cheater and was accused of assaulting at least two women during the time he was seeing me. Oh! He was also closet crack head who hid his drugs in plain site; inside of a marble turtle on a table in the middle of his living room. Every time I see one of those, I think of him and laugh. I'm thankful that I woke up and got away.

"Mom, I realize Frank is mature, he's smart, and he runs a multibillion dollar empire. He treats me like a lady and I feel good about myself when I'm with him. BUT at the same time, all of that is what scares me. Right now, I just want his friendship. He's one of the most sincere men I've ever known. That's enough, so stop."

I had to be honest with myself. The thought of Frank sent a flush of anxiety over me that I was embarrassed to admit to. I left my mother's house that night not understanding why. Truthfully I was almost mad at him for coming into my life and making things so complicated.

Over twenty-five, not his type

"Yeah, right here is good." The friend sat down as two servers worked the club house terrace, with him focused on the pretty young brunette who was seemingly trying not to notice. "Frank, you were saying…?"

The Golf Club was busy for a Wednesday morning, Frank's usual tee off with his friend Kip. He started the day at six with a bike ride exiting his Beverly Hills estate for a trek up Sunset Boulevard, to Greystone Park and back. By the time he circles, he's done five miles; usually getting to the club by ten to relax. No business, just clearing his head.

Frank grinned as he checked messages on his phone, and then glanced at the young woman now gushing over the attention Kip was throwing her way. Kip, a Buppie type, looked ten years younger than his forty-four years. His shaved head had something to do with that, concealing his receding hairline. The girl was probably already envisioning herself whipping up and down the Pacific coastline with him, in some sweet little ride. One thing for sure, he had taken many a young woman for a ride.

"What I should be saying is one of these days you're going to catch hell from your wife if you don't quit this." Frank gestured his head in the direction of the girl.

"Oh come on, Frank…it's nothing." Kip had that look in his eye like he wanted to pounce on the girl, who was twenty-two, tops.

Over lunch, Kip, not being much for beating around the bush, asked, "So when you settling down again man? Or are you just enjoying the buffet?"

Kip Matthews has been one of Frank's financial managers since the Nineties. He's a finance wiz with a competitive golf game, and Frank trusts him.

Brushing him off with a laugh, Frank answered as best he could without revealing too much, but just enough. "It's not like that, but since you brought it up, there is someone."

"Yeah?" Kip seemed surprised. "Well she's got to be something special to make you single her out as one, so who is she?"

"Let's just say she's beautiful, over twenty-five and intelligent. Not your type!" Frank teased, drinking his Evian.

Kip smacked the table, "Dammit! You got me there, man." He cut his eyes back at Pretty Young Miss.

Something Kip said made Frank realize that not only did he enjoy Candice's company, but he wanted her in his life. Even though he hoped she'd seriously consider his invitation, he didn't want to scare her off either. He could feel her interest in him building, but also knew she was afraid to cross the line into more than friendship. There was a wall up that he hoped he could break through.

Rayne: On second thought

*A*tlanta worked as a good stop on the tour for me. I took Trey's advice and decided to join Morgan on the road, for a couple of shows. When I told him my plans, he said, 'That's good baby, but why don't you spend Miami with me? We have a few days off after that show, and I know how you love the beach.' My suspicions told me he didn't want me in Atlanta. But trying to be positive, I was excited because I knew it meant that once we got the Miami show out of the way, we'd spend some much needed grown folks time away from the kids.

People always assume that the life of a celebrity's wife is roses. That everything is easygoing and since you have people waiting on you hand and foot, all you do is shop on Rodeo Drive, have spa days and sex all the time. That's an illusion, at least for me it was.

Admittedly, I have a housekeeper, a nanny to help with the kids, and a house in a lush canyon in Beverly Hills, the whole nine. The American Dream, especially for a little black girl growing up outside of New Orleans, in a less than desirable neighborhood like The Crossings. We had one grade school, one high school and lots of garbage bins lining the streets waiting to be emptied eventually. I wanted a better life for myself and my family: the good life. Well, I got it. I remind myself of that every time I hear *be careful what you wish for*, in the back of my mind.

I hoped Miami would be just what the doctor ordered, because my marriage was sick, and we needed whatever help we could get.

Candice: Done deal

On March 29 I arrived in Los Angeles for the big interview at USC. After weeks of preparing, becoming acquainted with the program and the school as best I could, I felt I had my presentation all set. All I could do is be myself and show that I was focused on excelling. I stayed with the friend who originally offered her home. I hated to break down and tell her I had another housing situation. I described it as long term house sitting. Who was I kidding? So that was weighing on me too.

She wasn't insulted but said, "An opportunity is just that. Grad school is tough. Working and going to school would be too hard, so good for you."

I made sure to get a full night's rest because if I hadn't, I would have woken up bitchy the next morning. I didn't want to give short and snappy answers. If I had blown it I would have died.

Up at seven-thirty, I had a couple of hours before my ten o'clock meeting with two members of the faculty. I chose a navy blue pantsuit and feminine blouse underneath and mid heeled pumps. My hair was pulled back in a sleek ponytail. I was careful about my first impression, and let my work speak louder.

Although I'd already submitted some writing samples and awards from DePaul on the disc I included with the application, I felt it was to my advantage to bring hard copies along, just in case. My friend let me drive her car around town for the visit. The more she did for me, the guiltier I felt for ditching her for Malibu.

Driving down Jefferson Boulevard I came to the realization that not only was I most likely going to start USC in a few months, but would finally be living in Los Angeles for at least the next couple of years.

The meeting went so well that it felt too easy. It wasn't until they mentioned the recommendations that I understood why. Professor Patton brought up the "stellar recommendations we've received...you'll be an asset." I had to fight the urge to drop my jaw when he continued, "Frank W. Swann, Chairman of Swann Industries says of you..."

I was floored. I hadn't even asked Frank for a recommendation. We'd spent a bit of time together over the weeks prior in Chicago, but he never let on that he was doing that for me. He took it upon himself. I didn't know whether to be elated or angry that he'd assumed to do that. I just chalked it up to him trying to use his influence to help the process. Truthfully, in the industry I was about to enter, who you know counts for a lot so I tried to be grateful for his gesture because he didn't have to care.

I called him as soon as I walked out of the building.

"Hello, Frank? I - thank you so much. I don't know what to say."

He softly gushed under his breath on the other end, "It's the least I could do for you. You did the work; I only helped put the exclamation mark on the end. So how's LA?"

I could almost feel his chest elevating as men do when women allow them to be our heroes.

Stopping in my stride, I instantly made up my mind.

"Perfect! And Frank... yes, I'll accept your invitation. It'll be a little bit of a drive, but I'm so excited. I can't wait to start my life out here!"

Frank went out of his way for me and showed that he cared about my future. I was starting to see him in a different light.

"Wonderful! You won't regret this, Candice. Now, enjoy yourself. Get to know your new town a little. We'll talk soon."

No matter what people thought, sometimes good things *are* handed over to you, and I was not saying no this time.

Bebe: Champagne afternoon

I must have walked through the doors of The Beverly Hills Hotel a hundred times. On this day, I was there to visit the spa and to have Camille's hands on me. She's the most skilled masseuse in LA, in my opinion. She's thoroughly attentive, and for sixty minutes, has complete control over my body. Camille knows how to not only help you relax, but how to guide you there. It's why I go to her when I need to escape.

Lying face down on the cotton sheet, my naked body covered only by a towel draped across my butt, I should have drifted off like I normally did. The aroma of sweet candles and oils in my cabana were intoxicating. Camille's warm hands glide in long full body strokes, subtly applying deep and heavy pressure at my longing joints. I felt guilty that I always enjoyed a private sensation as she gave attention to my thigh muscles. It felt good and I hoped she enjoyed the intimate access to my toned, naked thigh. I've worked hard to achieve these legs and I'm proud of them. I may have even slipped and released a slight moan, but she continued, unfazed.

Instead of drifting off, I started thinking about my relationship with Derek, even wondering if he'd want to do a couple's massage. Maybe that would connect us, even if for a short while. He'd been on another planet and I couldn't reach him. We merely co-existed in our home, and stayed out of each other's way to avoid an argument. I had my life, he had his, and we met somewhere in the middle. I didn't like it, but that's how it had been for quite a while. We hadn't had sex in six months. If it weren't for Camille's hands, I would have felt intimately abandoned.

That was the problem. Because he was focused on a couple of major projects, I realized Derek was in work mode and that I shouldn't try to penetrate it, so to speak. The music man could only tend to one thing at a time, music being that thing. That usually put me in second place.

But still, there was something else. I either *couldn't* see it, or refused to.

"Mrs. Fabian, how do you feel?"

I opened my eyes, and gazed at the inviting pool below me. "Fabulous, Camille. Thank you, darling."

"My pleasure, ma'am. I'll give you a moment to relax, and Jocelyn will be in to start your facial."

I put my robe on and enjoyed a glass of champagne before she came in. Not even Derek would ruin my afternoon of bliss.

Candice: Convincing myself

*I*t was August and I was aboard a flight to LA, about to meet Frank's daughter Karoline face to face. She wanted to pick me up at the airport, but I told her I'd better get used to driving around. I was really excited to finally get things rolling.

I'd officially been accepted into the graduate program at USC's Annenberg School, and I felt like my entire world was about to change. It was actually happening. At the same time, I was full of anxiety. Not because I was visiting and preparing to start school in the coming month, but because the circumstances of that move had changed. For six months, I'd undergone a long process of entrance exams, gathering letters of recommendation, financial processes, etc... Now, here's where things had changed for me, and for the better you could say. Two words: Frank Swann.

Two weeks before, Frank was back in Chicago and we had dinner. He has a way of making everything seem okay. He was charming of course, but almost fatherly as well. I don't mean because he's older than I am, but he's the take charge type of man I always needed in my life. Frank turned out to be nothing of what I expected. I thought he was a rich playboy, out to get every piece of ass he could buy. I was wrong about him.

No matter who I'd dated in the past, no matter the money they had, they were always expecting something of me; needing something. Frank needed nothing. He hadn't even tried to sleep with me. I was also sure that he had enough girlfriends stashed away that he was fine with our platonic friendship. He said he enjoyed my company and that I had a refreshing outlook on life that he hadn't seen in ages. I suppose I did, but over the years, I have to admit, my trust had been filed down.

I couldn't help but feel a bit like an opportunist sometimes, even though I knew that's not what it was about. I began to trust Frank. Apparently, the feeling was mutual, because we had a long conversation about opportunities in life. He kept giving me reasons why I should feel good about my living arrangements. Reasons like, my family would probably worry less because he could protect me, and he'd feel better about his daughter having someone like me around as an influence. I have to say, he really knew how to pour it on.

I'd be lying if I said I didn't appreciate the fact that a man like Frank wanted to help me along while I was in school. His support meant a lot. I felt like I'd been given a chance to start fresh. I hoped against all hope that I wasn't making a big mistake. But hey, why not? He'd offered and I'd always wanted to live in Los Angeles. Now I got to do that and go to school. The fact that I virtually had no overhead relieved half of the stress. There were no excuses for not doing well. It was now up to me to remain focused. It's easy to get sidetracked in LALA Land.

Rayne: Cake and eat it

"Oh my god, look over there - it's Morgan!"

I heard this screeching proclamation as we stood across from the boarding gate at the magazine stand, killing time as we waited for our Noon flight to Miami. In a knee jerk reaction, my head turned around, witnessing an eager little strumpet who was all of twenty-one, pop up from her seat in the American Airlines gate area, tapping her friend's arm. She adjusted her tight tee shirt, which was cut at the cleavage to allow her pushed up boobs to spill out. Tight jeans, tucked into knee boots, showcased her tiny waist and hips that were wide enough to be appealing to men who liked them a little thick in the right places. Her companion, who was dressed more conservatively, was just as excited but did a better job at holding her composure.

"Come on girl, hurry before he leaves!"

I couldn't help but think how aggressive that little white girl was. It didn't matter to her that I was six inches away from Morgan, who was seemingly oblivious to her excitement.

I tried to block them. "Babe, let's go wait in the lounge." I wasn't up to dealing with his fans.

Flipping through the rest of the Billboard magazine, he hurried and put it back on the shelf while the sales clerk watched his every move with stars in her eyes, like she wanted to say something, but refrained – thank God.

"You can baby, if you want to. I don't feel like being hemmed up, but Steve will go with you." He gestured to his bodyguard who was already approaching my side.

"No that's fine I can…" *What the hell?*

"Um, 'scuse me, hi… Morgan?" The fan sheepishly approached, but pretty much poked her head between us, not acknowledging me at all. I was fine with it because the fewer words exchanged, the quicker she'd go away.

I watched Morgan's eyes glance up from behind his Louis Vuitton sunglasses, purposely downplaying his assessment of the girl's curvaceous frame. I didn't miss that. He quietly smiled, trying to respect me standing there. I thought to myself that's why I don't go on the road.

"Yeah, how ya'll doin'?"

His attention was all she needed. The girl's lashes started batting over wide green eyes, and the tee shirt was pulled even lower, while the compliments spilled from her mouth.

"You were awesome! We were at both shows..." Again tapping her friend's arm, "...weren't we?"

The friend looked embarrassed but nodded in agreement. "And we'll be front row at the show tomorrow in Miami. I just love your music. We can't get enough!"

Then tight tee shirt girl finally acknowledged me. "So you're Rayne? You're so lucky!" She looked me up and down like why wasn't I as ecstatic as she.

"In the flesh." There I was, the inspiration behind Morgan's sexy ballad, Summer Rayne, which was always a fan favorite during his concerts. He'd sit at the piano, lost in the melody as the crowd sang along, and then stood up with the wind machines blowing his shirt open, revealing his cut abs as he belted out the lyrics. I gave her a forced smile.

She asked if I minded taking a picture of them with Morgan. He sure didn't mind - reaching his arms around the girls' waists as I performed my duties of the supportive wife.

"Thanks girls. What are your names?" He signed the tour programs that they'd pulled out of their totes, while continuing, "Alright...and make sure ya'll have a good time at South Beach." He winked at the bubbly brunette while squeezing my hand, moving towards our gate.

From his lips. They were honored at the instruction, and in unison declared, "We will!"

I swear my eyes must have rolled all the way up to the back of my head. I'd grown accustomed to playing the role, but it seemed the girls were getting bolder. The wife of a huge star is more of a technicality in their eyes. It doesn't deter them one bit.

As we sat in our first class seats with me on the aisle, the girls sauntered past us, waving and gushing at Morgan, who was laid back in his seat and already had his Bose headphones on. He was now in his private zone, so I chatted with an older lady across the aisle that was looking at a picture of her grandchildren. I thought it was sweet, and tried to forget about the tour, fans and the insecurities that were rising in me by the minute.

When we arrived at the Ritz-Carlton on South Beach, I didn't have to worry about anymore interruptions. It was just the getaway we needed. Morgan didn't have to work until it was time for his sound check the next day, so we made plans to meet Enrique and Claudine Martinez at The Forge at seven.

Early on in his career, Morgan wrote and produced two hit songs for Claudine. He was virtually an unknown, but his songs were chart toppers. We've remained friendly ever since. I learned a lot about the celebrity existence from them. Enrique and Claudine always kept their marriage first and the business second. I wish I could say the same about us. Morgan thought I should be jumping for joy because he was on top and 'making a good life for us'. I think sometimes he saw me as one of his adoring fans who lapped up anything he said.

How could I be happy when I was certain he was screwing around? No woman could be. Still, I felt stuck and backed against a wall.

Candice: Welcome to the 'Bu

I didn't exactly know how to get to Malibu from the airport but had rented a car with a GPS, so I was more secure about getting around LA. Once I got onto to the 405 Santa Monica freeway, I felt a chill come across my body and shivered like I was cold. The temperature in the Toyota Camry displayed ninety-two degrees outside. I guess I was just excited about the move. Smiling, I reached into my handbag on the front passenger seat and found my cell phone to call my sister.

"Hi, Annie! I just want you to know, I'm here. Yes it was fine. Anne please, tell me something...tell me I'm not making a mistake."

My out of breath sister put me on speaker, saying she was in the den working out.

"Okay, you there, Can? You know we're going to miss you like crazy, but this is an opportunity you'd be insane to pass up. You're starting grad school at USC! It's not like you dropped everything to get on American Idol or some craziness. You will be fine sis. I'm proud of you."

That's just what I needed to hear. But at the same time, I couldn't help but wonder why my usually judgmental sister hadn't insinuated the negative about Frank. I'd seen what serious money did to people - it changes their reasoning. I hoped that didn't apply to Anne, because she's the one person who always brought me back to my senses. If I started drifting, I counted on her to wake me up.

"Thank you...well I'd better focus on this freeway system. These people are in a hurry out here, and I have no idea where I'm going. Anyway, I'll call you later. I love you."

"I love you too! Bye..."

The drive towards Malibu was fast and easy. I remember that seeing the Santa Monica Mountains almost took my breath away as I inhaled the air around me.

"Ahhh, this is definitely home."

The directions were spot on. As I drove the Pacific Coast Highway approaching Point Dume, I felt a surge of calm, like I really was coming home. It's hard to explain the feeling.

Driving up the winding cliffs, I finally got to Birchwood Lane which is where the house is located. All I could see was the blue ocean behind the homes.

"Approaching destination, on your left..."

The robotic voice directed me to a house that was hidden by a wall of shrubbery and fencing with roses overlapping the top edges. The wood paneled gate at the driveway was closed and I could only see the shingles on the roof of the house.

Craning my neck, I looked out of the window and then back at my directions, "Alright, here we go." I turned into the driveway and pressed the buzzer.

After a couple of minutes a perky voice responded. "Yes!" I'd spoken to Karoline only twice, but recognized her voice from phone conversations.

"Hello, Karoline. It's me, Candice."

"Oh great - just a minute!"

There was a buzz and the gates slowly opened. Karoline met me out front in a white strapless sundress and bare feet. Her flowing auburn locks whirling in the breeze, she looked just as excited to meet me. I hoped that would last.

"Hi, Candice. Oh my god, welcome!" Clapping her manicured hands together, she giggled rushing over to hug me. "Listen, I'm interviewing a chef right now. He's in the kitchen and you can help me."

I wondered if she was serious about the chef.

Karoline was talking a million miles per hour. "I thought it'd be a good idea because our schedules are going to be so insane and right now I eat out almost every day, which is not good. We won't have a lot of time to do it ourselves. It's just a few days a week..."

Now that's one prospect that really appealed to me. Not having to cook every day. Fiddling with the pendant on my necklace and looking up and around the exterior of the modern bi-level structure, I told her, "That sounds great. Maybe I'll learn a thing or two. I'm a pretty good cook."

"Really?" She seemed surprised by that. We shared a laugh while walking into the house. "Good and remember this is your place too now, so please don't feel like a guest!"

Her blue eyes sparkled as she smiled; causing me to think how much she looked like Frank. Karoline was a young, free spirit who didn't seem to let privilege and money go to her head, because it's all she's ever known. She'd been sheltered from the so-called real world by her father. So to her it was normal to have someone come into your home and cook your meals.

I met Chef briefly, but let Karoline finish up, while I wandered about, checking out my new digs. I didn't feel I was ready to help hire staff just yet, because I was hoping to fit in myself.

Karoline was a complicated girl from the start. On one hand, a pampered princess who indulged the lavish lifestyle that her father provided her; like living in a five million dollar home rent free. While at the same time, she rebelled against those privileges and tried to downplay it.

For instance, she was accepted into Stanford University to major in Art History, but decided she would rather stay in LA and '...contribute to my community.' So she volunteered at afterschool kids programs as an art teacher and tutor. Then at night she partied. She and her best friend Brandon, another member of the lucky sperm club, were seriously tapped into the pulse of the LA social scene.

I'm sure that's where the troubles started. Frank thought Brandon was a bad influence on Karoline because he didn't do anything except spend his own family's money, party and drag Karoline off for days on end to Palm Springs and God knows where else. This is probably why Frank felt she needed someone who would set a reasonable example, living in the house with her. She's a good girl who always tried to save people, but is easily swayed in the other direction with her ending up being the one needing to be saved.

When I got inside the house, I immediately saw that the rear of the house faced the Pacific with its wall of windows framing the jaw dropping view. There was a deck with beautiful plants and flowers and chaise lounges. I remember how I couldn't take my eyes off the ocean, with the surface waves dissipating at the sand's edge. I smiled and basked in the moment. It all had to be seen to be believed. For a second I got caught up and wished I could see it every day; but realized that as far as I knew, I would be.

"Candie Kaaaane!" Karoline giggled walking in on me standing at the glass door in the living room area. "Okay, so I think we have our chef! What do you think? The house…do you love it?"

I turned around, "Honey, what's not to love? It's home!"

Karoline raised her eyebrows, "My father sure wants it to be!" She grinned, walking off. I wasn't sure how to receive her tone, and must have looked a little taken aback as I followed her. Then Karoline made an attempt to fix it.

"Don't get me wrong, so do I, but I'm not stupid. I realize you're here partly as my babysitter. I know my father. But actually I think this will work out great…really!"

I glanced at the floor and back at Karoline, "It's really not like that Karoline. But, your father does love you."

Karoline shrugged, like she didn't care. "Let me show you to your bedroom." We strolled down a narrow hallway, passing a few closed doors and at the end of the hall was a set of wooden doors. "I live on the upstairs level mostly, and there's also a third bedroom, but Daddy suggested you have the master."

I stopped in my tracks, "Karoline, I want you to know…your father and I, we're good friends. He's been wonderful to me, but I don't want you to get the wrong idea."

Karoline put a hand on my arm, "I don't have any idea. All I know is Daddy doesn't bring just anyone into our lives. He must really trust you. That alone makes me feel okay about this."

I thought that was sweet and smiled, "Well thank you. I feel the same."

Karoline reached at the knob and turned it, "Alright then…" She opened the door and all I saw was a sea of blue. The entire wall across from the bed was glass and the view of the ocean floored me. "Welcome to the 'Bu, Candice. I hope you love it."

The 'Bu. Malibu speak for the overpriced oceanfront community.

While I wasn't convinced that I deserved to live in such luxury as a student, I also felt like every dream I'd ever had had just come true.

It was the beginning of the rest of my life.

Candice: Too much reality

*I*t had only been four weeks since I'd arrived in LA, and with the exception of missing my family, Chicago was a distant memory. I'd even started socializing with new acquaintances from USC. One night I was at Clique having dinner with a guy I met in the student bookstore. Will (actually his name was Willy but I insisted on dropping the Y, because I just couldn't call him that) asked me out and I accepted. He's at least five years younger than me, but was so adorable when he asked, like he was shy about it.

Right in the middle of our date, my cell phone rang. It was Frank. I hadn't seen him since moving out here, but he told me he'd be in town soon.

"Are you coming to the beach house when you get back? We'd both love if you did. I'll cook dinner...well, maybe the chef will."

"Ahhh, of course... the chef." He teased me and I couldn't help but giggle when he sounded pleased that I was settling in.

Frank asked about school, but only passively, and then I cut it short.

"I'm actually out with a friend, but I'll be speaking with you." I wished Frank was there with me instead.

"Well, I'll see you soon then Candice. We'll spend some time together, okay?"

I told him I looked forward to it, and the call ended. I picked up my drink and glanced up at Will who tried to play off the fact that he was a little suspicious of the call. Men are a funny breed. They do the same to us and expect us to believe it's 'just a friend'.

After a couple of hours of talking about school, laughing and the typical flirting, we parted ways. I made a point of driving myself to the restaurant. Though afterward, I felt ashamed that I was going to drive home after three drinks, but felt okay to do so. I didn't feel tipsy or anything. It's just that ever since my little cousin Marty died at the hands of a drunk driver many years ago, I promised I'd never drive under the influence. Of course I'd broken that promise many times. Still, I felt bad every time, and this night was no different. I started the car, slowly pulling out of the restaurant lot onto Robertson.

I clicked on the radio in time to hear El DeBarge crooning *"All this love is waiting for you...."* Memories instantly flooded back hearing that song. The night air was cool and the wind hummed over my car, of which it felt good to be back in. I was so excited when the movers arrived with it a couple weeks before, along with some other personal belongings, furniture and such; most of which was put in storage.

I got home just after eleven and noticed a woman walking a large dog past the front gate. I checked my rearview mirror and she seemed to be hanging around, as if she was playing with the dog. She kept glancing through the gate, so I got out of the car and asked the forty-something blonde with obvious fake boobs if she needed something.

The woman wound her dog's leash tighter and flashed a phony smile, "Oh hi. You live here now?"

I couldn't help but wonder what the hell business was it of hers. I made sure to keep my car door open as the woman stepped towards the edge of the driveway, "Yeah, may I ask...?"

The lady laughed, "Oh, it's okay, I'm Bria. I live across the way. See, right there!" She pointed across the street as if I was really interested.

Glancing towards one of the houses, I nodded, "Right...well, nice meeting you!" I closed the car door and walked towards the house.

"Wait! I know it's none of my business, but I assume you're either Karoline's new guardian, or Frank's uh... friend?"

I exhaled; trying to conceal the rising anger, and with a light giggle shook my head, "Have a good night!"

I then noticed almost every light in the house was on and Karoline's Mercedes was parked in the circular drive with a black Denali behind it. When I got inside, I was greeted by the sweet smell of pot and it instantly pissed me off.

"Karoline! Karoline, where are you?"

I heard 'Oh dammit! Put that out...Brandon NOW...put it out!' Karoline strolled down the staircase in a tee and rumpled sweatpants hanging off her butt. "Candie Kaaaane...."

Her addressing me in that tone was starting to aggravate me. It was endearing at first, but now was condescending.

"Look, Karoline, I know this is your house, but whoever you have up there needs to go!"

Karoline's face scrunched, "Excuse me?"

Feeling bolder, thanks to the bimbo outside, I shot back, "You heard me...now! Please Karoline, I can't deal with this."

Just then a lanky figure appeared behind Karoline, "Yeah so uh, we'll be at Area if you want to stop by."

The tall blonde guy, who would have been cute if he wasn't so dorky, walked down the staircase staring at me.

"Wow, you're pretty... You look like that black chick from...what's her name? Tan...Tan something...?"

I rolled my eyes at him and looked back at Karoline who at this point looked embarrassed and instructed her friend, "Thandie Newton...now Brandon, just go!"

He threw a hand up, "God, it was a compliment. You two need to lighten the hell up. Okay I'm outtie." He slammed the door.

I gave Karoline a blank, disappointed stare and walked off towards the bedroom.

"Candice, what is wrong with you? What have I done besides roll out the red carpet to make you feel welcomed?"

I stopped and turned around, "I don't know what you really think of me, but this can't happen. I don't get high, and I don't like smelling it!"

Pursing her lips and looking bored, "Well, sometimes I like to have fun!"

I cradled my head with my left hand because by that time, I had a killer headache, "Look, do what you want. I'm really tired. Between that crazy chick across the street and this, I..."

Karoline looked confused, "What crazy chick?"

I told her about Bria confronting me outside.

"Oh forget her! She's just a jealous, hungry whore. She doesn't matter." Karoline then looked remorseful. "Candice I'm glad you're here, but please don't treat me like I'm ten."

I reached out and hugged her, "Fair enough...and be careful if you go out." I then closed myself off for the night.

Sitting on my bedroom balcony in a lounger, covered in a blanket, I inhaled the night air and sleepy sound of the ocean while I texted my mother and Faith, *Goodnight wherever you are. Thinking of you...Love, C.* Tears started flowing down my cheeks. I'd just witnessed a little too much reality for the dream I was living. Somehow I knew there would be more to come.

It was a Thursday night and I only had one class the next day - Literary Journalism. I finished my Chamomile tea and then turned in. I needed to stay focused, and was determined not to let the LA smog get to me.

Lying in bed, feeling alone and misplaced, I wondered where Frank was and exactly when he was coming back to LA. I couldn't bring myself to ask him when we'd spoken earlier, but I was rapidly feeling insecure in my new surroundings. He was the only person who had any vested interest in me out here, and I needed him.

Rayne: What is canoodling, anyways?

*E*very year, at the end of summer, Morgan and I invited our families to LA for a long weekend. I wasn't up to it this year, but if I cancelled, family tongues would wag from coast to coast. Half of them seemed to know more than I did anyways.

One of my girlfriends took it upon herself to tell me, 'Keep your eyes open, Rayne. That's all we're saying…' That was more than a year before. She read a blog online that said Morgan was seen canoodling with some girl in a club in West Hollywood. What is canoodling anyways? And, what made her think I needed to hear that? I told her it was gossip and that celebs are targeted all the time. She got mad at me for being so blind. I wasn't though. I actually believed every word. I just couldn't confront Morgan about it because I was afraid of the truth. I wouldn't want to put my kids through a public breakup. But in hindsight, I think Morgan was trying to do things to make me leave him, which brings me to Labor Day weekend. It was a disaster.

Beverly Hills is not the type of community where you put barbeque grills in the driveway and get rowdy in front of the house, like we did back in Louisiana. I spent a month finalizing who was coming, fine tuning the menus and agenda, and the décor for the barbeque.

On that hot Friday morning, two of Morgan's frat brothers arrived. I remember clearly that it was at least ninety degrees and smoldering. Morgan's friends had reservations at a hotel in Santa Monica, to be near the beach. But Morgan decided he wanted to show them a good time, so he handed over the keys to our Broad Beach cottage for the weekend.

When they got to LA, these guys leased two Escalades and rolled through the gates entering the Estates, like they owned it. The security guard's voice even sounded questionable as I gave the okay. I'm not a snob, and I'm not saying they're not educated, but one of the guys had the nerve to shout, 'I'm home!' from the street. Our house is at the end of a cul de sac, which is in a very high profile position as it is, and I can't understand why he felt the need to showcase the Negroes, as my friend used to say. Sometimes you need to leave that college hurrah at the gate. They buzzed the intercom and one of my kids ran outside to greet their 'uncles'.

Morgan was upstairs in the bedroom, but came out and stood at the top of the staircase, leaning over the railings hooting at his boys, like they were taking roll call. An hour later, I was looking for him and my son said, "Daddy left for the beach, but he'll be back."

I was humiliated. Our families were there to spend time with us and Morgan takes off. Well, we had a good time without him, as it didn't shock me that he'd pulled that. He always said, 'I can't handle the crowd', as if our families were strangers. I knew there was more to it.

My brother's teenage daughter wanted to go to Hollywood that night. My mother and aunts were with the kids so I said I'd take her and a few of the cousins for a drive down Sunset in Morgan's Hummer. They were impressed by that, though I personally hated driving around town with those glistening rims.

"Where's Uncle Morgan?" My niece wouldn't let up.

"He's at a beach house with his bruhs."

I turned onto Sunset towards Hollywood, when one of the girls in the backseat started waving her hands out the windows, flossing.

"Stop that, please!" I told them to play whatever music they wanted while I focused. It was actually nice to hang out with the excited young ladies who saw things so innocently. Not jaded, like me.

My cell phone rang. It was Morgan.

"I'm staying in Malibu tonight, just wanted to let you know so you don't think I'm hurt or anything."

I hung up instantly. I wasn't interested. *Sorry ass!* All kinds of images passed through my mind, but I was so mad because he used his friends as an excuse to do his dirt.

They finally showed up at four o'clock on Saturday afternoon, voicing how much they'd drank and that Morgan needed to sober up the night before. "We're looking out for our man. The media...you know?"

Media my ass... they were covering for him.

I had to make excuses to our family, but was running out of them. Then, Morgan's phone chirped on the kitchen island and I answered. Before I could say anything, I heard her voice.

"Hi baby. Morgan?"

The girl's slightly raspy voice was coated in a Spanish accent, and I was shocked to hear it. I couldn't fool myself into thinking that it was a business call. I thought back to that groupie backstage in New Orleans. This person was asking for my husband and I released the call, in a daze. My lips quivered and my mouth was dry because I forbid tears to develop. My focus was in one place. I stomped out to the pool, where everyone was, with fire in my eyes, and I aimed straight for the table of men who were playing cards. My brother looked up at me and saw the look in my eyes and tried to intercept, but I fanned him off.

Pointing to Morgan's friends, I yelled at the top of my lungs, "Get your black asses out of my house - now!" I didn't want them near me because they were enabling him, protecting him, and helping break up my family.

They looked at me like I was crazy. "What? Why...? Hold up..."

"Where did ya'll take him last night?" They started stuttering. "Right! He wasn't with you, because he'd never spend the night with a bunch of men. That's not his style anymore! Plus *she* just called. "I laughed, catching my breath to ward of hysterics. "That's what women do the day after...Now get the hell out!"

I looked up and I found Morgan standing on our bedroom balcony with an *oh shit* look on his face. But I couldn't deal with him right then. I was done with the charade and didn't want to hear his explanations or excuses. I ran into the house, snatched the keys and took off in the Hummer. I felt like crashing it just to hurt that bastard's feelings.

Speeding past the security gate, my mind was racing and tears were streaming down my cheeks at this point. I wanted to drive as far as my gas tank would allow me. I suddenly wished I were still in Louisiana. Things were simpler then. I would have never let him treat me like this.

I whipped a left onto Mulholland Drive and drove until I had reached one of my favorite spots –the Hollywood Overlook. I needed to calm down, but I cried the entire drive. I felt so betrayed, that I didn't want to go back to that house. I had seven missed calls on my cell phone and eventually, I turned it off. I was drained. There were no more tears. I got out of the car and sighed, shaking my head because there she was - Los Angeles in all of her glory. The city that had made all of our dreams come true had now destroyed mine. I loved Morgan, but could no longer pretend that what he had become didn't matter to me.

On that mountain Saturday night, I decided there was only one option for me to stay true to myself. I knew what I had to do.

Candice: Famous neighbors, crazy exes

*A*nne flew out to spend the weekend with me. It was the Sunday before Labor Day and the grocers at the Country Mart were already crowded with housekeepers and cooks, and other locals. The two of us went shopping for dinner. It had been a while since we'd cooked a meal together and I wanted to go all out.

"Oh my God, Candice, that looks just like…" She smacked my arm so hard; I didn't know what was happening.

"What?" I laughed, "Oh yes, it's him. His place is just up the beach and there's always half naked girls crawling around his balconies." Her shocked expression was priceless. "Annie this isn't Chicago. These people are on a whole different level out here."

Anne then got all righteous. "I just wish he hadn't made that tacky film, because his life hasn't been the same since." Still, Anne couldn't stop staring as the actor pondered over the produce. "Hey Candice, that guy you used to date…does he still live out here or is he back in Philly?"

Trying to focus on the organic strawberries, I was a little irritated that my sister would even bring this up. "Who? Wes? I mean, I suppose he lives in LA somewhere. I don't speak to him anymore, and that's fine with me. I can't believe you even remember him."

Anne looked at me like, *come on…* because she was there for the emotional rollercoaster Wes dragged me through. She felt he's responsible for my jaded view of men; that the inevitable is heartbreak. Get what you can, while you can. The memory of that relationship is painful to say the least.

One January, around ten years ago, I went to the Hype Street concert with two college friends. We had great seats, courtesy of the law firm one of the girls interned at. In fact, they were front row, stage right and we had a good time.

When the show was in the encore, a bodyguard came over and handed me a backstage pass and walked off. I grabbed his arm and said, 'One? My friends too or I'm not going!' I thought for sure he'd snatch it back, but he just stared at me and slowly reached in his pocket and handed my friends their own *After Show* passes. *Teenage girls behind us were upset that they were overlooked, but I didn't care. I knew what was really up, but I thought the guys were cute and I wanted to meet them. Maybe take some pictures. There was a meet and greet, but my friends and I were invited into the dressing room lounge and a little while later in walked Wes Donnelson, the so-called bad boy of the group.*

"How'd you manage to get back here?" He kidded me in the cutest east coast accent I'd ever heard.

We talked for a few minutes, discovering I was just a year older than he. The band was about to leave the venue and head to another town, but he asked if he could give me a call. My response was, "Why? You won't even remember me after this."

He had the nerve to look insulted and asked, "Why do you think that? Because I got a different girl in every city, right? That's what you think."

I felt bad after that. I apologized, and after visual boosting from my girlfriends, gave him my phone number. He called me that very night, late...and every day after that for two weeks. I never called him. He seemed confused by that, but it made him pursue me even more. That's when things took a turn.

He invited me to a show in Philadelphia. Though he was now living in Los Angeles, he said wanted me to see where he grew up. I have to say, Wes swept me off my feet. I soon was being introduced to his friends as his girlfriend. I didn't know what to think, but it felt good. Even if I wasn't the only girlfriend, his friends never let on. Wes was the boss and those guys did what he asked. They reacted the way Wes wanted them to. Period.

I got to know his family and they treated me like a daughter and sister. I loved that he had so many brothers and sisters, to my one sibling. His mother especially, embraced me and welcomed me into their lives. She told me 'my Wes needs a girl like you...somebody with a head on her shoulders, and some morals.'

Well, I tried to be that girl for him, but he brought out a side of me I didn't know existed. Sometimes for the worse. We were only together for a year and half, because towards the end, his personality shifted. He became erratic and paranoid. That's when I realized the affect fame could have on a person, especially that level of fame. He was a part of the most popular boy band in the world. He couldn't go anywhere without girls following him.

On a visit to LA one summer, I discovered an ugly someone I'd never known. Our entire relationship flashed before my eyes, and my heart was flooded with disappointment. It was all a lie; to his fans, me and the whole world. I was done and I walked away from him.

But, after the perfect apologies, I returned for more because I was a glutton for punishment. I was willing to dismiss Wes's behavior, because I thought I was in love with him and besides, he was world famous and a multi-millionaire, not like some junkie bum. Boy was I kidding myself. It only got worse and my visits less frequent. I couldn't handle it, not that he missed me much. I soon found out that he was seeing another girl. Some chick from New York. How did I find out? Randomly flipping through People magazine, I saw a photo of the two of them all hugged up in a paparazzi photo. The story he had told me before about going to LA was this: he was busy in the studio working on the upcoming record and couldn't see me for a while. I called him the same night and told him I never wanted to see him again. I didn't. A year later, he was married. Bastard! Never again would I give my heart away like that.

"Don't bring him up again, Anne, please."

That was over and done with years ago. I'd heard he ended up divorced, which wasn't surprising, but other than reading about him in gossip columns and seeing commercials for his television series, I had no idea what was going on with him.

Anne smacked her hands together. "Well, all I know is we're going to have a good time tonight. I'm in Malibu and we're doing it up, girl!"

I just shook my head and walked ahead. At least she was loosening up a bit. My sister could be a little uptight. If being in California had anything to do with it I was glad. "Let's not bring up anymore sad stories, you hear me?"

We got back to the house and prepped for dinner. I missed those bonding times with Anne. Back home in Chicago, cooking was like a ritual. But, wouldn't you know it would get interrupted?

"Those can go in the freezer Can, and I'll marinade these steaks. Karoline will be here for dinner, right?"

"She said she would be. Dangit! I forgot to stop for wine. We were just there." I hated to have to go back out, but knew it was a must.

The phone started ringing and I reached across the breakfast counter to grab it. "I'll go back because you know we have to have our wine girl!" I looked over at Annie who was already enjoying a strawberry mimosa. I hit the speaker button, "Hello?"

"Karoline please." The voice on the other end was cold and short.

"I'm sorry, she's not in. May I take a message?" I continued unpacking the bags.

"No. Who am I speaking with?"

I knew exactly who it was. After a cautious pause I offered to have Karoline call her back at the number on the phone. I didn't feel I owed any introductions after she was so rude. "I'll take a message."

"Just let her know that her mother would love to hear from her sometime soon."

"I'll be sure to let her know. Have a good day!" I looked at Anne with a mocking stern face, and we giggled silently as the call disconnected.

Anne's jaw dropped, "What's her problem?"

"I think *I'm* her problem!" I popped a strawberry in my mouth, thinking about the fact that this woman probably knew who I was as well. I didn't much care.

Karoline's mother had been a distant figure in her life. What's even sadder is she lived just three hours away in Santa Barbara, and the two rarely saw one another or spoke for that matter. Karoline is a daddy's girl through and through. The Swann's divorce was dirty and Karoline took sides with her father. I knew that I was destined to be caught in the middle of some nastiness.

Candice: Little Miss Sunshine

Karoline didn't show up for dinner on Sunday. In fact, by Monday afternoon she hadn't been home since Saturday night. It upset me. My sister and I had cooked a fabulous meal, which was Anne's idea of a thank you for Karoline's hospitality. When Anne got in on Friday, Karoline was the one who picked her up from the airport because I was in class. She showed her around and took Anne to lunch at the Ivy, which is about as Hollywood as you can get. Then, when the time came for Anne to fly back to Chicago early Monday morning, Karoline was nowhere to be found. Anne took it in stride and couldn't have really cared less, but I was hurt. I kept thinking, *who the hell does this stupid little girl think she is?*

When I got in from the airport, I slammed the keys on the wooden console entering my bedroom. I was livid. I stood in the middle of the room, looking around at my pretty new life, then, with one quick turn, headed down the hall and up the stairs to the loft. "I'm about to find out because something is off!" I wanted to find something – anything.

I looked around the cozy sitting area which was decked out in Shabby Chic décor. There was a plasma TV on the wall, and a huge painting of Karoline in a bikini lying on her stomach in the sand with her legs curled back and crossed at the ankles, facing her audience, giving the finger. I laughed and shook my head. I had to admit she was pretty feisty.

"Let's see what you do up here, Little Miss Sunshine." I crossed over the living room below via a walkway into her bedroom which faced the beach.

Karoline's bed was unmade and there were clothes with tags still on them, strewn across a chair in front of the glass doors leading out to the balcony. I wanted to make it quick, but just in case Karoline walked in, was prepared to say I was tidying up the entire house since I had some time alone. That was plausible since even though a housekeeper came twice a week, I cleaned my own bedroom. Those Midwest values never cease.

I nervously chewed my bottom lip, a crazy habit I have, zoomed in on a side table next to the bed and made a beeline for it. I slowly pulled the top drawer open, sifting through the contents. There was nothing but an empty Gucci sunglass case, some unopened mail, condoms peeking from underneath the envelopes and some money folded in half. I closed it back.

The bottom drawer told the story. I immediately spotted brochures from Promise Cove, a rehab center in Malibu. Then I found the folder. When I opened it I saw sticky notes with handwritten messages. Notes like *I will live my life, as I'm blessed with life* and *Darkness is in my past, I'm now living in light.* There was also a tiny laminated ID card that read Karoline F. Swann.

Karoline: a recovering addict. That explained why she dove into all of the volunteer work she did for young kids, which I thought was a wonderful thing, but back to the matter at hand. Staying away from home without so much a word smelled short of backsliding. I closed the drawers and went back downstairs in a hurry.

Karoline finally came back at around four o'clock. I was on the rear balcony with the glass doors open when I heard her come in.

"Karoline? Hey…you're okay. I was about to call."

Karoline looked puzzled, "Why? I'm fine." She was dressed in a long halter sundress with a bikini underneath, and her eyes hidden behind huge dark sunglasses. "Your sister left already?" She swung an arm up and sighed. "I'm sorry, I just…a group of us went to the Springs."

I shrugged and told her that it was okay. "Yeah, she's back in Chicago by now. She had a good time. I really miss her."

Karoline smiled, "Well she should visit again soon. I like Anne, she's nice."

Then she bolted upstairs and slept for a few hours. I decided I'd study for the rest of the evening, so I let Karoline be. But, I wanted to talk to her because it appeared she might be in trouble. It had to be timed right because I wasn't sure how Karoline would react, or how Frank would feel about my snooping for that matter.

At eight-thirty Karoline came downstairs wrapped in a blanket and joined me on the balcony.

"It's a calm night out, isn't it?"

I agreed and asked her to sit with me. I closed my book and turned off my laptop, sitting up in the chaise with my feet curled underneath me.

Karoline sat in the other chair just across from me and blurted out, "Are you mad? Don't be upset, okay?"

I leaned forward and told her I wasn't, and that I only wondered where she was. "I was more worried than anything, but I didn't want to call around looking for you, I mean..."

Karoline looked me square in the eye, "Right. So tell me Candice, what were you doing in my bedroom? I can tell you were."

She caught me off guard and I gazed into the ocean darkness.

"I wasn't meddling; I just wanted to straighten up a little bit for you. I was bored."

Karoline cut in, "So you went through my things? Did you find what you were looking for?"

I turned around, "I wasn't looking for anything Karoline! But, since you bring it up... honey I don't know if it's a good idea to hang out with people who get high."

Karoline scooted back in the chaise; finger combed her hair, pulling it all the way back. She was jittery. "Oh God here we go...I knew it."

I didn't say anything, just stared at her with concern.

Then Karoline continued, "You're serious aren't you? Did Daddy put you up to this?" She was very defensive. Totally not the girl I'd had gotten to know.

"Karoline, no he didn't. Okay, I saw the pamphlets and everything and I just...I don't know your story, but I want to make sure you're okay. That's all!"

She jumped up, tossing her blanket on the chair. "I'm going to let you get back to studying, alright?"

I suddenly remembered the phone call, "Oh - your mom called!"

Karoline walked into the living room and turned around, shrugged her shoulder and shouted, Goodnight, Candie!" She had really taken to calling me Candie. I think she knew I hated it.

Bebe: Troubled ground

I couldn't understand him. We weren't really fighting, but...everything was causing a rift right between Derek and me.

We had been tip toeing around each other for months. Trying to avoid the sit-down we should have long had. Something was definitely broken in the marriage, and while I wanted to shake Derek and make him listen to me, I was getting bored with it all.

Derek had always told me that when he's upset, he wasn't as productive, and that supposedly meant he risked everything *we've* built. I used to tell him I didn't care because I had my own life. Actually, I wasn't so sure. Some days I felt strong, and others, I was a nervous wreck, but I did a stellar job at hiding it. Truth was, if I hadn't had my foundation, I probably would have left him and this town behind a long time ago. Living this high profile life can be unbearable sometimes, but helping the children makes it well worth it.

I believe the height of our problems started a couple of years back, when after ten years of marriage I started feeling insecure. Derek had become the most sought after songwriter/producer in the industry. It wasn't unusual for him to have three songs land on Billboard at once. I knew he no longer needed me as a songwriting partner, and was even starting to feel he didn't need me, period. Derek would leave town more often than he used to. Jetting off to the Hamptons, and even Nassau, Bahamas where we still have a vacation cottage. The signs were there early on.

I surprised Derek one weekend by showing up in Nassau, and I ended up being the one surprised. He had houseguests. Two female singer/songwriters from London, whom he swore were going to be the next big thing. I haven't heard of these women since.

The girls, one British and the other African, were beautiful and suspiciously cold towards me. They lay around the pool all day, half naked. When I asked Derek to send them away, he became indignant, telling me I needed to relax and to stop blaming people for my unhappiness. I was so hurt by those words, and blasted him. "What do you mean...blaming people? You're shacking up here with strange women who supposedly are working with you! I'm not a fool, Derek, and stop making me look like the bad guy!"

He left the house, leaving behind his guests, and retreated to the Atlantis on Paradise Island. I threw the girls out and didn't care where in hell they went. It was one of the most humiliating episodes of my life. I flew back to LA the next day and did whatever I could to punish Derek for treating me that way. I withdrew and dove into work eventually starting a charity called Angels of Music Foundation.

My charity work filled me in ways that Derek no longer could. It gave me a sense of purpose. I felt good about myself again. It even seemed at one point, that our relationship had started improving, but now the ground was crumbling in again.

Rayne: Waves of excuses

I always tried to be home before the kids got in from school. My day usually involved running errands mostly revolving around my kids, and fitting in a regular fitness routine. Not one to sit around sipping tea and lunching with the girls as they say, I've always been pretty much a loner, and am okay with that.

My closest friends live back home in New Orleans and when I needed bonding time, I'd fly out to see them or send for them to come to LA. Morgan on the other hand, embraced the Hollywood lifestyle and had more than become absorbed by it. We were coexisting in separate lives, with him going about it as if Labor Day weekend never happened. I think he was used to me being upset one minute or, as he described it, 'flying off the handle', and then going back to normal, whatever that is.

"Hello?" I was surprised and irritated at the sound of Morgan's voice on the phone. "Morgan, well it's good to finally hear from you. How are things in Miami?"

Listening to his wave of excuses as to why he didn't answer in the hotel the night before, was turning my stomach. I knew exactly what was going on. He was ignorant to the fact that the people who work for him respected me a little more than they did him. He also had no idea I was actually friends with Trey.

What is that saying? The enemy of my enemy is my friend? I'm not alluding that Morgan was an enemy, but we were definitely on different sides at this point in our marriage. My heart was slowly growing cold.

"Okay well, I'm taking the kids to dinner, so...talk to you later."

I hung up before I lost myself, and I wasn't about to give him the satisfaction of knowing how truly hurt I was. As far as he knew, the lies he was feeding me were convincing. Boy, did I have news for him.

Trojans and the tabloid guru

*C*andice developed a protectiveness over Karoline that she'd never felt; not even for Faith. She was starting to really care about Karoline, and felt that something just wasn't right in her life. It'd been a week since Candice made the discovery of the stint in rehab, and she kept going back and forth on when and how to sit down and talk about it. Or, if it was even her place to do so. She felt like certain people, Brandon in particular, was a bad influence, and was trying to come up with a way to divert Karoline from him. She'd never shake her demons if she continued to encircle herself with her troubled crew.

On her way to USC one morning, Candice thought aloud, "She can tell me all she wants that she's trying to help Brandon, but who's helping her?"

She felt like she needed to talk to Frank. It was with hesitation because she didn't want to run to Karoline's dad, but at the same time, saw a problem that needed to be derailed before it started. So Candice called Frank's Chicago house. It had been a couple of weeks since they'd spoken, so she wasn't even sure he'd be there, but tried anyways.

The housekeeper answered, and told Candice that he was in Miami on business, so she impulsively called his cell phone and he answered right away.

"Candice Kane of Los Angeles, is that you? Is everything alright?" He seemed genuinely pleased to hear from her.

"Hi. Frank. Um, I don't think so. I don't know - how are you?"

"I'm good, in Bal Harbour, so what can I say?" He chuckled, and then got serious. "I can hear it in your voice. What's wrong?"

"Probably nothing, but... it's Karoline." Candice hesitated, not knowing how to start. "Frank did you know she'd had a problem in the past, and had been in rehab?"

"She's my daughter, of course I knew." He sighed. "Just tell me what's happened."

"Well Annie, my sister, was in town for the holiday weekend and Karoline was great. She really was, but then on Saturday morning she left and didn't come back. So Monday afternoon I was cleaning around the house and found some old papers from Promise Cove, and…."

He cut in, "She didn't come home all weekend?"

"No. No, she didn't, and when she finally did, I didn't want to pry too much. But that guy friend of hers, his influence…" All she could think of was Brandon and his glazed eyes.

"I had a feeling this was going to happen. She's been clean for a year then her mother started pushing!" The tone in his voice was one of disgust. Then he started whispering to someone in the background: "Give me a moment will you? Thank you…Hello, Candice?"

She couldn't help but wonder who he was talking to, while fighting the urge to tell him that his ex had called the house. "Yes, Frank?"

"I'm speaking at a conference in Salt Lake City at the end of the week, and then on Friday I'll fly back to LA."

"Good, I'm glad because I…she needs you." Candice felt relieved knowing he'd be coming to town. "Frank, I'm sorry I had to call you. I didn't know what else to do."

"You did the right thing by calling me. This isn't your problem and I don't want you to worry."

"Okay well, I'm at school now so I'll see you next week."

She attempted to end the call first, for fear he'd get bored of her and wrap it up. But, Frank definitely wasn't bored with her and kept talking.

"How are things at USC? Is it what you expected? The world of journalism, I mean?" The fatherly tone returned. That's not what she desired at that moment.

"It's amazing! I'm so happy here. Oh, and guess what? Harvey Levin from TMZ is lecturing today; the tabloid guru himself. I can't figure out why, but it should be interesting." She giggled at the prospect.

"Outstanding!" Frank mocked the idea.

"That's what I thought. I hear he's really smart though and what he does is actually considered some type of journalism, so... anyways, I'll see you soon."

"Have a good week and don't worry about Karoline, okay?"

"Alright, you too. Goodbye, Frank."

Candice quietly smiled while turning off her phone. She knew things would be better once Frank arrived, and she was finally admitting to herself that she couldn't wait to see him, and hoped the feeling was mutual.

Candice: Old ghosts

The thing about LA, is that no matter how tucked away you are in your private enclave; no matter if you shop in the valley or how far out of the way you drive - eventually you cross paths with the very things you were trying to avoid. That's the good thing about being new in town. You can hide in plain site because no one knows you; especially in a town like Los Angeles. There are lots of places to hide out. That's what I thought anyways.

It was early October and I had only two classes that day, so I stopped at Westside Pavilion to shop a little before heading home.

Pondering what to eat while I walked out of Nordstrom, I thought I'd seen someone I knew. My sister had to bring his name up and now I was seeing his face all over the place. Shaking my head, I switched one of my shopping bags to the other hand and reached in my handbag for my phone.

"Karoline, hi it's me. No, I'm okay. I'm on my way, but I was wondering if you wanted me to bring dinner. He did? Okay, well...see you shortly." Chef Mike had cooked dinner for us already.

I dropped one of my bags.

"Candice?"

I froze hearing that voice. That accent - and was immediately taken back to a place. Turning around I realized I wasn't seeing things before. There he was - Wesley Donnellson. The guy who had broken my heart into a million pieces.

Driving around for two hours on that cold Los Angeles night made my blood boil; especially when I'd been waiting for my boyfriend to finish playing stupid games with his hangers-on friends.

"What's your problem, Candice? Park the damn car!" With his arrogance on full display, Wes yelled at me at the top of his lungs. Pop star or not, I was so mad, I wanted to punch him out.

"Are you crazy? STOP yelling at me, Wes! I'm sick of you!" Puddles of tears welled up in my eyes; signs of anger coupled with disappointment, because I still wanted to believe in him.

I was trying to park in the awkward angular driveway alongside the tri-level house on Sunset Plaza Drive. It was late, and my friends and I had just arrived at the house that he now shared with his mom and eighteen year old brother. I didn't need him making me feel any worse than I already did. We'd made plans to meet up earlier that night to go swimming with our friends. He was nowhere to be found and the gate was locked.

The evening was shot because Wes never showed up. Instead he was on the other side of town 'taking care of something' with his ghetto ass friends. I knew what that meant; the so-called bad boy was crawling around the gutters scoring drugs. Wes's squeaky clean cover would be blown to pieces if word got out and he was too stupid to see it. Was too busy believing his own celebrity - that he was invincible.

"I'm not stupid Wes! I know exactly what's going on!" Yelling out of my car window, I wildly parked in the driveway and then let into him. "Wes, come here!"

He waved me off, "I don't have time for this, man!"

His hostile behavior was scaring me as he tried playing the tough role in front of his friends. But I was also furious, and had just about had it with him. He walked into the attached garage, while I stood watching him disappear into the darkness with only a flicker of light from the cracked door leading into the house. Less than a minute later, there was this loud snort. As usual, I immediately started making excusing for him in my mind, like I always did, as to what that could be. Maybe he has a cold? I knew better. He was snorting back a line of the white powdery substance for all it was worth. So there he was - Wes Donnellson, founding member of the worldwide pop sensation Hype Street: A coke head.

Embarrassed, I looked around at my girlfriends who at this point felt sorry for me. "You believe this?" I flung my handbag to the ground and ran into the opened garage, shoving him against the wall. "You are a fake and a liar! Look at you!" I gestured the length of his body, from the baseball cap covering his spiky blond hair, to the sagging designer jeans that were about to fall off his ass. "Your stupid teenybopper fans should see THIS!"

He laughed in my face, "What you talking about, Candice? Go in the house. My mother is in there." He elevated his voice, "Ya'll go in the house... damn! I godda' talk to my boys right quick." Wes was spiraling off the rails.

I cut an eye at Javier, "...the hell you lookin' at?" I stormed off, jumping in my rental car with my friends in tow. I backed out of the gate, screeching the tires, and then put it in drive to make a quick u-turn. Then, I stopped the car, "Wait, you guys!" The girls begged me to get back in the car but it was like I was possessed. "No I'm okay, hold on...Hey Wes!" I laughed almost hysterically, a side effect of my anxious rage at that moment.

His friends were standing between the garage and me. I raised my voice for the entire street to hear, "I should take this straight to press, you dumb ass idiot!" My nervously shaking hands on my hips.

Wes stormed out of the garage and walked right up to me. "Right! You ain't doin' nothin'. You know why, Candice? Because you love me, that's why!" He really believed that. His wanna-be rapper attitude was getting on my last nerve.

I took my finger to his forehead and shoved his head back, "Watch me!"

And with that, I turned and jumped back into the car and sped off. The next morning I hopped a flight back to Chicago.

By the time I got back, Wes had left a dozen messages on my voicemail. Apologies and lots of 'I'm sorry', while in a roundabout way, I knew he was really confirming that I was only kidding about going to the press. Hype Street was about to go on tour and he had around two weeks to clean his nose, so to speak. If I'd exposed him, his golden boy image would be ruined. Fact was, I never would have betrayed him. I'd learned how to hold tight all of the group's secrets. From the cute shy one who was secretly gay, to the youngest member who was seventeen and had an insatiable craving for older women.

Wes mustered up the apology of his life, which resulted in me going back to LA for the rest of the summer. He was the perfect boyfriend, but soon was up to his old tricks again and I was left feeling like a fool. It was the last straw. I was done. When I finally built the nerve to say goodbye I meant it. I never saw Wes again.

I put my focus on school and graduated at the top of my class at DePaul. I returned to Los Angeles to visit friends, and started running with a fast party crowd, even dating a high profile actor, which was the norm for our circle. I still believed in love and with each guy, *thought he was the one. It was only because they'd promised me that I was the one, they'd never met anyone like me, blah-blah-blah, and that whole spiel. Needless to say, heartache came at every spin. Disappointment mounted and I never quite looked at men the same again.*

The last time I was in LA, I vowed only to return if I got accepted to USC. Other than that, I had no further use for this town or anyone in it. That chapter in my life was over.

In a bit of shock, I glared at Wes for a few seconds before looking away to straighten up my expression. I leaned my head down to look into his car window.

"Wes? Oh my god, my sister was just asking about you." I hit the alarm unlocking the doors and put the bags on the back seat. I followed his eyes glancing at my license plate.

"So, you live here now?" I excitedly told him I was in LA working on my Masters. He looked surprised, "Good for you! You were always smart." Adjusting the bib of his baseball cap, he looked around nervously. "I never would have expected to see you again."

I thought it was easier to be cordial. "Yeah, funny isn't it? Good seeing you...I really have to go though. I'm late." I threw a wave up and closed the backseat door and opened the driver's.

He got out his SUV and walked up to me, now sitting in my car. "Look, I screwed up bad man. I know it. I wanna say I'm sorry. You look happy, Candice. You look good."

"Thank you, Wes. I think I'll like it out here. Oh, and I've seen your new tv series. It's really good, you should be proud."

For a second there was a spark of humility, as he rubbed the back of his head. "Thank you. Um, well LA suits you. Maybe we can..."

I cut him off before he started. "So you're married and with a child, right?" My heart was racing. I wanted to get out of there quick.

Watching him speak, and the curled corner of his lip, I started having flashbacks of Philly with him zooming down two lane roads in his red convertible Mercedes, and me leaning over kissing him while he drove. I always did that. But, diverting my eyes away, I quickly trashed that image.

"My daughter is beautiful; she's eight. But you know, sometimes it doesn't work, and now I'm in the middle of a divorce."

I watched him try to explain, while being sure it was his fault.

My face must have looked as if I wasn't surprised. "Sorry to hear that, really. Well, I have to go but, LA is a little big town, so maybe we'll cross paths again, huh?" I prayed we wouldn't.

He stepped back as I put the gear in reverse. "Right, I hope so. Take care, alright?"

I didn't say anything, just smiled. Slowly driving away, I looked in the rear view mirror as two young women walked up to Wes, almost frantically asking for a picture. By his grin and body language, he was more than happy to oblige. I giggled and thought some things never change.

I couldn't have driven off any faster, and was angry at myself as my eyes puddle from the nostalgia. I wiped my cheek. "God, come on girl!" I hoped I'd never see Wes again because there I was…in tears as usual.

Candice: The stuffed bell pepper

*L*ying in bed Friday morning thinking about my run-in with Wes, I pulled the covers up closer to my neck. Of all the people to run into, I hoped he didn't live anywhere near Malibu. Maybe he lived halfway across town, and this was the one in a thousand chance of running into him and I'd spent that already. He still reeked of a cheater and I wanted nothing to do with that. His poor wife, I could only imagine what he put her through. A woman needs a grown man, not a boy, which brought Frank to mind immediately.

I still tried convincing myself that Frank was my mentor. That he was just my friend, but the reality was...Frank didn't see me that way and I knew it, no matter how I labeled it.

Stretching my arms above my head, my fingernails glide across the leather headboard and something hit me. Why not Frank anyways? I was in that house for a reason other than convenience, and I knew it wasn't about Karoline. I couldn't contain my smile and I whipped the comforter back and got out of bed. I immediately grabbed my robe to cover my naked body. There's something about living on the beach that made me feel freer. The first thing I did every morning was click the remote that opened the drapes revealing the wall of glass facing the beach. It was heaven.

The other wall faced my neighbor's house, and granted me a front seat to a tittie show every night. Trust me, it was not appealing. Self-proclaimed retired supermodel Jorgie Vincent, well into her fifties, would come out and sit in her hot tub in a bikini, before discarding the top. Her boob job would have been perfect had it not been for the indentations that made them look like Nerf balls. Even seeing that hack job, I compared my own modest C cup to hers, before realizing they were good enough for me. For a woman in my early thirties, five foot eight and a size six, I was satisfied with my body. I can wear almost anything without looking vulgar. Jorgie on the other hand, looked like a stuffed bell pepper.

Watching the waves in the ocean, I thought about Frank, who would be arriving later. I wanted to make dinner for him as a sort of grateful gesture. Of all the men I'd gone out with, he was the only one who completely believed in me. He never felt threatened by my ambitions, but supported them; like he was preparing me for life. Now whether that included him or not, it was high time for Frank to meet the woman he's been aching to unleash. I was dying to know him better and hoped he sincerely felt the same.

There's one thing I've learned about wealthy men. Their decisions are not impulsive. It's like business, even with the women in their lives. I knew I wouldn't get anywhere by lying on my back. That's where women go wrong. I needed to be the woman he'd want to spend meaningful time with. I had to play my cards right. I stopped being afraid to be myself around Frank. It's funny, but whatever seeing Wes did to jar that new attitude towards Frank overnight, I felt like sending him a thank you card.

Still, I worried about Karoline. I'd watched people in my own family suffer through drug abuse and didn't want her life ruined by being surrounded with the wrong people.

Bebe: Stranger things have happened

I was getting ready for another brutal workout with my trainer, Danni. She always showed up at the house in low slung yoga pants and tank tops showing off her rock hard abs. I think she did it to flaunt her naturally skinny ass, to give false hope to her clients.

Danni was a little butch and I thought she was a lesbian, but she always bragged about her stunt man boyfriend who helped get her the A-list clientele she has. Quite frankly, she rambled too much. I would have tired of her had it not been for her miracle workout which I called squatting hell. It was the secret behind my highly photographed legs and tight rear end. I'm one of the few my age with natural curves, tight in all the right places.

Typically our session would end at around two, but on this day, it was interrupted early.

"Bebe, what the hell is Derek thinking? I never seriously agreed to perform in Las Vegas! Now I have a commitment, to Bellini Resort...headlining an entire week in February!" R & B super diva, Daphne Margot came dashing in, in a hysterical rant into the patio garden, with her assistant in tow.

Startled and quite frankly, infuriated by the uninvited intrusiveness, I in mid lunge, whispered, "Excuse me Danni, I'm so sorry..." All I could do was glare at Daphne, who was obviously having a crisis. "Darling, what are you talking about?"

"Bebe, I hope you don't mind my barging in like this, but I can't have Derek making decisions for my life like this." Glancing at Danni, who was noticeably uncomfortable as she downed a bottled drink a few feet away, Daphne hinted, "Uh, Bebe...I really need to talk to you, if you don't mind..."

How dare she come in and dictate my time; my private time. "Of course, just go inside darling...we can have a bite in the kitchen. I'll be right in."

Danni started gathering her things and was dialing on her cell before I could feel guilty. "Bebe, we can continue on Thursday, it'll be hot so I thought we'd do a pool workout. Fall in Southern Cali, gotta' love it, right?"

"Yes, that would be perfect, darling, thank you. I do apologize for this." I made a sorry attempt at concealing my aggravation, but failed. I made a stomping bee-line through the conservatory, and towards the kitchen. I didn't bother to freshen up because I wanted to get Daphne out of my house as quickly as possible.

"Daphne, there you are!" I grabbed an apple from a bowl on the island, and noticed she'd already helped herself to a snack from the fridge. "You've got to calm down firstly. It's not good for you."

The assistant was typing away on her laptop. "Daphne, I scheduled you for three o'clock with Aida. Is that good?"

"Bebe, talk to him, please…Yes, but make it two-thirty 'cus we're leaving now." Daphne gave me that *because you know he is an asshole* look.

I sighed, "Look darling, I would love to, but you need to talk to him yourself. I don't like to interfere, you know that."

"What?" She looked puzzled.

"Yes…you can talk to Derek. Let him know the schedule doesn't work for you. I'm sure it will turn out."

Daphne faked a glanced at her watch. "God, I'm so late! Well, thank you honeeey…" She pressed those inflated D-cups against me in a hug, and on queue her assistant got up from the cozy window bench at the bay window.

I don't know why Daphne really dropped in the way she did. I realize Derek was her mentor, the one who discovered her in Montreux France five years before. But, it made me wonder what could possibly make this woman think it was okay to show up unannounced at his home, and make demands of his wife. I doubt she valued anything I had to say. Derek didn't always keep things professional with his female artists, and the way she behaved that afternoon was like she knew he wouldn't mind. I always wondered about Daphne and her quick rise to the top. I shudder at the thought. I hoped I was wrong, but stranger things have happened.

Mr. Swann

Engrossed in the current Newsweek, Frank was tired and ready to get home. The flight attendant onboard his Gulfstream G500, handed him a hot towel and advised him that they were preparing for arrival in Burbank.

"May I get you anything else before we land, Mr. Swann?"

Frank glanced up appreciatively, "No, but thank you." He went back to reading, felt a jolt, and grabbed the arm of his seat.

Even enveloped by the luxury of his private jet, Frank was nervous about flying, and landing was the worst part. He'd flown all over the world, taken thousands of flights, and each one felt like the first. He hated flying, especially in private planes because there are fewer passengers. Like this day, there were only two other passengers. One of his assistants had thumbed a ride with her fiancé to visit family.

"That was entertaining!" Frank tossed the magazine, which featured a cover story on the pharmaceutical industry, on the plush seat next to him.

He was relieved to be getting back to LA. It had been a few months and honestly, he had some things to straighten out. Other than his daughter's recurring problem, his ex-wife didn't seem to understand that she was no longer welcomed in their lives. Karoline had told her to stay away, and Frank had all but threatened to have her thrown in jail.

Jackie Reese-Swann received a hefty settlement in the divorce ten years before, moved into a swanky Santa Barbara ranch and now she was crying for more. Between the parade of lovers and bad business decisions, her interest was dwindling. The day she turned twenty-one, Karoline inherited a hefty share of her trust fund, and should anything happen to her father, she will be the sole heir to Swann Industries. Of course, she'd most likely never head up the company a day in her life. Still, as the only offspring, she stands to inherit her father's shares in the company; hence Jackie's eagerness to rekindle their relationship. Frank feared that in a fragile state Karoline would cave in and open the door to her conniving mother.

Silently cursing under his breath, Frank leaned his head back against the rest as he felt resentment pulsating through his veins. He was going to make sure Jackie didn't get within earshot of his daughter.

Entering the gates of his estate, Frank was glad to finally be home. Home being a twenty two thousand square foot Spanish villa, tucked away on the gated Laurel Park Lane. Lake Forest is the Swann family home; where he lays his head when he's in Chicago. But ever since graduating from Stanford, he knew California was where he belonged. He still loves it, and it's where his daughter was raised. Only now the house felt very still, with no real signs of a family life.

Frank had purchased the four acre estate, hoping he and Jackie would enjoy living there for years to come. It's a shame she only spent two years there. The clock had run out on their marriage. Papers were served, and she was ordered out while Frank was in London on business. Twelve year old Karoline was in Europe with him at the time.

Near the end, Frank and Jackie both knew they were only together for Karoline's sake. While Frank was by no means the perfect husband, it was the last straw when Jackie's cheating elevated to blatant disrespect as she no longer hid her boy toys. She flaunted them around town on Frank's dime. He was forced to get rid of her for good, and when Frank brought the hammer down, it hit hard. Still, he provided her with ten thousand a month until the divorce was final. Jackie moved into a friend's plush guest house in Bel Air to save face. As for Karoline, she chose to stay with her father.

A light staff is at Swann Lakes year round, even when no one else is. Karoline would come back when her father was home, which usually is only six months of the year, including the holidays.

Loosening the tie around his neck, Frank stepped into the elevator leading to his master suite. His robe was laid out, bed linens turned back and bar stocked, exactly the way he liked it. Laid out on a silver tray on the mahogany console, were unopened invitations to charity events around town; some of them had expired. They just stack up until he returns.

He made himself a drink, and picked up an envelope with a familiar logo. It was for The Angels of Music benefit hosted each January by his friends, Derek and Bebe Fabian. Frank dutifully chose to attend with a lady friend, choosing at the flip of the coin, so to speak. This year, he hoped Candice would accompany him. Maybe he would even enjoy it this time around.

Rayne: Guilty as sin

"I wish I could stay up here all day."

I encouraged Cooper, our five year old Boxer, as I hiked through Runyon Canyon Park. It's there, that I get my personal time to disappear, to be alone twice a week. I get to clear my head and pretend life is perfect. Actually it is for a couple of hours, especially at Inspiration Point. I hike all the way to the top where the view of Los Angeles gives the celestial illusion of bliss.

"Come on, Coop! Let's go, boy!"

The hyper dog caught up and bounced ahead, ducking behind a shrub on the trail and tussling with something he found. I stopped, hands on my hips, feeling a little disgusted, then laughed. That silly dog chews anything. "Ew put that down!"

What he'd found was a snake's skin and decided to play with and then rip it apart. I jogged back down the trail and of course, he followed. It was nearly four o'clock and I needed to get back home to be with the kids.

Turning onto Clarendon Road, leading up to the house, I could already see the two vehicles out front. That meant one thing. Morgan was home and he'd brought the usual pack with him. Driving up to the gate, my lips tightened, and eyes squinted as it was all I could do so as not to ram my car into the Denali parked in my spot in front of our attached four car garage. I was so frustrated, that I almost put the car in park while it was still rolling.

When I got out, I couldn't walk fast enough to get inside the house. I was pissed because here Morgan had just returned home from tour; I hadn't even seen him yet, but instead of wanting alone time with his wife, he brings his boys home. Just then, I noticed the housekeeper entering the kitchen.

"Hello." She nodded, with a blasé look, and a hint of a smile.

I smiled trying to hide my frustration because this poor woman had definitely witnessed her share of drama in the Bryant household. "Hi Elsa, how are you?" I let Cooper off his leash and he trotted down the hall wagging his tail.

"I'm okay, Rayne. Mr. Bryant is in his studio." Elsa continued on to the laundry room just off the garage. I hated when she called him Mister, like he was some king. In all fairness though, she calls me by my first name, only because I insisted.

"Thank you." Smoothing my hair back with my hands, I walked into the hearth room and out the door leading into the garden. I could see that the door to the studio was open, and I heard loud voices. With each roar of laughter, my blood boiled. *Ugh, just getcho' trifling butts out of my house!*

I reached the detached room and went inside, knocking lightly. "Hellooo..."

The guys looked up, straitening their stances, and one of them jumped down off the counter that doubled as a bar. My side-eyed glance was cold as ice, so they started mumbling about having to leave.

"Alright man, yeah...I'll get with you guys in a couple of days. That track is hot, dawg!" *Dawg.* Just the sound of that being uttered from his lips sounded out of character. Then Morgan grasped hands and gave daps to them. I could tell he dreaded looking me in the eye.

"Yeah we gon' holla' atchu later, man." One of the guys tipped his Kangol hat at me in a supposedly respectful gesture. It was the least he could do. He knew I couldn't stand them because they encouraged Morgan's bad behavior.

They left and Morgan walked over to me reaching out for a hug, "Hey baby, I'm glad to see you." Gliding his hands around my waist, he pulled me close.

"Yep... so, you must have gotten here right after I left."

Suddenly reaching back and rubbing the back of his own neck, his body language was riddled in guilt, "I did. We got back to LA before one and I thought you'd be here. I wanted to surprise you." His tone was sly and I couldn't help but think *no you didn't just try to act as if you were thinking of me.*

I admit, his chocolate skin made you want to lick him, and there was no denying we still shared strong sexual energy. If it weren't for the fact that I knew he was cheating on me after all those years, my panties would have dropped quicker than the wind chill in Wisconsin.

I'd learned to block out a lot over the years. But, with the Labor Day weekend fiasco and everything that's been happening on the road, I'd never felt so disrespected in my life. Now I just had to gather my proof that it was all true. Morgan still thought he was playing me. The reality was I was just buying time.

Trust me, you'll love it

"*M*r. Frank, welcome home."

He glanced up at the petite Portuguese woman. His attractive, but matronly house manager Cecilia was standing at his bedroom doorway. She'd been with him since before Karoline was born. Cecilia used to constantly tell him that Jackie was sneaking men into the house and carrying on. Jackie hated her but could do nothing about it because Cecilia was one of the most loyal people in Frank's life. He depended on her, so she wasn't going anywhere anytime soon. Any new lady in his life would do well to beware. In her eyes, Frank Swann was like a god who could do no wrong. Even when he behaved badly, she closed her eyes to it and protected him.

Frank called Karoline's cell and she didn't answer so he immediately called Candice.

"Hi, Frank..." Her voice smiled through the phone.

"How are you?"

Just hearing his voice soothed her. "I'm good. Are you here?"

"I am. What's going on in Malibu?"

"Nothing much, I just finished editing a project, so you called at the perfect time." She giggled and instantly felt ashamed of her gushing. "How was your flight?"

"Terrible." He told her how he hated to fly and that there wasn't a strong enough drink this time. "Is my daughter home? I tried reaching her, but couldn't."

"Um, I haven't seen her in a few hours. I think she's at her art class. She looked good this morning; and happy. But of course she knew you were coming."

"Well, speaking of, what are your plans for dinner?" Frank really wanted to see Candice and hoped he would - sooner than later.

She paused, a little speechless because she wondered what he was about to say or ask. So she beat him to it. "I'm not sure, maybe we could all have dinner together?" She wanted to be as modest as she could be with her eagerness to see him.

"Actually, I was thinking more of just the two of us. We'll grab a bite and, I don't know…maybe go bowling later."

Candice was sure he was teasing her. "Bowling, you?" Not exactly the date she imagined.

"Trust me you'll love it. Have you ever been to Strike Three? It's great, and I'll whip your socks off in a few games." He smiled hearing Candice's laugh.

"Is that right? Hmmm…how could I turn that down? Alright, I'm in!" Candice refrained from revealing that she's quite a good bowler, thanks to her dad.

The sound of a woman actually laughing and not being phony was refreshing. "Okay then. Let's say I pick you up at seven?"

"I'll be here." She hung up smiling.

Strike three? Candice brought up Google and found the website of the upscale bowling lane, before wondering if she had been first on his list for the night. Insecurity tried to creep in but was dismissed. With women all over the world throwing themselves at him, Frank invited *her* into his life. Now he wanted to take her out on the town. Because face it, in the world of the super rich, a casual date is a public spectacle.

Frank shined like a mint condition coin and all eyes are on him wherever he goes. With Candice there on his arm, word was bound to spread like wildfire. Candice felt good about what the night might bring, because as handsome as he may be, she knew she'd be the star of show. That's one of the things she enjoyed about him. Frank allowed her to be a girl. All she had to do was show up. From the moment Frank sent her those flowers back in Chicago, he knew what he was doing, and now Candice was willing to accept.

She'd been in LA for almost two months and hadn't gone on what she called, a real date. Going for drinks with a school friend now and then didn't count. It was time for a night on the town with someone who knew how to make her feel like a woman.

What they do

*W*ith gentle, intentional strokes of her paint brush, the little girl had an accomplished look in her smiling eyes.

"That's really good Taji, now try this."

Karoline saturated her own hand with the oil based paint and proceeded to gently stroke the canvas with her fingertips. Eight year old Taji immediately mimicked her.

"Hey...it looks better!" Taji smiled broadly.

"Yes, it does. See...it now has a more natural look. The colors blend lightly, not forced."

Karoline spent most Friday afternoons volunteering as an art instructor at the Baldwin Park Elementary School after school program in South Central. She's loved art since she was around five years old at summer camp in Santa Barbara. That's when she first discovered her passion for creating. The kids she spent time with gave her a feeling of reliving that time of discovery; her own childhood innocence. They were so honest and untainted by the world and had fresh eyes. They saw what Karoline often forgot, and kept her mind focused on positives. Not the chaos that her own life usually brought her.

Karoline's cell phone sang out from inside her Mulberry messenger bag. "I'm sorry Taji, just a minute..." She fumbled and grabbed the annoyingly loud phone; stepping aside to answer it. "Hi, Daddy!" She turned into her dad's little girl upon hearing his voice.

"How's my girl?"

"Oh, I'm fine. Actually I'm with one of my school kids. We're working on an art project. You should see these kids Daddy, they're amazing."

"That's wonderful sweetheart; you sound good."

"Yeah, I'm so glad I have the kids. They think I help them, but they have no idea what they do for me."

"I know. Hey listen, I hoped you'd be home later. I'll be there at around seven."

"Really? Um, I might be gone by the time you get there. I have plans, but I promise I'll see you tomorrow. I'm happy you're home, Daddy!" She sped through the call quickly because she thought Candice may have summoned her father in to check on her.

"It's okay honey. I'm taking Candice to dinner anyway. We're…"

She interrupted him like she didn't want to hear the rest, "You're going out with Candice…tonight? Like, a date?"

"We're friends and I enjoy her company. Why? Don't you like her?" Frank waited during an uncomfortable silence.

"Of course I do. She's great Dad. Candice is really sweet."

Trying not to imagine Candice going out with her father, Karoline glanced back at Taji. No matter what he was trying to say, she knew it was a date because she knows her father. She just hoped Candice wouldn't bring up again what happened over Labor Day. "I'd better get back. See you tomorrow, okay?"

"Alright then…tomorrow. I love you. Goodnight."

"Love you too. Bye, Dad."

She adored Candice, but the idea of those two getting together felt uncomfortable. Not that she feared becoming second place. Karoline never came second to her mother, or any woman for that matter. Being that Candice was only ten years older than Karoline, she wondered if she had any idea what she was getting herself into. The world of Frank Swann wouldn't be easy. Things would get crazy, real quick.

Karoline put her phone away and turned her attention back to the project. "Okay Taji, lets finish up. Looking good…"

Bebe: Cabernet and Whatshisname

"*Just* keep talking, darling. I have to stay on this call. Paparazzo is outside the restaurant." Seething in paranoia, I hurriedly handed my keys to the valet at Porto Bello on Santa Monica Boulevard.

The photographer hopped out of his truck, with one camera slung over his shoulder, and another perched in his fat meaty hands while he snapped away at a safe distance of the restaurant. He aimed directly at me as I held the cell phone close to my mouth, head tilted in the opposite direction.

He beckoned: "Bebe, this way please...you look beautiful!"

What? I glanced up, "Thank you..." While thinking, *go away...there must be some reality star, somewhere desperately praying for you to show up...* "Have a good day, darling." Handing him a dismissive grin, I entered the restaurant, where I was meeting Sheila for a late lunch to go over plans for the gala. I had almost forgot she was on the line.

"Hello? Bebe? Bebe, are you alright?" Sheila's confusion shot through the phone.

"Yes I am. Why is this guy staking out this place? Mr. Chows closed or something?"

I giggled as the hostess ushered me to a cozy velvet booth in the rear of the restaurant. I never like sitting up front. I want to see what's happening in case I need to dash out the back way.

"Evidently...I'm only a block away hon. I'll be right there."

"Fantastic. See you soon."

The dimly lit Italian eatery was sparsely crowded for a Friday afternoon, ideal for a working lunch.

A few minutes later, I saw Sheila making her way through the dining room, capturing all eyes in her cream pantsuit and amped up cleavage spilling from the blazer. Her wide smile and enviable lips command attention. She stopped and chatted with a group of women seated in the middle of the room. Apparently I missed a goody, because Sheila cackled hysterically, and then covered her mouth in pseudo shame. I craned my neck when I realized one of the women was a Spice Girl. *How does Sheila even know her?* The whole scene was odd. But then, that's Hollywood for you.

When she got to the table, Sheila dropped her oversized Gucci handbag and sighed. "Honey, how are you?"

Watching Sheila fan her hands as she spoke, my thoughts flashed back to that guy, realizing he hadn't gotten out of his car until I arrived, and even addressed me, baiting a reaction.

"Sheila, do you think he was out there waiting around for me?"

"What? Noooo, they hover around these places like bees to honey. Don't worry about him."

I hoped she was right. I didn't want to wind up in the They're Just Like Us column. Last time that happened, I was climbing out of Derek's god-forsaken Ferrari and flashed my panties to the world. My mother reflecting her southern gentility always told us to make sure we wore pretty panties, just in case - and I do. I glanced back at that group. "Sheila, I didn't realize you knew a real life Spice Girl."

"Oh please, just barely. I mean every time I see her she's digging jabs at Whatshisname. Who even cares? He can't stand her. Are you having a cocktail Bebe?"

Sheila is a dear, but she could be harsh when she wanted to.

"Yes, I ordered a bottle of Cabernet for us."

"Perfect! So...what do you think? Will we get Frank to be the guest speaker this year? It would really be wonderful if he were." Sheila's eyes widened with the eagerness of a schoolgirl. She's been dying to get Frank to speak at one of our events.

"Well, each year he declines because of lack of time to prepare, or some other reason, and then makes an even heftier donation to supplement. Now he's out of excuses, and if he does it, that could mean five times the attention we'll receive, which equals more money for the kids!"

She clasped my hand, "So just tell him that. Frank knows how this works. He'll do the right thing. I'd hate to resort to getting on my knees..."

I think I gasped loud enough for the entire room to hear. "Sheila!"

"...and begging! Bebe, come on...I've never had to do that." She winked mischievously.

As the server poured the wine, I had a good feeling it would be the most successful Angels gala to date.

"Here's to strong arming Frank Swann!"

We clinked glasses and ordered our meal. Meanwhile, Miss Spice was still holding court with her pals, talking about Whatshisname.

Rich kid exploits

"*W*here are you right now? Okay, I'm on my way, bye..."

Karoline sped through Beverly Hills on the winding Sunset Boulevard in her Mercedes SL350, oblivious to the fact that she had just run a red light at Beverly Glen. She was anxious, and thoughts that roamed her mind about Candice and her father weren't helping.

"Oh whatever...that's their business. I don't care!" She clicked on her iPod and the Black Eyed Peas blared out, while she called Brandon again.

"Hey Bran, do me a favor? Get a room for me, okay? I don't feel like driving back to the beach tonight. No, I'm okay, it's just...I'd rather stay at Maison tonight. I need to be alone. Not a bungalow - a room. Thanks!" Click.

If you're ever in the mood to get into trouble, do it at the Maison Armand hotel. Karoline and her pals have done just that. It became a virtual clubhouse for her crowd and things rarely went well. Troubles began and peaked in those tucked away bungalows. For instance, a few years prior, Karoline was almost raped there. She still blames herself for someone else's violent behavior. The memory is haunting to this day.

That October, I was nineteen and a naïve little girl who thought my family name was a safety net against anything I did, and whomever I was with. A friend of mine, who was a professional footballer, was getting married so he and his fiancé hosted their bachelor/bachelorette soiree at Maison Armand. They threw a pool party with male and female exotic dancers as the eye candy for the night. There were dance platforms set up all around the pool and gardens. It was like a fantastic erotic dream, and everyone indulged to the limit. The drinks were heavy and whatever else you wanted was at your disposal. After a couple of drinks and chatting, this actor who'd just co-starred in the hottest urban comedy of the year, I and a few of my friends disappeared into one of the cottages, to talk to him about the film. Get the scoop so to speak.

One by one my friends left the room, and I was there alone with Dalen Stone, the comedian/actor and recurring host of The Comedy Jam. While far from being my type because he was too short, he was funny and I enjoyed talking with him.

Well, after he'd smoked a couple of joints, he took it upon himself to lean in and try to kiss me. I backed off, because while I was a little drunk and had probably taken some pill to curb the anxiety, I didn't want to kiss him. I jumped up and looked around hoping to see one of my friends, but they'd left me in there alone. I knew where this was going and I wanted out. He grabbed my wrist and yanked me back down on the couch. I yelled, "No...I have to go!" Dalen wasn't hearing it. He started forcing kisses on me, as I shoved him to get off me. I panicked when he grabbed the back of my neck and was trying to coerce me to into giving him a blow job. I kept yelling, "No! You got the wrong girl!" I then elbowed him and jumped up.

Then I heard knocks at the door. It was my friends who had all but abandoned me. I grabbed the knob opening the door, feeling sick and just shoved past them. I may not have been physically raped, but I was forced to see what the real world was, and how women get treated in Hollywood; even the rich ones. To this day I'm not sure if those girls know exactly what went down that night. The rumor mill said I was making out with him. I have an idea where and why those rumors started.

Needless to say, my dad found out somehow. Dalen would have been better off jumping off the roof that night because his career died. Daddy is chummy with some very powerful people in the industry, and needless to say Dalen Stone was over. Last I heard he was a host on the game show channel. Serves him right. The no good bastard!

Approaching the restaurant entrance of the hotel, Karoline saw Brandon waiting outside, smoking a cigarette. He was dressed in tight low rise jeans and a black tee, with Chucks on, and his hair meticulously spiked. She assumed he was portraying the Hollywood bad boy that night, as he would role play when he went out. One night he's preppy boy, the next, a male supermodel all decked out in Gucci.

The valet rushed over and opened her door, "Welcome to Maison Armand."

Cig hanging loosely from his pouty lips, Brandon clutched Karoline's hand, leading her through the large wooden doors and down a dark hallway, towards the bar.

"What took you so long anyways?" He let go of her hand and dragged on his cigarette.

"I'm here now, and stop that! You're going to die of lung cancer - I swear. Come on, you promised." Karoline yanked the stick from his fingers and flicked it, intentionally stepping on it.

Brandon scowled at her. "What's with you? You need a drink, girlfriend."

"No, I don't. Let's just...I want to sit on the terrace. It's nice out tonight."

They strolled in and a waiter immediately led them outside. The usual suspects were all there. Some random guy with a faux-hawk was bragging at increasingly audible levels about his script over which producers were supposedly battling. Two bleach blonde groupie girls huddled together, gulping 'tinis and stealing glances with the It Boy actor sitting with his equally slutty looking girlfriend who landed him because she was the groupie he couldn't resist.

The escalation from groupie to girlfriend is that one night It Boy feels down on himself, gets drunk and in steps Groupie Girl who rescues him. If he did it once, he'd do it again. The groupie girls knew they could lure him away if they just captured his interest. From the way he was looking over the girlfriend's shoulder, he was *very* interested.

These guys are always interested. The It Boy ego. It gets really sad when they start to believe their own hype. And if they pick the wrong groupie girl... it's over. If one thing can bring an A-lister down to a B in Hollywood is being caught with his pants down. The operative word being 'caught'. You can do anything you want - just don't get caught. One night gone wrong with one or more of these girls and he'll be back to weak rated sitcoms quicker than you can say career suicide.

Karoline spotted her friend Dominica Sogould, whom she calls Mimi, tucked away at a table in the corner along the shrubbery, waving them over, "Over here sweets!"

Mimi's family practically built Beverly Hills from the ground up. Olive toned skin and exotic looks; she used her beauty as a sword and lived out her role as a trust fund baby to the hilt. Great Grandmother Sogould single handedly financed the construction of the Bel Air Hotel over tea. Legend has it that the Sogoulds sold a bit of their land to develop what is now known as the Platinum Triangle: Beverly Hills, Bel Air and Holmby Hills. That means they have more money than the banks can hold.

Mimi got up and slid into the next chair, letting Karoline have the seat. Brandon recognized some guy across the room and decided to sit with him. Then they left after a few minutes.

Removing her cropped jean jacket Karoline adjusted her tank top. "Mimi, what's going on?"

Leaning back against the chair Mimi shrugged, "It's all good I suppose. You?" She ran her hand through Karoline's hair, while scrolling a phone text with the other. "You're stressed out, Kari."

Karoline didn't feel like sharing any news. "I'm just hungry." Gesturing for their waiter to come over, "Let's order. I haven't eaten all day."

Mimi leaned in and looked into her eyes suspiciously. "You don't look good. What'd you take?"

Irritated, Karoline rolled her eyes and snapped, "Nothing!" She thought about her mother and also wondered if her dad had gotten to the beach house already. She missed him but didn't feel like seeing him just yet.

Candice: Nothing, except...you

The mood already felt different. It wasn't our first date, but it was the first night out together in LA. I gave myself a pep talk like, "Be cool, he pursued you...don't be obvious about your interest...keep it classy and have fun. Most of all ignore the fact that his net worth is close to seven billion dollars. He is like *any other guy.*"

Who was I kidding?

The fact of the matter was, his money was an issue. How was I supposed to ignore that? At the time, I wished Frank wasn't so wealthy, because it would be easier for me to process. He was also more than fifteen years older than me, and could have been a friend of my dad, but I'd tossed that imagery out the window because there was no denying that I was seriously attracted to Frank. I wanted to have a good time and Frank was someone I trusted would treat me right. At the very least, I knew he wouldn't ask me to go Dutch on dinner.

Just then, my cell phone rang. It was Faith. Of course, as usual her timing was perfect.

"You gotta' have Faith..." I sang into the phone when I saw her number coming in.

"Just like Candaayyy...Hey honey, how are you?" Faith had an extra flair to her voice which usually meant she'd scored big and was dying to tell me about it.

"I'm good. I'm so glad you called, because I've been meaning to." Looking at the clock on the nightstand, I gestured for Faith to get to the point because I knew there was a point looming.

"So how's LA? Are you missing Chicago yet?"

"I miss my family, but other than that...not really." I could feel Faith leading.

"Well, I have to fill you in." Faith was on the verge of singing. Then she blurted, "I got married last weekend!"

My jaw dropped, "What? Married? When and who?"

"You met him. Donnie James -the Chicago Storm?" She said matter of fact like.

"The ballplayer… right. Wow, so fast. Well congratulations, sweetheart. Really!" I tried to hide my shock. Not surprise, shock.

"I know, thank you. We were in Vegas and he said let's do it. So we did."

Just like that, she'd landed her cash cow. From the tone of Faith's excitement, the biggest love she had right then was the love of his contract and I thought to myself, Donnie better hope it didn't run out anytime soon because, she might have.

"So Candice, do you ever see Frank?" She went from A to Z as quickly as she started.

"…in fact, I'm getting dressed right now. We're having dinner tonight."

There was a cold silence.

"That's great…I knew he liked you. Besides, white women have been stealing our guys since forever. Now it's our turn…and Frank will show you the world!"

"What?" I didn't know what Faith was trying to insinuate, but I didn't like it.

"You heard me!"

"Right. Well, I really want to talk to you but I have to finish up. He's on his way and I don't want to be standing here but-ass naked, you know?" I tried to lighten the awkward moment.

"Why not?" She laughed wildly. "Just kidding…Alright, well, I love you. Be careful." Faith had a hint of concern in her voice.

"Love you too and Faith, let's talk again this week, okay? I want to know more about this marriage." Rubbing the back of my head, I tried to process what just happened. But then again, it was Faith.

Sade's voice flowed from the stereo and I started gyrating to the beat around the room, stopping in front of the windows. Some kids were running down the beach after their dog. I slipped into my favorite Hudson skinny jeans and twirled on my tippy toes, turned my rear towards the dressing mirror to check the view. Rubbing my palms against my butt, I was pleased. No more flat-booty Candice. Those jeans were a miracle…and worth every penny.

When I heard the alert of an incoming call on my cell, I laid across the bed on my stomach to answer it. It was Frank.

"I'm inside, but didn't want to startle you."

I glanced at the half open door knowing he was somewhere on the other side. I tried to contain myself, by being nonchalant.

"Oh Frank...hi. I'll be out in a sec' okay?" I'm embarrassed to say this but I could feel blood flow to my face, as my eyes smiled. I quickly buttoned my cardigan.

"Take your time; I'm out on the deck."

I appraised my outfit as to whether I was underdressed or maybe overdressed for bowling night. But, decided that in LA there's no such thing as overdressed. We weren't going to the local bowling alley back in Chi town. Doing an onceover in the mirror, I was glad I kept the makeup minimal, and left my hair down. I undid one more pearl button on the cardigan, Just enough, but not too much. Stepping into my Tod's, I grabbed my handbag from the doorknob and headed out.

Frank stood on the top of the stairs leading down to the lawn that overlooked the beach. He had his hands in his jean pockets and I remembering thinking how sexy he looked from the back; more like a thirty-something and not someone who was almost fifty. He turned around when he heard me walking up behind him.

"Hi..." His smile killed me as he walked back inside to the living area. I could tell he was pleased to see me.

"How are you?" I reached out and hugged him quicker than I'd planned but couldn't help myself. With my arms around his neck, he rested his hands at my waist. He smelled like the men's fragrance counter at Neiman's, only better.

"I'm well and you? You look beautiful as usual."

I settled into the feeling of being safe with him. Frank was back and I didn't feel surrounded by strangers anymore.

"Can I get you anything?" Pulling away to reach for my jacket on the sofa, I checked him out on the sly and admired his black jeans and windbreaker, all Ralph Lauren Black Label. Very Frank, I thought.

"No, I'm fine. If you're ready, we can head out."

He took my jacket and held it up for my arms to slide into. Still trying to feel him out while enjoying every second of it, I was more than ready. When we walked outside, I saw the driver waiting for us at a black Town Car.

"You're not driving, Frank?"

"Do you mind?" He gallantly extended his arm out as we approached the car.

I smiled at him, "No, I don't mind. Are you kidding?" I looked back intentionally giving him a sexy smirk.

I then thought how cute the big hunky driver was, and then he greeted me, "Good evening Miss Kane. I'm Renee"

"Hello, Renee." And I loved that he knew my name.

I had had no idea where we were headed, nor did I care. I just basked in the luxurious sedan with my handsome date. Frank told me he wanted to take me for sushi and I remember being relieved that I liked sushi because otherwise I'd have to fake it. We were headed to a little place called Sushi Dokoro in Beverly Hills.

"Have you been there?" His eyes followed my hand as I adjusted the seatbelt across my firm and pushed up breasts. Thank you Victoria's Secret.

"No, is it nice?" I must have seemed eager to experience whatever he had planned for us.

He laughed under his breath as he squint his eyes scrolling through his iPhone, "I think so. I was there a few months back and the sushi is very good. So my theory is...if you find a place you like, stick with it."

Watching him speak, I nodded and agreed. I felt the same way about many things.

"So how was your day?" Frank intently focused on whatever was on the screen.

Trying not to be irritated at his divided attention I answered right away, "My Fridays are low key, so not bad."

He then looked up, noticing me watching his fingers type. "I'm sorry, Candice. One of my analysts is having a crisis that I don't really wish to hear about right now." With a smirk on his face, he dropped the phone in his jacket pocket, "No more...I promise."

I glanced out the window as the car continued on Malibu Canyon Road towards Pacific Coast Highway. I felt Frank watching me while I took in the scenic view.

"Are you enjoying LA? I know it's quite a difference from Chicago, isn't it?"

I turned to him, "It is, but like I said, I've spent a lot of time out here and I love LA. It's so...free, especially the people. I just love the people, and the pond out back ain't bad either." With a soft chuckle, I gave him a wink, and then he instinctively reached down and clasped his fingers through mine. I looked down at our hands and thought about Chicago.

"Frank, remember that first time we met? I wanted to think you were a jerk. Of course I didn't know you then."

He looked a little taken aback, "Really?"

Flashing a smile I assured him, "Yes, but I mean, that was based on my initial assumption." I meant his association with Faith, whatever that was.

He nodded, "Right, and now...?"

I squeezed his hand, "Well, I certainly don't think you're a jerk."

Realizing there was a long silence between us, as his eyes were piercing into mine, I nervously turned away. "Oh, we're in Beverly Hills already? That was fast." I softly exhaled, because something happened just then and I wasn't sure exactly what. But somehow I knew Frank and I were hovering into new territory.

At the restaurant, my back was facing the huge windows at the front of the dining room. It would have made me nervous if the driver wasn't just outside the door in the car. I felt other patrons staring at us as we sat at a table along the perimeter of the open room. Of course, Frank's presence demanded attention and I expected it.

"Do people always watch you when you're out Frank? I'm just curious."

He half glanced up, "Not everyone knows who I am, Candice. We aid the lives of millions, but those people don't know who I am when I'm on my private time. It's not like you think."

Grinning, I wasn't convinced, "I don't know..."

He leaned across the table, "Besides, the people in this restaurant are staring at you. Not me."

Just then I noticed a black man with a sharply groomed goatee looking at me with a questioning glare, and I just turned away, popping a maki roll in my mouth, nodding, "That's sweet of you, but..."

He kept on, "Look at you. You're a gorgeous, intelligent, sexy woman...." He looked down, grinning, "...but they probably *are* wondering why you're afraid of me." He raised his brow, waiting, because he knew he'd put me on the spot. You don't build a billion dollar empire mincing words. Frank was playing a strong hand. I didn't know what he was trying to pull.

His words triggered a shift in my demeanor, and I leaned forward a little, "Frank, what do you want from me?"

He sipped his glass of wine, "Nothing. I just want you." I sat back waiting for him to continue, because I didn't know what to say. But, he did. "I don't really go on dates, you know? I enjoy a night out with a friend occasionally, but my schedule is so impossible, then they get antsy and demanding. It's difficult."

I nodded, biting the corner of my lip nervously. I hate when I do that. It's such a giveaway but I was trying to figure out exactly what he was saying. "What makes you so sure that I'm not the same?"

"I'm not sure of anything. But, I do know that if I let you meet someone else, I'll regret it." Frank looked so serious.

Hearing him say that caused my heart to pound and I avoided looking him in the eye. I just stared at my chop sticks. It's like every guy I'd ever dated flashed before me, saying the same thing. Scrunching my eyebrows I finally spoke up. "Let's just take it as it comes…" I sighed, "…otherwise it'll go wrong, Frank."

He leaned in a little closer to me, "It won't go wrong. I promise. I want us to really get to know each other. You wouldn't be here, if you didn't feel the same."

I finally looked up, "So you're saying, what?" I wanted so badly to kiss his perfect mouth, but knew that would be a little too much. "We're steering off course and that's when it gets messy."

He sipped his wine, resting an arm on the table, "No, this is right, and you know it. Don't be afraid to show me who you are, Candice."

I reached over and patted his hand, "Let's talk about this later, okay? Right now, I just want to enjoy tonight, so that later…I can whip you in a few games."

He laughed, "Is that right?"

I felt a sudden urge and stroked the top of his hand with my fingers, "Yeah, it is."

Though I was drawn by his persistence, I was torn inside because if Frank was playing with me, it would be devastating. So many men had broken so many promises. Why would I expect him to be any different?

Get your mind right

After dinner, Karoline disappeared to her suite to get what she described to Mimi as privacy she couldn't get at home. Her friend recognized the tweaked look enough to know that at some point during dinner Karoline had taken something. She put her sunglasses on, as she usually did when she was trying to hide, and rambled on about her mother. Mimi offered to stay with Karoline but the offer was declined.

"I'll be no fun...I'm super tired. I just need to sleep and I can't do that at home. My whole routine is off, and now my dad is dating Candice! She's amazing but, she checks up on me. What the hell is that about? It's my house!"

Mimi helped her to her room, offering once more to stay. Karoline insisted she needed to be alone.

On the way out of the hotel, Mimi slipped the front desk guy a hundred.

"Do me a favor? Check on my friend later, even if she gets pissed at you, and she will." Mimi reached across the counter and scribbled down the suite number. "She's not well, do you understand? And keep it quiet."

Front desk guy knew exactly what that meant...*another junkie rich kid!* He promised to check in.

Back in her suite, Karoline got undressed, turned on Cartoon Network, curled up under the covers of her queen bed and settled into her self-indulged misery.

Karoline tried to go to sleep. Her thoughts were all over the place and sleep was for lack of better word, a dream. Surely the Xanax and glass of wine would help. She was going to see her father on Saturday and wanted to get her mind right.

She gazed at the flat screen television until it appeared to vanish from the wall. Karoline felt like she was floating. She then heard voices outside in the hallway. Pulling the bedding back, she tiptoed to the door and opened it. There was It Boy actor, the one from the terrace, making out with the two cheaply dressed bar-fly girls. Then they stumbled into the room across the hall, with the door slamming back against the wall. They just laughed as they tore each other's clothes off.

"Hey...hey!" Karoline slurred at them at the loudest voice she could muster.

The drunken trio looked at her like she was crazy for interrupting.

"You guys got food in there? I'm hungry and I don't feel like ordering up." She waited for an answer, not caring in the least what they were about to engage in.

It Boy released himself from the girls and slovenly stumbled over to her, "Yeah...why don't you join us." He had a greedy look in his eye. He was seriously stoned. "Hey, can I come in there?"

"No!" Karoline slammed the door in his face. She may have felt desperate, but the last thing she needed was to end up in THAT scandal.

Candice: Breakthroughs

"*A*nd you guys thought you'd show *me* how to bowl, didn't you?" I giggled while I stood poised at the tip of the lane for my follow up after a third strike.

"You've been holding out on me, Candice!"

I could tell Frank was amused watching me cut loose. He sat with his arms draped over the back of the leather couch, grinning at me. Renee had joined us in a few games. Good ol' Renee - I had decided this driver was more like Frank's bodyguard, because let's face it; billionaires don't exactly go on public outings guard down. Not even on a date. You want to walk amongst the people, but you have to be covered, so to speak.

Swann Industries is a very high profile company and no matter what Frank says, when you're that rich, people know you, and they get crazy. Either that or he didn't want to put me in an unguarded position. I'd been around long enough to know the difference between a limo driver and 'the driver'. Limo drivers don't wear holsters underneath their jackets. Yes- I saw that as Renee climbed into the driver's seat. Personal drivers take care of business when need be.

On the bowling front, I put them to shame. My father had taught my sister and me to bowl like champs. I was a little rusty in the beginning, but came back strong. The music and lights pumping made it feel more like a nightclub than bowling lanes.

When we finished and stepped onto out onto Hollywood and Highland, the night was alive and a homeless man rushed up asking for money. I felt sorry for him and reached into my wristlet, but Renee ushered me into the car immediately.

"Miss Kane, you can't do that!"

I snapped, "Excuse me? Oh Renee... you don't know me yet, do you?" My tone let him know I was irritated by that, as I climbed into the back seat.

Frank gave my hand a squeeze in the car, "See that's what I enjoy about you Candice. You care about people."

Renee turned around, "But ma'am, you have to be careful down here."

I blasted back, "Down where? I've been to Hollywood before, damn!" I then apologized, as I realized he was carrying out his job. Feeling effects of my cocktails, I lowered my voice, looking at Frank, "I think he feels I can't take care of myself. Do you think that?"

He reached his arm around, pulling me closer, "No I don't. You're considerate, which is wonderful, but he's right, you do have to be careful."

I nodded and settled into his side. "I guess, but I don't see things the way you do."

The connection between us was obvious without being outright. I felt comfortable in Frank's arms, and for him, it was natural to hold me.

When we got back to Malibu, the only light in the house was at the entry way, and the reflection bounced off the walls. Once we got inside, I lit candles around the living room. "I love the way this looks from outside. It makes me feel peaceful."

I could feel Frank watching me move around the faintly lit space. He walked over to the windows and slid open the doors leading to the beachside.

"Are you coming out, Candice? It's incredible here tonight."

The sound of the surf was hypnotic and the subtle breeze was just enough to feel good against my skin. Leaning against the glass rail, with one hand in his pocket, Frank extended the other to me.

I was curious and giggled, "What?"

There was so much anticipation, I started to feel flushed. I met his outstretched arm, and he enveloped me in a comforting embrace, with his hand on my lower back which gave me a tingle. He pulled me closer, staring me directly in the eyes as if he was about to confess something. Yet, me being me, I beat him to it.

"Frank, I want you to know that I heard you at dinner. I did, and…"

He leaned towards me so that our cheeks brushed and our lips hovered in front of each other. The energy between us was undeniable and then our lips finally met, in soft kisses. Feeling his tongue lightly massaging mine, I cradling the back of his neck, I encouraged him to kiss me deeper. The embrace was so intense that it manifested in the form of tears welling up in my eyes. I hoped to God he wouldn't see it. I remember thinking - never let him see you so emotional, so soon. Frank slid his hand up my back and I just leaned against him.

Then I pulled away and didn't say anything, with a feeling of breathlessness. I tightened my lips as I stared into his ocean blue eyes. He looked confused as to why I was shrinking back.

"Are you okay? I'm sorry if I..." He brushed strands of hair out of my eyes with his fingers, as I looked off into the ocean behind him.

"No, it's okay, I'm uh...I don't think I'm ready for this." I was inwardly mad at myself for letting those bastards in my past ruin our moment.

I didn't want Frank to see the tears in my eyes; the hidden pain. It was like I couldn't allow myself to believe he really wanted me. I was angry at myself for questioning his every touch, kiss and kindness.

"Ready for what? I'm not trying to rush you..." He pulled me close and hugged me, then felt me crying. "...but Candice, why do you expect to be hurt?"

"Why would you say that?" I leaned my head against his shoulder and hugged my arms around his back, tightly holding on. I couldn't look at him. "I don't expect that, but Frank I've gone through so many situations where I gave everything I had; all of who I am, to someone else. They started out perfect. So nice and..." I kept slowly shaking my head as I spoke. "...but they always wanted something else. I was never enough for them." I felt him tighten his hug. "I don't want to ever go through that again." By this time I was sobbing like crazy; almost oblivious to Frank.

"Look at me, come on Candice, look at me." I pulled my head back and he studied my tear stained face. I could tell he was trying to find the right thing to say that would help me understand who he was, and that he didn't want anything but for me to trust him. He continued his plea. "I'm not perfect. I've made huge mistakes, but I know finding you was not one of them. I need you to know that I care about you, and I want you to feel safe with me." He wiped my tears and kissed my forehead hugging me again.

I don't know if I did trust him just yet, but I wanted to.

"Okay. I'm sorry, I..." I finished wiping the tears away.

I calmed myself down by breathing deeply because an anxiety attack would certainly have sent him packing, thinking I was more broken than I actually was. I couldn't blame him if he had.

"I'm going to go now, but I hope you enjoyed yourself tonight."

"I did, thank you." I put my arms through his and we walked back inside.

I was sure Frank left the house hoping he hadn't pushed too far. At the same time, I was wishing he'd turn around and take me with him, but he was too much of a gentleman to do that. Not to mention, Karoline would be seeing him the next day. Wouldn't it have been something if I met her at the door?

I hoped I hadn't allowed Frank to experience too much of me, too soon. Kissing in itself is sometimes more intimate than sex because it lets the person into your soul...your heart. I dumped all of my feelings on him. I felt exposed. That stupid voice inside of me was prodding: *He'll lose interest now because the chase is over. They all do.*

I sat on the deck wrapped in a blanket enjoying the night breeze while dissecting what had just happened between us. I thought *what if Karoline had walked in?* Realistically, I knew it was a little too late to start back pedaling my feelings, but boy, was I going to give it the old college try. I was determined to go back to business as usual.

Rayne: Exchanging notes

"*S*top sliding on that floor! Go upstairs to the playroom or something, okay?"

Watching my kids run up the kitchen stairs, I smiled at their innocence. As far as they knew, they had the perfect life. However in the grownup world their mom lived in with their dad, it wasn't perfect. Not even close. I grabbed my cell phone and dialed Trey.

"Hi honey, how are you? Good. I know we said we'd have lunch next week, but I was hoping we'd get together this afternoon if you're free. I need to talk."

I couldn't take the guessing and assumptions anymore. And, since Morgan wouldn't talk to me honestly, I had to do my own detective work. I was sure of what was happening but needed proof should I decide to end the marriage.

"…the one on Beverly Drive? Okay, that'll work. See you in a half hour."

Glancing at the clock which showed one-thirty, I went upstairs to find the nanny to let her know I was going out.

When I pulled up to the Coffee Café I immediately saw Trey's convertible Volvo out front. He was engaged in conversation with some pretty boy on the sidewalk. They looked real chummy and when he saw me pull up, Trey hugged the guy and brushed him off before briskly walking over to get my door.

"Hey, lil' momma!"

"What's going on, Trey? Thank you for doing this last minute. I just…well, you know."

"Girl, it's okay. You know I gotchu." He looked me up and down admiring my low slung, fitted track suit that revealed my newly flat tummy. "Lookin' all cute!"

"What? No. I'm a mess…." I cling onto his arm. "Let's get in here so you can tell me what my trifling ass husband is doing."

He waved his hand and pursed his lips. "Gladly, even though I'm putting my job on the line, but wrong is wrong and you my girl."

I knew I could trust Trey to tell me all of the real dirt, even if it hurt a little. "Thank you Trey, for real."

When I met Trey, after he started working as Morgan's wardrobe stylist, we just hit it off. Morgan hated him being so friendly with me, even though Trey is gay. I think he knew Trey gossiped about everything and everybody, and feared he'd tell on him. He was right. Trey filled me in on almost every bit of nastiness that Morgan got into on the road. Trey told me his own father had cheated on his mother for decades, and now he was more than willing to hand Morgan his ass for, as he said, treating his black sista like this.

We sat in the café and talked for around an hour about the goings on of road life; particularly Morgan's new girlfriend being flown out to meet him. Trey even told me about the Latina who had all but taken on the role of his on the road wife. She called the shots and worst part is...she was *allowed* to do it.

"He's so damn stupid. Morgan rarely wants me to come on the road, saying it stresses him out, because he gets nervous with his wife there, and all that bull crap!"

I was so mad I couldn't even cry. I was beyond the tears at that point. It's not that I didn't care. I was just sick of his trying to play me. So, I started stacking my chips for the day I'd need them.

One way or the other, Morgan was going to pay.

Daddy's little girl

Karoline jumped up from a deep sleep, like she'd blacked out the entire weekend. She actually thought she had. Fact was it was only Saturday afternoon.

"God, what time...?" She tried to sit up but the room started to spin. Shaking her head, she fought the memories of the darkness she had clawed her way out of just a year ago. She knew she was headed back down that road. Looking around she saw the TV was still on, and her handbag was on the bed where she'd dumped everything out. She didn't remember doing it, but was sure she must have been frantically looking for something; the something that was causing her to see double. An open bottle of valium had spilled out. "Dammit!"

Karoline picked up her cell phone as the alerts of missed calls were getting on her nerves. Her mother called twice. Rolling her eyes, she mumbled, "What the hell do you want, Mother?" Karoline pulled her legs up to her chest, calling her back.

"Hello, my daughter." Jackie picked up on the second ring and the haughty tone of her voice sent chills through the phone.

"Mother..." Karoline hoped to get this call over with quickly because she needed to see her father.

"I've been trying to call you for a week. How have you been?"

Karoline was skeptical of Jackie's sudden interest. The last conversation they had resulted in yelling and Jackie threatened to leave LA and never come back. Karoline basically told her good riddance. She was sick of the bluffing. Jackie needed help and her condition was apparently worsening.

"I'm fine, Mother. What can I do for you?" The silence was long and uncomfortable because Karoline felt the usual mind game coming.

"Nothing. Things in Santa Barbara are wonderful. I've been riding again. It relaxes me."

Nodding, Karoline jumped in, "I'm really in the middle of something. You've been trying to reach me? Do you need something?"

Jackie changed her demeanor. "Why do you always think I need something from you? You're still my daughter, remember?" She waited for a response, and met silence. "Anyways, I left a message for you with someone I didn't recognize, but who seemed quite at home. Who was it?"

Throwing her hand up, Karoline was over it. "What do you care, Mother? Look, I'm really tired...I'll call soon."

She hung up before Jackie could pry anymore. No matter her own concerns about Candice, she wasn't about to let her mother dig her claws into her. The woman could be vicious and Karoline wanted her out of their lives; especially her father's. She helped him get rid of Jackie once, and was determined to do what it took to keep her away.

After an hour Karoline made her way out of the room and down to the front desk to check out. Hiding behind her dark sunglasses, she watched the clerk's judgmental eyes survey her. She snatched them off. "Something wrong, or...?"

The desk clerk pasted a fake smile on. "Uh, no ma'am...not at all." She quickly wrapped up her task. "I hope you enjoyed your stay and we look forward to your next visit."

Karoline grinned and walked off, still fuming from Jackie's invasive suggestions. She called her father as soon as the valet brought her car up.

Frank picked up immediately. "Hello, sweetheart."

"Daddy, how's your day coming?" Her voice awakened as soon as she heard him.

"It'll be better when I see you, pretty girl. Are we still on for today?" Her father was her one lifeline.

"Of course, um...in fact I thought I'd come now. I really need to see you, Daddy."

Frank's voice was full of concern. "Where are you, Karoline? Are you okay?"

Settling into the car, she sensed the worry coming from the other end, "Yes, I'm alright...I just need to see you. I've missed you."

Karoline felt like that twelve year old who idolized her father. As a kid, she would follow him around the house and sit in her own chair next to his desk in his office. Like many young girls, things were always better when Dad was there.

That being said, there were also times of resentment because business often kept him away. Now she was a woman and still felt the same way. Her loneliness overwhelmed her and he was the only person who reminded her that she's relevant in this world.

"Then come home, and we'll have lunch. I love you."

She smiled. "I know...love you too, Daddy."

Frank knew there was only one person who could have made his girl so down. One name: Jackie. Just thinking her name pissed him off. He wasn't about to let her send his daughter over the brink again. Jackie has been scheming for years to get back into Frank's good graces. He'd been cordial with her for the sake of Karoline and made the horrendous mistake of sleeping with her five years before. He's regretted that to no end. She's poison and he wanted her gone. The only way that would happen is if she knew for a certainty that he was over her. He also knew he'd have to make it known throughout their social circles that his romantic interests have *nothing* to do with Jackie. Maybe then, she'd back off. He just hoped Candice was ready for the inevitable backlash.

Spoiled and screwed up

"*D*addy...Daddy, are you here?"

Wandering the second level of the main house, Karoline called out, as she approached the study, knocking before pushing the door open.

"Hey, my girl..." Karoline's face lit up as he stood and reached out hugging her. "...I'm glad to see you."

Karoline was a softer, but mirror image of Frank, blue eyes and that jaw line. She inherited her mother's flaming red hair, but she's Frank Swann's kid through and through. She knew he always looked out for her, even when she didn't want his advice.

"Sweetheart, let's talk. You and me, okay?"

They went for a walk in the garden. The very one where Karoline had helped the landscapers with the flowers when she was a teenager. She practically designed the flower beds around the pool and tennis areas.

After they sat on a bench, not one to beat around the bush, Frank cut to the chase. "So, how are you really feeling, Kari?"

Karoline's face turned solemn. "I don't know, Daddy. I try to stay focused. I do my best to help people, like we always said we would, right? Then I just turn and it goes bad...." She cried. "...then Candice comes and she thinks I'm this spoiled, screwed up kid."

Frank shook his head, "No she doesn't. She's concerned, but she thinks you're amazing. The work you do with the children, everything..."

She pulled back and looked at him. "You know Mother has been calling me. I can't deal with her!"

Pulling his hands back, resting them on his knees he said, "Your mother doesn't exist, you hear me? You don't have to talk to her. She only hurts you. Candice is on your side. But...she did tell me about the other night." Nodding, Karoline told him she assumed as much. He hesitantly continued, "You haven't been using again..."

On top of the prescription drugs, she was being treated for cocaine use. Karoline almost died two years before. Brandon was there and to this day, Frank blamed him.

"No, Dad! No, I promise you. It's hard, but I'm trying."

Frank stood up, "Well for starters, you don't need to be around that crowd of yours, especially that kid Brandon. He's a bad influence and you know it."

Karoline knew her father was right, but it wasn't going to be easy. Brandon was someone who had always been there. Good or bad times, he's one of the few friends she could depend on. But deep down, she knew he was not conducive to her remaining clean for long.

She went back to Malibu on Sunday afternoon. Spending Saturday with her father, instead of her friends, was like a refresher. She felt safe at Swann Lakes. Though she still had her demons to ward off, knowing her dad was in her corner lifted her spirits.

Still, Karoline wasn't sure how she felt about his so-called friendship with Candice. One thing Karoline was certain of was that Candice would look out for her, even if only for the sake of pleasing Frank. She liked Candice, but was already feeling a tinge of jealousy when it came to her father's attention. Candice needed to keep her boundaries in check.

"Candice! I'm back!"

The house was still, with no sign of Candice anywhere. Karoline looked at the clock on the sofa table, which reflected two-thirty-five. Curious, she looked down the hall towards the master and pushed the partially opened door.

"Candice, it's me!"

Hearing a faint hum coming from the bathroom, she realized it was a hair dryer. Karoline glanced around the room and saw a half finished glass of wine, some open books and Candice's laptop at her desk. She couldn't help but think *she's actually serious about all of this journalism business…* It was apparent that Candice had spent Saturday studying. Karoline couldn't help but wish she would have found rumpled sheets with some sign of a man having being there; any man other than her father.

Hurrying out, Karoline wouldn't snoop; even though she wanted to, because Candice seemed too perfect.

A while later, Candice found Karoline fumbling around in the kitchen. "Hey, what's up?" Walking around the other side of the island, she sensed Karoline was either upset with her or just having a bad morning.

"Oh, Candice, how are you?" She nonchalantly glanced over her shoulder.

Candice shrugged, opening the fridge, "I'm alright…a little tired." She had a communications presentation on Monday afternoon and was up late working on the outline. She needed to enjoy her Sunday; and she would. Frank had called and invited her to spend the day with him, saying he wanted to show her where Karoline grew up. Then maybe she'd understand her better. Candice wondered how that would happen. Mostly, she wanted to spend time with him, and hoped that was his real intension.

"Okay, well I'm about to change and head over to Brandon's cookout. I know you think he's messed up, but he's really a good guy." Karoline seemed anxious, nodding as she spoke, as if she felt it necessary to convince Candice.

"I'm sure he is. Have fun and I'll see you tonight."

Karoline stopped, "What are you doing today? You should go out."

Sipping on her glass of orange juice, Candice side-eyed towards the windows. "Actually, I'm seeing Frank. He's leaving Tuesday so, he invited me over."

Karoline looked a little stricken, "Really? To Swann Lakes?" Then she realized how shocked her face must have looked, and smiled, "Um, that's great."

Candice clinched her robe tighter, "Okay well, I'm going to get dressed, but you look good, Karoline."

She walked by as Karoline's eyes focused on her back until she disappeared around the corner.

Ex games

"*I* know she's an adult, but I worry about her too."

"Of course you do." Frank felt his ex-wife's words weren't worth the oxygen it took to speak them.

"Dammit, Frank!" She put him on speaker, while she roughly brushed her thick, red mane.

"Jackie, what is it that you really want?" His tolerance was wearing thin. Candice would be arriving soon and he had nothing more to say. As far as he was concerned, Jackie needed help.

"I want you to stop treating me like an outsider! I *was* your wife, remember? She's *our* daughter."

"That's right, she is. It's just a shame you're now just realizing what all of that means. I have to go. Goodbye, Jackie." Click.

She swallowed hard with her back teeth clinching, tightening her jaw. Her mind started racing and conjuring up her next move. She had a feeling Frank was seeing someone, and it killed her. Not out of love for him, but of the thought of another woman in his life and all that came with it, when she had taken him for granted.

She threw the brush across the room. "You bastard!"

Candice: Thank god for do-overs

*W*hen I drove up Laurel Park Lane towards the palatial estate that announced Swann Lakes in brass on the stately gated wall, I couldn't help but think how it was exactly the way I'd imagined Frank lived. I buzzed, identified myself and moments later, the gates opened. They closed directly behind me, and I continued for what seemed like two miles up the winding palm lined drive past a breathtaking manmade lake.

I started to feel really nervous. It's not like Frank wasn't expecting, or wanting me there, but with every wealthy man, comes suspicious staff and friends that are sometimes less than welcoming. But, all of those feelings vanished when he walked out to greet me. I parked my car and got out, looking around and taking in the blissful setting.

"Candice, you made it…welcome!" Frank was dressed in khakis and a white shirt that hung loose. I thought he looked really tan and so sexy; more so than the other night. I remember being glad that I chose to wear the strapless Lilly Pulitzer dress with a cardigan covering my shoulders. "Could you be more beautiful?" He asked that, while I thought *could I want you any more right now?*

I hugged him, kissing his cheek. "How are you? Thanks for inviting me. This is all so beautiful, Frank."

He took my hand, "Well, come inside. I'll show around before dinner and please, make yourself at home. Despite what anyone thinks, we're pretty casual around here."

I wondered how he did it. How he made me feel so at ease every time we were together. It was one of my favorite things about him.

Our evening couldn't have been more perfect. That's until…

"Candice, I want to ask you something."

"Okay…" Raising my brows awaiting his question, I was anxious about what he was getting ready to say. With Frank you never know.

"The first week in January there's the Angels of Music benefit gala. It's a wonderful event that raises money for children's charities." My eyes surely smiled because I had already said yes in my mind. He gestured with his hands a lot, as he spoke. "Well, I was hoping you'd allow me to escort you."

I blushed, but didn't hesitate too long, "Of course, I would love to go. It sounds lovely, thank you."

We walked towards the front entrance just below the grand staircase and I took in my surroundings, "Frank, your home is really beautiful. I see why you love it here."

"I do, though it feels a little empty now." I stared at his eyes and tried to read the emotion behind them, but Frank is good at hiding his feelings, unlike me who spills it all out.

"I'd better go. I've got an early class tomorrow so…"

I noticed him watching my lips as I spoke. "Of course. Candice this has been one of the best weekends, thanks to you." I could tell he was stalling, not wanting me to leave. He slid his hands down my arms and grasped my hands and I responded by lightly squeezing his. "Stay with me."

I stepped closer, hugging him just to whisper, "I can't…" Then Frank released my hands and cupped my face, kissing me deeply. I swear I went limp, as my bag dropped from my wrist to the floor. When our lips finally parted I continued, "…besides, if I stay, you might not want me to leave."

He kissed my neck and whispered in my ear, "That's okay, too."

I caved, and nodded that I would.

The heel of my sandal got tangled in the strap of the handbag as I stepped, so I reached down and grabbed it. Frank took my hand and led me to an elevator in a narrow hallway.

"I refuse to walk up those steps. There's a million of them." He looked back at me and squeezed my hand.

I giggled at that, but still thought *Candice, what are you doing?* I couldn't help myself. I knew right then that I loved him, and though I was terrified, didn't want to fight it anymore. No matter the outcome.

We hadn't made it into his master suite a minute before he slid my cardigan off exposing my naked shoulders while we embraced the entire time. He kissed my shoulders, as I undid the buttons on his shirt, almost breaking one. Our breathing was heavy and the feeling was intense as the anticipation grew almost furious. I ached to be made love to like I never had before. The energy in the room was palpable, as we steadily made our way across the room, towards his bed where he laid me back, kissing what he always described as my soft, glistening skin.

My arms were outstretched over my head as his lips and tongue softly danced across my neck. – Okay first, let me say this -   I have to describe this like a bad romance novel, because well, you had to have been there to believe it. Frank was hungry as he reached underneath me, blindly groping my dress, before slowly rolling it downward revealing my firm breasts. His lips met my sensitive flesh and in anticipation, I began to rub my thighs together warding off a premature explosion. My fingers crawled from his neck, up through his cropped hair. I felt lightheaded and just dissolved in the moment.

Though he was still dressed I could feel his hardness growing, and I wanted him so bad. Frank was so intent on pleasing me and seemed to be fascinated by my body, like it was a new toy and enjoyed every inch of it. Finally working out of his clothes, he entered me with such force that I gasped. I released soft, pleasured cries, which motivated him to thrust even deeper.

"Ohmigod…" I couldn't remember the last time I'd felt so good. It was like this was the first time I'd ever made love. So as far as I was concerned, at that moment, it was a do-over for all of my past mistakes. Frank was a grown man who knew what I needed and didn't act selfishly. He was all about me. Somehow though, that voice in my head still managed to think *I know I'm going to regret this…*

Gliding my hands across his shoulders, I caressed the muscles of his back and lightly ran my nails across his skin. He moaned and responded by increasing the pressure. I thought I would faint, he was so amazing.

Then as we lay there breathing heavily, Frank revealed, "This entire year has led up to us being together."

I didn't know what he meant, and felt worried that in the midst of the intense sex, he wasn't aware of what he was saying. Even hearing the sincerity in his voice, those foolish assumptions flooded over me. "What do you mean?"

He repositioned himself onto his side and caressed my face with his hand, easing my concern a little. "What do you think I mean?" I turned towards him and said nothing. "Candice, when I return to LA, I want to know that you'll be here."

I sat up some, resting on my elbow, "I'm not going anywhere, Frank." I leaned down, tenderly kissing his face and then lips.

He closed his eyes and released a faint sigh, like my words soothed his soul. "My life isn't easy. Can you deal with all of this?" He seemed so serious.

I didn't really know how to respond, because it sounded like he was asking me to not see anyone else.

"I'll try. But, whatever happens, you have to always be honest with me. Don't ever play with me. Promise me…that's all I ask."

"Of course, always…" His face questioned why I said that.

I hoped he was being real with me. I wanted to be with him just as much. I fell in love with Frank long before that night, and stopped trying to fool myself otherwise, but I didn't know if I was ready for it.

Of course, we made love all night.

So, why then, did I sneak out of the house without saying goodbye?

Why do I always do this? Trying not to make a sound, I glanced over at Frank as he slept. I crawled out of bed, one leg at a time and tip toed across the room picking up my dress and other items off the floor. I gasped and almost laughed when I found my panties slung across a lampshade. I grabbed them and bolted towards the master bath on the other side of the room, throwing my clothes on, and rushed out with the quickness.

Unfortunately not quick enough before the housekeeper caught me in my walk of shame. What must she have thought? I gave her a questioning look asking how to get out of there. The woman pointed towards the staircase saying, "These stairs to the front, or the back stairs next to the media room."

Humiliated, I smiled, and in my bare feet sprinted out. Looking at my watch, I knew I was going to be late for class.

Fear got in the way

*W*hen Frank woke up in the morning, Candice had long gone. He couldn't help but wonder what she was so afraid of.

He also knew that what had just happened was an irreversible turning point in his relationship with Candice. It would either prove to be a beginning or the end. The entire time that they were just friends, all of the flirting and playful embraces were protected under that umbrella. Now, the veil had dropped and they didn't have anything to hide behind.

Frank had spent time with other women all around the world, but never had he cared whether they left without saying goodbye. The majority of the time, it was he who would graciously usher them out the door. Maybe Candice assumed that would be the case with her, so she beat him to the punch.

It's like it was easier for her to protect her heart by assuming that Frank didn't mean a word of what he said; that it was just the sex talking. He didn't want to risk losing her to that assumption, because the fact was, he cared deeply for Candice, and he was ready to prove it.

Take that!

*A*t eight-thirty, Candice came rushing into the house, headed straight for the shower. She grabbed the first thing she could match up, gathered her bag and was headed out the door by nine-fifteen. She knew she'd be late for her first class, so the excuse was lined up. The professor didn't police his students, so as long as the assignments were ready and complete; print ready, as he'd say. Candice was always ready. Except on this morning, she wasn't so sure. Her thoughts were all over the place.

"Good morning, Candie!" Karoline stood at the top of the stairs with a self-righteous look on her face.

Candice stopped in her tracks. "Hi, honey! Look…can we talk later? I'm so late!"

Karoline shrugged a shoulder and started walking down the steps, sipping her coffee. "Sure, I just wanted to say good morning."

Candice wasn't in the mood, so she opened the door and stepped out, fumbling for her keys.

"Oh, and Candie, the next time you stay out all night, call me. I was worried sick."

"Well next time, call your father's house!"

Candice triumphantly pulled the door closed while Karoline stood there with her mouth open from shock. Candice, her do-good housemate had all but told her *I'm screwing your daddy, little girl, so take that!*

Rayne: Ducks in a row

I sat outside of the cold starch building in downtown LA for at least fifteen minutes struggling with my own thoughts. So many years, so many plans, the kids, we were in love once, again, so many years… I came up with every excuse in the world to not move forward with the inevitable. Then the voice of that other woman rang in my head and my hurt and anger resurged. Morgan was going to pay for all of it, not just the infidelity. As hurtful as it was, I could have forgiven him for cheating, but it's the constant lying and deception that was unforgiveable. I couldn't be married to him anymore. However…first things first. I had to know how I'd fare once I walked away, which brought me to my attorney's office.

When we got married, Morgan was broke and I was the one who took care of us. I'll bet he kicks himself everyday over this next fact. No prenuptial agreement was drawn up because there was no money to consider. Then two years later his album broke platinum status and we became millionaires. I immediately got my own attorney. I'm an accountant so I knew exactly what I needed to do - just in case. I was sure the day would never come, but I wanted to be smart about things. Business is business. When there is this kind of money involved, the marital bed blurs into the boardroom.

"Hi, I have an appointment to see Vincent Albright." Self-consciously I glanced down at the receptionist's nameplate atop the mahogany desk, thinking she didn't look like a Liz. She immediately called back and announced me.

"Mr. Albright is finishing up a call, but will be right out, Mrs. Bryant. It's good to see you again." The thirty-something woman had a Colgate smile and a perfectly blow-dried bob that accentuated her high cheekbones. I didn't recognize her, but never let on.

"Thank you. It's good to see you, too." I took a seat in the chair in the reception area and watched her get up and walk over to me.

"Mrs. Bryant, I could bring you Starbucks from downstairs while you wait." I read her eyes and something told me she knew what was going down and wanted to make me as comfortable as possible.

"Oh, would you? That would be great. Thank you, Liz." There was no finding comfort in what was about to happen.

"So you're saying that should I file for divorce, *if* it ever comes to that, half of the estate will be mine? The money and property?"

Mr. Albright chuckled. "Half of the estate is already yours, my dear. The day Morgan and you said I Do, you were entitled to half of everything acquired during the marriage."

That was sweet music to my ears. I had to laugh. "That'll teach him."

There was a lot to consider. Most importantly, my children and how a divorce would affect them.

"If I may suggest, think long and hard about your future, your children's future. If there is any way to resolve the situation, counseling, whatever...consider those options."

I looked at him and softly smiled at the mature man's sincerity in trying to save a family.

"You know, Mr. Albright, I'm afraid it's beyond salvage at this point."

I fought back the urge to cry right then and there. I still loved Morgan, the father of my children, but Morgan, the star...he killed our marriage.

Coming to dinner

The Tuesday before Thanksgiving, Candice was in a quiet corner in the LA Times Reference Room, fine tuning the assignment for her Features Writing class. She was anxious to get finished, because she was flying to Chicago to see her family the next day.

"Have a good Thanksgiving, Candice!" A fellow student loudly whispered on his way out.

"Oh, thank you Mark, the same to you. Enjoy your family, okay?" He had a cute, innocent face, like the kind of guy she would have dated in high school.

Candice then felt her phone vibrate in her handbag on the table. It was Frank. Really needing to finish up, she wanted to let it go, but answered instead. "Hey, you..."

"Hi gorgeous, how are you?" Frank was calling from his gym after a workout with his trainer.

"I'm good, just finishing up in the library. Frank, I haven't even packed my things. Can you believe it?" She softly giggled, looking around.

"Yes, I can, actually." He laughed, teasing her. "In fact, I've decided to go to Chicago for the rest of the week, and hoped we could go together."

"I would love that."

"Great, there are some people I'm meeting with regarding a big merger, but we'll steal some time alone, I promise."

"Okay well maybe you'll get to meet my folks. They'd love to see you." Candice hoped she wasn't pushing, but she just wanted them to meet the man in her life.

"I look forward to it. Will you call me later?"

"Yes, of course..."

The most awkward moment - the end of the call when you can almost hear each other's thoughts. Candice wanted to say those three words she felt in her heart so badly, but there was no way she'd allow it. She'd been burned so many times. She felt that Frank loved her, but being *in love* was an entirely different thing. So for now, she was willing to take what her heart felt.

"I think this is as good as it's going to get." She snapped her laptop closed. The assignment was due the Tuesday after the holiday and she felt confident that she'd met the professor's expectations and more. She hoped anyways.

Swans in the ceiling?

*I*t was the first time Candice had traveled by private jet. From the moment they arrived planeside at Burbank, Frank's people treated her like royalty. An experience she'd surely never forget. People actually think that flying first class on a commercial carrier is living, but those people have never flown private.

Frank's world was an entirely different level of wealth and that scared Candice, just a little. She sometimes questioned herself and tried her best to not appear too in awe over it all. It was important for her to know that she loved him, not just his lifestyle. But what she didn't know is that Frank got off on spoiling her. He courted her to the hilt from day one when he showed up at her townhouse in his Bentley. Every girl deserves to experience that type of pursuit, at least once in her life.

When Candice called her parents to tell them she was bringing Frank to meet them while he was in town, Mrs. Kane decided that he had to come for dinner. Candice was sure he wouldn't feel comfortable with an entire evening with her family. She didn't want him to feel pressured, but when she mentioned it, he was more than pleased with the invite.

Hoffman Estates is idealistic suburbia but it isn't Lake Forest and definitely not Beverly Hills; which was what appealed to Frank when he arrived at the Kane's modest three thousand square foot colonial. James, his Chicago driver, drove him, but Frank asked him to return in a couple of hours. He didn't need backup. This visit was too special.

Candice greeted Frank at the door. Dressed in a suit sans the tie, he held the most breathtaking rose and calla lily bouquet in hand. Smiling, she reached for them, before he broke it to her that they were for her mother.

"What? Oh, you're in for it now. She's going to love you."

"That's the idea, right?" Frank winked, grinning as his dimples sank into his cheeks before giving Candice a kiss and admiring her petite frame in the high neck, Kay Unger faux wrap dress she was wearing. "You're beautiful. Let me look at you." He latched his fingers with hers.

"Thank you." She playfully did a half twirl and stance. "Okay, seriously. Come, I'll introduce you."

They enjoyed a relaxed evening, which left Candice feeling pleased that her parents got to meet Frank, even if it would be just that once. Mrs. Kane seated Frank near her, chatting and laughing with him as if she'd already pictured him as a regular guest. Mr. Kane seemed to approve of his daughter's friend, though cautiously. He even showed Frank the small guest cottage out back. It served as a man cave of sorts, especially for poker nights with his friends; as Candice recalled, was right up Frank's alley. She wondered what they talked about, but wouldn't ask. Her father had a tendency to run his mouth a bit too much. Either that or he laid down the law regarding his daughter. Both scenarios frightened her.

"I'm so glad you met my family, Frank."

In the foyer on his way out to the car, Frank stepped closer to Candice, caressing her shoulders, then sliding his hands downward, clasping their fingers together.

"There's nowhere else I would have been tonight. They're wonderful."

Her eyes smiled at his, "Yeah, I have to agree."

Gazing at her and taking in every soft detail of her face, Frank realized he'd never needed anyone as much as he did Candice. She brought calm to his life, and he was now feeling what he'd missed all those years. Before he realized it, in the midst of their goodnight kiss, he let her know how much she meant to him when he whispered, "I love you Candice."

She pulled back, and had to see that he meant it. She had to see his eyes. "I love you too." As her misty eyes smiled, Candice decided she was leaving with him. Releasing his hand, she grabbed her coat from a closet. "You're not leaving me here."

-

Being at the Lake Forest house again was very surreal because less than a year before, Candice halfheartedly met Frank for the first time, and now she was there *with* him; seeing it all through different eyes.

149

The staircase that wowed her at the entrance was still her favorite part, but she had completely missed the library to the right of the receiving room as she came in. To the left was the family room where she remembered following the housekeeper.

"Good evening, Mr. Swann." There she was. The same housekeeper who greeted Candice on her first visit was still there and Candice prayed those judgmental eyes wouldn't recognize her. "Ma'am." She nodded at Candice and continued past the staircase, disappearing through wood paneled glass doors.

As Frank led Candice into the huge room that was decked out in tasteful, luxurious furnishings, she looked up at the fourteen feet ceiling, with its ornate molding and design. Stopping in her tracks, she smiled. "Frank, are those swans?"

Chuckling, "Yes, they are. Apparently my father insisted on it. My mother thought it to be so gauche, as she used to say."

Candice couldn't agree more, though she never let on. She just thought, clever and rich it may be, but tacky...definitely.

"Ah, the staircase to the billiard room, right?" She smiled.

"You remember." Frank sounded pleased that she reflected on that fateful night without a snarl in her voice. He recalled that he'd hoped she'd return, and she had.

"Yes, I do." She brushed his arm with her hand, "Where's the master suite? It must be gorgeous."

He stopped and extending his arm out to direct her up the second staircase across the room. "Right this way. Candice, are you trying to take advantage of me?" He grinned with a look in his eye that said he wanted her right then.

"No, I just want to see how you live out here in bourgeois Lake Forest." She teased.

Candice took her coat off and handed it to Frank, taking the liberty of walking ahead, seeking out her destination. Reaching the top landing, she saw two hallways and looked back at Frank, who pointed ahead at the double doors.

"Is this it?"

She opened the doors to the eight hundred square foot room. The décor was spacious and inviting, masculine and elegant like an ad for fine living, but paled in comparison to the almost two thousand square foot bedroom suite at Swann Lakes.

Still it was impeccable. There were two sets of French doors that overlooked a lake in the distance. It was dark outside, but there was a clear view of the moon reflecting off the water.

Candice was lost in the gaze when she felt Frank walk up behind her, nuzzling her neck, while his hands slowly raised the hem of her dress. She felt a little exposed at the windows, since there was no telling if staff were within eyesight on another floor, but it turned her on to be a little bad. Feeling his hand graze her bikini line, she responded by gliding her Gucci heeled foot forward, giving her leg leverage. He pleased her, and her breathing escalated into slight moans. Working her dress up even further, Frank cupped her breast, as his body pressed so close that Candice felt him swelling against her. Leaning her head back against his, she reached back, caressing his face as her eyes closed, whimpering in ecstasy.

Gliding her hand down to his zipper and yanking it, she commanded him breathlessly, "Right here."

"There could be someone watching, baby..." He cunningly suggested.

"I don't care, come on..." Candice was burning for him, and amused, Frank played along.

"I'm sure they can't take their eyes off you."

Knowing full well there was no one outside, Frank turned Candice towards him, pinning her against the door frame. Her leg slid up and he met his goal, steadily stroking her, adding more pressure. Frank Swann certainly was no bore. No man had ever tuned into her desires the way he did.

Clutching the door frame, her body began to quiver.

"Oh my god, yes..." Nothing was more mind-blowing than a mutual climax.

Frank kissed her neck as she turned her head, peering out of the door into the darkness. Her breathing settled, wondering if anyone *had* indeed been watching.

Then out of nowhere, he asked, "How 'bout a game of pool? Just one game, I'll even let you win..."

Candice couldn't believe while he was still inside of her, he was talking pool tables. She couldn't help but giggle. "You're crazy. Alright, you're on."

Candice: Beyond the gates

*"H*ey, miss lady! Miss lady!"

"Are you talking to me?" I know I must have frowned something harsh.

Winking at me the man beckoned, "Yeah, I got something for ya!"

"You don't have anything I want!" My lips tightened, assuming he was being perverse. But as I walked across the parking lot and got closer, I realized the man was selling jewelry. Cheap jewelry packaged in sandwich bags in sets of clip on earrings, bracelet and necklace. Then waving and trying to be as friendly as I could, I told him, "No, not today...I'm good!"

Coming from Chicago, I'd seen my share of street vendors peddling their goods. It was just before Christmas, and I was at Ralph's on Crenshaw Boulevard where I stopped on the way home from class. The so-called hood doesn't scare me and I was a little sick of buying all of my groceries in overpriced Malibu. Honestly, sometimes I just plain missed being around black people.

I fought back the urge to laugh in the guy's face as he walked alongside me at a safe distance. I giggled and kept stepping. Irritated and mumbling to myself, "I thought these people weren't supposed to solicit incoming customers, anyways."

Finally reaching the doors at the market, I thought about what I'd just said... *these people*... I felt so disappointed by my own excluding words that my heart sank to my stomach. Mainly because everyone has a hustle, even me, and this was his.

Even though it's in different forms, it boils down to the same: getting ahead. I didn't say no when Frank offered to help me out. No matter the honest intensions, I knew that being associated with the Swann name would open doors for me. I still try to ignore the fact, but it is what it is.

On my way out, I stopped at the vendor, "Hey there, you know what? I just realized I needed a gift for someone..."

I bought two sets. I watched his chest puff out a little more as we made the exchange. His smile was genuine, and I think more than he...I needed it on that day.

I then tossed the jewelry in the hatch of my vehicle, knowing I'd never wear any of it, but hoped I'd given him the extra encouragement he needed to keep it up.

Out of nowhere, I started thinking about my friend Faith. How she was the only person who really knew me. After I moved to LA, we rarely spoke, because I met new people and became so absorbed in my new life. Not to mention she was now married. Faith was like a sister to me, so she'd always be there. That was my thinking.

I slowly felt my real self disappearing. I didn't want to just be Frank's girlfriend, with no identity of my own; totally dependent on his world to define who I am. That's not the person I was in Chicago, and that's not who I wanted to be in Los Angeles.

Candice: Just as fake

*A*s I savored the feel of the cool, moist sand between my toes I couldn't think of anything besides Frank, and going to the Angels of Music Ball on Saturday night. The New Year had just ringed in and I anxiously looked forward to the gala. I hoped the new year would be just what the doctor ordered; a new town and a promising relationship with a wonderful man. Things were starting out good so far. The fundraiser was the biggest ticket of the social season and unbeknownst to me, Frank's way of presenting me to Beverly Hills society and his friends. I dreaded it, but also realized that in Beverly Hills, who you know is everything.

There I was walking barefoot in the sand in the middle of winter, while my family back in Chicago was freezing. I didn't miss those winters one bit.

Frank was in London and I had only a few days before he got back to LA, which was a good thing because I had a heavy schedule at school over the next couple days. I wasn't about to put off my hard work for anything or anyone...not even Frank. Still, the pressure was on to decide which gown to wear to the ball, because I knew it needed to be perfect. I had a private fitting scheduled that afternoon at Monique Lhuillier, and was hoping to find something to compare to the gown I brought back from London.

Over the Christmas holiday, Frank invited me on his weeklong business trip to London. It was romantic, and felt really good to be there with him. He introduced me to an aristocratic world that I'd never imagined. From our grand suite at the Dorchester to dining at his long time friend, steel magnet Lashi Mallak's opulent mansion in Kensington Palace Gardens. Bel Air has nothing on that place, which is aptly referred to as Billionaire's Row. It's bourgeois, but appropriate. Yet, I'd never want to live behind those gates. It was too stiff for my taste. No matter how beautiful, I'd longed for our life in Los Angeles by the time we left.

Our relationship became much more defined during that trip. Frank made sure I was comfortable in every sense and his colleagues did the same. Stacy his assistant was with us and she and I took the Eurostar rail to Paris for a shopping trip.

Our first stop was Rue Cambon, home of Coco Chanel. Ever since I was a little girl, I dreamed of shopping at Chanel. The local boutique on Michigan Avenue in Chicago was fine, but the birthplace of the brand - that was the fantasy. I think Stacy and I burned holes through our credit cards. But, the pinnacle of the entire visit was being treated to a brief tour of Chanel's legendary apartment. There are no words to describe the feeling, so I won't even attempt it.

Stacy is all business when it comes to her career, but she's also free spirited and fun, and boy can she shop. She's also very discrete when it comes to her boss's personal affairs. I always thought that must be a heavy burden.

I always refused to speak of money, because it made me uncomfortable. Though Frank's generosity was apparent, Stacy never outwardly judged me. She is loyal to Frank, and that trickles down to those in his personal life. Stacy probably knows more about his life than even he does and it's a safe assumption that she is paid handsomely for that accommodation.

Out of nowhere a skinny little brown dog aimlessly ran across my path; stopping and twirling in circles in the sand.

"Hey little one, come here." I squatted down; beckoning her to come to me but the pooch ran off. Being the dog lover that I am, I took off after her, "Wait, come back little baby!" I was sure she was going to dash towards the water, and wash out. "Silly rabbit!" Giggling I just stopped trying; putting my hands on my waist. I was still laughing because she was so cute.

"Gigi! Gigi, come back! Come to Momma!"

A voice behind me was yelling with her hands clapping for the dog. My head turned around and found a tall, lean glamazon of a brunette in her early forties I assumed, in full makeup.

I smiled, "That's your dog?"

The woman pouted her full lips in frustration as her cascading hair blew in the strong breeze, "Yes, she flies down the stairs of the deck and just goes - every time!"

Keeping an eye on the dog, I noticed Gigi stop and turn around, then sprinted back towards us, "Oh good…here she comes."

The woman knelt down and scooped up her prized dog and with an almost screeching tone, "My babyyyy…." Then she looked at me and stood up, extending a manicured hand, "I'm Hunter…Hunter Goldman."

Relieved that she was cordial, I responded, "Candice Kane, nice to meet you."

Curiously surveying me with suspicious eyes, Hunter nodded, "Me too. You live here on the beach or…?"

Pointing in the opposite direction, I told her I lived at the edge of the bluffs.

Hunter gave an approving smile then eyebrows raised like a light bulb went on, "Wait a minute. Are you Karoline Swann's new housemate?" I was a little taken a back because, how did this woman know anything about me? "Oh don't get the wrong idea. I decorated the beach house and I know her mother. She mentioned Karoline was excited about her new housemate, is all."

I swear I felt a chill sweep over me. "That's sweet. Well I'm going to head back. Hope to see you again."

"Yes! I live right here. We should have lunch sometime."

She giggled, pulling out a card from the tiny wallet in her track suit pocket and handing it to me. The little dog started jumping and twirling on her hind legs. Hunter excused herself; jogging back towards the house. It was a huge bi-level structure of windows and steel; shielded by palm trees, exotic flowers and umbrellas. Watching her strut off into her little paradise, I thought, Hunter Goldman - That name can't be real. Surely, it was as fake as her breasts. Silently scolding myself for being so catty, I reached down, picking up a random coral colored stone and headed back towards the house.

"Karoline, so what do you know about Hunter Goldman?" I was sitting at the kitchen island, scrolling through my cell phone.

"Hunter Goldman? How do you know her?" Karoline's tone sounded a little suspect to me.

"Oh, I don't. I met her on the beach just now. She gave me her card. It's funny though, she knew who I was."

Raising her eyebrows, she leaned over the counter. "She's married to this big movie producer. But besides that, she's an amazing interior designer. Daddy knows her."

I softly sighed, "Of course he does, Karoline, and you just couldn't wait to tell me that."

"Oh, not like that, Candie. I didn't mean…"

"I'm sure you didn't." Pulling open the garbage drawer, I tossed my half eaten apple in. "I'll be working if you need me."

Karoline sipped her tea and I felt her watching me exit the kitchen. I think she admired me for having the guts to enter their crazy world. She told me once that she envied that I had my life together. But at the same time, she was a daddy's girl that iced me out sometimes, like I was competition. I didn't want to compete; I just wanted her to trust me.

Bebe: Runway, don't want it

*I*t was the afternoon of the Angels ball and my house was like Grand Central. Crews were in and out all day: florists, caterers, event stagers, security, and most urgently my stylist, Heddy and her assistant.

"Bebe, hun…how do you feel? Is it too tight at the bust?"

"No, I'm fine darling, really. But, do you really think this is the one?" I didn't love the dress then, like I did in the showroom.

"Hmmm, you're not feeling it, I can tell."

Heddy gestured to her assistant, whom I watched in the three way mirror trot over like an eager to please puppy.

"Let's try the backup, shall we? Oh, and bring the crystal Dior strappies as well, okay?" She turned her attention back to me. "Bebe, you will love this one, and may God strike me if you don't!" She pushed her rhinestone encrusted specs up on her nose, smiling confidently.

Heddy was over the top glam, like a lovechild of RuPaul and Marilyn Monroe. Tall and curvaceous, with a style direct from the old Hollywood sound stages. Her motto was: *Hun, if it looks fresh off the runway…we don't want it!* If it were new, it had better look as if Lauren Bacall wore it forty years prior. A self-professed vintage whore, Heddy kept my closet so packed with goodies that more than one Hollywood starlet has literally banged on my door to borrow for awards season.

Slipping off the gold Marchesa gown, as beautiful as it was, I knew it wasn't right for the gala. I needed to be more subtle, and demure. The perky little assistant approached me holding up the most breathtaking strapless black and white Dior gown. The matching shoes dangled from her fingers.

"What do you think of this one, Ma'am?"

I couldn't take my eyes off of it. I knew it was my Angels gown. The Marchesa would have to wait.

A knock at the dressing room door interrupted us. It was my house manager advising me that Daphne Margot had arrived, and was about to begin rehearsing with the band. I didn't want her anywhere near me. Still, Daphne was our star performer so, I graciously sent welcomes to her, and arranged for a gift basket to be waiting in her guest suite. Daphne kept an apartment in LA, but I needed to keep an eye on her, so to speak. Our girl had a tendency to show up when she wanted, or *if* she wanted. This night was too important. I wasn't going to let the likes of Daphne Margot and her diva tantrums ruin it.

Little did I know, Daphne would be the least of my worries by the time the night was over.

Candice: Beauty shop talk

"So, tell me about this fabulous party you're attending, Candice."

I was awakened out of the daze, because having her hands tend to my head felt so relaxing. Straightening my naturally curly hair with the blow dryer, my stylist was bringing the magic. While I inherited that so-called good hair, my curls fought back sometimes. For the polished 'do I desired, I sought out the best hairstylist on the West side. Being a woman, especially a black woman, it's all about the hair. I wanted to look spectacular for the evening and with Stacee's help, I would.

Stacee James, owner of Glam Lox Salon in West Hollywood, is the queen of hair on the Hollywood circuit. Especially ethnic hair and she'd worked on major scalps in the industry; from the R&B divas to award winning actresses. She was responsible for the famous hair cut on the historical night when a black woman won Best Actress at the Oscars some years back. If that cut was Stacee's doing, I knew I needed her. I had a classmate, whose hair was always perfect, and I asked her point blank, 'Who does your hair, girl? I need the best!' She led me straight to Stacee, the follicle goddess who also, rumor has it, introduced the lace front wig to Hollywood; black and white, women *and* men.

"Well, I'm attending the Angels of Music benefit at a private estate in Beverly Hills, and…"

"Oh, yes of course, it's huge. A friend of mine will be performing in the band. Sorry, go ahead, sweetheart." She continued brushing and tugging at my hair.

"Really? Well, I'm going with a friend, and he's the guest speaker." Looking straight ahead at my reflection in the mirror, I tried to hide the spark in my eyes when I thought about Frank.

"A friend, huh? He must be some friend to make you glow like that." Stacee raised an eyebrow like, *spill it…*

"What? I'm not…" Blushing, I glanced up at Stacee's reflection. I wasn't about to go into details with my hairdresser. I love her, but they're the biggest gossips on the planet.

"What's his name? He's got to be somebody if he was invited to speak before that crowd."

"Frank, and he's wonderful." Glancing down, I realized I had completely reshaped a bobby pin with my fingers.

Stacee continued pinning my curls up. "Frank? Hmmm, does he have a last name?"

I was hesitant but was sure Stacee didn't give a damn about who Frank Swann was. "Swann..." I almost whispered it.

I saw the light go on in her head. "THE Frank Swann? Girl, he's gorgeous! I'll tell you one thing, if I was going to date a white man, he'd be the one, that's for sure! The fact that he's seriously loaded doesn't hurt either." She gave me that matter of fact look.

"Stacee!" I was a little embarrassed.

"Well, he is!" She went on saying Frank was the lucky one and not to ever let him forget it.

"Thank you for that. Now hook me up!" I grinned at Stacee's reflection and nudged back on my chair, teasing her.

"I'll tell you one thing, honey. Mr. Swann is going to flip when he sees you tonight."

I hoped so. I realized that it was important for him to attend the gala, but having me on his arm was sure to send the blogs to buzz. Even in this age, nothing makes for better gossip, than a billionaire and his much younger love interest. It's all so silly, but sadly, true.

Three hours, a tight up do and a glass of champagne later, I was ready to knock Beverly Hills off its feet.

Angels of Music Gala

*F*rank stood at the full length mirror in his study, surveying his image as his tailor put the finishing touches on his Prada tuxedo.

"Make sure I look great, Arnaud. I'm counting on you, my friend." Looking down at the tiny Italian man tapering the hem of his slacks, he nodded and winked.

"Of course, Mr. Swann…T'is perfect already."

With a tape measure hanging from his neck, he worked like a master making certain that his favorite client was pleased. His English was bad, but he was so excited to be working with 'Meester Swann', as he pronounced.

"Good…because this is a special night and I can't show up looking like a slob." The two men chuckled.

It was the night of the Angels ball and Frank had it all planned to a T. Not having spoken to Candice since the night before, he was anxious to see her. She wasn't part of the typical Beverly Hills social set. She wasn't fighting to belong. Most of all, Candice still had a joy and passion about life that he hadn't seen in many years. Not until Candice Kane walked into his life.

There was a knock at the door. "Yes, come in!"

Cecilia entered holding a velvet box with gold embossing of the name Fred Leighton. "It was just delivered. This is for tonight, I assume?"

Eyeing the box, he grinned and nodded, "Yes…on loan. She'd never allow me to buy her something so extravagant."

Cecilia raised her eyebrows giving him an inquisitive look, wondering what was in the box. She didn't dare ask since he didn't volunteer, but she was sure whatever it was, was exquisite. "She must be very special to you. I haven't seen that smile in your eyes in ages."

"She is, and, thank you, Cecilia." Frank knew Cecilia had seen and heard a lot in his life and appreciated her loyalty.

"Of course, Sir." She sensed he would not give up any information about his lady, and turned and left the room.

Frank opened the box and rubbed his fingers across the contents thinking how beautiful it would look on Candice. They'd enjoyed a fairly private relationship, as best they could, being that he was away quite a bit and she had a full schedule at USC. But it's that time apart that made him realize how much he loved her.

Across town, Candice glanced at her Gucci Signoria watch, which displayed four-fifty. "Oh my god...it's getting late!" Frank would be there for her at six-thirty and she had been postponing the shower for fear she'd get her chignon wet. If her hair got wet she'd have to change her look, and she didn't have time for that drama. Carefully placing a huge bonnet on her head, she jumped in the shower.

Later, sitting at her dressing table, she thought about the party and wondered who would be there. Beverly Hills can be intimidating when it comes to the social scene. They would surely gossip about who she is. They'll assume it was a sex-off from the word Go. Especially the women. Frank was the jackpot catch: Good looking, established and very wealthy. That's how most of the women size men up in this town. They'll want to know how an unknown landed one of the richest men in the world.

Candice knew she was about to walk into the lion's den, but she also knew that the Swann name would ward them off a bit. They'd play nice. If one thing is true, it's the fact that people of Beverly Hills love money and you never slight the lady of a titan like Frank Swann. He's known for his charitable generosity, and to piss him off they risk millions.

Elbows on the table, Candice rested her head on her clasped hands and gave herself a pep talk.

"You can handle these people, girl. This is not your first waltz." She started thinking about Miami, and all of the upper crust vile she managed to crawl out of.

Four years ago, I was in Miami Beach with a girlfriend and we got invited to a cocktail party at a waterfront estate on Fisher Island, belonging to a Colombian "diplomat", is what he titled himself. I say that because everyone knew he was a drug kingpin. In Miami, if you have the money, they don't care what your origin is...as long as you have the funds to gain entry. Common party girls and hip hop moguls rub shoulders with Middle Eastern tycoons and the denominator is money, honey.

This particular night, while enjoying the festivities with other partygoers, in walks the Prince: a real life Arab prince, son of the Sultan. I really didn't recognize him until buzz spread across the patio like a wildfire. To me he was a little twerp of a guy, but with money and power like his, he may as well have been ten feet tall. The kid had a harem and he traveled with an assistant who scouted more talent. Having heard tales of his raunchy habits and kinky exploits, I was almost sick at the stomach upon sight of him. I grabbed my drink, practically tiptoeing out of his vicinity, but not before hearing a famous actress bragging about how he had sent for her to Dubai. Saying he was disgusting, but she walked away with a half million just to party with him for one night. She laughed and drank some more, like it was all good – prostituting yourself out. I scooped up my friend, who put up a fight, but we got out of there before he started collecting new booty for the weekend. I hate to admit it, but thinking back on it, I was probably so intent on getting out of there because I couldn't be certain that if had he chosen me, I wouldn't have caved. That kind of money and power does strange things to women. We're willing to lose ourselves then fall to our knees and pray about it in the morning.

If the likes of an Arab Prince didn't faze her, the gala would be a cakewalk.

Finishing her makeup, Candice walked into her closet and gazed at the red Monique Lhuillier gown she'd chosen. The asymmetric neckline and fluid back showcased her lean neck and shimmering complexion to seduction. The boutique associate helped her with the decision when she said, "This dress will make him fall in love with you, if he isn't already."

Actually Candice felt Frank loved her as much as she did him, and since the night was set to a fairytale, she knew she may as well live it to the hilt and dazzle him. She pulled out her diamond stud earrings and matching tennis bracelet as the only pieces of jewelry because 'too much is just too much'. She, not the jewelry, needed to hold his attention.

She pranced around the house in her robe until around six-ten, eating cereal, her favorite snack. Plus it wouldn't ruin her appetite for dinner. She also thought how glad she was that she wasn't on her period because she'd be so self-conscious all night, fearing looking bloated, or worse. Fact was, her size six frame couldn't look bloated if she forced her stomach outward intentionally.

Karoline walked through the door at six-twenty and offered to help her into her dress. Even though she was still processing the fact that her father was dating Candice, she offered to help her. Candice was suspicious but was pleased with the kind gesture. She figured it was Karoline's way of letting her know that she was fine with it all. And deep down, she was.

Frank chose to ring the doorbell instead of letting himself in. Candice could hear him talking to Karoline in the living room. Giving an onceover in the mirror, she felt confident and ready for the night. She grabbed her Jimmy Choo clutch and walked towards the living room, holding onto the outer layer of the dress that fanned as she walked, for fear she'd trip over it.

"Look at you. They're going to hate you..." Frank teased as she entered into the room.

"What?" Candice looked worried, and then giggled.

"You're so beautiful." He reached out for her to settle into his arms.

"Hmm...I bet you say that to all the girls..." She rubbed her manicured fingertip across his bow tie. "...and may they eat their hearts out." She kissed his inviting lips.

She inhaled softly and became a little intoxicated by his fragrance. Frank's tux fit him to perfection that even he knew he looked good. Arnaud the tailor had done his job well.

In the middle of the kiss Karoline walked in on them, clearing her throat, "Are you two leaving or...?" As they walked out, she realized she hadn't seen her father so happy in years.

When they settled into the backseat of the waiting Rolls Royce Ghost, Frank pulled out the velvet box. Candice's eyes fixed on it in anticipation. "Frank, what is that?" He opened it and inside was the most dazzling diamond sunburst choker. She softly exhaled past pouty, glossy lips. "It's beautiful...you want me to wear it now?"

Smiling, he tried to make her feel at ease about it, "It's just a loan, but I knew you had to have this for tonight."

Candice stared at it and raised an eyebrow in awe of the necklace. It was worth nearly two hundred thousand dollars and though she didn't know that, she wasn't very comfortable wearing it, but it was too beautiful not to. She wanted to please Frank. *So much for just enough* she thought. "Thank you."

Turning her back towards him on the seat she felt a tingle come over her as his fingers graze her skin as he secured the necklace around her neck. Then he kissed the nape her neck. "I promise you'll have a wonderful night. The Fabians are lovely people. You'll like them."

"Okay, I trust you're right." Candice turned around and gazed at him, silently wondering what she'd done for God to bless her with such a beautiful man; someone who cherished her. She hoped it would all last; the kindnesses...because they rarely did.

Looking out the window she began seeing Beverly Hills signs and she knew they were approaching the estate, and the feeling was daunting. Nervous about what to expect when they got out, she reached down and clutched Frank's hand for comfort. She felt like a complete newcomer, which she was.

"Don't be nervous. First of all, the women could take a note or two from you, trust me. As far as the men...they won't be able to take their eyes off you."

Candice blushed hearing that, but still didn't buy it. She was sure she might be walking into a coven of snooty, rich bloodsuckers.

The car turned off Mulholland Drive and continued past the security gates of the exclusive Beverly Park. The Fabians boast one of the most lavish estates in the community. It was almost disgustingly so. Swann Lakes, in her opinion was much more elegant.

Valet met them, but Frank told the driver to give them a few minutes. He wanted to talk to Candice alone.

"We won't get a chance to really be alone until later. I want you to know how much I love you. You do know that, right?"

Candice nodded, looking into his eyes, and stroking his jaw line. "I do know that, I do."

As far as she was concerned they could have skipped the event all together. They kissed until she remembered the chiffon on the gown; that it was probably crinkling the longer she sat. Her entrance had to be perfect. "Frank, my dress!"

Frank tapped the window and the driver opened his door. Photographers were waiting and Candice knew from that moment forward she'd be known publicly as Frank Swann's girlfriend. She almost dreaded it because she didn't want the attention and everything that came with it. She just wanted him.

He grabbed her hand, helping her out of the car and they walked towards the steps and huge opened doors of the French chateau style mansion, stopping briefly on the carpet for photos.

A photographer shouted out requesting, "Mr. Swann, can we have a few of the lady alone? Over here, Miss!"

The flashes were blinding but exciting at the same time. Enjoying the moment, Candice channeled Billy Flynn and gave 'em the old razzle dazzle... She graciously smiled and posed at their beckoning and then put a hand up, "Thanks, guys!"

Frank looked on, grinning with pride and then escorted her inside. He looked at her and she securely put her arm through his. He teased, "See...putty in your hands. She playfully nudged him. All of her anxiety slowly dissipated.

"Good evening, Sir. Cocktails are on the terrace. Enjoy your evening."

The petite blonde hostess greeted them graciously but looked bored, like she'd rather be somewhere else. But then, repeating the same words to five hundred people who are most likely not interested in you, can do that to a person. Candice gave her a smile and the young woman returned one, nodding.

They continued through the grand atrium which was decked in crystal chandeliers and floral arrangements. The aroma was heavenly. The well-heeled guests filed in, heading towards the huge French doors leading out onto the stately terrace which appeared the size of the stage at the Hollywood Bowl. There was a live jazz ensemble performing in one corner, and more flowers along the stone railings and down the staircase leading into the garden. It was like an art museum rather than a private residence.

"This is quite a showplace. I can definitely handle this." Candice laughed playfully.

Looking around, Frank nodded and whispered, "See Candice, this is what people do when they have too much money." He laughed, almost making fun of his own wealth, trying to downplay it.

One thing Candice knew about the Fabians is that they are not billionaires. They're rich, but by old boy standards, were new money. The Swanns are old money, people who made money and hand it down to generations. Which is often more appealing because they tend to be more humble, if that's possible. They don't flaunt it. Candice loved that Frank never played the mine-is-bigger game. That's what turned her off about every other man of means that she's known. They bought nice things to impress others, not because they sincerely enjoyed them. It was as if they weren't used to anything.

Candice giggled at his remark, "I see."

Couples approached them, greeting Frank at which point he introduced Candice to them. They were cordial and inviting. The women issued compliments, 'your dress is divine darling', that type of graciousness. She recognized a few faces, like Kenny "Babyface" Edmonds, who smiled and nodded as he walked by. Candice tried not to appear star struck. Then there were your tabloid socialites who make it a point to attend every event on the circuit, which is acceptable, so as long as they come strapped with a sizeable check for the cause.

When they reached the terrace, Candice recognized someone else immediately. Hunter, who upon sight, raised her glass and smiled. That's until she noticed who Candice was with. That smile went cold, real fast.

Same ol' troubles

*"K*aroline, I'm coming in!"

Brandon showed up at the beach house at around eight-thirty to pick her up for a movie at The Grove. They were laying low instead of driving to Palm Springs like they'd planned. He tried calling to let Karoline know he was pulling into the driveway, but she didn't answer. When he got to the front door, it was unlocked, so he kept in. It wasn't really like Karoline to have the house open while she was there alone, so he got a little worried and put his cigarette out, before walking in.

He could smell her perfume in the air so he knew she had to be around. Checking the rear deck, he found no one. Then he headed towards the loft stairs, but not before grabbing a fistful of red and green M & M's from the crystal dish on the table in the living room. Then he heard a little rumble, like something was falling over upstairs. Brandon must have skipped three steps getting up there.

"Kari! Honey, where are you?" Brandon found her stumbling from the sofa trying to make it to her bed. She finally lay down on the sofa, curling up under a blanket.

"Heyyyy Bran'...I'm okay. I'm just..." She coughed, and with the husky sound of her voice dragging she continued. "...am tired. Can we skip the movie?"

"Sure." He stood in front of her with his hand on his hip, "You're not okay. Look at you!" He was sure he knew what was happening and it was nothing good. Brandon looked around the room and zoomed in on the table next to her bed. He read it: *Hydroco...* He sighed loudly. "Nooo, Karoline! How many of these did you take?" He glanced back at her and she had fallen asleep. He immediately woke her up, and pulled her off the sofa. "Nope! Not sleeping..." He walked her to the bathroom.

She was almost dead weight and Brandon struggled a little. Groggy, she cursed him, "Get your damn hands off me, Brandon...stop!"

Brandon was in a panic because he'd watched her almost die before. He ran downstairs to the kitchen and grabbed a glass and filled it with mustard and salt;

more than any one person should be able to handle. Then topped it off with water. Rushing back up to Karoline, now on the floor in the corner, he handed it to her. "Here honey, drink this. It's good for you."

She pushed his hand away but he kept on, so she gulped it down to get rid of him. "Sonafabitch! What are you doing? Get out of here!" Suddenly she hurled over, crawling towards the toilet, and then vomiting chunks all over the seat.

"I'm sorry, I had to. I'm not going through this again!" Karoline fell back on the floor, still out of it, but fairly lucid. Brandon knelt beside her. "I'm not going anywhere. You can go to bed, but I'm staying."

It was like Brandon was completely oblivious to the fact that he should be calling 911 or at least taking Karoline to the hospital. He cleaned her face and brought her bottled water to rinse her mouth, before helping her to bed, where she passed out shortly after.

Brandon thought about how pissed Candice would be if she were there and would probably blame him. So he had to make sure Karoline was back in shape by morning. Standing over her bed, with his hands against his forehead, he pleaded, "Karoline, you've got to control this!"

The Swann effect

There Hunter was. Her body draped in a jaw dropping Alexander McQueen gold crepe satin gown, sashaying across the terrace, making a beeline for Frank and Candice.

"Well, what are you two up to?" Frank mumbled something under his breath, bracing himself for what was surely to come. "Candice, helloooo..." Hunter reached out with one arm, greeting her with a kiss on the cheek before glancing at Frank. "Frank..."

Candice almost felt a frost come over her. "Hunter, it's good to see you again."

Frank stood dumbfounded, looking at Candice, "You two know each other?"

She softly touched his sleeve, while Hunter's eyes followed the gesture, "Actually we met earlier in the week on the beach." She giggled and continued, "We were introduced by the sweetest little dog."

Hunter gave a sly grin. "Naughty puppy...but she's my baby." She shot Frank an ice cold stare while keeping her smile intact. She glanced behind him and noticed her husband Harold Goldman, movie producer and studio executive, coming over. A tall, stocky man with a reputation for being a pig when it came to the ladies joined the group and Hunter straightened up her face. "Sweetheart...you know Frank Swann."

The men shook hands, "Of course, Frank, how are you?" Frank responded but ol' Harry didn't hear a word as he couldn't stop staring at Candice, who suddenly felt uncomfortable.

Hunter linked arms with her husband, "We'll see you two later, yes? Candice, you look gorgeous." The Goldmans started walking away, but not before Hunter took it upon herself to whisper to Frank, "I hope you do better by her than you did me."

The ink on Frank's divorce papers wasn't dry before Hunter, a thirty year old interior designer from Laguna Beach came knocking at his door ten years before, offering the proverbial shoulder to lean on. They'd met while he was married to Jackie. Hunter was dating another man, but craved Frank. He had the power and social status she wanted. She dreamed of becoming the queen of Beverly Hills. That was until Frank left for Europe and didn't return for three months. He never once asked her to join him. Frank had seen Hunter coming long before she got to him. She was too hungry and it turned him off. She never sealed the deal, and feeling spurned, it killed her that he didn't want her. Beverly Hills is an intimate circle and Hunter had a reputation for being a social climbing fortune hunter; aptly named. He didn't feel he owed her anything. A few months later, Frank read she'd married a Hollywood heavy weight. He felt for the sorry schmuck.

Aggravated by her threatening tone, Frank shot back, "Oh, I plan on it." Hunter then rolled her eyes and moved on.

Frank turned to Candice hoping she hadn't heard that exchange. He assumed she hadn't because she was swaying to the beat of the jazz trio performing on the terrace. He was going to make certain that Hunter didn't ruin their night with her stupid games. Just then, he saw Derek and Bebe Fabian making their way onto the terrace. "Come on, I want you to meet my real friends."

The grandeur of the Fabian's world would have to be seen to be believed. Candice still couldn't believe it. The house was certainly beautiful, but leaning towards Frank as they entered she kidded, "This isn't my taste, but it'll do."

Dinner was in the three thousand square foot ballroom which was added onto the main house six years before. Frank and Candice were seated at the head table with the Fabians. Interesting enough, Bebe took to Candice immediately because something about her was a reflection of herself. Not to mention she personally despised Jackie, and was one of the biggest supporters of the divorce. She made a point of telling Candice how happy Frank looked, and that Jackie put him through hell.

"Oh, I'm sorry...I won't bring her up again, darling."

Candice shrugged it off, "No, it's fine."

Candice sensed that Bebe was someone she could trust. She hoped anyway. A friendly ally is good to have in these parts. Not only was she beautiful, but Bebe was smart, well connected and on top of her game; especially when it came to her charity work. She had perfected the art of getting people to let go of millions of dollars. The

172

two spoke about how Angels of Music came about. Candice was impressed that Bebe had accomplished so much on her own, without her husband's direction.

"So, how'd you two meet?" Bebe seemed sincerely interested in the details.

Candice sighed, "Well it's a long story but, I'm from Chicago and a mutual friend introduced us. Then I got accepted into USC's graduate journalism program and..."

Bebe interrupted, placing a hand on hers, "Oh good for you darling, that's wonderful."

Candice felt comfortable with her, "Thank you, Bebe. We got to know each other better once I moved here. He's amazing."

Bebe was pleased. "He's a good man and you must be very special. I can see how he adores you."

Candice glanced over at Frank who was chatting with Derek, before preparing to take the stage as the guest speaker. He looked over at Candice and winked, as she discretely clutched her hands together giving dual thumbs up.

Sheila Ericson approached the platform and introduced him. "Now, a few words from a dear friend of the Angels of Music Foundation. It's my pleasure to introduce Chairman of Swann Pharmaceuticals, Frank W. Swann."

As the audience applauded his approach to the podium, Candice felt a warmness come across her body as she watched him standing there commanding their attention. Her smiling eyes reflected how proud she was to be with him.

"Good evening, ladies and gentlemen. It's an honor to be invited as guest speaker for the fifth annual Angels of Music Foundation charity gala. It is a great pleasure for me to be here tonight. I would like to seize the opportunity to congratulate the beautiful Bebe Fabian and her team of Angels on launching this outstanding fundraising campaign of which many educational institutions will benefit. The children of our communities, locally and nationwide are reaping the benefits of your giving hearts. Your selfless donations this evening have amounted to more than five million dollars." The roar of applause filled the room. "Yes... you deserve that. Five million dollars, the sum that will be distributed to music programs not only in the greater Los Angeles area, but schools around the country who would have otherwise had to cut programs in the arts from their curriculum. That would be tragic; to halt the dreams of talented boys and girls who are our future. The money will be used for new musical equipment, additional classrooms where needed, and opportunities to attend musical events such as field trips, that would normally be out of their reach due to a lack of funds. The goal of the Angels of Music Foundation is to decrease the number of children lost and dreams shattered because of lack of extracurricular activities. This is done through education. Alongside their parents, we hope to inspire young people to not only dream, but plan their paths as they strive for greatness. Ladies and gentlemen, this is why music and other art programs are so important. Life is a beautiful gift, and God gives us talents which add to the joy of life. If our children cannot nurture these gifts, again...it would be tragic. Together, with our mutual efforts and support, we are honoring these young people...and it makes me proud to be a part of something so great. In closing, I wish to thank all of you, the sponsors and donors, for your considerable generosity and hard work. Thank you all for being here tonight. Nobody throws a party like Bebe and Derek!" The crowd cheered. "Enjoy the rest of your evening. Thank you."

The audience came to their feet with applause. Bebe stood stage side and hugged her friend, thanking him. She made a brief announcement as Frank returned to the table, sitting next to a beaming Candice. As the music started and guests approached the dance floor, Bebe made her way back to the table. She placed her hands on Frank's shoulders, leaned down towards him and whispered, "Don't let her get away, Frank. She's a keeper, don't you think?" She giggled lightly, while Derek looked on, almost bored.

Frank turned to Bebe and said, "I won't. You have my word."

He stood up and took Candice's hand, knowing how much she loved to dance. The male vocalist's voice was smooth and hypnotic and Candice was lost in Frank's arms. It seemed light years ago that she had given him the cold shoulder and described him as too bold and arrogant. He truly was not that man. They swayed closely, absorbed in each other, almost oblivious to the other guests.

"Are you having a good time?"

"Yes, I am. This night is perfect, and Bebe is so sweet."

"She is, and she feels the same about you."

"You think so?" Candice glanced over at their table.

"Oh, I know so. She told me…" Mocking Bebe's voice, '…don't let her get away Frank.' His eyes smiled.

Candice giggled, "Is that right?"

"Yes, and I told her, I won't."

Frank stopped dancing, and held both of her hands with his. The music was still playing and everyone danced on. "I meant it. I love you Candice, but I don't want to be your boyfriend anymore. I don't want to date you, I don't want take you home afterwards. I want us to be together."

Candice was about to respond, but then watched him step back and kneel down on one knee. Her legs went weak underneath her gown. "Frank? Oh my god, Frank, what are you…?"

With a hand up to her mouth she looked confused, like she thought he was playing games. He wasn't. Her eyes became flooded by tears, her lips quivering, while not wanting to mess up her makeup. Not at this moment. There were gasps and slight cheers coming from around the room and the music stopped. A spotlight was put on them. She glanced over at Bebe with a puzzled look like *is he really doing this?* Bebe, hands clutched together under her chin, was smiling ear to ear, nodding at her.

Frank reached into his lapel pocket, pulled out and opened the velvet Harry Winston box, and took her left hand. There were flashes popping off around the room. "Candice Kane, will you marry me?"

His smile was directed up towards her as she stood there, legs trembling and heart beating rapidly. Frank waited for her answer, which seemed to take forever as every moment of their friendship and relationship flashed before her eyes, but she was sure this was right. She squeezed his hand, and stared into his eyes until tears started falling from hers.

"Yes -Yes I will." Candice bit her bottom lip, laughing and crying as he slipped the platinum and eight carat diamond onto her trembling finger. She couldn't believe the size of the ring. She was almost embarrassed.

The crowd applauded and raised glasses and some guy shouted, "Well done, man!"

Frank stood and hugged her close, shielding her from the glaring eyes in the room. Softly rocking, her said, "I promise I'll do whatever it takes to keep that smile on your face."

She looked into his eyes, "You have already. I love you, Frank."

He'd never felt so free to reveal himself to a woman until Candice, and she felt just as secure with him.

Bebe took the stage, "Wow… On that note let's celebrate for the children and for the future Mr. and Mrs. Frank Swann!" She blew kisses at them with her perfectly manicured hands as her own bling reflected the lights.

As they walked off the dance floor, a half drunk Hunter approached them, "Congratulations, you guys. Really, I'm happy for you."

Candice thanked her but was no fool. She'd put two and two together and knew exactly what Hunter's problem was. She read it in those conniving eyes the moment her phony smile froze upon seeing Frank. Candice didn't give another thought to Hunter and her silly behavior. Who Frank chose to play with before her was his business. She wasn't about to give Hunter the satisfaction.

Candice and Frank ducked out of the ballroom and into a lounge down the hall. She was still in a little bit of a haze and sat on the edge of a leather chair near the fireplace, admiring her engagement ring.

"Were you planning this the whole time?" She waited, watching him close the doors.

With a hand in his pocket he rubbed his chin with the other, "Not really. I told your father I was going to wait until after the party tonight. I had the whole thing set for a moonlight proposal on the beach, but I couldn't help myself just then. It felt right."

Her face lit up, "My dad knew?" Thanksgiving flashed before her eyes. No wonder Frank was so eager to meet her family. But Candice never expected this. Not so soon. She blushed as he sat in the chair, gently pulling her onto his lap. Reaching her arms around his shoulders, she rested her head against his, "Frank…"

He brushed her lower back with his fingers, "What is it sweetheart?"

In all of her love and excitement in thoughts of marrying him, the reality of possibilities loomed, "Promise me…that we'll never let anyone come between us. Not even us."

Realizing she was serious, he held her closer. "I promise. I knew we'd be together from the moment I first saw you. It's been about you and me from the beginning."

For the first time, Candice trusted a man completely, that his words were real. She gave her heart to Frank; hoping to finally let the emotionally battering relationships of her past stay there…in the past. "You didn't give up on me, even when I tried to push you away. I love you."

Candice knew it wasn't always going to be a fairytale, and she'd have to fight against people who would feel she didn't deserve the life that Frank would provide her. A gold digger, they'd assume. Especially once his ex-wife caught wind of this engagement; which she probably had already. Surely one of her spies had already phoned in the highlights. In Beverly Hills, loyalty is a casualty of a privileged life.

After a few minutes alone, they returned to the ballroom just as Daphne Margot joined the band for a set then closed with a few of her chart toppers. At the onset of her hit song, Love Me Some You, she proclaimed, "Felicitations pour tes fiancailles! May your life together be blessed and full of love."

Candice had a hard time containing her excitement because Daphne was one of her favorite singers and there she was in the flesh, honoring them. Candice mouthed *thank you* towards the stage, blowing a kiss with both hands. The sad reality was, the songstress couldn't have cared less about Candice Kane, but felt the future Mrs. Frank Swann had earned her attention.

At the end of the performance, Derek and Bebe took to the stage and Bebe spoke.

"We can't thank you enough for joining us this evening for this momentous night. It's been truly magical. Now, enjoy more music, dancing and champagne!"

She pointed to the flowing fountain that had been rolled in at the rear of the room, flanked by a decked out table of gourmet desserts. It was time to party and no one does it better than the Beverly Hills set; especially when they've been drinking.

Not so perfect after all

*S*lipping out of her Choos in the back of the Rolls, Candice pulled the mink throw over her legs, as it was a cool night.

"Frank, I'm a little hungry, aren't you?" She'd hardly eaten anything at dinner. Gesturing her hands, she proclaimed, "I'm dying for a Cobb salad."

Undoing his bow tie, Frank laughed, "Where do suppose we'll find this salad?" He glanced at his Patek Philippe, "It is well after midnight."

Candice's face scrunched, "I could make something at home. We have food...I think."

He kissed her forehead as she laid her head against his shoulder, "You can have anything you want."

When they got to Malibu, the car entered into already opened gates and Frank saw the black SUV parked in front of the house. "Who is that?"

Candice looked through the front window past the driver, and mumbled in irritation, "Brandon. What is he doing here?"

The driver got out with them. "Mr. Swann, would you like me to check things out?"

Frank threw a hand up, "No, it's fine."

Candice didn't bother to put her shoes back on, just held them and tip toed all the way to the front door where Frank was waiting. When they got inside, there was a dead calm. The only sound was coming from the outside, faint crashes of waves against the bluff. They noticed the deck doors were open. Then they heard a loud cough, a man's cough.

Candice rolled her eyes and shook her head in disgust. "I told you."

She stared at Frank wondering why he was just standing there instead of making it up those stairs to send Brandon packing. Instead he took his jacket off and walked towards the kitchen. Candice lifted her gown above her ankles, and made a beeline up the stairs. Frank knew she was annoyed and followed her.

The loft was a mess and Brandon lay stretched out over the sofa, with the only light flickering from a couple of candles and the moon shining through the wall of windows facing the beach.

Candice reached down touching his arm, startling him. "Brandon, where's Karoline?"

He seemed disoriented, "She's um, sleeping. She was sick."

Frank turned and sprinted across the landing that led to the bedroom. He sat on the bed to make sure Karoline was alright. But she didn't just look asleep, she looked pale and he smelled vomit on her clothes. He knew she wasn't alright.

"Karoline, Karoline..." He shook her but she was unresponsive. Frank then yelled towards the other room, "Call help - now!" He knew she was still alive because her chest was moving lightly, but he didn't know how long she'd been in that state. Candice ran downstairs and called 911, while Brandon ran into the room speechless. Frank was furious, "Brandon, what happened? What?!"

Brandon was frightened, because to say the wrong thing would be assuming all blame and he knew Frank disliked him already. "I got here earlier and she'd already taken some stuff so I made her throw up. I don't know..."

Karoline started waking up, but fell under again. Her body was very limp as Frank tried sitting her up.

"Kari, what'd you take, sweetheart?" He thought *Dear God, not again...* He had been through the scenario before and last time, she almost died.

"They're on their way!" Candice was terrified, so turned back and went down to her bedroom to change. She yanked off the necklace and tucked it away in a drawer in the closet. Throwing on a pair of jeans and a long sleeved tee, she grabbed sneakers and ran outside when she heard the sirens from the road. It felt like forever, but two minutes later the paramedics were in front of the house, turning into the driveway.

Two men jumped out. "Hello ma'am, where is she?"

Candice ushered them inside and up the stairs where Frank was holding Karoline in his arms, trying to keep her alert. One of the medics said, "Okay Sir, we'll take it from here."

Frank laid her head down on the pillow and got up, standing back with Candice. Brandon in a panic was holding a cigarette in his trembling hand.

"Don't you light that!" Candice felt the urge to kick Brandon and his cigarette out.

"Hon, what's your name? Come on Karoline, talk to us. Can you hear me?" The paramedic was trying to keep Karoline alert while his partner checked her vitals. She was lapsing quickly. Looking around at the group he asked, "Do you know what she took?"

Brandon spoke up. "When I got here I found um…" He ran into the bathroom, where he'd taken the bottles earlier. "…these! She took these. I don't know how many, or if she took both." He handed one of the medics the bottles of Hydrocodone and Xanax.

Just hearing this set Frank off, "Why didn't you call for help when you found her? " Brandon was speechless.

Watching Karoline on her bed in the state she was in caused a wave of anxiety to come over Candice. She sat down on the sofa in the other room, clutching her hands together to offset an attack.

Frank came and knelt down in front of her. "Kari's going to be okay. She has to."

She looked up at him, "No, she's not! She's not going to be okay if this keeps happening. Karoline is going to lose, Frank!" He could tell Candice was frightened, so he hugged her.

"Her pulse rate is weakening…" The medics were talking among themselves and one of them called ahead to the hospital. A few minutes later, two more techs came up the stairs with a stretcher. Karoline had passed out again. "We're taking her to UCLA Medical in Santa Monica."

Hearing that, Brandon went outside and was on his cell phone when he saw the others come out. "Mr. Swann…I'm sorry! I swear I would never put her in danger. She's my best friend. I love her!"

Frank glared at him and kept walking towards the car. Candice felt compelled to hug him, "Brandon just go home for now. We'll call you, I promise." Frank sent his driver on and he and Candice followed the ambulance in Karoline's car.

"Frank, what's happening? How did this start?"

In an apparent daze, he blurted, "She's going back in and this time she's staying!"

Candice's head swung to the left, "In where...rehab?"

Staring ahead as he drove close behind the emergency vehicle, he nodded, "Yes! Only this time she's not leaving until she's better. I just let her..." He sighed, "It's like I don't know what to do. But, I'm not going to let my daughter die."

Candice reached over and clutched his free hand. "I'll do what I have to do to help her. I mean..." She sighed and laid her head back on the rest. It was too much, watching someone slowly kill themselves.

Almost two hours later the doctor told Frank point blank that Karoline is walking a tightrope and she wouldn't survive next time.

"What are you going to do? What can we do?" Frank, distraught hearing those words, asked a thousand questions, while on the inside consumed more blame. The divorce, he being away most of the time...it was too much for Karoline to handle.

"Mr. Swann, Karoline needs help; serious help. We're going to keep her tonight, to make certain that she's stable. Tomorrow she needs to go directly into a detox program."

Candice placed her hand on Frank's forearm, and stepped forward, "What?"

The doctor just told them straight out, "Karoline has a codeine addiction."

Frank's heart sank. "Oh my god, will this program really help her?"

The doctor told him that a representative was on the way from the Promise Cove center in Malibu. "They have one of the most intense programs specifically designed to treat these addictions. I think it's best for her. They'll fill you in. Meanwhile, you can see her now."

Frank grabbed hold of Candice's hand and they rushed down the cold hallway into one of the rooms. Karoline was lying there connected to a monitor and a drip, with an oxygen tube in her nose.

Frank leaned over and kissed her forehead, "Baby, what happened? I thought you..."

She just stared at him without a word. Then a tear streamed down her right cheek, "I'm sorry, Daddy…" Then realizing he was still wearing his tux minus the jacket, she looked past him at Candice who was standing there, holding her hand to her mouth trying not to cry. "Candie, I'm sorry I…"

Candice walked to the other side of the bed, "No honey, it's alright. You just get better, okay?"

Karoline felt completely drained and had to catch her breath. She then noticed Candice's hand and her eyes widened, "That ring…" She looked up at her dad, "You?"

Candice brushed some strands of hair out of Karoline's face, "Your dad is incredible, but you already know that. We were going to surprise you tomorrow."

Karoline nodded and faintly smiled, then fell back to sleep. Candice pulled up a chair and sat next to her.

"Mr. Swann?" A bohemian looking brunette in her early forties walked into the room.

Frank turned around. "Yes, I'm Frank Swann." She introduced herself as Joanie, a clinical admissions specialist for the program at Promise Cove. "Of course…thank you for coming." He gestured towards Candice, "My fiancée, Candice Kane…"

The woman nodded, "Miss Kane." Candice nodded, but went back to keeping an eye on Karoline as the woman spoke. "I thought I should come here tonight because…and the doctors agree, it's important for Karoline to come in tomorrow." She glanced at Karoline, "She's a very sick young woman. She needs our help or it'll get worse. She can't do it on her own and you can't help her at home."

Candice glanced across the room at Frank, giving him a supportive look, then spoke up. "Joanie you have our cooperation. Just please, help her. Please."

The woman nodded, "We'll do our very best to get Karoline the help she needs. You have my word." The woman was there all of ten minutes.

A nurse with too much makeup on came in and checked the monitors. "She's stabilizing…" She scribbled in her chart, smiled and left.

Then there was a knock at the door. "Is this Karoline's room?"

Frank and Candice looked up. An exotic brunette was standing there, visibly distraught and clutching her huge Hermes handbag with all her might.

"I'm her father. I'm sorry, you are...?"

She looked over at Karoline sleeping in the bed. "I'm Dominica, she calls me Mimi. I'm her friend." She started crying. "I knew I should have gone to her house earlier. She was so upset. We had a fight and she was so upset."

A few hours earlier, Karoline showed up at Mimi's Bel Air Road home to surprise her with dinner and a quiet night in to make up for being so distant lately. Surprised to find the door unlocked, Karoline walked in and put the food in the kitchen before looking for Mimi upstairs. When she opened the master bedroom door, there was Mimi, lying naked underneath some random surfer boy toy. Karoline ran over to the bed and started kicking and hitting at both of them, cursing and screaming. Mimi threw the guy out, but Karoline couldn't handle it and took off.

Frank then realized Mimi was the girlfriend he hadn't met.

"Then Dominica if she's upset, I don't think you should be here when she wakes up. We'll be in touch."

Frank caught sight of the shock on Candice's face and tried to play it off. Mimi and Karoline had been on and off for over a year.

Mimi ignored the brush off. "Is she okay?" She fought back tears when she saw Karoline lying there with an oxygen tube in her nose.

"We hope so. She's going back in tomorrow. How'd you know she was here, Mimi? How'd you get back here?" Frank issued no sympathy.

"Brandon called me, and I told the nurse I was family." She ran her hands through her lush dark locks, looking extremely jittery and nervous. "She has to be okay, you know?"

Glancing over at Frank, Candice got up, feeling sorry for Mimi. "She will be, and don't you worry." She tried comforting the frazzled friend.

"Alright, well I'm going to go, but please, will someone call me? Let her know I was here." She looked at Candice pleadingly, hoping for assurance she wouldn't get from Frank. Mimi left, with her clicking heels echoing down the hallway.

Candice wasted no time asking, "Frank, do you think this relationship is why she's having a hard time?"

Frank shrugged like he either didn't know, or didn't care. "My daughter takes things to heart. Everything..." He glanced down at Karoline, still sleeping. "She bottles up, and gives off this facade that it's okay, but it consumes her."

Another nurse walked in whom reminded Candice of an aunt back home and the lady caught her staring at her. "We're taking her upstairs to a private room so she can rest peacefully. One of you can stay, but we'll watch her all night, Mr. Swann."

Frank thought they should stay, but Candice encouraged him to go back to the beach house. It had been a long night and she just wanted to take care of him. "We'll come back first thing, sweetie...but now you need to rest. Karoline is in good hands."

Candice: Speechless

"*Y*ou've been quiet. Talk to me." Frank was trying to get me to discuss what happened. He could tell I was shaken up about it.

It was well after three in the morning, and the drive back to Malibu was tense. He worried that too much reality had just tanked an otherwise perfect night. At this point the gala was almost a blur.

Still riding the jolt of getting engaged and ending up in the emergency room all in a three hour span, I was exhausted and wanted to shut the world off. I looked out the window, realizing we were on the Pacific Coast Highway. Gazing out into the darkness of the ocean, Malibu no longer felt like the privileged haven I'd fallen in love with. It felt more like a dirty little secret; a place where our own version of reality was not so pretty. It was supposed to be one of the happiest moments of my life. Instead, I felt heavy.

"Huh? No, I'm just a little tired."

I must have turned towards him with such emotion in my eyes that he reached over and massaged my neck. "I know this is a lot to deal with, isn't it?" I tried to muster up a smile, but it failed.

Entering the gate, we discovered we'd left all of the lights on in the house. I felt anxious and couldn't help but feel a little irritated that Karoline lost control on that night, of all nights. I loved her even then, but at that moment, I selfishly felt like someone intentionally peed on my party, so to speak. Of course, I knew that wasn't true. That child's downfall had nothing to do with me. However, in my lapse, I felt like my night was ruined. Frank sensed how upset I was and tried to ease the situation.

"Candice, I want to show you something." He gestured for me to take his hand. We went outside and walked over to the corner of the lawn just at the cliff, which was barricaded by plush mid-height shrubbery and fencing.

"Sweetie, it's four in the morning. We can't see anything."

The moon was bright and it was a cool misty night, so he pulled me close. Spanning the perimeter he assured, "Yes, we can. We might have to...there!"

I followed his pointing finger and saw nothing at first. "Oh my god...what is that?"

Enjoying my reaction, he laughed, "It's a whale, sweetheart. See, there's another one!"

It was dark, but I could see the shadowed figures leap up out of the ocean and submerge into the hazy darkness. Whales migrate into the area from around December to March or April and unbeknownst to me, I had one of the best seats in the house. Point Dume is like a winter home for the giant mammal.

"You can see them better during the day, but this is beautiful, isn't it?" His excitement was soothing.

I just nodded and let myself be consumed by the moment, "This is by far my favorite thing since I've moved here... well, and you of course." I snuggled against him and he tightened his embrace.

It all reminded Frank of why he chose the house. Karoline woke up one morning proclaiming to the world that she wanted to live on her own. That meant it was time for Daddy to buy her a sweet little hideout somewhere. He shared that memory with me.

"I remember when I found this house a couple of years ago. March it was, and I'd sent my broker out hunting for a beach house because I knew how much Karoline loved the ocean. There were two properties in the area that she liked, so I came back and did walkthroughs to see which was right."

I could hear the melancholy in his voice and instinctively wrapped both of my arms around his waist, comforting him as he continued.

"When I walked onto this property it felt peaceful, and Karoline needed that. When I came out here and stood in just about this very spot and saw whales, I knew this was it. I hadn't even seen the rest of the house, just walked from the front door to the back of the house. It was perfect for Karoline, so I bought it."

"She loves it here, baby, and so do I." I tried steering the conversation back to us. Just to have some time with my man on what was left of our night. "Let's go inside and have a glass of wine, then get some rest, okay?"

"Mmm, that would be nice..." He grabbed my waist from behind, his fingers creeping underneath my tee and softly grazing my flesh.

The touch of his hand was titillating to say the least. "We're never going to get to sleep if you keep that up." I meant that.

Walking behind me, Frank watched me as I loosened my hair. "You promise?" As I stepped inside the house through the patio doors, he grabbed a belt loop on my jeans, which made me want him right then.

Teasing him, I gestured with my index finger for him to follow me, "Why don't you come see for yourself, Mr. Swann."

We had a few drinks and despite Karoline being in the hospital, we found comfort in each other and fell asleep. I remember waking up with a headache. The sun crashed through the windows and the sound of seagulls filled the air. Frank was asleep, and we were both still dressed.

That's when I realized I could probably expect to face a few more nights like that one in my new life in Los Angeles. I'd never admit to anyone, but for a moment, I longed for Chicago.

Bebe: Married to a stranger

*L*ying on my side in our satin covered bed, my tear stained pillow was beginning to feel cold and uncomfortable, so I got up. Walking across the room passing the huge ornate mirror, I caught sight of my reflection and everything that surrounded me. There I was, living the dream in one of the most coveted manors in Beverly Park. All I ever wanted. In passing, I grabbed hold of the robe that lay across the chair in front of the fireplace and draped it on to cover my nakedness.

The night before, Derek and I hosted the annual Angels of Music gala at our estate; a ten thousand dollar per plate fundraiser. I always try to give back and put my heart out to the community; especially when it involves the children. The Angels of Music Foundation has single handedly kick started music programs at inner city schools, allowed terminally ill children and adults to live out their dreams of performing before a live audience, and last year AMF donated more than ten million dollars to children's hospitals around the country as well as to the Make- A-Wish Foundation and Boys and Girls Clubs of America. These are the projects that give real meaning to my life. The night should have been the highlight of my year. Derek was charming for the most part and seemed proud of me. He knew I had worked very hard in planning the evening.

It was a beautiful night, which is why I couldn't understand why he ruined it by getting so rough with me in bed afterwards. He's a fantastic lover, but on that night, he wasn't making love to me. It was hardcore sex. I was enticed for a moment, but then felt humiliated.

After midnight I walked upstairs and headed to the master bedroom to unwind. Most of the guests had left, with the exception of a few who decided they wanted to swim and party a little more.

When I got into the bedroom, Derek followed behind me. "You're turning in already, sweetheart?"

I began unzipping my evening gown. "Yes, I'm exhausted. Tonight was great though, wasn't it?"

I stepped out of the dress, laid it across the settee at the foot of the bed, and wearing only my La Perla bra and panties, crawled in. Derek stood there with a cocktail in his hand and a hungry look in his eye, watching me. He undressed as well and joined me. Feeling his warm body against mine, I scooted closer to him and sighed as his hand slid up the side of my thigh and continued towards my breasts. I felt his breath on my neck but he never kissed me, just kept caressing my body. Though the stink of the liquor was strong, and could have turned me off, when he undid my bra I helped him by lifting myself up a little. Once it was off, the stroke of his hand became stronger and not even in a sensual way.

"Calm down Derek, I'm not going any…"

He pulled me back and said, "Shhh…don't talk, just let me enjoy you."

He was too aggressive, but it had been a while, so I was willing to play this new game. His hand continued down my stomach until I felt his fingertips brush across the top of my panties. I could feel my own moisture building at his touch and my hips slowly rotated. Then he shoved a finger inside of me. It felt good for about a minute, but he quickly snatched my panties off and coerced me onto my stomach and entered me from the back. His penetrations grew ferocious and trying to pull away, I yelled at him.

"Stop, dammit! This is not fun!"

He slurred at me, "Come on…play along, Bebe."

He didn't stop, and eventually his strokes started to please me again, my fighting subsided and my moans encouraged him even more. I rolled over and he climbed on top, shoving himself inside and grabbed hold of my legs, pulling them apart, before stroking me at a rapid pace. I was now turned off and punched his chest.

"Get the hell off me! You drunk ass fool!"

He wouldn't stop, but kept huffing, and viciously kissing and sucking my breasts until he finally came. I shoved him off. I didn't recognize this behavior. I was shocked by it, but more so hurt that he had disrespected me to this level after all of these years. I'd told him to stop and he didn't; making me feel like a two-bit whore. After a few minutes I looked over and noticed he had already passed out.

I didn't know what to make of any of it. Derek Fabian had just gone too far. Feeling like I had just been crapped on, I cried myself to sleep.

Fueling the fire

"I thought you'd want to know before you saw the papers or hear it around town. I was just as shocked when I witnessed it last night. I'm so sorry you had to find out like this, Jackie." The friend wasn't sorry, but thrived on all the drama.

Not revealing that she'd already seen it, Jackie stared at the Lifestyle section of the morning paper. There, with his arms draped around a beautiful, young beauty, was Frank. But it was the caption that sent a surge of rage through her body: *Billionaire Frank Swann proposed to Candice Kane at the Angels of Music Foundation gala last evening.*

"Oh, he's just going through one of his phases. She's like a shiny new toy and it won't last. He's not even over our marriage yet. That's why he's being so cold towards me." Jackie could feel her blood flowing through her veins, she was so on edge.

Almost feeling sorry for her desperate tone, the friend sympathetically added, "Jackie, he's getting married…to someone else. I call that moving on, honey."

"He's not moving on! It's his way of getting back at me. And, where did this girl come from? They can't have anything in common. He'll realize that!"

The friend giggled, realizing that Jackie Reese-Swann was even more delusional than even she'd thought. While at the same time, knowing Jackie could be the key to stirring up a little trouble in paradise. "Well, I don't think she knows what she's getting into."

Shaking the ice in her cocktail, Jackie glared out the window of her bedroom, at the surrounding mountains. "Well, she will. I've got to go, sweetheart, and thank you!" She released the call.

Jackie was drinking again, and in her unbalanced mental state, that was a toxic mix. She was hell bent on punishing Frank for leaving her all those years before. Knowing that he was marrying a woman many years younger than she, had her all fired up. "You're not getting away with this, Frank. I promise you that."

To move forward, you go back

*I*t had been eighteen days since Karoline entered Promise Cove and she was finally tugging at the root of her troubles. She hadn't even given much thought to how she dove into that dark hole. All she knew was that she was comfortable there. It felt normal to hurt. But there's nothing normal about waking up wishing you *hadn't* even woken up. The pain of carrying a torch of unworthiness ever since she could remember came to a crashing head.

"Karoline? Do you need a moment? We can stop."

"No. I'm fine, it's just…" Her face tightened and her brow furrowed, fighting back painful memories she hadn't faced in a decade. "…hard to talk about her sometimes. She's so damn evil."

"Your mother?" The therapist leaned forward in her chair. She felt Karoline was approaching a much needed breakthrough.

"Yes." Karoline swallowed and a tear fell from her eye. Then anger painted her face, "She used to try and make me feel bad for loving my father so much. He's the only person who's ever cared about me!"

"What would she say to you, Karoline?"

"Say?" She laughed, "You mean what she would do?"

"Alright…"

"My mother is very paranoid and frantically insecure because she knows she's an awful person. I realize that now, but all those years she took it out on me. She told me once when I was little that Daddy traveled so much to get away from me. How could someone say that?" Karoline started to break down and the therapist handed her a box of tissue.

"Did you ever feel that your father traveled to get away from you?"

"No… never! He divorced my mother because I begged him to get rid of her. Finally, I told him what I saw." Her posture changed in the large chair, as she pulled her legs underneath herself.

"What was that Karoline? What'd you see?"

"I was twelve and Daddy was in Chicago working. My nanny had picked me up from school." Staring at the floor, shaking her head, she continued. "I ran into the house yelling for my mother because something really good had happened at school. I wanted to tell her, so I ran up to her bedroom where she slept during the day. She wasn't there, but then I heard laughing outside at the pool so, I went to the balcony and looked down and..." She paused at the flashback, "...she was in the pool with some man. They were naked, and making out and laughing...in my father's house!"

The therapist sympathetically removed her glasses. "Karoline, we don't have to go back there."

"See, this is what she did...I yelled 'I hate you!' Mother got out of the pool and ran into the house to find me. She told me if I told Daddy, she'd send me away to boarding school out East, and that it's what he wanted her to do anyways. I knew she was lying. So, I called him at the Chicago house and he flew back the next day."

"Did you feel caught in the middle?"

Reflecting, Karoline shook her head, "Not really. A few days later he took me to London for a month and when we returned she was gone. He had her thrown out of our house. Daddy divorced her and she's hated me ever since. "

"Well, I'm not sure if she hates you, but it certainly sounds as if she's tried her hardest to punish you for what she sees as betrayal. You must know this Karoline...you've done nothing wrong. You were protecting your father. The one who made you feel safe, secure and loved. And, that's okay."

"I've tried my best to reach out to my mother, hoping she'd changed. But she only responds when she needs something."

"Do you love her?"

Karoline thought about it for a second, twirling her hoop earring with her pinky, "Of course, because she's my mother. But at the same time, I don't trust her and I don't want her in my life. My father was right when he said she's poison. She started doing it again some months back...calling and trying to make me feel bad."

"You're saying you think pressure from her triggered the over medicating?"

194

Karoline gave her therapist a blank stare. "What do you mean? Nooo... I was having problems sleeping; pain from the accident two years ago. The stress makes it worse, and it's hard to sleep." Karoline didn't want to talk anymore and cut the session short. "My friend is coming to see me. We're having dinner."

The therapist scribbled some more, "Mimi, right? You're ready to see her?"

Karoline hadn't spoken to Mimi since the night she went into the hospital. She halfheartedly refused her phone calls because she felt betrayed. Now she feels it's time to talk.

"Yeah, I think so."

Bebe: Even Elvis couldn't break me

Glancing at the clock in my bathroom, I realized I'd slept longer than planned. It was already ten o'clock and I would be driving up to Santa Barbara in a couple of hours. After the crazy month I'd had, getting away from LA for a few days was just what I needed, so I made reservations at San Ysidro Ranch. Even in February the area is beautiful. An avid horse rider, I'd often run off to lose myself there. San Ysidro boasts some of the best horse trails on the entire coast.

Derek had already left the house, which was just as well, because I didn't want to see him. Sweeping my hair into a ponytail, I dipped a toe into the hot bath I'd drawn, prepping for a quiet hour or so to myself before I left. It was my time, in my private sanctuary, complete with the custom designed garden tub that has the initials BB embossed in gold in the marble. As I lay my head back against the pillow, I began thinking about everything that was happening, and how Derek took me for granted.

I thought back on when I was a young woman in Nashville. I grew up on a ten acre ranch in Arrington with my parents and two sisters. Still, I always wanted what I thought would be a better life. Not that the life I had was shabby. I was blessed with wonderful and attentive parents who enjoyed their daughters living at home, and didn't push us out the door. And praise God - I didn't have a shortage of guys to go out with either. I should have been satisfied, but instead I had ideas, big ideas. I used to go to concerts at the auditorium to see all of the huge stars perform: Frankie Valli, Dolly Parton and even Elvis Presley. Speaking of which...

When I was fourteen, a girlfriend and I met Elvis before a show as he was walking into the venue with an entourage of what seemed like fifty people. When he saw me, he said something to the effect of 'put this little girl up front; I want to sing to her all night.' I couldn't believe it, and the entire time felt like the whole concert was for me. Little did I know he had decided I, little Bobbie Bradwell, was the chosen one for the night. I was later summoned backstage to meet the King of Rock and Roll. I guess I shocked the whole crew by bolting out before Elvis came out of his dressing room. I admired him but felt Elvis was just

196

too old. I do realize I looked all of twenty and I knew it, but I just wasn't interested in getting into that kind of trouble. I've never regretted that night, because I could always say that I left Elvis waiting for little old me. The memory still makes me proud.

I couldn't help but wonder why I'd allowed my husband to break me down. After all I'd achieved in my life, which included helping Derek accomplish so much in his own career, I was starting to feel a surge of worthlessness. We hadn't been intimate since that shameful night. I could almost vomit to think about it. We'd had our problems, but he was now acting like a filthy bastard. The more I thought about his behavior, the more disappointed I became, because I loved him and was confused by it.

Climbing out, I tip toed over to the vanity, still dripping of water and stared into the mirror. There I was, a successful woman who had the world at her fingertips, but all I wanted was for my husband to love me. I felt completely alone. In the back of my mind, I knew Derek was doing something and I was determined to find out what. Meanwhile, I packed my things and got out of the house before he returned. I was ready to clear my head and have a good time before coming back and facing the ugly truths.

Like old times

Standing at the windows in her suite overlooking Beverly Hills, Faith pulled out her cell phone to call Candice.

"Come on girl, answer…" She was anxious to speak with her friend and tell her the news.

"Hello, this is Candice."

"Hey, it's Faith!"

Candice giggled upon hearing her friend's voice. "I know…you doing okay? How's married life?"

"Girl, it's fabulous! Donnie is incredible. We're adjusting, but big things are happening. In fact…"

"Okay, here we go - in fact, what?" Candice braced herself.

"I'm in LA - right now!"

"You are? Why didn't you let me know you were coming?"

"Well I'm calling now. Anyways, I'm moving out here."

"Really? How's that going to work for you guys?"

"Just fine 'cus Donnie has sealed a major deal with the LA Starz!"

"Wow, I…well congratulations!"

"Yeah, I'm house hunting this week, so…" Faith could hardly contain herself as she spoke.

"Faith you are something else, but I'm happy for you. And, I'm glad you'll be close."

"I know, right? Who knows, we might be neighbors." She laughed under her breath.

"I'm still learning the area, but let me know if I can help. So where are you?"

"I'm at the Iberian hotel. Maybe we can get together."

"Well, right now I'm at school and will be here kind of late, but let's have dinner tomorrow."

"That would great. I'm going to rest up a little and go for a drive around town. Call me later, okay?"

"Will do. I'm glad you called."

As excited as Candice was to chat about Faith's new life, it all felt a little weird. There she was about to marry Frank, the man her best friend once marked as a sugar daddy. It made her head spin to even think about it. Still, it was nice to have Faith back in her life.

Better than us?

*"W*hat did she do to make him fall in love with her? I mean, she's beautiful but..."

Hunter shrugged and put the call on speaker while she finished getting dressed. "I was told she's not impressed by the quote-Beverly Hills lifestyle- at all. Like, she thinks she's better than us!"

The woman on the other end giggled, "She wants Frank Swann all to herself and I can't blame her, but I'll be damned if this Candice Kane didn't sneak in through the back door."

"Oh come now, don't be like that. She's just a girl who played the game well, and now it's paid off."

"I don't know Hunter, they look happy. Maybe they're *really* in love. Stranger things have happened around here."

"Hey, I'm rooting for them, but we'll see. I mean, I hope she's as sweet as Frank thinks she is, and isn't after his money." The mischievous tone in her voice said she was up to more than just rooting for them.

"Well if not, the truth will come out."

Hunter giggled, "Yes it will...even if it needs a little nudging."

Sisterhood

"*H*old it for thirty seconds…you're doing great, ladies! Now, just thirty seconds more. You feel it? Extend…extend…and releeeease…."

That nasal British accent was getting under Candice's skin. *I only have thirty more seconds in me…now, come on!* Glaring at the Pilates instructor, Candice reached into her deepest core to find the energy to finish the session. The spasm gathering at the base of her back was literally getting on her nerves. She didn't want to hold onto anything, but let go of the band, and let her legs fall.

The session was tough but she craved it…that time for herself. Karoline was back home and doing better; school was out on break, and Candice was taking full advantage of it.

"Whew! I think she tried to kill us today."

A pretty and petite, cocoa complexioned woman wrapped a towel around her neck and reached for water in the standing cooler against the wall.

Candice twisted the top off a grape juice and swigged it down. "She was a little zealous, wasn't she?"

"I'm telling you." The woman introduced herself. "I'm Rayne."

"Oh sorry, I'm Candice, nice to meet you, Rayne." Candice couldn't help but feel a sense of familiarity.

"Are you new to this club or…?" Rayne dabbed her mouth with the towel, curiously waiting.

"Yeah, I am. I usually just hike Point Dume or run on the beach but, I needed a disciplined class, you know?"

"Great, well you'll like this one. I've been working out here for…" Rayne's cell phone vibrated on their way into the locker room, "Shoot, I'm sorry, just a second. Hello?"

Rayne started whispering and Candice hung back a little to give her privacy since it was obvious by her body language that the call wasn't a pleasant one.

Rayne looked pissed. "Bye!"

"Are you okay?" Candice thought she saw tears.

"I'm fine. My husband's not coming home today like I expected. He's been gone for two months girl, but trust me, I'm fine."

"Oh…" Candice drank more juice so as to not look uncomfortable, but she wished Rayne hadn't volunteered so much personal info.

"He's on tour. Excuse me, *was* on tour. He's all of a sudden in New York working on a song with a so-called…" She sarcastically used finger quotes, "…hot producer!" From the shake of her head, this was a repeat occurrence in her life.

Candice changed the subject. "I don't know if you're in a hurry, but I'm having lunch at the terrace restaurant at the Iberian Hotel across the street and you're welcomed to join me. I'd enjoy the company." Candice giggled to lighten the mood.

"You know what, I will!"

They agreed to meet in thirty minutes, and hit the locker room to freshen up.

The Iberian, an uber chic boutique hotel, is the type of place where you can slip in and out virtually unnoticed. A-list celebrities and bored housewives alike can get into just enough trouble without making it into the tabloids; unless they want to. And, sometimes…they do.

A few years back, a certain blonde "actress" was caught making out on the roof garden with a revived pop singer whose new record was about to drop. Paparazzi zoomed in from nearby balconies and those two desperados ended up on the cover of every major rag the following week. Needless to say, his cd went platinum the first week after release, and she got her very own reality show. That was a choreographed stunt if there ever was one. In Hollywood getting caught is almost always a staged event.

"Rayne, I'm over here, hon!" Candice waved her new friend over to their table at the center of the terrace. The overdressed glitterati lunch crowd was out in force, and the two women took their place front and center, where they could see everything and everyone.

"Hey…" Rayne hugged her and was glad to finally hang out with someone who seemed real. She plopped her Bottega Veneta handbag in a chair, looking around the terrace. "Look at them! They're wondering who we are and who our men are."

She laughed under hear breath, shaking her head. Rayne rarely did the Beverly Hills social thing, but still enjoyed her status as a celebrity wife, because membership definitely made life cozy.

Giggling, Candice felt like she'd inhaled a breath of fresh air with Rayne around. "Oh my god, I know!" She looked up at the server waiting for their drink orders. "I'll have an apple martini and easy on the vodka please." She feared getting tipsy too early in the day.

Scooting a little closer towards the table and fluffing her shoulder length hair, Rayne was ready to dish. "So! I've got to get nosey. What do you do? Or better yet, *who* do you do?" She widened her eyes and mischievously giggled. "I'm only kidding! Seriously, you don't seem as, excuse me for saying this, fake as these chicks around here." She sipped her Margarita waiting for the answer.

Looking up from her menu Candice smiled, not even offended by the comment. Their interaction was natural. "Well, if you must know I'm from Chicago, that's why I'm not fake." They both laughed. "I've been here...hmmm, seven months now?"

"Really? So you're fairly new in town."

She pulled at the cherry with her teeth, "Um hmm, I'm in grad school at USC."

"Aaah, little sis has got a plan. Good for you, sweetheart. Are you seeing anyone?" Rayne wouldn't let up.

Candice's beaming eyes told it all. "Yes, I am. Actually, I'm engaged."

Rayne instinctively glanced down at Candice's finger, "Oooh nice... Yeah, I remember that feeling being so in love - mutually in love." She reflected while rejecting an onset of tears. "Congratulations."

"Thank you. I'm learning it's not as easy as I hoped. I mean, there are so many things to combat, you know?"

Rayne was sympathetic as Candice swirled the glass of her now second martini. "Why do you say that?"

Candice thought long and hard in the five seconds before she spoke. "My fiancé is...well, it's a struggle to keep everyone out of our relationship, you know? Especially around here, I've learned that I have to."

"Humph! You'd better." Rayne raised her eyebrows and flipped through the menu. Rayne had experienced the good the bad and the ugly of this town and wouldn't wish it on anyone. "Is he here in LA or...?"

Candice was a little hesitant but continued, "Yes, he divides his time between LA and Chicago, which is how we met. It can be a little trying, but so far it's amazing." She smiled, thinking about Frank.

Rayne nodded, listening. "Well, from the looks of it he makes you happy, so that's great. What does he do?"

Damn you're nosey! "He runs a business and it gets pretty hectic sometimes, so we..."

"Excuse me ladies, I am so sorry. You're Candice, right?"

Saved by the interruption, Candice looked up at the fifty-something woman who had an eager expression on face, anxious to get her words out. She was so thin that her hip bone poked against her tight wrap dress, as her horrid breasts spilled from the neckline. "Yes, and you are...?"

"Nadine... Nadine Paley?" For a split second you could hear crickets. "Frank and my husband are acquaintances. We met at the gala, and you were absolutely radiant my dear. I want to extend congratulations to you both."

Candice glanced over at Rayne, who had a look of wonder across her face. She turned attention back to Nadine. "Oh, of course, I remember." She lied. "Thank you. It's so good to see you again."

Nadine Paley graciously excused herself, as Rayne curiously stared at Candice, crossing her legs.

"Okay, I have to ask. Candice, who is this Frank? That woman practically drooled while talking to you."

Candice giggled, "Frank Swann. Don't tell me you know him." Candice continued sipping her drink.

"Ahhh, it all makes sense now. No wonder you're so secretive. I don't blame you. I met him once, at a Grammy party I attended with my husband. He seems really nice. I'm just...wow, it's a small world, isn't it?"

All Candice could do was nod and smile. She was relieved to find that she and Rayne had a lot in common, and hoped they'd become good friends.

The perils of Mimi

"*And*, there she is..."

Mimi pulled the door open to let Karoline in. They hadn't seen each other since the brief visit at Promise Cove back in January.

"Hello, Mimi." Karoline tossed a chilled greeting, still not sure why she was asked to stop by. She thought maybe Mimi wanted to try and fix what she'd broken; the trust in their relationship.

Looking around the living room, Karoline noticed that once again, Mimi had redecorated. Her posh Bel Air lifestyle seemed perfect, but when life got less than, Mimi rearranged everything, including the people. As if it makes all the bad in her life right; to deflect from reality.

"Kari, you look good, babe." She sat down on the sofa, crossing her legs. Her emerald eyes surveyed Karoline's hair and then her eyes. "You cut your hair. Nice..."

Rubbing her hands through her locks, "It's just a trim. I needed something fresh and Brad at Felipe's is very talented." She hated when Mimi did that. The distracting compliments. "So Mimi, why'd you call me over here?"

"Because, I'm sorry!" Scooting forward Mimi repeated the words as her hands shook, while ferociously trying to light a cigarette. She took a long drag and blew curls from the corner of her pink, glossed lips. She rubbed her temple with the cig holding hand.

"Careful, you don't want to set your hair on fire again. Just...stop!" Karoline reached over and snatched it from her, putting it out in a crystal tray on the coffee table. "I thought you quit."

"I did - Kari I made a mistake! God, I didn't mean for this to happen! It was nothing to me. He was fun for a minute, you know? It's like I couldn't help it. You and I were having problems and there he was."

Laughing at the crazy logic, Karoline grabbed hold of her Skye handbag, which Mimi couldn't take her eyes off of, and headed towards the door. There was a photo on the mantel of her with Mimi and Brandon, in Palm Springs. Karoline impulsively swept it onto the floor and stormed out.

Mimi followed her. "God, Kari! I can't believe you're acting like this. It was nothing!" She stood there with her hands on her hips as if what she'd said was really a justified come back.

About to climb into her car, Karoline looked back, "Nothing my ass...it was everything! I don't know what I thought you were going to say when I got here. I hoped..." She threw her hand up, "You know what? You're selfish and I can't do this anymore, Mimi. It's stupid and I'm over it!"

The perfectly coiffed Dominica Sogould stood in her doorway with tears streaming down her eyes. She actually was sorry, but hadn't a clue as how to show it, nor how to deal with it. She closed the door watching Karoline's Mercedes exit the gates, and picked up the picture frame from the floor. Through tear soaked words, she repeated, "I'm sorry..." Mimi realized she had lost one of the most important people in her life, because of a five minute lapse of judgment. Everything seemed like a lapse in her world, and she felt like it was spiraling down a drain.

Mimi walked up the stairs and through the sitting room situated at the top of the landing. She started sobbing and reached for the phone on the table, but decided against it. Karoline wouldn't want to speak to her. Not ever again, is what she said.

"I have to get out of here." Mimi mumbled as she began undressing, walking towards her bathroom. She turned the shower on. A hot steamy cloud of mist filled the master bath, fogging up her mirror at the vanity. As she sat down, with her naked flesh sticking to the white leather stool, she opened a drawer and pulled out an antique Tiffany compact. Instead of a cosmetic, there was a tiny bamboo straw and a white powdery substance. She sighed and unsnapped the straw, then leaned down, snorting back with a vengeance, one line up each nostril. Feeling it approach her nasal cavity, she closed her eyes and enjoyed the high, still feeling lonelier than she ever had. Though short lived, it gave her what she needed: a blockage of the hurt that consumed her.

Mimi remembered the running water, ran and turned it off and went into her bedroom to call New York.

"Hello, Brookie? Hey sis, listen…I need to visit for a couple of weeks, just to get away. I miss you."

Mimi called for a car, and packed what she could fit into a Vuitton weekender. The driver took her straight to LAX, where she flew to New York City so that she could hibernate in her socialite sister's Upper East Side apartment and try to heal, yet again. Only this time, Mimi wasn't so sure it would work.

Let the games begin

"Thank you for having me over, Bebe."

Admiring the plush greenery surrounding the charming little patio near the pool, Candice felt so much calm. Bebe had become like a surrogate mother to her. In LaLa land, where almost nothing is real, she treasured Bebe.

"Oh, darling, I'm just happy that you accepted on such short notice." Bebe smoothed the hem of her Elie Tahari crepe skirt as she sat down at the table. "So how are you feeling? You're still in school, right?"

Candice wondered why she asked her that. "Of course, and everything is going great. This is my second semester on the Dean's list, so I guess I'm doing okay." She shyly giggled, looking down at her empty salad plate. With everything going on in her life, it's been difficult to focus on her classes. "Actually, I've been thinking about what to do after this semester. I mean, with the wedding and all…"

"Speaking of, have you two settled on a date?"

"Yes, we have…August." Candice almost laughed at the look of horror on Bebe's face. "I know, I know, there's so much to do. Thank God for my mother and sister because I'm a nervous wreck!" She picked up a red velvet petit four and annihilated it.

"Darling, that is just around the corner and it's almost May already. What are your plans?"

"That's just it. We wish we didn't have to wait, Bebe. Frank wanted to elope to the South of France, but I said no because my family would kill me!"

The two women laughed but Candice was serious. Frank knew she wouldn't live with him without being married, which on her part probably had more to do with sealing the deal than morality. Not to mention she didn't want people getting the wrong idea about her. Besides, regardless of what Candice felt, it was important to both of them that their family and friends be a part of the occasion.

"We've decided Swann Lakes is perfect. The gardens are so beautiful and romantic, and that's all I want. So we'll have an intimate ceremony for three hundred of our closest friends..." She shrugged a shoulder, "...because we can't leave anyone out."

"Oh, of course! It's going to be breathtaking. I'll help you find the right planner. It'll be perfect." Bebe had been Candice's biggest cheerleader, especially since she was aware of the evil brewing in the background. Pausing, she asked, "Candice have you met Jacqueline Swann, Frank's ex-wife?"

Candice sighed. "No, but we've spoken on the phone briefly. I don't know what to think of her." Why would Bebe bring her up, of all people?

Bebe got up and sat next to Candice, with seriousness in her tone and in her eyes. "First of all, she's not well, and I mean that. The woman is off, and she won't stop until you are miserable. She's already scheming. Jackie is convinced Frank is still in love with her and..."

"Are you serious? No wonder Karoline stays away from her and Frank despises her." Candice's face showed her frustration.

"Oh, darling, I have no doubt. Don't you worry about Frank, he loves *you*. Just..." Bebe paused shaking her head, "...be ready for anything. She's going to try to get in your head to plant doubt. She's insane!"

Candice's heart sank. "Why?" Then she wondered how Bebe knew this stuff. "How do you know this?"

Bebe sipped her tea, stalling then looked up at her. "Sweetheart, just know that not everyone who smiles in your face around here, is your friend. I've learned that the hard way."

Candice knew full well who Bebe was referring to. "You mean Hunter?" Candice waited for confirmation, but Bebe just raised an eyebrow while dabbing her mouth with a napkin.

"Look, just focus on your life with Frank. He loves you. I've never seen him happier." Bebe gave Candice a supportive hug. "They're jealous, like stupid school girls, so don't give them the time of day. They'll back off eventually, and Hunter needs to tend to her dirt-bag husband!"

Candice couldn't help but laugh, "Well, I'm glad you're on my side."

"It's only right. I've been there. Now, let's talk about this wedding. I'll help you and it will be exactly what the two of you want. Not to mention your engagement gala." Bebe's eyes sparkled with her smile, because if there's anything she knows is how to throw a party.

"Engagement party? Do we have to?" Candice shook her head, giggling.

"Of course! Make your presence known officially. After that, these bitches will be licking your boots." Her laugh was sugar coated evil and for Bebe, that was just her way of telling Candice she always has her back.

"Right." Looking at her watch, Candice was anxious to see Frank since he'd be getting in from Chicago that evening. "Oh, I have to get going, but I'll call you tomorrow, okay?"

"Of course, when you're ready, darling."

Chicago was never this complicated Candice thought to herself as she walked towards her car. Glancing around the Fabian's stately manor, she soaked in the reality that in Beverly Hills it was a whole new ballgame and she hoped she was equipped to play.

Candice: Beverly Hills 101

I continually replayed Bebe's words over and over in my mind. *Not everyone who smiles in your face is a friend...* While that statement was isolating and immediately caused my guard to come up, it triggered a realization in me. The women I'd met so far took interest in me for one reason and one reason only. I was about to become Mrs. Frank Swann.

"No, I don't like this one. It's nice, but the bust is not flattering for me."

I flipped through racks of exquisite vintage couture at Gabriella's Closet on Burton Way, like I was at a flea market. Impatient and on edge, I couldn't focus. Our engagement party was in two weeks and my schedule was completely full. A classmate and I were set to fly to Sacramento the next day to interview the governor's wife, and my family would be coming to LA the following week.

"Candice, what do you mean? That would be gorgeous against your skin. Look at that fabric, darling. It was meant to hug you."

Bebe is the most convincing person I've ever met. She was practically salivating over the fluid, satin navy blue Halston masterpiece. I held the fabric against her. We are just about the same size. I'm an inch or so taller, but that dress deserved Bebe's ample breasts. Not mine.

"I think you should take it, Bebe." I signaled for the associate who stood a few feet away. "Miss! Mrs. Fabian will try this one. Thank you." Bebe was surveying another dress on a mannequin. "Well now Bebe, at least you've found something." I was bored of the hunt. "Sorry, I'm just tired, you know?"

Bebe gave me a sympathetic look, and then fanned her manicured hand. "You have an appointment with Elizabeth tomorrow. She'll take care of you. We have two weeks darling, you'll be fine."

Elizabeth, being LA's queen of vintage couture. My fairy god mother promised me I'd be fine, so I believed her.

The twenty-something brunette sales girl, who had introduced herself as Nina, clicked over in her four inch stilettos. "Fabulous choice. It's an original Halston, circa

1980, from the collection of Bianca Jagger." I suppose that was meant to seal the deal. She then disappeared into the dressing lounge in a hurry.

Obviously having overheard the tidbit about Elizabeth, when she returned, Nina approached me with a suspiciously triumphant look on her face, like she was holding the golden ticket or something. I smiled, encouraging her to spit it out.

"Miss Kane..."

My eyes responded, though I didn't. "Oh, didn't I say, what?"

"Well, if I may take the liberty..." Nina's unnaturally plump lips outlined her veneers and glossy smile. "...I think I have the perfect dress for you."

Now, I couldn't help but wonder if she knew who I was, or more so, who I was marrying, because she was not just merely attentive, but she was practically tap dancing. In Beverly Hills, you are assessed by your name and net worth, and not necessarily in that order. Unfortunately for me, I was about to inherit both to the tenth degree.

My eyes widened as I thought *where is this fabulous dress?* "Really? Good, because I'm having a hard time with all of this. I'm running out of time."

Bebe, while texting on her phone, glanced up at me and winked.

"I'll be right back, ladies." Nina appeared a short while later, and invited us into the dressing lounge. When we walked through the draped entry, my eyes fixed on the dress form before us. I hoped it was my dress.

"Now, I want you to know that Angelina Jolie's assistant is expecting this as one of the choices for the film festival, but I think...this is definitely *your* dress Miss Kane."

Just like that, I beat out ol' Angie.

"I couldn't..." Giggling, I knew I wouldn't turn down Valentino's slice of couture heaven with its fitted bodice and cascading chiffon layering. The party was black tie and I knew my entrance had to be dazzling. I was ready to play the part to the hilt.

Nina flapped her hands, "Oh, I can come up with some excuse, trust me."

That little girl was scandalous, and part of me admired that in her. Then leaning towards me she whispered, "You will do it more justice, if I may say so."

"Well, thank you." Amused by the obnoxious suck up, I also knew that had I not been in the position I was, she would have pulled out some random frock worn by a now nameless Oscar winner of years past.

"It's a size six, but if you need it taken in a bit, of course we'll accommodate." Handing me that gift wrapped compliment, Nina's eyes appraised me head to toe, coming to a screeching halt at my ring finger.

"Candice, the color is perfect for you, darling." Bebe caressed the pale hued organza overlay. "We only have fifteen minutes, so let's do a run through of the gown...and Nina? Have the Halston delivered to my home." Bebe winked at the overjoyed sales associate.

"Of course, Mrs. Fabian."

Being a self-professed vintage connoisseur, Bebe had decided she had to own that piece of fashion history, even if she'd never set an arm in it.

Nina helped me into the gown, and I couldn't wait to see it in the three way mirror. I fell in love instantly. Not to mention my modest cleavage seemed to have inflated significantly thanks to the magic of priceless couture and my padded Fleur of England bra.

I had found the dress that would formally present me as the future Mrs. Frank Swann. As pretentious as that sounds, even to me, I also knew I could not show up in any less than a one of a kind piece. Editors and photographers for Town and Country and Ebony magazines would be there, recording the event for feature stories. Frank and I agreed to give only these two magazines the exclusive rights to photograph our engagement party.

During a conference call with one of the editors, she bluntly gushed, "It's not every day that a blue blooded billionaire marries an African American princess. I want our readers to have the fairytale!" Is that what we were to them? Still, somehow, I was not insulted by that declaration. When I was a little girl, I, like many, dreamed of marrying a prince. Black or white, I didn't care. The editor and her staff were over the moon excited. I didn't see it as a huge deal, but evidently to the rest of society - it was.

"Oh Nina, you were right. This is the one." Smoothing my hands across the luscious organza, I knew Frank would love it as well. "Wait until my mother sees this dress."

Nina displayed a sigh of relief. "I'm so happy you love, it Miss Kane. We'll have it delivered at your specification, ma'am." As happy as I was with the gown, I was also ready to get out of that shop.

Settling into the chauffeured Town Car, I turned to Bebe, a little confused about what just happened. "So, this is what it feels like when you can't be sure someone is sincerely interested in *you*, or just your name and credit card?" I wasn't used to people dancing for me the way that sales girl did.

Bebe placed her hand on mine, "Unfortunately. But, there's only one person you should care about Candice, and that's Frank. None of this is really important. Do you hear what I'm saying?" I could tell she understood what I was feeling.

I looked through the front windshield at the palm lined street ahead. I was now living the dream. I diverted my eyes down towards my legs, the way I used to when I sat in the back seat of my dad's car. For a moment I was just Candice from Chicago, not Frank Swann's fiancé. I felt a familiar comfort. I wanted to hold on to it forever.

Bebe: Something's not right

"Sweetheart, where are you? Bebe!"

I quickly hung up the phone when I heard Derek roaming the hallways of the master wing, yelling for me. When he got to our bedroom, I went into my closet.

"You didn't answer your phone, what's going on?" He put his hands in the pockets of his slacks waiting for me to respond.

I gave as pleasant a smile as I could and kissed his cheek, "Nothing is going on." I knew he sensed I was still upset so he treaded lightly to avoid a fight. The old fool still didn't get it.

"Good, because I thought we'd have dinner. Let's go to Malibu. It'll be nice."

I shrugged a shoulder, "Sure, why not Derek."

The infectious smog hovering over Beverly Hills is like a virus that creeps into your soul and cataracts your outlook on all the good you used to believe in. It had now saturated Derek. I was sick to death of him at this point, because he'd really taken a dive and I couldn't figure it out. If he kept this up, he was going to be reintroduced to the girl he found on the onset of our relationship; the one who was always on guard and didn't trust a word he said.

Back in 1996 when we first started dating, it took months for Derek to tap into my heart. It was still bruised from the emotional turmoil of my previous relationship. We met at a party that I attended with a couple of girlfriends. I kind of had the reputation of a cold ice queen and would beat him at every angle. If he tried too hard to wine and dine me, I'd cancel plans. When we finally started getting serious, Derek shared his entire life with me, but I only let him scratch the surface of mine. Little did I know this drew him in more, and he didn't give up on me. He wasted no time letting me know he wanted me to marry him, but I was terrified to let him in. I did enough to remind him that I cared about him, because I didn't want to lose him. It was just going to take some time and he allowed me that. I fell in love with Derek.

Now, there was an unsettling feeling that something was going on with Derek because I'd noticed subtle shifts in his character. His demeanor was different, like he was going through a mid-life crisis. He was almost sixty-one and should have been past that phase. Derek was zipping all over LA in his Ferrari, when he usually kept a more modest profile in one of the Mercedes or at least the Range Rover. He rarely drove the Ferrari, but it was now his favorite toy; except when we went out together, because I didn't want to be seen in it anymore.

"Yes, we need a night out, Derek, because we have to talk."

He sighed. "Bebe, come on... I'm trying to have a nice time with my wife."

"That's right I'm your wife, not somebody you force yourself on!" Derek wouldn't talk about what happened, so I refused to sleep with him after that night. "Derek, I can't believe you did that to me!"

He laughed, "What? Oh, now I can't even make love to you or god forbid, try something new?"

He was delusional. I'm getting upset to think about it.

"It wasn't making love. Derek, you were too rough with me, and you damn near made me have sex with you! What's happened to you?"

He turned around and walked out of the room, throwing his hands up, "Bebe, you know what? I'll be in the studio. I've lost my appetite!"

I was left standing there seething as he turned his back on me leaving behind only the high priced stench of his cologne. It stank as bad as the smell of deceit that he cast off. I felt disposable, and like I'd been put on time-out once again by the great Derek Fabian. It's like he didn't understand nor care how this was hurting me and destroying our marriage. Also, he was evasive, like he was hiding something.

I stepped out of the bedroom, watching him stomp down the hallway as his cell phone rang in his coat pocket, and I could hear his voice clearly. "Hello? Yes." Looking over his shoulder as he approached the staircase, he answered, "I told you...tomorrow. No, it's alright. Goodnight."

I was sure he was having an affair, and I couldn't bear to go through that pain. Somehow I had to find out the truth.

Twisted intimacy

*F*licking his arm to check the time on his Omega, Derek was aggravated by the conversation he'd just had with Bebe and seemed just as irritated by the call he just received. As he neared the rear of the house, Derek stopped mid stride, turned and dashed out the front door. The screeching spin of his Ferrari could be heard as he exited the front gate. He was in a hurry, and wherever he was headed, he went from wanting to have a nice dinner with his wife, to speeding off in his car without her. All in a ten minute time span.

Derek put the car phone on speaker. "Hello...yeah, I've uh, decided to take you up on that. I need to talk, so I'm on my way."

At the stop entering Mulholland Drive, Derek fingered his graying temples, tussling with a couple of strands. A pretty young thing caught his attention in the rear view. She nodded and raised her sunglasses to acknowledge him, dropped them and looked away. He didn't like that and grumbled, "Little tease." Derek was hostile. He was now even more anxious to reach his destination.

~

His fingers frantically strummed along the keys of the piano and created a melody so hypnotic, so tight, that Derek impressed himself with the piece that he'd improvised as he went along. He'd just had a fight with Bebe and was now in a creative free flow.

"So, why are you really here, Derek? Because I know it's not just to play that piano." Leaning against his back, the young woman pressed her inflated breasts against him. He stopped playing, gazing ahead at the Renoir, an obvious copy, on the wall of the plush suite. She continued, "You said you need to talk...we could have some drinks in the bar."

He turned and shot her a look that said that's not going to happen. "No, let's just relax a little, okay?"

She shrugged with a sensual smirk and calmly strolled over to the sofa, crossing her legs and patting the space next to her, "Come here, baby. Talk to me then. That's what I'm here for. What's going on?"

Derek sighed and turned in her direction. The fair haired vixen licked her glossy lips and raised her perfect eyebrows, enticing him to join her. Once he reached the sofa, she helped him out of his jacket and laid it on the chair next to them. Comfortably laying his head across her exposed thighs underneath her silk robe, Derek's legs flung over the edge of the sofa.

"I can't make this woman happy! I used to, but she doesn't understand what I need anymore. I just..."

She stroked his hair and temples with her manicured fingers as he continued to disclose details of how he suffers through his pitiable, privileged life. *Selfish bull* is what she thought of that, but this is what he needed from her; a kind of twisted intimacy. It wasn't the worst thing she'd endured. Besides, he paid her handsomely and she was willing to reciprocate; earning every penny, so to speak. Even if it meant she had to play psychologist every now and then.

The Game

*A*t seven o'clock Candice walked into Via Allegra on Canon Drive, looking around the noisy room for Faith who is notorious for being late. While she waited at the bar and ordered a drink, some old man talked her ear off while his eyes fixated on her cleavage peeking up from the low front of the fitted black Michael Kors dress.

"...and I said, why do you live here if you hate it so much?" He drunkenly chuckled to himself.

Candice tried not to laugh in his face, so she nodded while praying for Faith to show up quickly.

"I think my friend is coming in. Nice speaking with you."

She turned around to walk away and then froze when she saw Wes sitting at the end of the bar with a male friend. Candice wanted to bolt out of the restaurant, but with a room full of people didn't want to look like a fool, so she fake scratched the side of her temple, shielding her face while walking back outside to wait.

"Hey! Candice!"

God! She sighed because he'd seen her. "Huh? Oh Wes, hi." Acting surprised, she wished he'd just leave her alone, especially now.

"How you doin'? You look good as usual."

"Thank you. I'm um...I'm waiting for my girlfriend. She should be here any second."

"You wanna wait with us?"

"No!" Realizing how rude she sounded, "I mean, I'm early and I'll just wait for her outside. It's a little crowded in here anyways."

He stood, nodding and checking her out. "Right. So it was what, six months ago that I saw you? What's been going on?"

"Actually, I got engaged!" She shoved her bejeweled finger in his face.

Instantly glancing down at her hand, "Engaged to who?" His forehead wrinkled as he seemed irritated.

"Why do you care? Wes, I have to go, but it's good to see you." She turned quickly, and saw Faith walking into the restaurant.

He grabbed her arm, "Wait! Hold on, I just asked, man."

Candice yanked her arm back, "Get your hands off me!"

Just then, camera flashes popped off in the doorway. Candice never saw a thing.

She turned back and waved at Faith, and fled the scene before it got too ugly. The old possessive Wes had surfaced. She'd almost forgotten him. She also missed the paparazzi standing outside the entrance that spotted Wes Donnellson in what looked like a heated argument with a mystery woman. He took a slew of shots and Wes, even though he saw the guy, didn't warn Candice. He just sat there with a smug look and sipped his vodka and energy drink concoction.

"Faith, I'm here!" She kissed Faith's cheek and hugged her, trembling.

"Hey girl, you okay?" Faith glanced over Candice's shoulder, wondering what got her so flustered.

"I'm fine, crowded rooms just get to me sometimes. Come on...I'm so glad you're here." Candice linked onto her friend's arm, as the hostess ushered them to a table in the corner of the dining area.

"This is perfect, thank you." Candice plopped down in the chair, wishing she could hide.

"Candice look - Kim Kardashian! She's cuter in person."

"Yeah, she's alright..." Noticing the starlet glancing in their direction, Candice gave Kim a friendly nod before her eyes cut to Wes walking out of the restaurant. She sighed of relief. "So Faith, how's the new house coming? You love it?"

Faith started rolling off details and Candice could only think how complicated her own life was becoming. The game was different, and she wondered if her defense was strong enough.

Nothing

There's a saying…A man doesn't pay a prostitute for sex. He pays her to leave.

So what's the difference between a prostitute and an elite escort? Nothing. Money men fool themselves with the notion that they just have a professional and drama free girlfriend on the side, when in actuality she's a hooker dressed in Versace with the equivalent of a mortgage on her feet. The rules are all the same: No money…no honey.

Derek Fabian on the other hand, didn't try to disguise it. His was an insatiable craving for call girls. He put down major cash for a few hours. Usually he bored her to death with his sob stories, then as a reward he screwed her brains out. That's why his secret had been so safe, for so long. He's filthy rich, dresses well, usually has clean breath and packed a big stick. Afterwards, the lady gathers up everything, including his baggage, and you guessed it….she leaves.

There's just one problem. Derek broke the number one rule by bringing his dirty games home to his wife.

Bebe suspected he was seeing another woman, but what she was about to discover was even more than she'd imagined. While he was out one day, she had just enough time to search for the truth. If Bebe knew one thing about Derek, it was that her husband held onto keepsakes. Just like he kept the napkin that she'd scribbled her phone number on when they met. She found it in a desk drawer four years after they had married.

"I don't know what you're up to, Derek…" Quickly pulling out island drawers in his closet, she could almost smell it. "…but I'm going to find out."

Nothing! Hands on her hips, she almost gave up. That's until she remembered – the watches. He kept his prized timepieces in a separate velvet lined case next to his shoes. She unlatched it, and pulled out the little ring drawer. Tucked away underneath his Rolex box, there it was. The business card: Holly Taste, Elite Companion.

"Oh my god..." Bebe's face scrunched. She couldn't fathom why he'd go there, but now, it was all starting to make sense. "...you sick sonofa..."

At that moment, she was filled with disgust, anger and deep hurt she'd never felt. This topped the Bahamas twins. It was now in the open what he'd been doing behind her back. Still, she felt stuck. It wasn't the time to have the media all over their lives. Candice's wedding would be ruined by gossip, and Derek would have too much time to spin the situation. Once again, she'd end up being the bad guy. Bebe knew she had to keep her discovery to herself for a little while. But when the time was right, Derek was going to pay.

In Hollywood, perception is reality

*"H*ello, Kari? Well, I hate to say this, but I think your dad's girlfriend is playing dirty, honey. Hold on..." Brandon transmitted the link to her phone.

Kari opened it and saw the picture. There Candice was with a famous actor in what looked like a lovers spat. "What the hell is this?" She tried not to jump to conclusions but, it looked pretty obvious. "Brandon, I have to go!" She hung up and called Candice's cell phone.

"Hi, Karoline. I was just..."

"You had us all fooled, Candie, but I'm not going to let my dad go through this again!"

Candice felt defenseless, like she'd been sucker punched. "Karoline, what are you talking about?"

"I think you know. I want you out of our lives!" Karoline hung up before Candice could say another word.

Candice's mind was racing because she had an inkling it was about what transpired the other night. But, how did Karoline know?

Then she got the call from Bebe. The story was on the gossip blogs already. *Bad boy Wes D: Caught in a fight with gal pal Candice Kane - fiancé of billionaire Frank Swann!* It was accompanied by photos that splashed across the online celebrity blog read by millions around the world.

"Hunter couldn't wait to call me with this. What's going on, Candice?" Bebe scrolled the site and told her to look at it as well.

On the other end of the call Candice was silent, and didn't know how to answer. She pulled up the site and saw it for herself. There she was, pushing Wes away with the top of her dress falling open, partially exposing a nipple.

"I can't believe this is happening!" She naively hoped Frank would never find out about the pictures. The truth would have sounded like a lie, and to lie about it would make it worse. "Bebe, nothing is going on! I don't know who took these, but it's not what it looks like. He's nobody to me, just an idiot ex-boyfriend." She shook her head in disbelief.

"Why were you with him?"

"I wasn't with him! Bebe, come on, I was meeting Faith. I was in the wrong place at the wrong time. Wes saw me and started in, and I snatched away. You have to believe me, please."

"I do believe you. Darling, you don't have to convince me, but I'm sure everyone has seen this, and you know what's going to be said."

"What should I do?" Candice was too shocked and upset to cry.

"First thing you do is not let it upset you. It was bound to happen, because people see how happy the two of you are. Just get to Frank first and make him understand what happened, because there will be others who will try to convince him otherwise."

That's exactly what Candice was worried about. That he'll believe the lies. She was terrified to face what was happening. So, she jumped in her car and left before Karoline got home, and rushed over to Faith's house in Pacific Palisades. The last thing she needed was a faceoff with Frank's daughter.

Glass houses

"You have about thirty seconds to spit out a real answer, so let's try this again!" Frank hadn't been so angry in years.

With her face frowned and mouth quivering, Hunter Goldman was seething at the commanding tone Frank blasted through the phone. "Why are you so confident she's not trying to work you over?"

"Because I trust her. I'm not going to let the stupid stunts Jackie pulls change that. So... what did she do, Hunter? Now!"

"Alright! Jackie is pissed about you marrying Candice. It's like she's lost her mind, and she won't stop, Frank. Then she calls me because there is nowhere else to go." That alone proved how crazy Jackie was to trust Hunter: she of zero loyalty.

"Well, I find it amusing that she confides in you, of all people."

"There's no reason for you to be so cruel, Frank. But, don't worry - I'll make sure your own little secret stays safe. I'd hate to see poor Candice heartbroken. The girl won't know who to trust."

Frank's pen practically dug a groove in his Smythson portfolio, listening to the underhanded threat. He picked up the handset and calmly spoke directly into the phone.

"Let me tell you this, Hunter. You'd better hope Candice doesn't so much as shed a tear over anything else, or you'll regret it. Not Jackie...you! That's a promise."

He slammed the phone down, knowing that if Candice found out about what happened all those years before, it could cause serious doubts within their relationship.

~

"Faith, he's never going to believe that I wasn't there with Wes." Candice leaned over the breakfast table in Faith's ultramodern home in the Highlands of Pacific Palisades. Her head rested on her hands, with tears welling up as she spoke. "His daughter has so much influence over him, and now she's convinced I'm sleeping around with Wes!"

Faith knelt down in front of her. "Then you get up and call Frank. Don't sit back and let this happen, Candice, you hear me?"

"It's already done. Once it's out there that Frank Swann's gold digging fiancé is playing him, they're going to be thrilled to tell him." Candice's body was trembling as she looked pleadingly into her friend's eyes.

"You think he's already seen it?" Faith was worried for a second, even blaming herself for Candice meeting Frank in the first place.

"I don't know." Candice kept shaking her head. "I do know him though. He's probably thinking déjà vu…a repeat of his ex-wife and that scares me Faith, because I love him."

"I know you do, honey. Look, Frank's not that guy. He'll listen to you."

"I don't know if I can." Candice clenched her hands together, looking down.

"Well you have to try…right now!" Faith picked up Candice's cell phone. "Here, call him. Don't give these people time to trash your name. Call Frank, right now!"

Just then, an incoming call rang through. It was Frank. Candice waved it off, got up and rushed out of the room. Faith answered it.

"Hi, Frank, this is Faith."

"Okay - so where is she, Faith?"

"Candice is here with me, and she's upset and scared. You can understand that, right?"

"I appreciate you screening calls, but I was hoping to speak with *her*."

"Well you just remember this, Frank Swann. I've known Candice all of my life. She loves you and wouldn't do anything to hurt you. I probably would have, but she wouldn't."

"Yes, you sure would have." Frank's attempt at mocking failed.

Faith was serious. "Frank, I know you love her, and she feels safe for the first time in her life. Don't let this happen to my sister."

Frank paused for a few seconds. "That's why I have to speak with her. I'm at home, so have her call me, okay? Thank you, Faith."

"Alright..."

Frank hung up before Faith could say goodbye. She tried to understand from his point of view. Still, it reeked of a setup, and she wasn't about to let her friend's life fall apart over some bull.

Perfect nightmare

Candice woke up early the next morning after repeatedly going over the tabloid story. Curled up on the bed in Faith's guest room, she hoped it was all a bad dream. She had imagined everything under the sun, but mostly that Frank would break it off, believing she'd been seeing someone else; and Wes, of all people.

Candice knew right then what she had to do. She took a quick shower, trying to work out the anxiety that was pumping through her.

"Faith! Where are you? Faith!" She went yelling through the house.

Faith rushed into the living room still in her robe. "What is it? Are you okay?"

"Yeah, I'm about to leave. You're right, I have to face this." She hugged Faith and left.

When she got to Swann Lakes just after eleven, Candice sat in her car at the gate for a good ten minutes rehearsing over and over what she'd say. She finally rang the buzzer. "Hi, it's Candice Kane."

The gate opened and she sped past the security shack, up the winding drive and to the front door where a housekeeper met her.

"Good morning, is he upstairs?" Candice entered in past her.

"Yes, ma'am, I'll go…"

"No, it's okay, I'll find him. Thank you."

Candice dreaded the walk, but knew she had to do it. What will be, will be. She was so irritated by the size of the house, the long hallways and huge rooms. She knocked at Frank's bedroom door, but there was no answer. "…he's probably in the study." Thinking out loud, she kept walking down the hall.

"Candice?"

Startled, she swung around to find Frank standing in the middle of the hallway, with his hands in his pockets. She figured the housekeeper had announced her roaming presence. "Frank, you're here. We need to talk." She felt anxious.

Frank watched Candice standing there; sensing her nervousness about what would come next. "Okay, let's talk."

Candice couldn't move. "Look, I can only imagine what you're thinking." She swallowed back tears because it was not the time, but she was about to lose the fight because they started welling up. Frank didn't say anything; just kept looking into her eyes, like he was searching for truth. "Frank, say something…please."

"Come with me." He reached for her hand and led her to the study. He went back to his desk, sat down and pressed the button to resume a call, asking Candice to give him a minute. Speaking to the person on the phone, his eyes remained focused on her. "Are you there? I need you to call me in two hours. Okay, thank you, goodbye."

Candice sat in the big club chair across from his desk. "I've never felt so blindsided in my life. I only hope you don't believe any of it."

Frank stood and walked over, wrapping his arms around her and kissing the side of her face, and then he stopped. It was like he wasn't listening to her. Then he said "We're fine. I love you and…"

Candice pulled away. "I didn't ask if you loved me, Frank. I need to know if you trust me." Realizing she'd have to live with whatever his response was, she was ready for it.

"…and if you'd let me finish." His fingers grazed her collar bone.

"Go on." She was getting frustrated with his prolonged speech.

Frank softly chuckled, "Alright, so you were at a restaurant meeting Faith, right?"

"Yes, I was. I didn't even know that fool was there."

"I know. The reason I know is because a friend of mine recognized you and witnessed the whole thing. He called and wanted me to know that my fiancé was in a bit of a sticky situation."

"When did he tell you about it?"

"Yesterday morning."

Candice looked puzzled, watching the magnetic balls dance on his desk. "What? Why didn't you say anything then?"

"Why would I? Candice, you don't have to prove anything to me. We love each other, and that's enough for me to know the truth." He resumed hugging her, and felt her body relax in his arms.

Candice started to explain about Wes, but Frank jumped in.

"Look, just be careful. This seems like the perfect life, but once you're in it…can be your worst nightmare. You understand what I'm saying?" He massaged her shoulders.

"Yes, I'm starting see that." She clutched one of his hands and kissed it. "I love you."

"I love you, too. So - here's the bad part. That call just now? I have to leave for a few days to New Jersey, and then back to Chicago. Are you going to be alright?"

Nodding she assured him, "I'll be fine. Except that now Karoline thinks I'm a gold digging whore." She tried to laugh it off.

"No, she doesn't. She's just a daddy's girl." He patted her shoulders and headed towards the doors, "Oh, and Candice?"

She scooted around in the chair, "Yes, babe?"

"The next time you fight off an ex-boyfriend, make sure your tits don't spill out." He chuckled under his breath, and exited the room.

"Frank, don't say that!" Candice was horrified that he'd actually seen the photos. Still, she was intrigued by the fact that even though she'd flashed half the world, he didn't seem that phased by it. Frank was definitely not insecure, and she prayed he stayed that way.

Bebe: My three-way marriage

I came up with a million excuses for Holly Taste's phone number being in my house, but they all dead ended. I was fooling myself, but what woman could come to terms with the fact that her husband had been having sex with someone else?

Another nasty little fact - if he was screwing around, then so was I. Married people usually don't use condoms, and I'm sure he never used them with *her* either. Derek used to say it ruined the mood. He's is a stickler to what he believes in and that scares the hell out of me. It should scare him too. Oh, and forget about him being afraid of getting a disease. Derek would be more afraid of getting caught. That's exactly what happened. I caught him with his pants down. Literally.

After I found the card in his closet, I could think of nothing else. Sure, I kept busy helping Candice with the wedding, and was able to put up my strongest front. I pray something like this never happens to her. Can you imagine being fairly certain that your husband is not just cheating, but having sex with a prostitute? It's like slowly dying inside. *How could he?* That question was on repeat in my mind.

What is strange even to me is that I never cried about it. Not one tear. I was so hurt, I didn't allow it. Then that hurt turned into anger. I couldn't stand to look at Derek anymore. When I did, I'd find him staring at me, like he knew the gig was up. I never let on, and I certainly didn't let him touch me. I pulled up every excuse in the book, from migraines to yeast infections. I needed to figure out what I wanted, and I had to act fast.

All that matters

*F*rank sat behind his desk in Chicago, staring at the monitors as he dutifully listened in on the conference call. He could only think about the fact that soon he'd be marrying Candice and was anxious to see her. Glancing at the small clock on his desk, he was ready to get back to LA.

"Excuse me, ladies and gentlemen; I'm flying out in an hour so I'm logging off now. Dr. Grayson, Dr. Reid, thank you for your time this afternoon…and I'll speak with all of you in a few weeks." Click. Frank dialed Candice's cell and got no answer, so he called her at home.

Back in Malibu, Candice mindlessly went over the guest list for the ceremony. They had two hundred and seventy-eight guests on the list and she wished they had narrowed it down to fifty, but there was no doing. Her head was pounding, and not only because of the intense workout at the gym. Frank would be back soon and there was still so much to be done. She thanked God that Bebe was so involved, because it was overwhelming and gave her anxiety like nobody's business. She hoped Frank wouldn't even talk about the wedding.

"God!" Upset with herself, she shut down her laptop and hurried to her bathroom to take an ibuprofen. Resting on her hands at the sink she stared at her reflection. Feeling the surge of panic and tightness in her chest, she sat on the edge of the tub. "What the hell's wrong with me?" The phone rang and she made her way out to the bedroom. The ring only irritated her more and she snatched it up. "Hello!"

"Candice, it's me. Are you okay?"

"Sweetie hi…uh, ye,s I'm okay. There's just so much going on; the wedding and everything. I really need to see you."

"I know, baby, I'm on my way to the airport. I'll see you tonight. I've missed you."

"Me too. I love you…" Hearing Frank's voice was calming, but she so wanted to tell him how stressed she was about the wedding, but thought against it. "…call me when your plane lands."

He quietly smiled at the sound of her voice. "Okay. I love you, too...see you soon."

Looking past her bedroom door, Candice hung up and could hear Karoline fumbling around in the kitchen. "Kari?"

"Yes, Candie, I'm in here!"

"What are you doing, cooking?" She was surprised to see Karoline scribbling on a pad.

Karoline just giggled, "Not yet, but, what...is that so strange? I learned a lot from the chef, remember?" She closed the Sub-Zero with a grin on her face.

Leaning against the island, with one foot perched on the stool, Candice shook her head, "Right. Oh! Your dad will be back tonight."

"Yeah, I know. I thought I'd make dinner. I'm going to the market now."

"Wow, you're a regular Rachel Ray, aren't you?"

Karoline rolled her eyes up, giggling. "Do you wanna come?"

Without hesitating Candice stood up straight, "Yes! I need to get out of here." She offered to drive, and on the way, Karoline's cell rang.

"Hello, Mother." She looked over at Candice with an apologetic look. "What? I have no idea. No, look, I'm sorry, I have to go." She hung up.

Candice gave her a sympathetic look and tried changing the subject. "So, I thought I'd make key lime pie for later. It's super easy and my mom's recipe."

Karoline didn't know how to break it to her. "Candice, she knows all about the wedding and she's going crazy."

Candice raised an eyebrow. "I know, but it's okay, don't worry. It doesn't bother me and I don't want you to feel in the middle, okay?" She put a reassuring hand on Karoline's arm.

Jackie had been calling everyone in the vicinity of Frank's circle, giving off the transparent impression of being happy that he'd moved on. She didn't realize, or was too insane to know that those same people had a greater interest in Frank than in her. The walls were closing in and she was getting desperate.

~

"Mr. Swann we'll be taking off in ten minutes."

Frank looked up as the flight attendant handed him his drink. She blushed when making eye contact with him. He noticed that type of thing with women who work for him, but never reciprocated, no matter how attractive he found her. He knew it could lead to a bad situation if he took it too seriously. The last thing he needed was to appear to be another skirt chasing billionaire and end up on CNN.

Sitting his drink on the walnut tabletop, he got up and removed his jacket, tossing it on the leather seat across from him.

Frank started thinking about marrying Candice. He was pleased that they wouldn't have the big wedding fiasco, with five hundred guests in a church, the lights, camera, and action of it all, like he had before. One of the things that almost destroyed his first marriage right out the gate was that Jackie got so caught up in the grand display that she forgot about him. Their wedding lacked any real sign of romance.

He hoped Candice wouldn't do the same. But whatever she wanted, he was willing because he loved her. Frank felt for the first time he found someone who truly loved him; flaws and all. He was ready to give her the world.

~

"Kari, I want to tell you something." Pressing the graham crack mixture into the pan, Candice looked over at Karoline who was rolling her ingredients for the sushi.

"What is it?" Karoline was a little hesitant because ever since she came home from rehab, they'd tiptoed around what happened.

"You look good and I'm really proud of you." Candice smiled, turning attention back to the crust.

"Thank you." Karoline sighed, "It hasn't been easy. I won't even pretend it has been, but I feel better."

"Well, I'm here for you, you know that, right?"

"Yes, now I do. I didn't know what to think of you at first, but I realize now that you were just looking out for me." She flipped her hair off of her cheek. "I'm glad you're here, Candice. You're good for him." Karoline paused. "I also want to apologize for..."

"Nope! It's nothing...we're good. I love you, kiddo." Candice then giggled. "I was just thinking how in the beginning I fought him off. I tried my best not to fall in love with your father." They laughed and she settled into a more serious tone. "I didn't want to get hurt, but Frank is different from any man I've ever known. I can't imagine being with anyone else."

Karoline smiled watching Candice confess her love for her father.

Candice thought about the parade of characters she gave her heart to, only to have them cheat or reveal their true ugly selves. The recollection almost pained her stomach. It made her more anxious for Frank to come home, even though their love made her dizzy sometimes, and that's what really scared her; the intensity.

Frank's plane was landing at Burbank in an hour and Candice set the table on the patio. The warm breeze whispered and the flowing fabric of her maxi dress felt good against her skin.

Karoline popped up at the threshold of the open doors, "Okay, well...I'm out, so enjoy your night, Candie Kane. Oh, and I spoke to Daddy and he sounded excited to get home."

Candice smiled but was confused. "What do you mean, aren't you staying?" Gesturing at the table she wondered why Karoline was suddenly ditching out. "What about dinner?"

"I did this for the two of you. Besides, I have my own plans." She smiled, turned around waving and sashayed towards the front door, "Have fun, doll!"

Candice was happy that she and Karoline were becoming friends. She hoped from that point on, they'd be family.

Candice: Wedding jitters

"I'm going directly to Malibu, Renee."

Renee looked in the rear view and nodded.

Frank was finally back in LA and it was like regardless of the smog, he was actually breathing again because Candice had brought something back into his life that he'd missed...an emotional intimacy that made him feel secure. When you're worth as much as Frank Swann, you're rarely secure in romantic relationships. Even *those* are usually based on business. Sad, but true.

Frank took a call from one of his analysts, but with so much on his mind, rushed him off the phone.

"That's fine. Have Stacy set something up for a few weeks. Oh and Chuck, you owe me a rematch because you swindled me last time, man!" He laughed and clicked the phone off.

~

Candice was curled up in her chaise chatting with Anne online when the feel of hands gliding across her shoulders startled her. "Oh, my god!" She looked up and Frank was there, "Hey, lover..."

Massaging her shoulders, Frank glanced down at her fingers as they typed *Have to go. See you soon! Hugs xo* She sat the laptop on the side table and reached up for a hug.

"Hey, yourself..." He leaned down and they locked into a deep kiss. "...now, that's what I missed." Sitting at the foot of the chaise, he draped her legs across his lap. Candice still got a chill over her body when he touched her.

"Mmm, me too..." She seductively ran a finger down his shirt buttons. "So, we made sushi! Well, Kari did mostly."

"My Kari?" Frank looked shocked.

"That's what I said." Playfully nudging his leg, "We had a good time, come on..."

After dinner, she brought him up to speed on the wedding. "Frank, you've got the good end of the deal. All you have to do is write the check." Raising a brow, she giggled. "Seriously, this is a lot to keep up with. I wanted to keep it sweet and simple, but I realize it wasn't possible. Not in this town."

Linking their hands, the two shared a laugh. They were on the threshold of being married, and Candice hoped she was ready.

Bebe: Germaphobe

Our summer barbeque was always another great Fabian production. This year, Derek had been in France for two weeks and returned just in time for the big July 4th weekend. We would be hosting our friends for a day of swimming, golfing, spa treatments for the ladies, food catered by Wolfgang, and at night, fireworks over Beverly Park. We did it up big. Of course, Derek exited the party early. When he took off in the Ferrari I knew exactly what that meant.

I tried to figure out where he'd meet her. I say *her* because, and I laugh at this, Derek is a germaphobe. He couldn't stomach diddling more than two women at a time. Any more than that, and he wouldn't be able to keep track of hygiene habits. He'd find it disgusting in his own twisted mind. So on this night, it had to be no one but Holly Taste. I was pretty certain of that.

One of our business entities, DBF Holdings, owns a three thousand square foot loft apartment in Downtown LA. I hadn't been there in three years, since Derek and I last worked on a project together. The space was great for the creative process. We sometimes leased it to artists who came to town to record for extended periods, but mostly it was never used. Or, so I thought.

My gut told me he was at the loft with Holly. It terrified me to follow through, but I borrowed Candice's car to go meet Derek's "new artist who is performing at a club…" She seemed a little suspicious but didn't question me. I thought going to see a singer at eleven at night in LA, was a reasonable lie.

I pulled up to the twelve story luxury building located near the Staples Center and parked out front. The doorman ushered me in. I prayed I'd prove myself wrong this time.

With the click of my key, I let myself in and…

"What the hell! Bebe, you followed me?" Derek had the nerve to question me while he lay in bed with his slut.

Shaking my head and breaking into hysterics, I laughed and threw the key at the woman, as she scrambled to cover her naked body.

"No, don't run! Stay…we own you tonight!" I wanted to scratch her eyes out, but decided Derek deserved my attention more than she.

The cocky bastard just lay there, with a drink in his hand, cursing and yelling for me to get out. It felt like an out of body experience. The only thing I remember about what happened next is Derek ending up with a huge cut across his arm. Holly must have made her way out at that moment, because I only recall Derek in the bathroom holding a towel to his bloody arm.

"How could you do this? You stupid sonafabitch!" I snapped - kicking at him until finally, I felt defeated and tears finally flowed from my eyes.

"Bebe, she's just…it's nothing, baby." He was so calm.

I pointed a finger in his face and screamed, "If you say that again, I'll kill you!"

I turned and left, passing the broken glass lamp on the floor next to the bed. I assumed that's what cut Derek. I was a mess, with speckles of Derek's blood on my white halter jumpsuit.

Refusing to waddle in my sadness, I went home to my guests. I sped all the way, making it back just in time for the grand finale fireworks. Some of our more festive guests didn't go home…as usual. Both guest houses were occupied. Like always, I made excuses for Derek.

The scenario was getting old and I knew it was time for some changes. I couldn't let him do this to me anymore.

Candice: Wouldn't be complete

*I*t was August 5th, the night before the wedding, and we gathered for a private party in the Polo Lounge at The Beverly Hills Hotel. It was a wonderful evening, and the staff went out of their way to assure everything was perfect. There's nothing jazzier than cocktails in the bar, and singing along as the legendary Derek Fabian plays a medley of some of his most famous compositions on the piano. He even invited Faith, who was now sporting a new cropped pixie haircut, to sing with him. I think she shocked even her husband with her voice range; a gift she inherited from her mother who in the late Sixties and Seventies, performed with a quartet in New York.

By ten o'clock we were all feeling pretty festive. I recall not being able to find Frank, but Rayne told me he was outside on the patio with some of his relatives, so I went to join them. His father's youngest brother Edward Swann, who is just a little older than my dad, met me with an over eager embrace.

"Ahhh, my new niece! You are one beautiful girl. You'd better be careful, Frank, or I'll steal her away!"

I saw the glazed look in his eye and pulled back as Uncle Edward planted a wet one on my cheek. His wife looked on in horror, trying to apologize for his behavior. Frank just laughed at my reaction, while puffing on his illegal cigar.

I looked into the dining room where a few guests were having drinks in a booth, while being entertained by my visual discomfort. "Alright then, Uncle Edward, okay!" Needless to say he was a little drunk. He's a dear man, but I sure as hell didn't want to know him so intimately. He overstepped his boundaries with that kiss.

My parents had already left the party and returned to Swann Lakes. They were sensible and wanted to rest up for the next day. It's a good thing they did.

At around ten-thirty, while I was enjoying another apple martini, there was a commotion at the entrance to the lounge. Actually only one belligerent voice rang out. I saw thick, red locks flinging back and forth and it wasn't Karoline, as she was clearly in my view. I knew it could only be one person, and was headed in that direction when Bebe cut me off at the pass.

"Darling, look, why don't you go sit with your husband-to-be on the terrace, huh? Steal a quiet moment while you can?" She made an attempt to distract me and I love her for it.

"Bebe, is that Jackie over there?" I craned my neck to look to the door.

"Yes, but she doesn't deserve your attention, Candice, please."

I ignored Bebe and briskly walked towards the hostess stand in my bejeweled four inch Derek Lam heels, which were killing my feet. I was so pissed that I think I must have been running on pure adrenalin at that moment.

"Excuse me!" I gently place my hands on Karoline's shoulders, guiding her out of my way.

Karoline turned around, "Candice, she's leaving." She turned back towards Jackie, "Mother, just go!"

Frank's driver slash bodyguard was standing there and tried to spare me, "Miss Kane, it's under control." Another security guard approached from behind.

Jackie glared at me with a drunken smirk; the corners of her emerald green eyes, riddled in crow's feet. "I just want to wish the lovely bride a beautiful day tomorrow."

"No, it's alright, Renee..." I was smiling, trying to be as graceful as my soul allowed, but pushed past him and walked directly up to Jackie. We were eye to eye, almost bumping foreheads. "I don't know who you think you're dealing with, but let me tell you this. He's not your husband anymore, so stay out of our lives! If you don't you'll be sorry, I promise you!"

Jackie gave me a hard stare, looking me up and down. If I didn't know any better, I would have sworn she was about to grab my drink and dash it right in my face. Instead, she glanced at Karoline who was shaking her head. Then that cold gaze cut past her and stopped at Bebe.

Jackie yelled, "Bebe! Why don't you tell her what a great friend of the family you've *really* been all these years!" She was drunk and becoming vile.

I turned around, waiting for Bebe to say something, but her eyes were now spitting fire at Jackie. She wouldn't look at me, but screamed at Jackie. "You bitch! Can't you let anyone be happy?" Bebe then turned to me, with a sorrow in her eyes that spoke volumes.

Faith rushed up to me. "Candice, are you okay?"

I spotted Rayne, sitting at the bar with her jaw now dropped and watching me. She saw the look in my eyes, and then gave me a sympathetic look. She evidently had heard Jackie's rant. I shook my head for her not to react any further.

I didn't know what to think. I was confused and felt like the joke was on me, but I knew it wasn't. I also didn't need Faith defending me with a Chicago-style beat down at the epicenter of Beverly Hills. That would have gone over really well, so I chose to save that for a rainy day.

"Yes, sweetie, I'm fine. She was just leaving."

I knew what that drunken ass piece of trash was insinuating, so I tried not to show my confusion and embarrassment and said nothing else. I gave a visual signal to our driver friend, and he escorted Jackie towards the lobby and out the doors. Swallowing back tears, my emotions were all over the place. Not ready to confront Bebe about what Jackie was saying, I walked past her without so much as a glance. I found Frank on the patio, where he'd missed what happened, and I made sure he wouldn't know. I wanted to be the only somebody on his mind that night.

"There you are…" He pulled me in for a hug.

I hugged Frank tight but tried not to look at him, because he would have surely seen through the forced smile, every bat of my eye that concealed the upset. "I was just saying goodnight to our friends."

He pulled back to see my face. "You're not worried, are you?"

"About what?" Looking into his eyes, I tried to dismiss the images in my mind.

"You're tense, sweetheart." I racked my brain for a response, but couldn't come up with anything. I looked at him, with no words. "Look, I'm nervous too, but I can't wait to marry you." He kissed me, and as corny as it sounds, settled my insecurities.

Just before midnight, Karoline and I were driven back to Swann Lakes. We had blocked several bungalow suites for the weekend including the presidential, where Frank stayed that night and we'd spend the next couple of days. The other suites were for some of Frank's business associates, Uncle Edward and his wife, my father's sister and her husband, as well as two armed bodyguards. Other family and friends were accommodated throughout the hotel. My parents, sister and two aunts stayed at the house with me. Not everyone in my family was invited because if I never heard from you before my headlining nuptials, there was no reason to at this time, and that's how I feel about it to this day.

I should have slept peacefully that night. Instead, I replayed Jackie's words while visual assumptions played around in my head.

I hoped it wouldn't ruin my wedding day.

August 6th ~ Wedding Day

*T*he entire entrance to Swann Lakes had been guarded like Fort Knox since the day before. With the exception of the wedding party, security, decorators and caterers, no one was allowed inside before five o'clock. News of Frank Swann and Candice Kane tying the knot was the hottest buzz around Los Angeles.

At four-fifty Candice was sitting anxiously in the dressing area of the master suite with her mother, Anne, Faith, Rayne and Bebe. The women were helping Candice into her exquisite Ramona Keveza gown. The whole while, the scene at the party was still on her mind.

"Don't you start that mess!" Faith playfully scolded Anne who was about to cry looking at her baby sister preparing to walk down the aisle.

Bebe and Rayne thought the other women would appreciate some time alone, so they excused themselves to the sitting room.

"Ladies, we're going to give you a moment together. Candice, I'm going to check on the music."

"Bebe's so sweet. Not what I expected." Millicent Kane wasn't one for phonies, and could spot one a mile away. To admit liking Bebe Fabian was a big deal. She felt the genuine friendship between her and Candice.

"Faith, can you go ask Bebe to come back for a second? I just need her help with something, please."

Bebe strolled in with her pale gold Badgely Mischka gown flowing in her stride. "Darling, you asked for me?" The others had left the room and they were finally alone. As soon as the door closed, Bebe sat down in front of Candice. "I know what you must be thinking."

"I don't know. That's why I need you to just tell me what Jackie was talking about, because right now, I *don't* know, Bebe."

Bebe sighed and stood, "It was a painful time. Ten years ago, after they separated, Frank and I...it was a terrible mistake. That's it - one night. Jackie found out and has been holding it over our heads ever since." She pleaded with Candice, "I promise you. It was impulsive and reckless and never came close to happening again."

Candice listened and turned towards the mirror. It all reminded her of the affair with a married man years before. She was twenty three and found out he was married but didn't stop because the sex was too good. The guy was a jerk and she knew it, but enjoyed it until things turned crazy. He became so possessive that Candice threatened to tell his wife about it if he didn't leave her alone. So with that history, she felt hypocritical for being upset about something that happened before she came into Frank's life.

"Bebe, listen to me, I don't want to ever talk about this again. I never want Frank to know that I know, okay?" Bebe nodded dabbing her eyes with her pinky finger. Reaching a hand out to assure Bebe that they were okay, Candice smiled and asked that her mother come back into the bedroom.

Bebe rushed towards the door to let her in, but not before turning around once more. "Candice, Frank loves you with all of his heart. You always remember that, regardless of what you face. Then, you face it together." She meant every word. Regardless of anything that happened in the past, Bebe loved Frank and Candice, and wanted them to be happy.

~

"Look at my beautiful baby girl."

Fluffing the delicate veil over the off the shoulder sleeves of her daughter's gown, Mrs. Kane couldn't believe the day had arrived. Candice was actually getting married. She'd witnessed so much pain in years past and thought her daughter had vowed never to give her heart to a man again.

Candice got serious. "So Mom, how's Dad? He seemed a little quiet at breakfast."

"It's hard for him to let you go, baby. But, he likes Frank and sees how much he loves you. Dad knows that you'll be okay."

Hugging her mother one last time as a single girl, Candice got choked up.

"I hope you're right Mom. I love you."

Meanwhile, just up the road, Derek came knocking at Frank's bungalow, to lend what he felt was helpful advice to his friend.

"I want to talk to you; before it gets crazy. Honestly, I didn't think you'd take this walk again, my friend." He stood there in his expensive sunglass reading specs, holding the drink he'd just made for himself.

Derek had been there for Frank throughout his tumultuous marriage to Jackie and sincerely looked out for him.

"I sure as hell didn't think so. She's wonderful, isn't she?" Frank's eyes smiled as he spoke about his bride.

"Yes, Candice is a beautiful woman. We adore her, and Bebe can't stop praising her, that's for sure." Derek chuckled, raising his drink to his lips.

Frank stood at a mirror, checking out his reflection. He looked distinguished in his custom Gieves & Hawkes tux, direct from Savile Row, London.

Then Derek spoke. "Frank, just tell me one thing."

"What's that?" Straightening his tie, he felt the leading tone in Derek's voice.

"You've taken care of business, right?"

Frank stopped, cutting an eye in Derek's direction. "What do you mean, man?"

Derek laughed walking towards him, with his hands in his pockets. "I think you know what I mean. An agreement?"

Frank turned around; looking a bit pissed that Derek had the audacity to ask this on his wedding day, as if he was casting judgment on his wife to be.

"Derek, would you say I'm a fairly smart man?"

"Damn right, that's why I'm asking."

"So, things are in order, but I appreciate what I assume is concern."

"Good!" He patted Frank's shoulder and went over to the sofa.

"Look, Candice will be my wife in one hour. Not that it's any of your business Derek, but our attorneys have met and IF anything should happen, I'll do more than right by her."

The driver yelled from the dining room, and into the bedroom. "Mr. Swann, whenever you're ready."

Frank irritated, walked out of the room. "Derek, are you coming?"

"Hey Frank, I wouldn't be a friend if I hadn't asked...just precautions. Though I doubt you'll need it." He reached out and shook Frank's hand. "Alright then, let's get you married, buddy!"

Derek couldn't have whittled a comeback any faster to climb out of the hole he'd just stepped into.

~

Guests began arriving at the estate at around five o'clock. Limousines, Rolls, Bentleys and the occasional Mercedes paraded through the front gates of the Swann estate. Security checked names and invitations before the guests passed through. It was like the Inaugural. Once a guest's vehicle made it to the valet at the main house, they had to present their invitation and identification to one of the coordinators before being ushered into the plush garden where the ceremony was to take place. A photographer from Beverly Hills Life & Style caught the guests as they arrived. The nuptials were to be covered in a forthcoming issue.

At five-thirty, Frank and Derek arrived, and the driver took them along the opposite driveway leading to the rear terrace. Frank watched guests milling about and taking their seats. He was filled with emotion, as he was about to marry the woman he loved. Finally, he'd gotten it right.

Frank walked up the stately stairs and greeted Candice's father, who was standing there with a concerned look in his eye, overlooking the activity. The two men greeted with a handshake.

"I'm giving my baby girl to you today, Frank. You'd better take care of her."

"I promise you I will. I can't lie, my life isn't always easy, but I'll do whatever it takes. I love her."

"I know you do." If there was any time Clinton Kane felt his daughter was safe in the care of any man, other than himself, it was now.

At five-forty, the ladies prepared for the big moment.

"Okay, before we all destroy our makeup, I'm going to go downstairs. You have a few minutes, Can. I love you so much." Anne's eyes started misting as she squeezed her sister's hand.

"Candice, you look beautiful. I love you girl. See you in a minute." Faith hugged her friend and whispered, "I can't wait until ya'll have little blue eyed babies. Won't that be something?" She giggled.

Candice laughed, "You would say that!" She watched Faith disappear into the foyer with her violet chiffon gown fanning behind her.

Her dad knocked and peaked in, "You ready, baby?"

"Yeah, I think so, Dad."

Mrs. Kane then entered the room and handed Candice the full bouquet of white and peach roses. Just then, Candice started feeling queasy and light headed. "Mom, I have to sit down. Hold on..." A wave of anxiety and nervousness came over and she slowly settled in the plush chair. She focused on calming herself and letting it subside. Embarrassed, she pulled it together, holding on to his arm. "Okay Dad, I'm ready."

~

As Candice strolled towards him, Frank knew she was the woman he'd spend the rest of his life with. She was radiant. Her hair was swept in an elegant up do, adorned with sparkling Harry Winston diamond butterflies, which shone through her fingertip length veil. Her smiling eyes were reminiscent of the first time he'd seen her, and he hoped she'd always have that.

With each step down the rose pedaled aisle, to the heavenly strums of the two harpists, Candice felt like she was living outside of herself. Every eye in the garden was fixed on her. Including the judgmental, feeling she was unworthy of the life she was gaining. Still, she convinced herself that she was the most adored girl of the day.

She also noticed the musical strings were overpowered by smooth and familiar vocals. They belonged to Lola Owens, Candice's favorite singer who is also referred to as the first daughter of soul music. Lola inherited her father's gift to move a crowd with a single note. Candice had asked the Fabians to use their power to get Lola to come and perform at her wedding, but Bebe later broke the news of a schedule conflict. She wondered what magic they worked to get her.

Clinching her father's arm, Candice tried her best to conceal the excitement sweeping over her and the huge smile painted over her face. Until moments like these, it was easy to forget that Beverly Hills was an entirely different world. All things are possible.

Mr. Kane had finally reached the moment he secretly dreaded. Frank took his bride's hand as she stepped up to the floral covered alter. In an instant, she was no longer little Candice from Chicago. Her life would never be the same.

Frank and Candice took a moment to share their feelings between each other before the ceremony continued. You could hear a pin drop.

"I love you, Candice. You've made me the happiest man in the world." Frank's eyes were intensely focused on hers. He could feel her love in return. "I look forward to spending the rest of my life with you."

Candice stroked his face, "I never stopped believing in love, even when I wanted to. I know God brought us together, and I thank him for that. I love you so much." Frank took her hand and kissed it.

At six-twenty-five they were pronounced Mr. and Mrs. Franklin W. Swann, Jr. Clearly heard were the sobs of Candice's sister who was standing to her left, and then of her mother. Glancing over at Bebe who winked at her smiling broadly, Candice watched Derek come to his feet, smiling and applauding. She didn't have a strong connection to him, but Derek was one of the first to approach her after the ceremony.

"Frank is a lucky man. Congratulations..." She assumed that was Derek's way of giving his blessing. Not that his approval mattered. "...and give him a couple more kids, huh? This place is a museum, for god's sake! Don't end up like Bebe and me, huh?"

All she could do behind that was laugh, because she wasn't sure what he meant by that. "Okay, Derek. I promise. Besides, I don't think you two are so bad. We kinda' love you." Candice kissed his cheek, and for the first time, heard emotion in his voice; as if he was regretful of something.

After the congratulations subsided, the wedding party ascended to the terrace for more photographs.

Looking around, she found Bebe standing near the steps. The women engaged in a tearful hug.

"Bebe, I love you. You're forever my family, you know that, right?"

"I do, and I just want you to be happy. I know you will be." Bebe seemed a little distracted, hiding behind her perfect smile.

Karoline walked up and pulled Candice over to the staircase as the photographer snapped away.

"Look, I know it's been hard dealing with me." Candice tried cutting in. "No Candie, I know it has...but I also want you to know that you've brought something special to our lives. I've never seen my dad so happy."

"Well, we're family now." Candice hugged Karoline tightly. "I love you sweetie, and..."

"Ladies, hold that please!"

The photographer gave thumbs up. The two of them giggled because they'd forgotten their every move was being photographed.

Meanwhile, guests were in awe as they entered the party tent. No cover story could give justice to the wonderland designed by eccentric Beverly Hills event planner, Lovell Lenox. They were welcomed by two live mannequins, dressed as ballerinas. Crystals spilled from layers of exquisite fabrics at the top of the tent, in raindrop formation. White roses in crystal vases were the centerpieces of each table, and as the lighting changed color, so did the flowers. It was truly dazzling.

After a few hours Frank and Candice were ready to sneak off. But, not before Lola dedicated her hit, Our Forever Lasting Love, to them. Then the DJ kicked the party into high gear.

Frank took the microphone, as he held Candice close, and announced, "We want to thank you for being with us on this perfect day." Candice nodded, holding back tears. "We love you and hope you're having a good time. This party doesn't end yet, so enjoy... Just, don't burn our house down!"

The guests roared with laughter. Even the stuffiest of guests were on the dance floor getting their party on, as they say. It wouldn't end until well after Midnight.

On their way out, Frank and Candice approached Anne standing near the lake chatting up some guy who didn't appear to hold her interest at all. He was good looking, but she gazed right past him as he spoke.

"Sorry, give me a minute." Anne lifted the hem of her dress and ran over to her sister. "Wait!" Giving Frank a kiss on the cheek, she told him, "Welcome to the family, Brother-in-law." She hugged Candice as the bodyguard looked on, waiting to escort them to the hotel. "I love you both, now go!"

Inside the party, Bebe approached the table where Candice's parents were enjoying Faith's performance with Derek accompanying her on piano. Karoline and Rayne were also sitting there.

"I'm so happy for them!" Rayne declared, as she sipped on another glass of vintage Bollinger champagne.

Karoline agreed, "I know, they're perfect for each other."

Bebe raised her glass in agreement, "Yes, they are..." Derek glanced in her direction and she looked away.

The wedding was romantic and very elegant without being ostentatious. It was the talk of the town. One of the most eligible men in the world has taken a new bride; someone who only cared about being with him. Candice couldn't have cared less what *society* expected of her because none of it would make a real difference in her life. She also knew now that people would treat her differently, and may not always have her best interest at heart. There's a lot of backstabbing in a privileged world. Candice just hoped that wouldn't include the people she trusts most.

Bebe: The last straw

*I*n the limo, I felt unusually calm for the first time in months. Derek sat across from me loosening his tie, and then looking at his watch.

"Nice wedding, huh?"

"Yes, it was. They're so in love." I watched him pour a cognac from the bar. I felt so far removed from the bliss of the wedding we'd just left.

"I think you're right." He looked up at me and I turned away, staring out of the window. The night had been just about perfect. I glanced back and my eyes burned into him. "What is it, Bebe?" He was clueless.

"Just a hectic day, Derek, that's all." A smile quietly crept to my face as I was reeling the courage I'd been trying to muster up all weekend.

The limo drove through the gates and up to the house. When I got out, I asked the driver to wait. I turned to Derek as he climbed out the other side. As he approached me, I looked him square in the eye, and calmly declared: "I want a divorce."

His lips tightened, "Not this again!" Derek was smug and confident. So used to running the show, he lit a cigarette and kept walking towards the house.

"This time I'm serious, and I don't want you here tonight! I can't live like this." I was terrified, but held firm.

Derek squint his eyes at me and yanked his tie off, returning to the car. "I'll be back tomorrow when you get over this...whatever!"

I slammed my crystal Lieber bag to the pavement, rushed back to the car and leaned in. "Why do you treat me like that? Like I'm stupid!"

"Bebe, what the hell do you want? I made a mistake! Besides, you're one to be so self righteous. I forgave *you*... remember? " The look on his face was as if he was apologizing for spilling wine on my dress.

"Don't you dare do that to me! This is not a mistake. It's a dirty habit you've fallen into. You're so used to calling the shots. I won't say that I can't believe you did this because honestly, I'm not shocked. I'm just hurt that you actually try to make excuses and lay the blame on me. Well, no more!"

The buildup of tears stung in my nose, like I was about to erupt. I glanced at the driver who was looking at Derek, shaking his head. I picked up my handbag and pulled out Holly Taste's card, threw it in Derek's face and walked away. "Call your whore! Maybe she'll let you crash at her place!"

He called my name as I rushed into the house. Then it's like the adrenalin crash kicked in, because as soon as I got inside and closed the doors, I fell to my knees, in tears. I thought I could stay strong, but I couldn't.

In my heart, I still loved Derek. I just didn't want him anymore. My marriage was over.

Mrs. - No hyphen

"*F*rank, are you awake?"

Cradled in the warmth of her husband's body, Candice experienced a security she hadn't felt in ages.

He rubbed his hands against her skin and kissed her shoulder. "Yes, I am..."

"Okay, so I've decided. I know you said you wouldn't mind if I wanted to keep my maiden name."

He giggled, "Right, I won't be insulted."

She rolled over to face him, "But that's just it. I married you...with no hyphens." She giggled as she felt his hand glide inward of her thigh. "Are you listening to me?"

"Yes, I am Mrs. Swann, and whatever you decide, I love you. Every inch of you..." He firmly kissed her lips, then slid his body downward while stroking her breasts and making his way towards her stomach. His lips glide across her belly button and bikini line, sending chills across her body.

"Hmmm, really? Then show me how much you..."

Before she could finish her sentence, he showed her. Frank grinned to himself watching her clinch the pillow as her body squirmed with delight as he played with her. "You mean like this?"

She almost begged him. "Uh huh...just like that."

So consumed with each other, they were oblivious to the fact that the doors of the bedroom were open leading out to the pool outside of their bungalow, where they'd been hiding out for two days. Candice, a self-proclaimed screamer, feared the sounds of their lovemaking may have been heard by nearby guests.

"You're a bad girl..." Teasing her, Frank's eyes moved upward as he enjoyed watching her facial expressions as much as he was turned on by her moaning.

She managed a laughed, "Ohhh... you have no idea."

The sex got so intense that she dug her nails into his back, which seemed to encourage him even more, until their limp, sweaty bodies fell flat across the bed.

Frank made his way out of bed and towards the bath, but not before turning towards Candice, who had pulled the cover up and was close to dosing off. "Would you mind calling the concierge and checking the weather in the Turks over the next week?

She raised her head, leaning back on her elbows, "What? Is that where we're going?"

He winked in confirmation. He'd told her the honeymoon location was a surprise, so she prepared for anything, but had no idea where.

"You are too much...I love you baby, thank you!" She excitedly hurried out of bed and joined him in the shower.

Frank was ready to spoil and pamper Candice, and started by surprising her with their honeymoon on the private island of Parrot Cay in Turks and Caicos, where they would spend a week in a fully staffed villa. They were scheduled to fly out the next day, and she was very ready.

~

"Will you be having champagne, Mrs. Swann?"

Candice hung her jacket and handbag in the closet of the G500 and glanced back at the smiling flight attendant with a look on her face like she wasn't sure that she was addressing her. "Oh yes, thank you."

"My pleasure, Ma'am." The perfectly coiffed young woman sashayed down the aisle towards the men seated at the rear of the aircraft.

Situating herself in one of the overstuffed leather seats, Candice turned around and waved at the two beefy gentlemen. Frank's personal handlers, if you will.

"Will they always travel with us?" She hoped not.

"At least one of them will." Frank reached across the aisle and rubbed the top of her hand with his. "It's necessary, because I want you to always feel safe."

"I understand." Nodding, Candice lied, and had already begun planning how she'd ditch them. Having babysitters wasn't her style.

The fact that the so-called one percent, of which Candice was now counted amongst, don't travel like the average tourist, still took some getting used to. Those extreme luxuries made it almost impossible for her ever-present guilt to fade.

Champagne didn't always agree with Candice, and after just one glass, she settled in before takeoff. There was close to seven hours of flight time ahead, and she knew she was going to pay for that drink.

"See Candice, there's a reason I don't drink during long flights. You're going to regret it." Frank smiled at her and continued checking emails.

"It's okay. I'm willing to chance it. I'll be asleep, anyways."

It was their beginning, and Candice felt like it was time to be a lot more adventurous. Truth was – she was curious about what was to come, but feared it just the same.

Being Mrs. Swann

*I*t's been said that no woman marries for money, because she's smart enough to fall in love first.

That's certainly true in Candice's case and then some. Irrespective of the fact that he is one of the world's wealthiest men, she actually fell in love with Frank. Despite his generosity when she first arrived to LA, she paid her own way and refused to take a dime from him. She lived off the ten thousand dollars she had from her savings and what she borrowed from her 401K. That means she never *had to* rely on anyone for money, but yes, Frank accommodated her handsomely and she knew it. There was access to the best of everything, but he didn't push, knowing it made her uncomfortable.

That all changed once they got married.

The morning after they got back from their honeymoon, Frank walked into Candice's dressing room while she was changing, and presented her wedding gift. The diamond Fred Leighton choker he had borrowed for the gala.

Gazing at it, she was confused because she'd assumed he'd returned it. Tucked underneath the eye popper, was her very own Centurion card, better known as the Black Card, with her name embossed in gold lettering. Almost embarrassed, it took Candice a minute before she looked up at him. When she did, she smirked and said, "You know you don't have to go to such lengths to get me to do that thing you like..." Frank winked at her while she teased, "...and the necklace is a nice touch, too."

"Well, after I saw it on you, I knew no one else's neck would do it justice. It was always yours."

She reached her arms around his neck, "And, *I* was always yours."

~

There were major renovations taking place at the Swann estate. They sought out the best and Candice was given one name: Kevyn Brodzik. The Beverly Hills interior designer had decorated some of the most famous homes on the planet, and Candice knew he was the only choice.

There was a reconstruction of the master wing to accommodate a mistress suite, which includes a spa bath and lounge, luxurious closet and dressing room, along with Candice's office that overlooks the gardens and tennis court. The latter prompted her to take lessons with a pro that came to the house once a week. She talked Faith into being her tennis partner.

Standing in the hallway just outside her office, casually dressed in a Betsey Johnson romper and sneakers, Candice was a nervous wreck.

"Oh, my goodness! See, I told you, it's not going to fit through the door." Her hands were flailing all over the place, then onto her hips. "Look, back up and turn it sideways or something."

"Ma'am, trust us. We got this."

One of the movers tried to calm her down. He was cute in a rugged, blue collar kind of way. Sporting dreadlocks up in two ponytails, the way Busta Ryhmes did when he was hot.

"Are you sure?" Candice then threw her hands up, realizing she was acting like a maniac and mouthed *sorry*.

The guys tried not to laugh at her. "No problem, Mrs. Swann."

She apologized again. "I'm sorry. I just want to make sure it's okay."

It had been nearly a month since the wedding and she had finally gotten some of her things out of storage. Candice had the antique armoire, once belonging to her great grandmother, delivered that morning. She chose to put it in her dressing room where she'd use it as a 'purse closet', as her mother called it. To Candice it was an emotional care package from home. Swann Lakes is heaven on earth, but those twenty thousand square feet took some adjusting to. Something, just a part of it, needed to feel familiar.

"Let me show you where I..." Her phone vibrated in her hand. "Just a second...hello?"

"Hi, Candice, how are you?" It was Hunter Goldman. Candice couldn't help but wonder what brought the call.

"Hunter? What a nice surprise. I'm good. Getting settled, actually arranging some furniture as we speak." She giggled, but could almost feel Hunter's eyes rolling through the phone.

"Oh, that's wonderful. I'm sorry I wasn't there for the happy occasion. We're all so elated for the two of you."

You weren't there because you weren't invited. "Aren't you sweet? Thank you, Hunter." Almost gritting her teeth, Candice braced herself.

"In fact, I'm calling to invite you to my house on Saturday evening. Kind of a girl's night, dinner, drinks...you know, let our hair down without the men!" She did that obnoxious giggle of hers.

"Well, I'll double check our plans, but it sounds fun. Thank you for thinking of me."

"Of course. It'll be good for you to meet more of the ladies. They'll love you. Besides, Frank has got to loosen that grip some time."

"I don't know. That grip feels pretty good, know what I mean?" Candice giggled in triumph.

"You naughty honeymooners, do tell... So see, you have to come. I'm texting you the address now. Oh - and bring a friend!"

"Thank you, I will. Have a good day, Hunter."

Candice hung up wondering how this conniving woman would really benefit from her being at the party. Something told her Hunter was trying to maneuver into her good graces. Whatever it be, a new Candice Swann was about to emerge and show she was nobody's fool. She called for backup immediately.

"Hey Rayne B, how are you?"

"Candice, hi...I'm good. What's going on?"

"Well, I'm not sure...but I was wondering if you'd want to go to a party with me on Saturday."

Rayne could sense a motive. "Okay, I'll bite. What's the deal, because I can hear it in your voice, baby girl."

"Stop it, you cannot." Giggling Candice couldn't wait to spill. "Okay listen...Hunter just invited me to a little soirée which won't be anything but a bunch of women gossiping and stirring up mess, I'm sure. But it's in the Hollywood Hills, so..."

"Wait, two-faced Hunter Goldman?" Rayne laughed "What does Frank think about her sudden interest in you?"

"He doesn't know yet, but doesn't trust her any further than he could throw her. Still, I feel it's time for me to break the ice so to speak. So come on Rayne, I need you."

"Because you know I have your back. The king of Beverly Hills fell in love with someone these women feel is an outsider and it kills them, plain and simple."

"I don't buy that. I think Hunter is just a shit stirrer! But it's time they know I can hold my own!"

"Okay, I'm in!"

"Great!"

Sacrifices

$\mathcal{A}$t the beginning of the new semester, Candice decided to take leave from school. Not permanent, just until she got her new life situated and to figure out what her goals were. Still it was with mixed emotions that she withdrew from USC after all of her hard work.

"I'm sure you feel I'm making a huge mistake, Mr. Brookside, but it's best for me right now; my just getting married and all. You do understand?" Candice wished someone would rush into the office and stop her.

"Yes, I do, and I don't believe in mistakes, Candice. However, I have to say I do hope you reconsider. You're one of our brightest."

Candice glanced at the stack of books on the department head's table. "Thank you and like I said, it's just temporary. I love this program and it's been my dream forever. I'm not throwing it away. I'm just...taking a little break."

He smiled and nodded his head at her, "You've done well. I'm sure we'll see you again."

"You will, thank you." She stood and draped her handbag over her arm. "Okay then…"

Brookside took her hand, patting it, "Your husband is a lucky man."

"Thank you, I appreciate that. You've all been wonderful."

Walking out of Annenberg, Candice couldn't help but feel irresponsible. But part of her was anxious to dive into her life. This little sacrifice would surely lead to a blessing. She trusted that motto and believed it. Driving off in her new Audi, she felt a resurgence of confidence. When she got home, she ran upstairs to Frank's office and flung the doors open.

"Sweetie, I think it's time I got to know some of the ladies around here."

Frank, engrossed in whatever was on the monitors, glanced up at her with a half grin as she stood waiting in the doorway. "Really?" Studying the smirk on her face, he looked pleasantly suspicious, "Okay, what's going on?"

"Oh, nothing, just…Hunter invited me to her place on Saturday. I don't know - it might be fun. I'm going with Rayne."

Candice, being sure that Hunter was partly responsible for fanning that tabloid fire, knew the invite was more out of malice than sincerity, but was ready to beat her at her own game. *Kill her with kindness* She just hoped it wouldn't backfire in her face.

The sins of a husband

"*Y*ou guys were awesome, man. Thanks!"

With an approving nod, and flashing that captivating smile of his at his music director, Morgan turned the bib of his cap backwards and continued towards the backstage area after rehearsal at the concert theater at The Palms. His demeanor changed as soon as he hit the dressing room.

"Damn, I gotta figure this out!"

Throwing the towel across the room, he felt hemmed against the wall. His girlfriend Eva had just arrived from San Diego and insisted on being in Vegas all week for the shows. He picked up his cell phone and dialed his assistant.

"Hey, where are you? Okay listen, Eva is in town. Yes, Vegas and she's driving me crazy. I need you to get her a room. No, Rayne's not coming. I just don't need her staying in my suite."

Eva came on the scene two years before while she was in LA working for the PR firm that represented Morgan. He saw her on set of one of his photo shoots, pulled her to the side, fed her his line and the rest as they say is history. The twenty-five year old Brazilian hottie was about to get herself into a whole mess of drama. Morgan was careless when it came to who he screwed around with. He thought everyone would keep their mouths shut and that Rayne would never find out. Now, he was tiring of Eva but didn't know how to avoid her running to the tabloids airing his dirt. The golden boy of the music industry would be another stereotypical case of sex, lies and destruction. Morgan even had a backup plan in place just in case that very thing happened.

"Okay, thank you. Bye." He kicked back on the sofa and started dialing out on his cell phone.

~

Sitting by the pool underneath the covered patio just off the hearth room, Rayne's phone started ringing.

"Don't play too rough in there!" Yelling at the kids, she noticed it was Morgan and hesitantly answered. "Hello?"

"Hey, baby…"

"Oh, Morgan, how's Vegas?" Rolling her eyes, she shook her head; never letting on that his very voice sickened her.

"Okay, I guess…it's a tough schedule."

"Right, I can imagine."

"I just finished rehearsals and was thinking of you guys."

"Aw, that's sweet. I thought about flying out for a few days but I can't leave the kids, being that they're just getting settled into the new school year and all. I have a lot going on so…" She could have sworn she heard him sigh of relief.

"You're a good mother, Raynie." Addressing her by the nickname he penned for her back in Louisiana.

"Yeah, well… Morgan I have to go, but call after the show, okay?"

"Sure thing. Hug the kids for me, and I love you."

"Me too." She hung up.

Rayne felt bad that she couldn't say she loved him, but there were mixed feelings because while she wanted to believe he was making an effort, she could also tell that he was trying to cover his tracks before he laid them. Making sure she *wasn't* coming to Vegas. She didn't need to because her pal Trey was taking what he calls 'hoe notes'. Still, she fought the urge to jump a plane and surprise him.

Business as usual

ⅅerek called Bebe and practically begged her to work on a song with him. Though caught by surprise she was very interested in the project. It had been three years since she had collaborated on anything with Derek.

"I've changed up the bridge. See, I want it to be something like..." Eyes closed, with her lean fingers gliding across the porcelain keys of her custom made Steinway in the music room of their mansion, Bebe was lost in creation. Music being her real passion, nothing was as stimulating as the euphoric feeling that flowed through her body while composing a melody. "...you know something like that." She shrugged modestly, turning in her seat towards Derek.

"Her vocals are going to be fantastic on this piece, Bebe." Laid back against the mound of plush pillows on the sofa, arms flipped over the back with his legs crossed, Derek gave an approving nod. "I just hope she gets back to the flippin' States in time to get the track down. I don't want to be off schedule again!"

Bebe and Derek wrote the song for Daphne Margot, who was recovering in the French Riviera from what the tabloids penned as, "the Montreaux incident". During an interview backstage at the music festival, she started ranting about her estranged movie star husband and practically forced herself on the reporter right in front of the cameras. She later performed her set and then passed out stage side.

Lending no sympathy to Daphne's condition, Derek made his way to his feet and buttoned his sports jacket. "I have no problem giving it to Mariah! Alright, I'll see you tomorrow."

Derek then leaned over Bebe, planting a soft kiss on her cheek. Though it was his way of being tender with her, Bebe wished he wouldn't seemingly ignore their problems. It's one thing she hated about him – the way he lived in pretense. She still couldn't figure out why he wanted *her* to write the song he'd been asked to produce as the theme for an upcoming film. It was all like business as usual.

Probably a couple of factors came into play. One - he felt guilty, or two - it was a romantic comedy and the production called for a love theme. Truthfully no one wrote a love song like Bebe Fabian, even Derek knew that.

He had been making subtle efforts to fix what he'd done to Bebe, because "I'm sorry" just wasn't enough. Bebe hoped with the new project, maybe they could have a fresh start. Only time would tell.

Candice: Girl's night out

"I shouldn't have gotten this dress - look!"

Rayne's brows furrowed, like she thought I was crazy. "What are you talking about? It's perfect on you."

"I know, but...I mean, the dress is awesome. I just don't like the way I look in it."

I harshly critiqued my reflection in the dressing mirror. Tugging at the single shoulder Tracy Reese dress, I was unsure and self-conscious. "Just let me change, okay? It looked much better when I tried it on in the shop last week."

Texting away on her Blackberry, Rayne frantically typed but called me out, "You're stalling, Candice!"

"What?" Glancing at Rayne's reflection I put a hand on my hip and responded, "No, I'm not."

"Yes, you are. Girl, the dress looks fantastic, now let's go!"

I saw Rayne catch a glimpse of her own reflection, taking pleasure in the fact that even after two kids, the pinched silk Dolce and Gabbana dress fit her petite frame like a glove. No sense in girl's night out if you can't make a couple of them jealous.

As our limo made its way up Sunset, I rolled the window down a little, for the breeze. "Do you mind, Rayne? I need some air." A surge rolled over me, which made my nerves hype up.

"You okay, Candice?" Rayne saw the look on my face, which I'm sure looked like I was in another world.

"Yes, I'm fine." I sighed out, smiling and changed the subject. "So how's Morgan? You guys okay or...?"

Rayne did that giggle, a mask for her feelings. "Or is right." She pouted her lips, shaking her head. I didn't know how to respond, so I didn't. Just gave a sorrowful face of support. Then her facial expression changed. "Candice, he's having an affair and...I put him out. He's living in Malibu while we take a break to figure things out."

"Oh, girl..." I put a hand on my friend's arm, "...I'm sorry. What the hell is wrong with these men?" I then realized maybe I shouldn't have blurted that; perhaps just play the listener role.

"Don't be sorry. He's the sorry ass!" Rayne wasn't upset, she was mad. I almost felt sorry for Morgan because I saw vengeance in her eyes.

The news had me stumped. I rarely saw Morgan, but this... I prayed Frank never did anything like that to me.

The closer we got, I dreaded the party because I'd been so tired and irritated, but I had to make my presence known. Hunter and her friends were not going to intimidate me. I needed to let them see that.

A lil' birdie told me

The limo turned onto Doheny Drive, winding upward towards what is known locally as the Bird Streets, which boast some of the most coveted views in Los Angeles. Hunter's prized estate on Lory Drive reigned supreme. It definitely was not as laid back as her beach house. This one was the trophy, and there were cars out front to match.

The driver pulled into the circular drive and opened the passenger doors. When Rayne got out, she started tiptoeing up the slate walkway, fearing she'd slip and fall in her sky high Louboutins. "This is a horrible material to have out here. Whatever happened to plain concrete? My goodness!"

Candice giggled at Rayne's blunt assessment and rang the bell, which sounded like wind chimes. As they went inside, they were met by Hunter who was barefoot and wearing a fitted floor length printed maxi dress with a deep neckline. Curiosity peaked in Candice's mind because Hunter's boobs appeared more balanced and a little higher. She was obviously showing them off.

"Helloooo..." Hunter greeted Candice with cheek kisses then glanced over. "You're Rayne, yes?" Hunter embraced her as well. "Welcome, I'm so happy to finally meet you." Hunter seemed eager to make up for the dirt she'd allowed to happen to Candice.

The women exchanged pleasantries and passed through the expansive Moroccan styled living room. Straight ahead was the patio which was set around a tranquil pool surrounded by fountains and floral filled vases. The backdrop was the most breathtaking vista in all of Hollywood. Walking onto the patio, which extended almost to the hill, Candice soaked it all in, with the sunset and a sea of twinkling lights at her feet. It gave an illusion of floating above the city. She thought Hunter didn't deserve such a gorgeous view.

"This house is insane, Hunter. The views really are unfair!"

Hunter gushed, "Oh, thank you. Well, what can I say? My husband's a whale, and he needs to feel like he's looking down on everyone." She rolled her eyes which revealed contempt for her darling hubby. She quickly pasted a smile back on. "Come, ladies..." Waving her claws in the air, she gathered attention, and told Candice, "...I want to introduce you." At which Rayne and Candice exchanged suspicious glances.

There were only six or seven other women there, some of whom Candice recognized from social events around town. Then one of the ladies approached her as she stood near the edge of the lawn, gazing out into the night. It was a little startling as she turned around.

"Oh, hi...how are you?" As the familiar woman stood before her, Candice smiled and extended a hand. "Candice...and you are Marlene, right?"

"Yes, that's right." The moderately attractive woman appraised Candice with her eyes and couldn't wait to get her words out. "You know, I was acquainted with Frank and his former wife years ago. He and my ex husband are friends from the East." She sipped her cocktail and reminisced, glancing off over the hills.

"Is that right?" Irritated at the underhanded reminder that she was new, Candice was about to walk away, until Marlene backpedaled.

"You seem a lot more pleasant than Jackie ever was." Marlene, a second wife herself, assumed she understood Candice's position. "Well, it's nice to see you again, Candice."

It was no secret that Marlene married well and divorced even better. Bumping into her at the party made Candice realize that their social circles are very small, and nothing is really confidential because so many relationships are entangled.

"My pleasure, Marlene." Candice looked around, desperate to make an exit because suddenly she felt like she was on display. A little cautious to get too chummy with Marlene, she sought out Rayne.

"So what do you think, Candice? Hunter's changing sides, or what?"

"No, she's not. I think she knows I'm onto her and is trying to put the fire out. She's not sorry. Besides, I don't really care. " Candice lied, because it did bother her.

Rayne giggled. "Most of the ladies here seem nice enough. Let's just have a good time and get the dish on Hunter." Rayne laughed, and then noticed how pale Candice's face became.

Lifting the lid of one of the chafers, Candice asked the server, "What is this, scallops?" She then caught a strong whiff of the aroma and slammed the lid down, feeling dizzy. "Eww, I'm sorry." She felt nauseous and excused herself signaling at Hunter, who came rushing over.

"Yes? Candice, you don't look so..."

"Hunter, where's your powder room - the closest one?"

Candice quickly headed inside, hoping she'd make it to the bathroom. Hunter watched her disappear down the hallway where she closed the door and rushed over to a settee. It was more like an ultra lounge, with a huge window framing the view outside. Candice laid her elbows on her knees with her head down, breathing deeply hoping she didn't get sick.

There was a knock. "Come in, Rayne!" It wasn't Rayne.

"Are you okay?" Hunter peered past the door suspiciously gazing at Candice.

"I'll be fine. I just think everything is catching up with me. It's been a busy couple of months." The last thing Candice wanted was for Hunter to ask questions.

"I'll bet." She nodded, walking over to Candice and sitting down. "You know it's none of my..."

"Hunter, what do you want? I mean, why'd you invite me here? We're not friends!"

"What?" She had the nerve to look insulted.

"It was you, wasn't it? You had that photographer follow me around hoping to catch something."

"Candice wait - I can explain..."

Fanning her off, Candice got up and started towards the door but was immobilized by a feeling of vomit surging up her throat. "Oh my God!" With her hand to her mouth, she ran and opened a door which led to the toilet.

Hunter still barefoot, ran over and held her hair back. "I've got your hair!" She couldn't believe what she was doing.

Candice stopped puking for a second and was breathing hard, "Go get Rayne. Please!"

A minute later Rayne rushed into the bathroom, "Candice, sweetie what's..." She watched Candice lift her head and look at her with glazed eyes. "Oh my god, you want me to call Frank?"

Candice grabbed her arm, "No!"

Hunter was at the vanity wetting a cloth while looking like she'd caught prey in her mouth. "Candice, a little birdie told me that... you're pregnant."

Candice looked back at Hunter with a threatening look in her eye. "What?" Reaching for the cloth and water Hunter had brought her.

Gesturing towards Candice, Hunter wouldn't let up. "It's obvious, look at you! But I promise, I won't breathe a word." A remorseful hint of sincerity showed in her eyes.

Rayne smiled at Candice, quickly glancing at her stomach, "Oh you are...Does Frank know?"

Candice shook her head. "Not yet. I just took a test this morning and it was positive. I'll tell him tonight, because he'll probably find me slumped over sick in the morning." Her smile was sprinkled with worry.

On the way out, Hunter said she'd make excuses for their early exit. She then pulled Candice to the side. "Like I was going to say, I didn't do that. But I didn't stop it either, and for that I'm sorry."

Candice didn't know how to take that apology, but had other things on her mind at the moment. Hunter was the least of her concerns.

When she got home she found Frank in the indoor pool. Waiting for him to finish his lap, she grabbed the towel from the lounger.

On his way out, he asked why she was home so soon. "Did Hunter make an ass of herself again?"

"No, actually she was surprisingly helpful. Here you go."

Drying himself, Frank chuckled, "What do you mean?"

"Babe, let's go inside, I can't stand smelling the chlorine."

When they got to the attached game room, Candice sat on a stool at the bar, prepping her words. "I may as well just tell you now." Frank flipped the towel over his shoulders, looking worried. "I kind of hoped it would be next year, but... Frank, you gave me a little something more than that necklace as a wedding gift."

He instinctively glanced at her stomach. "Are you sure?"

"Not a hundred percent, but both tests this morning said I was. Not to mention I just threw up all over Hunter's bathroom. I'll see my doctor Monday."

Shaking his head and grinning, Frank caressed and cupped Candice's face, kissing her lips. "I love you so much. You're happy, right?" Frank was beaming, but he could tell she was concerned.

"I am. I didn't expect it so soon, but of course, I'm happy."

Candice got more joy out of watching his face light up like it did. She just wasn't sure she was ready for the next seven months. Not looking forward to the actual pregnancy, she even hoped she'd be able to conceal it for at least another three months. Mostly, she was terrified that she wasn't ready to be a mother. But the news made Frank so happy that she was willing to cast all of those fears aside.

She called Faith while running a warm bath.

"Faith, I want to tell you before it hits the fan...I'm pregnant!" She held the phone to her ear during dead silence.

That's until she realized Faith was crying.

"Oh my god, Can, this is unbelievable. Everything is happening the way it should, don't you see?"

"I know, and that scares me." Candice was terrified.

"You're going to be good mother. And damn, Frank didn't waste any time did he?" She laughed, "I'm so happy for you guys!"

"Thank you, Faith." It felt so weird thinking back on the past couple of years. "If it wasn't for you, I wouldn't be in this place in my life."

"Well like I said, everything happens the way that it should."

Candice believed her. Life seemed perfect.

Better than ever

Karoline planned a bon fire on the beach. There's nothing like a Sunday night clambake in Malibu. Some of her friends were visiting from San Francisco and a party was in order. It's the first time in a year that she'd felt like entertaining.

"So do you know if Mimi's coming?" Brandon nibbled on a pretzel in the kitchen, watching Karoline fill one of the sinks with ice.

"I don't know. I left a message on her service. We haven't really spoken in a while, Brandon. But…it's okay." Waving her hands in front of her, "I just want to let bygones be bygones, you know?"

"No, you're right. Life's too short!" He shoved a couple of bottles of wine in the ice.

Karoline hadn't seen nor spoken to Mimi since the blowup at her house. Honestly, she almost didn't care about any of that anymore. She missed Mimi. They'd been friends before anything else.

She shrugged. "Maybe she'll show. What time is it?"

"Almost six." The doorbell rang. "Ah, I'll get that!" Tugging at his low rise jeans, Brandon jogged to the front door to let the first arrivals in.

It was going to be a great night. No pills, no drama, just the ocean and a good time.

Rayne: Boiling point

*I*t seemed to take forever to get a cab. I can't tell you how much I hate McCarran Airport. Stupid ding-ding-dings the moment you step off the plane and tourists shoving their last few dollars in the slot machines before going home with empty pockets.

"The Palms, please."

The taxi driver grabbed my small overnight bag and placed it in the trunk. I didn't even care that it looked like it hadn't been cleaned since coming off the assembly line.

While Candice's family was growing, mine was about to become one member less.

Glancing at my watch, I realized it was just about time for Morgan to go on stage. I knew this because Trey ran down the typical time line for a show. Tidbits like, at ten-fifty they'd be saying their goodnights to the crowd. That gave me just enough time to be waiting outside of Morgan's suite when he got there.

I woke up that morning and something came over me. I knew it was time to confront Morgan and finish it. I reserved my room at The Palms, as well as booked my flight. After hanging out with my kids all day, I drove to LAX to catch my seven-thirty flight. I told the nanny that I was going to see Morgan's concert as a surprise to him. It was a surprise alright.

By the time I got to my Palms Place suite, it was just after ten. Morgan was in a penthouse suite and I needed to have access to that floor without bringing attention, especially as his wife. I wanted no one to know I was there. Trey told me he'd text me when Morgan was on his way up to the suite after the meet and greets with fans. I was counting on that.

I had dinner brought up to my room before I got changed. At eleven-thirty-five Trey's text hit my phone. I wore the tightest fitting knee length black spandex dress I could find and paired it with my trophies, the Christian Louboutin rhinestone peep toe sling backs I wore to the Grammys. Hurrying out of my room, I knew I looked good because as I walked to the elevator, two guys in their twenties almost broke their necks looking at my booty, which is not bad for a forty year old mother of two. Morgan was going to miss me, I convinced myself.

I had two floors to go up and his suite was at the end of the hall. I would have a clear view of him coming. At just before midnight, a ding echoed down the hall. I heard voices coming from the elevators, then a man's clearing of the throat the way Morgan always does. They turned the corner and headed towards me, as I leaned against the doors with a smirk on my face. Morgan looked like he'd seen a damn ghost. Then I saw *her*, holding onto my husband's arm like she owned it.

"Morgan, who you got there?" Smiling, I postured up, walking towards them. I glanced in the familiar looking girl's direction, "Oh, I'm just the wife, don't mind me." It took all I had so not to smack the piss out of her, standing there looking down her groupie nose at me.

Then the girl tried to use a tone with me. "Excuse me?"

I leaned forward. "Excuse what?"

I was two seconds from decking that classless, sloppy piece of trash. Morgan grabbed my arm and gestured for his handlers to take his girlfriend somewhere.

"Don't show up here throwing tantrums and shit, Rayne! You claimed you couldn't come!"

"Oh, is that why? Huh? I couldn't drop everything, so you replaced me?" I wanted to throw his trifling ass through a wall.

He laughed under his breath, looking away, "Look, she just came in to see the show and..."

"STOP lying! I know everything!" I was so upset I couldn't cry, but was trembling something crazy. "I want you to hear this. I'm leaving you and I want you out of my house for good!"

"*Your* house?" The smug look on his face was priceless. It gave me just the buildup I needed.

"Yes, MY house. When I'm done with you, you're going to have play Vegas on a regular just to make ends meet." Pulling myself together, I turned away and quickly strutted down the hall. He came after me, grabbing for my arm.

"Rayne, wait!" His voice sounding as if he knew he'd messed up.

I turned around and smacked Morgan dead in his face, giving him a gash under his eye from my ring. "Don't touch me!"

"Ugh! What the…" He fell back into the door of another suite. His blazer falling off as his arms went limp. I didn't realize I had that much fight in me. Apparently, neither did he.

My lips were tight and I showed no remorse. "I knew that ring served some purpose!" I rushed to the elevator and saw the girl standing in the corner with one of the guys. Her overly lined eyes wide open in fear, like she'd heard me kick Morgan's ass down the hall. "He's all yours! But from what I hear honey, he was about to dump you!"

One of the bodyguards smiled at me and nodded.

I stepped onto the elevator and went back to my room, sleeping like a rock before waking up at four-thirty Monday morning. I was back in LA in time to see my babies off to school. There was no time for tears right then, but I knew there would be plenty later.

I filed for divorce the next day.

Six months later, after much battling between attorneys and the custody agreement, the divorce was final. I was free. Morgan showed no remorse and made it easy for me to move on without him. I was ready for a new beginning and thanks to having no pre-nuptial agreement, there were twenty million reasons and a vacation home, as to why I was confident that I'd be okay.

Now, what about Trey, you ask?

Trey was the first person who called me when the divorce became finalized. He'd helped me find the truth and I am grateful to that kid. Morgan fired him, of course. Trey's now a celebrity stylist with a modest office in West Hollywood and all of the clients he can handle. He even styled a nominated actor and his fiancé for the Oscars this year.

Trey is also my unofficial wardrobe stylist. Okay, he gave me a complete makeover once I got rid of Morgan, but I needed a new look. Trey talked me into "un-weaving" as he calls it.

I love my new haircut, my new outlook, and my new life!

Candice: A dream revived

I slept in a little later that Tuesday morning. I'd just gotten confirmation that I was seven weeks pregnant, which calculations mean I got pregnant on my wedding night or honeymoon. I actually think I knew when I didn't get my period in September. I'm never late, but thought maybe it was just the excitement of everything going on in my life. That was until I started feeling sick, which moved me to take the tests.

After the initial shock wore off, I felt like I'd been given a chance to be the person I was born to be: a mother *and* a journalist.

Where does journalism fit into this scenario? I received a phone call that morning, and was handed an offer I couldn't refuse.

"Hello, Candice, this is Destinee Mathews. We met the other night at Hunter's place?" I vaguely remembered meeting her.

"Oh right, how are you?" I was still lying in bed. The room was dark, with sunlight hinting around the closed drapes. I hate the sun in the morning. The housekeepers don't come knocking until they see my door opened a little. I had to sit up and turn my lamp on. "What can I do for you, Destinee?"

"Actually, I found out from my brother Kip that you're a journalism student, or was... and I was a little surprised, but impressed by that. No offense."

"None taken. Yeah, I majored in journalism back in Chicago, and up until recently was in the masters program at USC. I decided to take time off, just for a while."

"I understand. Congratulations, by the way! I heard the wedding was beautiful."

"Yes, it was. Thank you. We're really blessed."

"Well I was hoping we could meet for lunch soon. I'm starting a new magazine and would love for you to be a part of it."

I sat up in the bed and couldn't believe my ears. "That's exciting. Congratulations to you and yes, I'd love to hear more about this project." I think I was grinning ear to ear.

"Great. Tell me what works for you, because I want to meet as soon as possible."

"It's short notice, but if you'd like we can have lunch at my home tomorrow. How's one o'clock?"

"That's perfect, Candice. I look forward to it."

"Me too Destinee, see you then."

Just from a brief phone conversation, I now felt confident that I would be able to avoid the role of a pampered princess. That's not who I am, no matter how much I enjoy living in Beverly Hills. I was ready to let people know that.

Destinee Matthews is the sister of Kip, Frank's friend. At Hunter's party, I was so sick; I barely remembered speaking to her. She turned out to be someone who actually believed in my abilities and dreams. I hoped it would all work out.

Candice: New beginning, tragic end

Destinee arrived right on time, and when she got out of her car I was met by one of the most stylish women I'd ever seen. She appeared much younger than her forty years. Her cocoa complexion was healthy and glowing, like that of a girl twenty years younger. Her jet black hair parted in the middle, cascaded past her shoulders, framing cheekbones to die for. The strapless black and white floral dress complimented her almost six foot frame. Destinee was stunning without pretense. She also had soft smile lines, which I found refreshing.

"Hi, Destinee! Welcome." I was happy to meet her. Not just for the career aspect, but hoped we'd become friends. So far, it was promising.

"Hello, thank you for inviting me, Candice." She greeted me with a friendly hug, glancing around. "This place is unbelievable, girl!"

I laughed, "Thank you so much. We're in the midst of making a few more changes, but I'll show you around."

Destinee briefed me on the basics. "So, I thought we'd call the magazine Beverly Hills Woman."

Nodding, I liked it. "It's a strong title; it's about us - real women, not the cloned mannequins the world thinks all women in Beverly Hills are."

"Exactly! I want this to be more than a glitz and glamour magazine, although we'll have that because it's Beverly Hills after all. Am I right?" She fanned huge gestures with her hands.

"Right..." I was becoming more and more intrigued by the idea, and her.

"But the important thing is for us to reveal the pulse of Beverly Hills. This town does so much good, but outsiders think we're phony, self-centered housewives. That's not who we are."

I couldn't have agreed with her more. "There are a lot of amazing women here who work very hard. They just don't get the credit they deserve."

"We're going to be up against a lot of competition, but it's time for people to see the heart of Beverly Hills." I could tell Destinee was dedicated to her mission.

"That's the Beverly Hills I want my child to know." Destinee's face expressed question. "Oh, I just found out that I'm almost two months pregnant." I rubbed my hand across the top of my Marc Jacobs skirt, which was a little snug.

She glanced at my stomach, which wasn't really a noticeable bump yet.

"Oh my god, congratulations. Frank must be thrilled! See...that's another thing, we're mothers and wives who are raising families - just like everyone else."

"I want people to see that. So, what timeline are you looking at to get things off the ground? I'd love to be a part of this."

One of the housekeepers brought out tea and little sandwiches and placed them on the small round table before us. Destinee got a kick out of hearing her tease me about eating too many. Saying the baby might not like them as much as I do. The people who work here are like family, not just employees, and we treat them with respect. I insist on it. These are men and women who assist in the wellbeing of our child.

"I'm glad to hear that because I was hoping you'd be a feature writer. I have a couple of other people onboard already. It's going to be fabulous. Things are moving really fast."

"Great! I was thinking too, maybe we can even feature women from other parts of LA. I think that would be positive. Not to mention bring a broader reader base."

She smiled and nodded, reaching out to shake my hand, "This is going to be fantastic!"

The magazine would surely be something that Beverly Hills had never really seen: lifestyle, glamour, entertainment and philanthropy presented by African American women. When I called Frank in Chicago about the magazine, he was impressed. So much that he had me arrange a meeting with Destinee about investing in the project. Beverly Hills Woman was about to break serious ground. Everything was falling into place.

Then tragedy struck.

Karoline called that night while I was sleeping. She was screaming frantically. Her friend Mimi had been found dead in her Bel Air home - an apparent overdose. I immediately called Frank and asked him to come home. He said he would fly back the next morning. We both knew Karoline wouldn't get over this any time soon.

It was almost midnight and I called Faith to meet me in Malibu. It felt so unfair. I think I cried the entire drive.

~

"Kari?" I walked around the quiet space trying to find her.

Brandon and some girl I didn't know came down the stairs.

"Hi Candice, she's um…she's upstairs." He looked wiped out. I could tell he'd been crying.

"Okay." I hugged him. "Why don't you go and get some rest, honey." I told him how sorry I was, since he was so close to Mimi as well. I gave a sympathetic look to the girl with him. Just then, I heard a car pull up front. It was Faith and she rushed in as they left.

"Candice - oh my god! Girl, is she okay?"

Faith had on black leggings and a long oxford shirt with the sleeves rolled and sneakers. Tell signs that she threw on the first thing she found. It looked like one of Donnie's shirts, because it hit almost to her knees.

"I just got here. Come on…" I impulsively rubbed my stomach, like I was shielding the baby from bad energy.

We got upstairs and Karoline was curled up in a ball in her bed. I sat next to her with Faith at the foot of the bed. I lightly touched her shoulder, "Kari…"

She opened her eyes, which were red and swollen. She quickly reached up, hugging me tightly. We didn't say anything. I just held her while she cried. I remember wishing Frank was there. I was sure he wasn't sleeping at all back in Chicago, worried about his baby girl.

"Sweetie, did you speak with your dad?" She nodded that she had. I looked over at Faith, who had tears welling up in her eyes, watching us. It was so sad. Karoline was helpless.

We stayed with her all night so that she could get some sleep.

In the morning when we woke up, Faith made us breakfast. I realized how necessary she was to my life; my friend for more than twenty years, was still there. I don't think I could have made it through that night without her.

"Karoline, I want you to come home with me, to Swann Lakes. You need to be with us and for as long or little as you want. No pressure, just...I think you need to be with the family."

"Yes, I want to." She nodded, with tears streaming down her face.

I clutched her hand. "Okay, and your dad is on his way back." I packed what I thought she'd need for a couple days and we'd figure the rest out.

I don't think Karoline realized how rough the next few days would be for her. I'd been there. I know how painful it is to suddenly lose someone you love, so tragically. It would prove to be a rough road.

Bebe: A new leaf?

$\mathcal{D}$erek and I had been talking about our marriage and how it had gotten to the point it had. I hadn't been the perfect wife, but when and how does a man begin paying for sex? Trying to find a way to piece it back together, we began seeing a marriage counselor. After everything, we didn't want to give up. I wasn't ready for him to move back into the house, but was agreeable to try and work with him on this. Maybe there was some glimmer of hope for us.

The therapist came to the conclusion that Derek had a sexual addiction. Why on Earth does everyone in Hollywood use that cop out? I wasn't buying it. My husband did these things because he could. He got away with it for quite a while. He's a powerful man, with a huge ego. That's almost always a toxic mix. It allows a person to do what they what, when they want, because they can.

We treaded through a lot of our issues. We fought. We battled, accused and cried. The results?

Somehow, we're still together. There's no one who can deal with Derek Fabian the way I can. He's back home and it's working - for now.

To live and cry in LA

𝒦aroline moved back to Malibu in late December, after the holidays. Candice practically nursed her back to health, so to speak. The first week Karoline didn't sleep at all. Maybe an hour here and there, but she mostly sat up crying and blaming herself. Candice even slept in her room a couple of nights, having known how it was to feel alone after such a tragic loss. She didn't offer advice, just her sympathy and love, almost neglecting her own wellbeing.

One night, with a pounding headache and tightness building in her chest, Candice sat up on the side of their bed trying her best not to wake Frank. She had been up late watching It's a Wonderful Life on the classic movie channel and had only been in bed an hour. Looking at the clock, she noticed it was after one in the morning. She closed her eyes, trying hard to control her manic breathing.

Reaching over towards her, a groggy Frank asked, "What's wrong, sweetheart?"

"It's nothing, Frank. Just go back to sleep."

He rolled over and did just that.

Making it to her bathroom, Candice closed the door and ran water in the sink, to mute any fumbling. She sat on the marble ledge of the tub. Her hands were trembling and she had a hard time catching her breath. She huddled over, sliding to the floor. Feeling like she was about to throw up, she almost crawled to the toilet and ended up with her hair brushing against the seat. Something that would have normally disgusted her was on this night a desperate act to feel better. She suddenly got scared.

"Frank! Frank, wake up!" She could hear the bedding whip back and him running towards her bath.

"Candice!" He slid over to her and knelt down holding onto her while reaching for the phone on the wall.

"No, what are you doing?" Still holding her stomach, she started crying, "No, no..."

"I'm calling the medics!" In his mind, he feared the worse. That she was losing the baby.

"No, don't…just sit with me, Frank, I don't want to go!" She leaned against him, clutching onto his arm and crying profusely.

Frank called downstairs, waking the live-in housekeeper to alert her that paramedics were coming. It seemed to take forever, but they were at the gate within ten minutes. They stabilized and calmed Candice before taking her to UCLA Medical in Westwood.

After talking with Candice about her symptoms and history of them, the doctor made a general determination that she was suffering from an anxiety attack disorder. It was no surprise to her. Since living in LA, she'd had more and more attacks. They had heightened lately. She even tried to hide her episodes from Frank.

Bebe's marriage was in trouble. Rayne's marriage was over. Then Mimi died so tragically. Though she didn't believe in it, it all felt like a curse. Candice was sure she and Frank were next in line, and she wanted to get out of Los Angeles as soon as possible.

They flew to Chicago two days later. After being with her for two weeks, Frank returned to LA before flying to London for a week.

It was then that Candice told him: "I'm not going back to LA. I'm done."

Full circle

𝓕rank hadn't taken any calls from his office, and his assistant had been texting and calling for three days. He didn't care about any of that. His wife, the only woman he'd loved so deeply, decided she didn't want to live in Los Angeles anymore.

He flew directly from London to Chicago. Candice had been hemmed up in the Lake Forest house for three weeks, refusing to see anyone other than her parents and sister. She even went so far as to leave word with the staff that she was not available if Frank called. It was like she no longer believed in their love.

Frank punched the back of the seat, "Can't you drive any faster, James?"

His driver James looked in the rearview at him, "Mr. Swann, I'm getting there, but we need to make sure you get there safely, alright? " He shook his head at the franticly impatient man in the back seat.

Frank broke down and called the house. Something in him wanted to know for sure that Candice was there and that she and the baby were okay. She was five months pregnant and on the verge of what seemed like a breakdown.

"Hello, Swann residence."

"Benita, this is Frank Swann, how are you?"

"I'm fine. Mr. Swann, are you okay?"

"Of course - is my wife there?"

"She is. She's resting, Sir. Should I…?"

"No, no don't wake her. She doesn't know, but I'm on my way. I'm almost there, in fact. Do not wake her."

"Mr. Swann, she wouldn't want me to say but…you should know Mrs. Swann's doctor was here yesterday… at the house."

Frank sat almost numbed with worry. *She's lost the baby. All because of this nonsense!* All kinds of thoughts swam trough his head. Already blaming himself, he released the call.

When the car turned into the estate, he put his coat on because the January wind was gripping, and the outside temperature was a frigid three degrees.

At the screech of the stop, he opened the door and jumped out of the backseat, quickly walking to the door and was met by one of the housekeepers.

"Good afternoon, Sir."

He waved at her and sprinted up the staircase and down the hall, where he sat on a plush bench in the hallway outside of the master suite. After what seemed like an hour, but was only ten minutes of thought, he opened the door and walked in looking for her. No one was there. *Where are you, baby?* He then thought about the modest guest room on the opposite wing of the house. The one that was Candice's favorite because it reminded her of her bedroom growing up, with its canopy bed and simple, cozy décor. When he got to the room and walked in, he saw her asleep, on her side, curled up peacefully. He wanted to wake her, but decided against it.

Sitting in the chair across the room he thought about what he'd done wrong. While trying to give her the perfect life and help her settle into his, he'd forgotten who Candice Marie Kane really was and why he fell in love with her in the first place. She always showed how much she loved *him*, not just the life they lead. That's what made her different, and he took it for granted. He kept piling on the gifts and the luxuries, the way he'd had to do all of his life to keep women happy. And worse, he left her alone in LA more often than he should have.

"Frank? What are you doing here?" Candice tried sitting up, holding her stomach, and he rushed over helping her. "No, I got it. I'm okay. Why are you here?" Her eyes were puffy, obviously from crying.

"What do mean? Did you think I wouldn't come after you?" At this point he wasn't sure if she'd even wanted him to come for her. "Are you okay? The baby..?"

Holding back her inner pain, she swallowed her tears, "We're fine."

He sighed of relief.

She looked down with a sorrow in her eyes. "My mother told me Chicago isn't my home anymore." Shaking her head, Candice looked sad when she spoke of the conversation she had with her mother the day before. "She told me my home is wherever my husband is."

"And what do you feel?" Frank was so regretful that it had come to this.

"I don't want to go back to LA. I'm not ready, not right now. Everything is falling apart there. I don't want that to happen to us." Tears began to puddle in her eyes as she reflected.

Candice had become the victim of her own dream.

Frank sat beside her on the bed. "We don't have to, sweetheart. But your mother's wrong about one thing. Chicago *is* home. Your family is here, and I know that's important to you, right? We can stay here for as long as you need to."

He rubbed her face but she lightly pushed his hand away, and leaned back against the headboard.

"Frank, remember the night we got engaged? We promised we'd never let anyone come between us...not even us. We messed up." Hot tears were now streaming down her cheeks. "I got so caught up in being Mrs. Swann, that I lost sight of the reason I married you. I thought I was okay with you being gone so much."

"I'm sorry...I was so busy and didn't pay attention to what was happening." Frank's face revealed a deep pain that she'd never seen. "I don't have to be away so often. I was just used to living my life."

When he was married to Jackie, the woman didn't care if Frank was there or on the moon, so as long as the money was close by. That's not how Candice felt about it. She truly loved him.

"Frank, it was me too, I just...I felt alone. Like I had been abandoned to that huge house, so I needed to make you pay attention to me." She pulled the cover back and he started to stand up to help her. The baby was more than a bump now; he was making his presence known.

"Be careful. Have you seen the doctor since you've been here?" Frank secured his hand at her waist, helping her up.

Candice looked at him suspiciously, "Don't act like they didn't tell you the doctor was here..." The corners of her mouth curled up as a smile made effort to appear. "...and yes, I have." She sauntered ahead to the bathroom. "You're staying, I take it?"

Frank clutched her hand, "For as long as we need to." He was still holding on to her hand, and she released it.

"Okay." Closing the door, she gazed into the blue eyes she fell in love with nearly two years before.

"Alright, I'll be right here." Frank pulled out his cell phone as he stepped out of the room. "Hello, Karoline. How are you, sweetheart?"

"Daddy, hi…I'm good. I'm better than ever, actually." He could hear in her voice that she was healing inside and out. Perkiness had reappeared. "Are you in Chicago? Is she okay?"

"Candice and the baby are just fine." Frank knew he had a lot of fixing to do. Like being a more attentive father because he knew that had been part of Karoline's problems and he didn't want to start wrong with the new baby. They're the most important part of his life and he was determined to keep his family together. "I was hoping you could come here to be with us."

She paused, "To Chicago? Why Daddy, is everything okay? You guys are working it out, right?"

"Oh no, it's nothing like that. We'll be fine; I just think Candice would love to see you."

"Sure, I'll fly out Saturday then. I'm working with the kids again and I want to finish the week up."

"Of course. I love you and I'm so proud of you."

"Thank you, Daddy." She paused. "You know, it's because of Candice that I worked my way back. My own mother didn't care."

Frank thought about that. All of the nights Candice spent taking care of his adult daughter when she could have shut her out.

"I realize that. Candice is a good woman and I'm not losing her. When the baby arrives it will be a new start for all of us."

A new addition

"*H*e's the most beautiful little thing I've ever seen." Mrs. Kane couldn't stop gushing over her first grand baby.

With Anne and Karoline sitting on either side of the bed, Mr. Kane nudged his son-in-law. "Well done, old man. Congratulations." They both proudly stood guard over Candice in the suite at Lake Forest Birthing Center.

The room was filled with so many balloons and flowers that the nurses had to take some away, because the smell was overwhelming and Candice kept sneezing. They feared she'd rip a stitch. She asked them to deliver some of the arrangements to other mothers at the Center.

Candice and Frank had been in Chicago for almost four months leading up to the birth. On May 4th, their seven pound, three ounce son, Franklin Wendell Swann III arrived. Six days early in fact.

On that day, Frank was hosting a business lunch for Swann's Chicago Vice Presidents. They were bringing their spouses and despite being more than eight and a half months pregnant, I insisted on dining with them. I wanted to get better acquainted with Frank's team, especially the women. I looked forward to the afternoon, even arranging to have my favorite eatery, Flatbones Deli, in Lincoln Park, cater the luncheon. It's a shame we never got to enjoy it.

I was sitting on the built-in of the shower, with the water streaming over me. It was very relaxing, especially when almost everything else was irritating and uncomfortable. Sudden sharp cramps hit my upper abdomen and my lower back started aching. I'd been having cramps since the day before, but my doctor told me that would happen more often the closer I got to my due date. Well this hurt like hell, and I couldn't catch my breath. My stomach felt tight and I could hardly stand up. I stepped out, grabbed my robe off the hook and made my way to the vanity where a phone was. I called downstairs, and one of the housekeepers answered. "I need someone up here now, please hurry!" I was clinching the handset.

Next thing I knew, Frank was there in the bathroom, as well as Karoline who had returned to Chicago two days before. The housekeeper called my doctor at Frank's direction.

"Honey, what do you feel? Are you in pain, or...?" He stood there for what seemed like minutes, before he realized he'd better help me.

I looked at Frank like he was crazy. "Of course I am! What are you talking about? My water just broke!"

I knew what was happening because I felt and saw it as the pain hit me. Water streamed onto my thighs from the shower heads, but I also saw water gushing from between my legs.

James got me to Lake Forest Birthing Center in ten minutes flat. It was just before eleven. A nurse met us at the entrance and I was taken to the birthing suite immediately, where my obstetrician Dr. Lee was waiting for me. Frank called my parents and sister. A million regrets of getting pregnant roamed through my brain because it was the worst pain I'd ever experienced in my life. Of course all of that went away when I heard my son's cries.

"Mommy, here...let me have him." Candice giggled, reaching up as her mother settled the infant in her arms. She playfully spoke to him, securing his plush blanket, "You're so beautiful, and I love you so much. I do, yes I do..." His tiny body slightly writhed at the sound of his mother's voice. Candice often spoke to him when he was in her womb, so he recognized her voice.

Just four hours old, the baby's lids were just barely opened, but his blue eyes peaked through vividly.

"You know, I'd really hoped he'd have my eyes. I just hoped - but Frank overpowered me!" Candice gushed, looking up at her husband who was chest-out with pride.

"Actually Candice, my mother's genes may have kicked in on that one, too." Mrs. Kane had a point. Candice's grandmother was biracial and her eyes were as blue as the sea. "She would be so proud of you right now."

Smiling, thinking about her grandmother who passed away fifteen years prior, Candice turned towards Frank. "She would have just adored you. She would have sat you down and recited the rules, right Mommy?" They laughed in agreement. "...but she would have loved you, Frank."

"Well Candice his hair is brown and curly like yours, and he has your mouth too. God, he's so cute!" Karoline lightly stroked a finger across her baby brother's head, which was amassed in swirls of lush curls. Being an only child for so long, she was now a big sister. Karoline leaned over and kissed his mitten covered hands. "I hope you're ready for this, little brother. It's not easy being in this family." She doted and beamed, playing with his toes.

Baby Frank's life would be one of privilege and wealth, but Karoline hoped he'd bypass all of the loneliness and confusion she had faced growing up. She was pretty sure his mother would put him first, unlike her own. One thing was for certain; he had breathed new life into their family.

~

Everyone had gone home for the night and the nurse was with the baby, so Frank took a moment alone with Candice who was exhausted from the strenuous day. She lay asleep and he leaned over her, admiring how beautiful she looked. Her skin still glowed like it did when he first met her.

"Thank you." He whispered, not wanting to wake her.

"Why are you thanking me?" She opened her eyes; still groggy from the pain medicine she'd been given.

"Oh, I didn't know you were awake."

She nodded a little, gazing up at him. "Uh huh…How are you?"

"I'm great." He took his hand out of his pocket and sat next to her bed.

"We've been through so much haven't we, Frank?"

He kissed her head, rubbing her hair, "Yes, we have. I love you." He paused. "Karoline loves you too, you know."

Candice smiled, still swept up by his charm. "I know. Hey, did you hold him?"

"I did. He's pretty amazing. I already know he'll be at the top of his class at Harvard." He laughed.

"Oh Frank, please…" She giggled at her husband's jesting.

Just then, his cell phone rang. "This is Frank Swann. Oh yes, I'm sorry, I was going to call you. Stacy, he's beautiful. Thank you, I will. Okay, goodbye." His assistant called, checking on the baby. "That was Stacy. She sends her love. By morning the entire company will have word of the newest member of our family. "

"Well, when you hang up your boxing gloves, he'll be the head of Swann one day, so it's fine. " She kidded, realizing in the back of her mind that it was actually a likely reality.

"You're okay with that? What this all means for him? I won't force him of course, but he's the future. His great grandfather built all of this…for him."

Candice shook her head, smiling, "Okay, okay…down boy. Just kiss me, alright?"

They were still so in love and it felt like the first time they'd kissed. Talk of their son's future would just have to wait.

*

EPILOGUE

"*F*rank, do you see? He's trying to walk, honey!"

Candice, sitting on her knees, reached out to her son as his little legs wobbled beneath him while his father held onto his arms. Seemingly proud of his one step accomplishment, he held his arms out and made gurgling sounds with 'Mama' mixed in there. His smiling eyes were fixed on reaching his mother.

"That's right. Yes, come on sweetie...Mommy's got you."

"Candice, he's not trying, he's doing it. See! Leah, will you help him, while I get this?" Frank picked up his handheld video camera and excitedly edged the toddler on. "Look at him... eleven months and he's walking already!"

Looking up at his nanny Leah, who has been with them since the family returned to Beverly Hills, little Frankie kept stepping, unaware that he was now standing on his own. Leah had released his hands seconds before, but spotted him just in case he fell. He did of course, but he tried again making a couple more steps than before. Candice scooped him up and hugged him like no tomorrow.

"Good! Frankie, that's so good, baby!" She held onto his arms letting him stand on his own again. Looking over at a proud Frank, Candice waved into the camera, "Hi, Daddy..." Frankie was determined to master those steps, independent of his mother. After a couple of tries he started wobbling over to his father.

Frankie had a jumpstart on life from the beginning. He was destined and ready to claim his place as a Swann from birth. If he follows his father's footsteps, Frank W. Swann III will be a force to be reckoned with.

At thirty-four, Candice is already leaving quite a footprint of her own. She's an attentive, loving wife and mother, while at the same time enjoying a thriving career as co-publisher and contributing writer for Beverly Hills Woman.

She refused to be another Beverly Hills stereotype of the sad, drunken, plastic, used up mannequin housewife. Candice had witnessed enough of that in her three years of living in LA. They all expected Frank Swann's pampered, young wife to lose herself to the good life. Either that, or hightail it back to Chicago for good. She came close, but decided she had too many plans of her own to let that happen.

There was also a bit of business to be dealt with regarding Jackie Reese-Swann. A while back, Candice was having lunch at Mr. C's with a very pregnant Faith when a polished, yet overtly sexy woman asked to speak with her. She introduced herself as Holly, and assured Candice that she would appreciate hearing her out.

Holly ran down the plot to destroy the Fabian's marriage. About how Jackie found her through a male escort friend, and hired her to carry out her treachery, with the intent of turning attention to Candice as the next target. It was all to serve as "payback" for Frank shutting Jackie out.

Holly lured Derek into her web, which was like dangling candy in front of a baby. He fell head first and got hooked. The next step was to send Holly in Frank's direction. What Jackie hadn't counted on was Holly reading about the wedding in the cover story of Town and Country, with the fairytale striking a chord in even her tainted heart. Holly refused to carry it out, and was pretty certain that even if she'd walked in front of him naked, Frank was so in love with Candice that the attempt would fail. Holly excused herself from that dirty plot. She also knew that trying to screw over a man like Frank Swann could mean she could wind up in handcuffs, and not in a good way. Jackie was furious.

As far as Candice was concerned, it wouldn't end there. How did Jackie think she could get away with the pain she'd caused her family and friends? Not to mention, trying to destroy her life with Frank. There were too many sacrifices made, and Candice wasn't about to let anyone interrupt the life she felt she'd earned. There was no way a piece of garbage like Jackie Reese was going to kill it. That said, Jackie was like a disease that had to be quarantined.

So, how'd Candice do it? Beverly Hills Woman did a feature story on the unfortunate popularity of elite companions saturating Hollywood and quoted a call girl: "A desperate socialite named Jackie approached me a couple of years ago to break up the marriage of a very high profile entertainment couple. Then, the pinnacle would be to move on to and demolish the reputation of her newly remarried ex-husband. I have the phone logs and texts to prove it. Of course, I had to do the right thing. I told her I wanted out."

Just like that, Jackie Reese-Swann was stripped of everything she craved. The Beverly Hills set didn't dare go up against Candice Swann - not to her face - so Jackie was shunned by not only Karoline, but her so-called friends, like Hunter Goldman, were now outwardly Candice's and Frank's biggest supporters. Again, loyalty is often a casualty in Beverly Hills and Jackie had lost at her own game. All Jackie had now was a fabulous last name.

Matthews-Kane Publishing is a flourishing entity and Candice and Destinee are the It Girls of the magazine world. In the time she's been involved in the project, Candice has hustled to make a name for herself. She even uses her maiden name professionally. Things are moving up so quickly, that they are about to launch a secondary periodical, Beverly Hills Man in the coming year. Bebe and Rayne were swift about giving their friend the speech on having it all. Candice is determined to balance her professional and home life, but she's not willing to sacrifice her family for the sake of her dreams. So far, she has no regrets.

*

www.ingramcontent.com/pod-product-compliance
Lightning Source LLC
Chambersburg PA
CBHW032150190626
46814CB00005BA/1930